BEASTS OF COURTH

Ravek Hunter

First Edition, August 2020

Copyright © 2020 Ravek Hunter Literary LLC

All rights reserved.

ISBN:

978-1-948782-18-0 (paperback),

978-1-948782-19-7 (ebook)

www.WorldsOfAtlantis.com

For Mrs. Wife,
who gave me two incredible boys
that I hope will be proud to read their father's work one day.

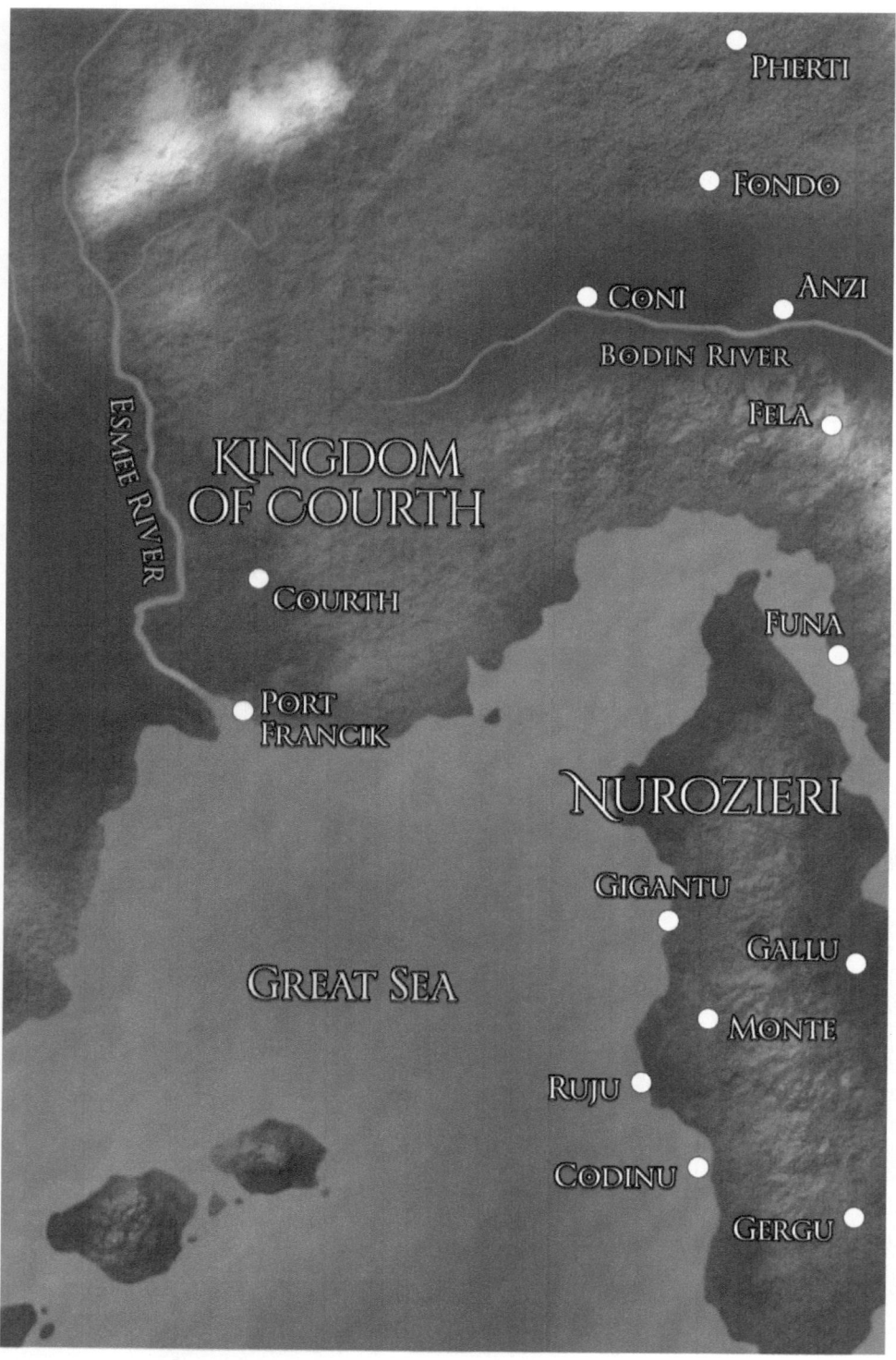

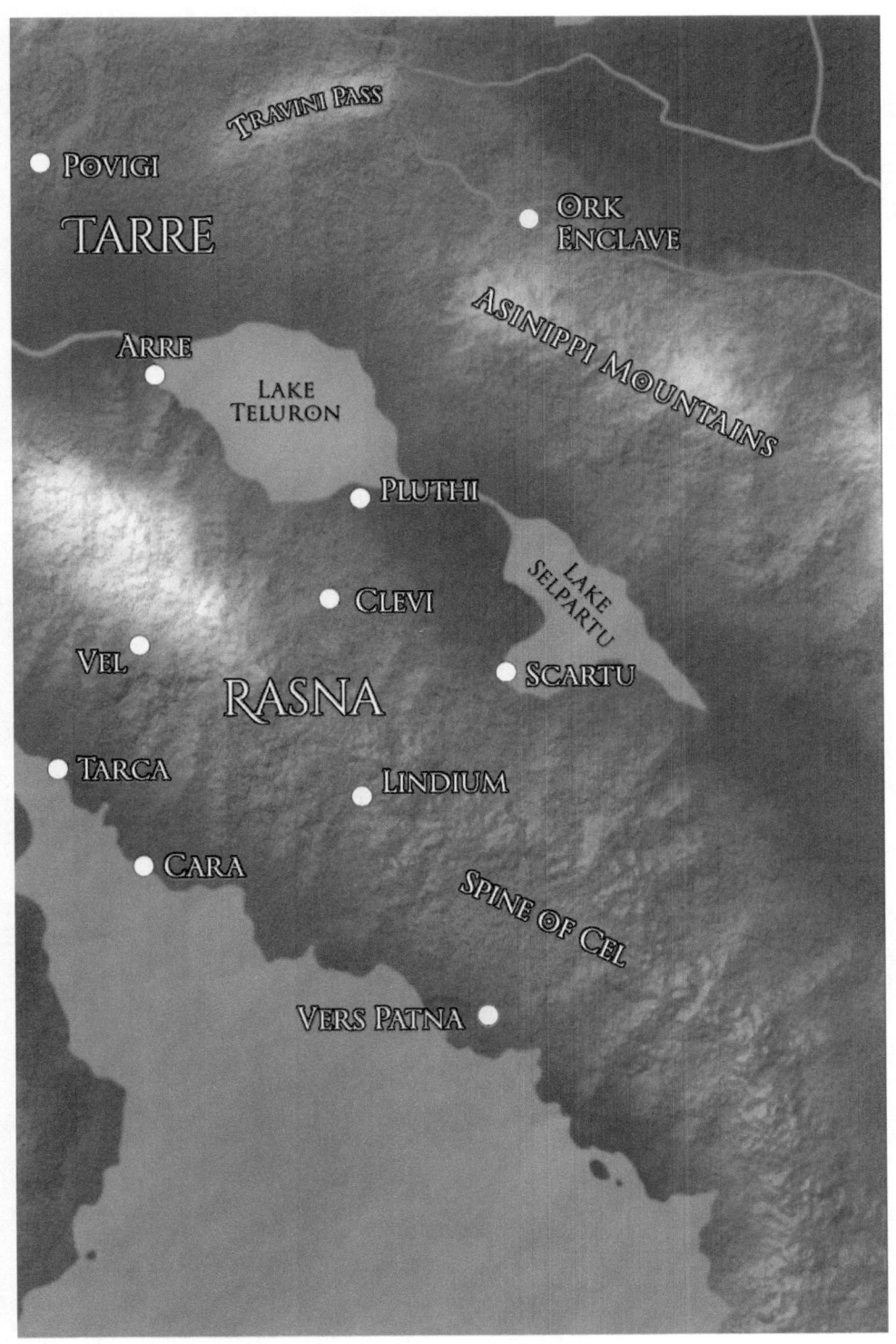

Fantasy Novels by Ravek Hunter

Red Wizard of Atlantis

The Fallen

Saving Eridu

The Imaziyen Druid

Shadows of Lyonesse

Beasts of Courth

Ys (Coming 2022)

If you enjoy reading books by this author, please remember to leave a review at your favorite bookseller!

To learn more about the backstory, mythology, and character development in these stories or to view world maps visit us at:

https://www.WorldsOfAtlantis.com!

Table of Contents

Children of Atlas

It was from the stars they came, out of the vast darkness of the Primeval Cosmos, plunging from the sky in a great wingless beast consumed by smoke and fire. It fell with a thunderous crash upon the earth plowing a long black rift across the open plain before it came to rest in a final shudder of sparks and lightning. The smoking shell of the massive creature lay shattered, yet from its broken maw came hundreds of odd-looking figures that crawled through the acrid haze and stumbled disoriented onto the lush green grass of a new world.

The Sylvan watched the arrival of the newcomers from the quiet repose of the forest. They scrutinized these strange bi-pedal aliens with blue-tinted skin and elongated heads and large almond-shaped eyes that had come uninvited to their tranquil isle, until now isolate and protected from intrusion by the vast expanse of the Primal Sea. They observed how the slender forms worked as a collective to remove the shiny scales of their battered host piece by piece to make shelters, how they buried their dead, how they mourned their passing.

When that was done, they brought red glowing crystals that shown bright even in daylight from the metallic frame of the silver beast's remains. The crystals they handled with great care and reverence, depositing them in caverns deep in the earth near an inlet on the coast. It was there too, that they began to build with stones.

These were a people with no hope of return or rescue, determined to survive and resolute in their struggle to make a place for themselves. A permanent place that would bring irrevocable change the Isle. To the land, to nature, to a way of life that had existed since time began.

Still the Sylvan watched.

The prophesies spoke of events such as these that would herald the beginning of the Fourth Age, the Age of the Golden Aspen, the Age when the winds from the north would bring an icy chill even in the summertime. And end the elves isolation from the rest of the world forever.

In time the Sylvan learned that the unusual blue-tinted people called themselves the followers of Atlas, the one who had risen among them and offered up hope for a new future. They would name the spine of the island in his honor and build a shining city on the sea that would become known as Atlantis.

And they thrived.

***Recorded in the Fourth Age of the Golden Aspen
by Watcher CrellianRafkarSil of Avalon***

Prologue

The morning light was just beginning to illuminate the dark room where Tanais, Arch Priest of Courth, was sitting at his well-organized desk lit solely by a small light-globe hovering in the air above it. He wrote with deliberate care on parchment with a quill pen, his left arm resting on a neatly stacked pile of new parchment opposite a much taller stack of completed work to his right. He had been up all night working on the Temple budgets. In a few days he was scheduled to present the documents to King Sarou Francik for approval and it was up to him to put the final polish on the plan his Temple clerks had been working on for weeks. Tanais enjoyed the challenge of it. He was one of only a few in the Temple that was educated in writing numbers and the frequent task of reviewing the ledgers kept his aging mind active and energized.

Focused as he was on the figures crowding the parchment before him, he nearly missed the furtive knock on the door to his study. Slowly, he set down the quill. It was odd for anyone to be at his door at this hour, unless . . . "Come!" he shouted.

The heavy wooden door opened slowly and a young servant popped his head in, "Your pardon, Holiness, I am sorry to disturb you at this hour."

"I am awake and you are here, so it must be important. You bring news?" the Arch Priest arched one dark eyebrow high on his forehead.

"Yes, you're Holiness. An officer of the Guard brought an urgent message for you." The boy quickly walked over and handed the folded parchment to the Arch Priest.

Carefully unfolding the note, Tanais read the short note then slammed his hand forcefully onto his desk sending papers scattering across the floor. The servant jumped from the sudden noise but did not move.

"They have taken another one, this time from a village north of the city. Say nothing of this boy." The Arch Priest dismissed the servant with a quick wave. Without hesitation the servant bowed and left the room nearly at a run.

Tanais was livid. Recently, the city and surrounding villages had been plagued with a rash of abductions. Oddly, not a single resident living with any of the missing persons had been awakened during the night to witness and only the next morning becoming aware that their loved one was gone. At first it was assumed the people had either wandered off or left due to a domestic situation. But after some investigation, which had turned up multiple boot tracks and witness reports of shadowy figures near the victims homes, was it determined that they must have been taken against their will. King Francik had ordered the night-time patrols doubled and the citizenry warned to lock their doors and be more alert during the night, yet the abductions continued unabated. So far, none of the victims, nor any evidence of them, had been recovered.

Enough was enough, Tanais would speak to the king this morning and demand that he appoints a special commission to oversee the examination of the crimes. They needed more man power including competent Bayles to investigate, make inquiries and form recommendations that could lead to the capture of whomever was taking innocents in the night. This problem was well beyond the capabilities of the city guard.

Leaving the scattered papers where they lay, Tanais retired to his adjoining bed chamber to get a few hours of sleep before he set out for the palace. One of his scribes would have his office organized before he awoke and he would get back to the work later. Compared to the abductions, the temple budgets suddenly seemed much less of a priority. Quickly changing into a sleeping robe, Tanais pulled his blankets up close to his chin and willed the light-globe to go dark. Even with the first light of dawn approaching, the widows of his room in the tower faced to the west and the light would not reach them for a while. Staring into the darkness, his imagination conjured fears of what he could not see and what he could not know and even though he knew the Temple was one of the most secure buildings in the city, it took some time for him to drift to sleep. He couldn't get the abductions out of his mind or prevent them from entering his dreams and he couldn't shake the feeling that these were no simple crimes, but something very unnatural at work.

~~~

Tanais arrived at the palace while the morning sun was still low in the east sky. He managed to sleep only a couple of hours before his active and worried mind had him up and dressed to meet with the king. There was no delay, Tanais was ushered in to the royal chambers without appointment or fanfare. It was part of the balance of power and interdependent relationship they shared that no matter the time of day or night they would each have complete access to one another, within the reasonable confines of decorum and appreciation for circumstances that demanded privacy, of course.

King Francik IV was still in his night clothes seated at breakfast in his private dining room when Tanais arrived. Except for a few servants he was alone, idly moving his spoon through his porridge making artless shapes with the blueberries that floated on top.

He looked up at Tanais with nervous anticipation clouding his eyes, "I expected you earlier."

Usually jovial, there was a hint of irritation in his voice this morning, not necessarily directed at him, but for the grave situation they would find themselves addressing this morning.

"I was up the entire night working on budgets and needed a few hours of rest before I came to see you." His excuse sounded silly hearing it out loud. He should have known the king would have been awakened with the distressing news about the abductions just as he was.

"Sit down, Tanais." The King motioned to a chair near him at the long table. "I suppose you have some recommendations? I have already spoken with Commander Duraunt and he suggested more patrols during the night hours, especially around full moons. I hope you have some better ideas."

Tanais sat heavily in the chair offered by the king, "I do, your Majesty. It seems we cannot leave this matter in the hands of men used to battering down doors and chasing footpads. Instead, you need to appoint a special commission to take control of the matter. Of course, with our oversight."

The King eyes stared again into his bowl of porridge. He was much younger than Tanais by nearly three decades and had only ascended to the throne a few years earlier after the previous king, his father, passed away. Still, he was turning out to be a very intelligent and thoughtful ruler that cared deeply for his people and country. The Arch Priest was glad for it, since it made his job of guiding and advising His Majesty that much less difficult.

"Agreed," King Francik finally responded. "I will order a special commission formed today and I will make whatever resources they require available. But I would like for you to head the commission yourself and choose its members." He stood from the table and put his arms through a housecoat offered by a servant.

Tanais stood as well saying, "I will accept the responsibility and give the matter the necessary attention that it deserves. May Sunna guide our faithful hands to end this reign of terror across our land sooner rather than later."

Before the end of the following day, Tanais had gathered together seven men and women from the kingdom that he considered competent to serve on the special commission. Their backgrounds were varied and included Commander Duraunt to represent the city guard, High Priestess Rhalia from the Temple, a distinguished Magistrate, two highly respected and successful merchants, The Duke of Toulliou – a northern territory of the kingdom and The Earl of Berci in the West. Each one brought intellect, cunning or resourcefulness to contribute ideas about the abductions, the motivations behind them, how they were being carried out and most importantly how to stop them. Tanais was sure the two merchants, in particular, might have inside information about all of it, except that they would be reluctant to speak in the public setting of the commission. In fact, they didn't want to be on the commission at all and only accepted because they were compelled to do so by Tanais. Outside of the commission meetings, Tanais planned to meet with them on a regular basis in private to get their unfiltered thoughts. Although they appeared to everyone else, even the king, as wealthy and influential tradesmen, He knew them for what they really were – Guild Masters of the shadowy criminal underworld in Courth.

"Have you sent Bayles to interview the families of the missing people and inspect the place where they were abducted, Commander Duraunt?" the Duke stroked his long raven-black mustaches as he spoke. It was a well-known characteristic of the man that was often parodied by the common-folk in Courth.

"Of course, we have," the Commander stood from the large table they were all gathered around. "Aside from the boot prints and unusual figures roaming the night, there is another less-recounted detail that we have discovered."

The Dukes eyebrows raised high on his forehead. "And what is that, prey tell?"

"In every case, there was an illness at the home of the abductee," the Commander paced to the edge of the room and back as he spoke. "Each time, a healing priest was summoned from the temple to provide a remedy. The symptoms of the illness always suggested the possibility that it might be contagious and a potential threat to others in the kingdom. The priest would treat the ill person and the entire household with a curative potion and instruct them to quarantine themselves until the morning. After the priest's departure, the family usually went straight to bed and the next morning someone from the home would be missing."

"Is it the person with the illness that is usually gone?" The Earl asked.

The Commander shook his head, "Sometimes, but not always."

"And what about these priests?" It was the magistrate that spoke next. "Have your Bayles interrogated them?"

High Priestess Rhalia cut-in, "Commander Duraunt came to me a week ago with this information and together we spoke to the four priests and priestesses involved. None of them were any more likely to be summoned than another to treat the illnesses and it is not unusual to treat an entire family when there is illness in the house."

"We do not see a connection with the priests at this time," Tanais confirmed. "Although it is possible that whoever, or whatever, is abducting people could be causing the illness in the first place and taking advantage of the household's vulnerability."

"Vulnerability?" hand on his mustaches again, the Duke's voice rose a pitch.

"Yes," the High Priestess addressed the Duke. "The curative potions administered by the priests have the side effect of putting people into a deep healing sleep for several hours. But again, not unusual."

Voices rose in speculation one over another at once from several members of the commission.

"There is something else," Tanais spoke loudly to quiet the group. A hush quickly settled over the room. "One of the Bayles is a ranger who is skilled in tracking. He was able to follow the boot prints from the missing people's homes into the forest, but not much further."

"Is there any clue as to who these men are?" The Earl had a fearful look upon his face.

"Not yet," Tanais was also troubled by the tracks they had found and where they might lead. "The citizenry refers to them as Night People."

"Don't we have a ranger capable of tracking them further into The Wilds?" the Duke demanded. "If we can find their hovel, lair or whatever hole they come from Commander Duraunt can lead a force to exterminate them to the last!"

"Gaurin Rand," the magistrate spoke quietly. "A legend of a ranger if there ever was one."

The Duke threw his hands in the air. "Then fetch him to us! Offer him gold, land or both. Whatever it takes to secure his service for a few weeks."

"Sadly, there is no force on earth that could compel him to serve," the Commander echoed the magistrate's sullen tone. "He passed from the coughing illness last winter."

"Is there no other?" the Duke was pulling at the side of one mustache so furiously that Tanais thought he might detach it.

"There is one," Tanais forced his eyes from the spectacle of the Duke. "And I am willing to bet he has the talent, if not the experience, of his father."

Chapter 1

Visitors

Sylvan Year (SY)5490

I have been many places in my life and I have to say that summertime in the Kingdom of Courth is among the most pleasant. The cool winds that blow south follow the valleys separating the high mountains east and west where the river Esmee flows past the logging camps, the City of Courth and all the way to Port Francik before emptying into the Great Sea. The temperature is mild and the humidity is low enough that my old bones find comfort even when it's a little chilly after nightfall. If I were to ever retire to a remote cabin or tower, this would be the place.

Wodanaz the Wanderer

Sounds of movement on the dirt road approaching the simple stone and thatch dwelling were the first indication that he was about to have company. Enguer Rand glanced out the kitchen window where he sat mending a broken strap from his father's studded leather armor and his heart sank. At least a dozen horses approached carrying heavy men. Armored men.

It was the time of day that old Mrs. Eibhlin, his closest neighbor from across the field separating their homes, usually dropped by with a basket full of freshly baked bread, cheese and sometimes meat. And always, always she brought pie. Mrs. Eibhlin was never shy about expressing her opinion and the latest gossip and news from the city, but mostly she assured him that a spot of pie would lift his spirits. She was right. Enguer did feel better after one of her nearly daily visits.

He smiled at the thought. Mr. and Mrs. Eibhlin had always been good to him and his father. They shared the vegetables and pork produced on their farm, even when the winters were long and food was short, while Enguer and his father made sure they had furs to keep them warm and wild venison to fill their bellies in trade. After Enguer's father died, only a few weeks previous, Mrs. Eibhlin had decided that it would be her job to look in on him regularly and keep him well fed. Enguer almost laughed out loud. If he let it go on much longer, she would have him married to one of her many daughters and tending a field before the end of summer.

A heavy knock at the door echoed loudly through the small quiet house. Enguer rose from his chair and opened the door without fear. He knew who these men were.

"Hello Enguer," an older man, about the same age as his father, greeted him with a sincere smile. His name was Tanais and he was the Arch Priest of Sunna in Courth. "May I come in?"

Enguer eyed the cluster of priests and armored soldiers crowded in the yard behind him before making a quick bow, "Your Holiness, how can I serve you today?" He opened the door wider for the older man to come in.

The Arch Priest entered with his entourage a quick step behind to follow, but he waved them away and closed the door leaving the house empty except for the two of them. "I have not seen you since the burial of your father. Are you well?"

"Yes, you're Holiness. I am well. Please sit." To the surprise of everyone, the Arch Priest had seen to the funeral ritual himself and even wept at his father's burial mound when he thought he was alone. Enguer had watched from a distance in the forest contemplating vague memories that only hinted as to why the Arch Priest was so emotional over his father's death. Enguer remembered the man from when he was a priest not yet elevated to the head of the Temple of Sunna in Courth. He used to come to their home quite regularly. Of course, Enguer was a small child then, but he still remembered his parents talking and laughing with him for hours into the evening. A few years later he was elected to the position of Arch Priest and didn't come around any longer. Enguer supposed that the duties of an Arch Priest were very time consuming with little time for a social life and although his parents would see the Arch Priest at important religious ceremonies, it was different, and he would often overhear his parents speaking about how they missed their friend.

The Arch Priest removed his hat, a white Biretta with the symbol of a yellow sun on the front and sat down casually in a chair. He waved for Enguer to sit, as if it were his home they were in. In truth, Enguer was a little intimidated by the stature of the man sitting in his father's chair. The priest was second only to the king himself in power and influence and it was said that even the His Majesty deferred to his council much of the time according to Mrs. Eibhlin.

"It's been a few years since I last sat in this room." The Arch Priest appeared to study every detail. "I remember when you would play near the hearth there as a small child," he smiled warmly. "Not too many people know this but your father and I traveled and explored many exotic places when we were younger. Even beyond the Emerald Isle. Perhaps he told you stories."

Enguer sighed, "Not really. My father didn't tell too many stories. Mostly his talk revolved around teaching me the ways of a Ranger and being a good tracker."

Sadness dimed the priest's eyes for a moment. "Your father changed a lot when your mother died, taken by that terrible illness that ravaged the kingdom in those years, the rest of us were lucky to survive it. But your father took it hard. You were just old enough to start going out with him into The Wilds and sometimes we wouldn't see the two of you for weeks. It was an escape for him, a way to ease his mind in an environment that comforted him."

Enguer ducked his head in a quick nod, "I learned to hunt and trap in those days. It seems a lifetime ago, but the time alone together in the wilderness after my mother died was good for us both. My father couldn't stand the sympathy in every word and every eye that he passed. Now I know how he felt."

The Arch Priest studied Enguer closely. "He taught you well so I've heard."

Enguer shrugged and the Arch Priest went on, "What are you doing now? Trapping and hunting like your father did? Or do you have other ambitions?"

Feeling uncertain about how he should answer, Enguer said, "It's a good life. It is what I know, and I love being close to nature. Besides, I don't know what else I would do."

Leaning closer to Enguer, the Arch Priest spoke just above a whisper, "I knew your parents well. Especially your father, and they would not want this secluded life for you. In fact, because of the relationship I had with your father I feel somewhat responsible for your wellbeing."

"What would you have me do?" Enguer asked.

"You know about the Night People and the trouble they are causing?" the Arch Priest asked in a way that didn't quite sound like a question. Mrs. Eibhlin spoke of almost nothing else in the past week or so. "The special commission appointed by the king needs a few of the best rangers in Courth with the ability to track these criminals back to where they are hiding. You may be young, but already I would count you among the best, and it would be a good opportunity for you Enguer. Don't waste away in the house your parents built. They and I expect more of you." The Arch Priest stood up and applied his Biretta.

"How long can I take to decide?" Enguer asked.

"As long as you like", smiled the Arch Priest, "but if you are not in front of the Temple at dawn when they leave tomorrow it will be too late. I've already told Commander Duraunt to expect you. Don't let us down boy, we need you."

Walking toward the door, the Arch Priest paused, putting a hand on Enguer's shoulder, "I am the Arch Priest of Sunna in the Kingdom of Courth. But to you, I would like you to think of me as family and if you need anything, you know where to find me."

Turning, the Arch Priest walked out the door, leaving Enguer again in the silence of the lonely house.

So the rumors are true, Enguer thought to himself, old Mrs. Eibhlin was not just prattling away about gossip she had heard from some overzealous townsfolk.

Enguer sat down again to resume his work on his father's armor as he listened to the horses stomping recede into the distance. This would be his armor when he was done. Thoughts swirled inside his head making it difficult to concentrate on the task at hand when there was another knock at the door. He barely had a chance to open it before Mrs. Eibhlin breezed in and pushed the leather armor aside to set down her food-laden basket. Enguer was always impressed by how gracefully she moved for a heavy-framed woman.

"Who were those men Enguer? Is everything alright?" She cast a studious gaze around the kitchen with an eye that took note of every dirty plate and crumb. "This place is a mess! I will have to send over Jeanna this afternoon to tidy things up."

Enguer groaned on the inside. Jeanna was a very pretty, thick-bottomed daughter of the Eibhlin family only a year or two younger than he. She was pleasant enough, but her personality was much like her mother's and she was not shy about expressing her desire to get married. He was certain that Mrs. Eibhlin already had it all worked out and was doing everything in her power to encourage the match. Enguer wasn't ready to get married and he certainly didn't want to be tied to a farm.

The Arch Priest was right. He needed to decide on a direction to take with his life and despite all the wonderful memories made in his home, his family was gone and it no longer felt the same. Without realizing it, Enguer had made a decision.

"The king is collecting men to chase down the Night People . . ." Enguer began.

"Yes, yes, I know, dear." Never one to stand idle, Mrs. Eibhlin was busy clearing the counter of dirty plates and cups. "Gaurin, your father I mean, would have been the first fool to line up with them. No disrespect to your father, of course, that's just the way he was built. An adventurer and all that nonsense." She brushed by him and pat his cheek. "I'm glad his son has more sense than that."

"Mrs. Eibhlin . . ."

"You're a good boy. Settle down and have a family." Mrs. Eibhlin tossed the leather breast piece onto a nearby chair and opened the basket she had brought. The scent of fresh bread and pie was distracting. Especially the pie.

"Mrs. Eibhlin . . ."

"I know, I know. Jeanna is strong willed and a bit on the chatty side, I can't change that about the girl, but she would be a fine wife to you and she has those wide hips good for making babies . . ."

"I'm going with them." Enguer quietly interrupted.

Mrs. Eibhlin stopped, cheese in one hand, a link of sausage in the other and just stared into the basket. Enguer didn't know what to say, he had never seen her like this before. He waited for what seemed like an eternity until Mrs. Eibhlin finally exhaled a long sigh.

She turned to look directly at him, maybe for the first time since she had arrived and spoke in a calm, motherly fashion. "I suppose the apple doesn't fall far. And you spent so much time in the wilderness with your father after your mother died it shouldn't come as a surprise you crave more than this." She raised her arms to take in the whole of the room, sausages dangling with the movement.

"This is not the life for me, Mrs. Eibhlin. I'm sorry. I know you had plans, but I need the forest around me, that is my real home."

Mrs. Eibhlin smiled sadly, "Jeanna will be so disappointed. Will you not return after this mess with the Night People is done with?"

Enguer shifted uncertainly. "No. My path will lead me away from here. To where I do not know yet. Perhaps some time in The Wilds would be good for me."

"Such a dangerous place, child." A fearful look painted her face.

"It is more than just a place for me, it is part of who I am." Enguer smiled. "Besides, my father trained me well enough."

Mrs. Eibhlin put down the sausage and cheese and wrapped him in a big bear hug holding him tight. "I wish you only the best in your travels, Enguer. I know your father would have been proud of you." She pulled back a little and smiled slyly. "And someday, when you come back, maybe one of my younger daughters will catch your eye!"

Enguer stifled a groan in his chest that was begging for release and smiled nervously sending Mrs. Eibhlin into fits of laughter followed by more hugs.

Later that night, after packing his gear and more than one helping of pie, Enguer lay awake in his bed staring at the ceiling. He thought about how many nights he had stared at the same spot over the years through good times and bad. His mother always described him as a contemplative boy with a strong sense of balance and appreciation of nature. Enguer still wasn't sure what she meant by that, but like most things during his early years, she was probably right.

He smiled at the thought of her and tried to will his recollection of their time together to be sharper and more vivid. The memories of her – how she looked, the fragrances she wore and the sound of her voice – seemed to fade a little with each passing year and he feared that one day he might forget those intimate details altogether. Enguer was young when she died. Eight or nine years old, he wasn't sure since his father would never speak much about it. Enguer remembered how happy she was, full of life and energy, and much younger than his father. He knew she was a dancer in a local theatre in Courth and often practiced new acts with him that she would perform on stage. At the time, Enguer was unaware of his sexuality and unashamed, but his father was not so happy about the display. His mother assured him that it was okay because it made her happy to dance with him and they were in the privacy of their own home. His father never argued the matter.

After his mother died his father began to take him camping in the forests and instructing him in the ways of a ranger with particular emphasis on the art of tracking. The years of training and education in The Wilds was both arduous and rewarding in more ways than he could possibly express and by the time he reached maturity Enguer had managed to become a competent ranger, tracker and a pretty good dancer.

One of the last things his father told him before he died was that he recognized something different about his son in the forest. He described it as a natural intuition that bordered on the mystical. It was true, the forest would silently speak to him and show him the way. Never once did he struggle to find food, water and shelter in the forest and nature always revealed details only he could see when tracking his prey. On the rare occasion that his father spoke of Enguer's abilities in The Wilds, he expressed his certainty that his son would grow up to be a better tracker than he. It was one of the highest compliments Enguer could have received, all the more so considering that his father's skills as a ranger were considered legendary.

That time was passed. Both of his parents had died from illness during winter months. His father elderly with a life well lived and his mother young and in her prime. It made no sense to him why Sunna would set their suns so far apart. He didn't question the goddess. What would be the point? He simply accepted it as her will.

Now he was alone with no family to speak of in a dark and lonesome house on a plot of land on the outskirts of Courth that had never been farmed. The Arch Priest was right. He needed purpose. Tracking the Night People would certainly give him that, if nothing else. Despite what Mrs. Eibhlin and the Arch Priest said he was still a little skeptical. In the rural area well south of the city where he lived there was no sign in the fields or forests of the creatures. All he knew was that people were disappearing from their homes and fields with alarming frequency. Even firsthand accounts were hazy and unclear with the details of the abductions if that's what they were. Of course, Mrs. Eibhlin's story telling was based entirely on hearsay and the Arch Priest had not offered any particulars.

At least it promised adventure. Probably nothing like the famous stories penned by Boeger Penhallow or Vyvyan, but an adventure nonetheless. He glanced over at the crack of light that entered through the space of the slightly opened door to his room. Once he could hear the murmur of his parents' voices through that opening, later the persistent stroke of stone on metal as his father sharpened the blade of his short sword and now lonely silence. With no little sadness he realized that night would be the last one spent under this roof for some time and he drifted off to sleep imagining that he could still hear the happy sounds that once made this place his home.

~~~

A small red flame streaked across the night in the distant sky. It was too far away to discern any detail, but that didn't matter, Myrllin knew exactly what he was looking at. He shifted his weight on the back of the massive red dragon that served as his mount, although he never would have referred to the dragon as a mount. At least not in his presence.

"What are we waiting for?" the tone of his brother's gravelly voice was characteristically impatient.

Myrllin sighed, they had been through this already. "We are not fast enough to chase it down, so we must anticipate its course and intercept it. Preferably without it noticing our approach."

"It's already incinerated a dozen Vikja villages between here and Tirnan Yog," Wodanaz pat the neck of the strange eight-legged horse he sat astride reassuringly. "But don't worry, Sleipnir and I are ready whenever you get around to giving the word."

Myrllin ignored his brother's cranky reply and eyed the massive black stallion. He still wasn't sure if it were a physical beast or a magical beast the way his brother summoned it from out of nowhere anytime he needed a ride. And all those legs. Somehow it was able to travel three times as fast as the best conditioned horse Myrllin had ever ridden and to his utter surprise, fly just as swiftly as the dragon! It was just as well, Myrllin doubted that Dergo would have been willing to carry two.

"Be patient, it has to turn north. There is nowhere else for it to go unless it decides to cross the Primal Sea."

From their vantage point high on a volcanic ridge overlooking the southeastern edge of the Vikja homeland Myrllin could see as far as the frigid waters of the coastline. Luck was with them this night. According to Wodanaz, the peaks where they waited were usually enveloped in a halo of clouds and a plume of volcanic smoke. The locals referred to the mountain as the 'Gates of Hell' because it was so often concealed.

"There is an island a few leagues off the coast," Wodanaz pointed southwest. "The Phoenix may have gone there."

"Is it settled?" Myrllin feared that another village would burn while they watched, but there was little they could do. Every time they chased the fiery bird it left them in its smoldering wake.

Wodanaz shook his head, "Not that I recall, but that might have changed sense I was last here."

Myrllin's gaze swept over the distant horizon, "It will pass this way. I can feel it."

"Waking dreams now, Myrllin?" Wodanaz scoffed. "You were insufferable enough when you slept for centuries at a time."

Myrllin let the comment pass. Wodanaz was only like this when he was scared. He would never admit it and Myrllin was wise enough not to bring it up. They shared a bond that, no matter where they were in the world, they would each know the other's whereabouts and general condition. That was thanks to their father and the Liafal Stone in Eriu.

"This one is not like the others, you know," Myrllin's tone dropped to nearly a whisper. "Something with the blood-magic and the Dwarfs three-faced man, the wizards he captured and the energy trapped within Tirnan Yog has given the demon power he should not yet possess."

Wodanaz's snort never achieved the level of a snicker. Another sign that he was more worried than he let on. "It is but one. Our father trapped seven of them and another thirteen chaos demons. We can handle this."

His brother was correct. Their father had lured the named demons one-by-one into a prison that became a Pithos many centuries before. What Wodanaz failed to acknowledge was that there was a dozen Tuatha De Blood and a host of Atlanteans, Dwarfs, Elves and humans to back him up. Unfortunately, through a series of events that still baffled Myrllin, the Pithos was broken and the demons were free once more.

A spark of light rose above the horizon and Myrllin stiffened. "Ready yourself, it is coming."

The spark slowly grew into a blaze that itself grew into a ball of fire until Myrllin could make out the distinct shape of fiery wings, head and savage claws. The Phoenix flew at an astonishing speed through the cold air at an elevation similar to their own and Myrllin knew that he would have to time their move perfectly if they were to successfully intercept it. His mind carefully worked through the complex mental calculations and when the bird was less than a league away, he gave Wodanaz the signal.

"Go!" Myrllin called to his brother.

The red dragon carrying Myrllin launched into the air followed closely by Sleipnir with Wodanaz. They flew a pre-planned route taking deliberate care to conceal their silhouettes against the dark terrain far below. Myrllin's strategy was simple: take the Phoenix by surprise and if they had the luck of the gods, kill it.

The gap between the demon and the brothers closed quickly. Ready for the assault, Myrllin spoke a charm and an icy bolt streaked away from his upraised arm. The impact on the unsuspecting phoenix was nothing short of phenomenal as the unerring bolt struck it squarely in the center of its fiery breast. Almost as if it had collided with a wall, the Phoenix's flight ceased mid-air and tumbled wildly out of control. Myrllin, seeing an opportunity to strike again, did not hesitate to press the advantage. Mentally guiding Dergo to dive after their quarry, bolts of lightning cast forth from his finger tips to ensnare the plummeting Phoenix in a tangled web of electricity. The demon-bird screeched in pain and rage at the assault, struggling to break free of the deadly current that surrounded it and arrest its rapid descent.

"Brother," Wodanaz's voice boomed from behind. "Pull away!"

Myrllin suddenly became aware that he had pushed Dergo too close to the Phoenix and he urgently pulled the great dragon away a second before a blazing tongue shot out and cracked the air they had just vacated. Myrllin cursed his own foolery for the near fatal misstep and joined Wodanaz hovering in the air on Sleipnir several spans above him.

"That would have made for quite the tale for one of your songs," Myrllin uttered cynically.

Wodanaz gave him a withering look. "And I am the impatient one? I need my brother alive more than a song."

Myrllin stayed quiet. He was the elder of the two by less than a minute, but Wodanaz had always assumed the role of protective older brother from the time they could walk. Maybe it was because he was always so much stronger and physically larger than the wiry frame under Myrllin's robes. Whatever the reason, they had both done their part over the years looking after each other.

The Phoenix fell through the clouds like a streaking, crackling meteor and struck the ground with a jarring boom at the base of the 'Gates of Hell' with nearly the same impact. Earth and fire erupted into the air forming a great mushroom-shaped cloud immediately followed by the rush of hot air and a shockwave that roared over Myrllin and Wodanaz with enough force to send them tumbling into the night sky. Myrllin held onto Dergo with every bit of strength he possessed until the red dragon managed to regain control and level out. Off to his left he spied Wodanaz and Sleipnir rolling a short distance further before they too came to a stop.

Sweat saturated Myrllin's face, shoulder-length black hair and airy robes. A small measure of the intense, unnatural heat touched his skin despite the protective bubble Myrllin had cast over Wodanaz and himself earlier due to the subzero temperatures that flowed on the bitterly cold winds from the glaciers just a few leagues to the north. He opened his mind to Dergo and was relieved that no harm had come to the dragon. The impenetrable red scales that safeguarded the beast from extreme cold had also shielded him from the extreme effects of the magical heat.

Wodanaz rode up next to Myrllin, sweat glistened on his heavy blonde beard and brow and Sleipnir looked no worse for wear. "That was too easy," his tone thick with apprehension.

Myrllin agreed. If they had killed the Phoenix, the demon's essence would have been released and he could have captured it for disposal in the Ourea. Unfortunately, if that were the case, the still billowing mushroom cloud would have obscured the demon's essence long enough for it to escape to find another body to possess. What concerned Myrllin the most was that the Phoenix was not a physical creature of this world. It was a supernatural creature conjured out of the molten rock beneath Tirnan Yog with corrupted Dwarf enchantments known as blood-magic. What Myrllin knew was that however it had happened, this demon was far stronger than it should be, but he still had no idea if they could separate it from its host the same way they had done with the other demons they had captured and disposed of.

"Here we go," Wodanaz rumbled.

Chapter 2

The Hunt

Sunna brought light upon the earth and with the light that slowly spread across waters, mountains, hills and rivers of the land came the stirring of life that heralded the beginning of a new day.

Enguer Rand stood in line with a contingent of ten soldiers of the king's elite guard, a pair of Bayles, two Fire Priestesses and four rangers gathered on the steps of the Temple of Sunna to receive a blessing from the Arch Priest, Tanais. It was dawn and although it was well into spring, a brisk wind sweeping over the nearby mountain range would permeate every seam and fold with icy chill until the sun rose high enough to offer some relief with its blessed warmth.

When he first arrived, there was a stir among the gathering. Somewhat apprehensive, Enguer at first thought the heavy wolf-hide cloak flung over studded leather armor oiled against the damp weather drew their mockery. The only other notable equipment he carried was a short-sword and axe at his waist and a bow with a quiver of arrows along with a small travel pack over his shoulder. The mount he led was his father's horse, a Lambei from the Emerald Isle different from all the others – strong and nimble and three hands taller. The unusual horse was capable of crossing great distances without tiring and fantastic bursts of speed when needed. They were bred by the Enlightened One's, although Enguer read once that they originated in a land far across the Primal Sea beyond even the Emerald Isle. Yet, the powerful steed stood out for another reason; it transported no additional packs. This was how Enguer always equipped himself when going into The Wilds with his father. Some of the soldiers openly snickered among themselves at his apparent lack of preparedness, considering they were carrying at least eighty pounds of gear on their mounts. Even the rangers expressed surprise at how light he was travelling. All of them were older than he and carried at least a thirty-pound pack on their mounts.

One ranger known to Enguer and only a few years older approached him. "You know we might be in the wilderness for several days, right?"

"Of course," Enguer responded.

"Then why are you packed so lightly?"

With absolute seriousness Enguer responded, "The wilderness is my home. Everything I need is already there."

"Enguer Rand!" a voiced bellowed from behind, interrupting his conversation. It was Commander Duraunt. "You will take the rear left."

Enguer sighed. That meant that he would trail the other 'experienced' rangers on the left flank looking for any signs they might miss along the way. A low buzz of whispers spread through the ranks. They all knew who he was now, thanks to the commander, and given his father's reputation they would surely expect miracles – or the opportunity to humiliate him.

He didn't have time to dwell on it as the Arch Priest made his appearance and everyone's attention shifted to the top of the steps. It was Tanais, dressed in the robes of his office, just as Enguer had seen him the day before. With arms stretched toward the rising sun the Arch Priest delivered the morning benediction. It didn't last long and almost as soon as it was over, Commander Duraunt was shouting for everyone to mount up. Enguer took his position and rode with the small company through the quiet city streets.

Courth was just beginning to wake up, but already the scent of baking bread wafted on the breeze and several lights shown in windows along the way. By the time they exited the city, tradesmen and farmers were rumbling down the streets in wagons and merchants were beginning to open their shops to early risers. It was an odd way of life to Enguer's thinking. Constant noise and the press of bodies on crowded boulevards mixed with the stench of horse dung and livestock. He was glad they would be out of the city before the majority of the population poured into the streets to go about their daily business.

Once beyond the high suffocating walls, Enguer sucked in a chest-full of the chill, fresh air and allowed his gaze to follow the line of trees that marked the edge of the forest a league to the west. Beyond it, he could barely make out the dim outline of high peaks that most city-folk considered the borderlands of The Wilds.

Memories cascaded through Enguer's mind of the years he had spent with his father among the trees and elevations. Mostly, a few leagues south of where they rode now, but much of it looked the same. In an odd way, Enguer felt the familiarity of going home and he longed for it. He had not returned to The Wilds since his father died and it was far past the time for him to remedy that.

The rangers he accompanied fanned out ahead of the small force following the various trails leading into the forest. To his dismay, Commander Duraunt requested that he stay with the main group in case any signals were sent from those ahead. The rangers of Courth shared a universal system of signaling over distance and in the cover of the forest that allowed for basic communication.

"I knew your father," the Commander glanced over at him from astride his tall dusky war horse that was still a hand or more shorter than the Lambei.

"My father was well known."

"All these men learned much of their craft from him," the Commander gestured vaguely ahead where the other rangers were riding through the grassland with their heads down tracking their prey. "Although, I would bet that you are already far better than they will ever be given the years you spent under Guarin's wing."

Enguer felt heat rise to his face, "Then why do you hold me back when I could serve more effectively out there with them?" he kept his voice calm and respectful despite the irritation he felt toward the officer.

"They have been loyal subjects to the crown for years, serving his majesty without complaint whenever he has called." Commander Duraunt shrugged. "Regardless of your famous name, we must respect those who have proved themselves."

Enguer responded with a begrudging nod. Of course, the Commander was right. What right did he have to trade on his father's good name without proving he could live up to it?

"Don't worry," the Commander smiled. "I suspect you will have the opportunity to earn your oats sooner rather than late."

Commander Duraunt rode beside him on in silence for a while until they reached the dark edge of the thickly forested tree-line. There, four rangers were gathered together waiting for them.

"Commander, there is a trail leading further in that appears more recently used than others. We believe this is the one to follow." The old ranger adjusted the bow on his back so that it clung closer to his body. Enguer had already done the same in anticipation of entering the forest.

"Very well, Suri," Commander Duraunt's eyes peered into the dark wood as if he could somehow see beyond their tangled foliage. "We will stay closer together in case of ambush. Enguer, join your brothers marking the path ahead."

Enguer eagerly kicked his horse forward to stand with the other rangers. To his great relief, none of them rolled their eyes or appeared annoyed. They were all focused on the business ahead. *Good men*, Enguer admitted silently to himself.

"Let's go," the old ranger called Suri was clearly in charge. Enguer and the other rangers took his que and followed closely behind.

Once under the dark canopy of thick branches, Suri ordered one ranger to scout their rear in case anyone followed and two others to shadow their flanks. Enguer knew it to be a standard patrol exercise to avoid being taken by surprise by anything that lay ahead or circle around behind.

"You and I will scout ahead," Suri pat him on the shoulder. "Let's see if you have your father's instincts."

To Enguer's surprise, Suri allowed him to lead. Then it dawned on him that he was being tested. If he failed, none of the rangers would ever take him seriously again and his unearned reputation would be ruined. The pressure was high, but Enguer had learned well how to compartmentalize his fears and anxiety and he pushed his Lambei to the front, concentrating on the narrow trail ahead.

To his eyes, the trail was easy to follow with clear indications that it had been used recently as evidenced by multiple human sized prints pressed into the soft earth. Eyeing them closer, he realized there was something strange about them.

"The people that travelled this way were not your typical bandits or raiders."

Suri was watching him closely. "Why do you say that?"

"They wore sandals." Enguer pointed at the tracks on the ground. "And look there, those wavering lines next to them, caused by heavy robes."

"You have a good eye," Suri sounded impressed. "None of the others caught that. Can you guess a number?"

"At least seven," Enguer studied the tracks closer. "but the freshest tracks lead out of the forest."

"Very good," Suri gave him a wink. "You may prove a match to your father yet."

For the next two hours they followed the trail deeper into the forest. When they came to a shallow stream, they stopped to rest and eat the cold rations they brought with them. Enguer spent his time canvasing the opposite side of the stream, but there were no other signs of passage except for the trail that continued deeper into the forest.

Moving on, they rode less than a quarter of a league before Enguer detected the faint scent of smoke in the air. "Smell that?"

Suri nodded. "Barely. It is close by and at least a day old. There is something else . . . ."

Enguer agreed. There was an underlying pungent odor that belied it as more than a simple cooking or campfire. It was not something he had experienced before, although there was something oddly familiar about it.

One-hundred strides later, Enguer stood with Suri at the edge of a small clearing. In the center stood an elevated altar constructed of stone that was black as a starless night. Carved on its surface and in lines that encircled it, were unusual symbols that appeared to glow from some internal luminescence. On one side of the altar sat a thick stone step and on the other a shallow pit which held the charred remains of what Enguer could only assume were numerous animals.

Trailing Suri, they moved slowly closer to the altar. Within a few feet, Enguer noticed a dark stain on the surface of the altar. Bile rose in his throat as he realized the intent of such a stone forcing his gaze to follow the crimson path into the pit beyond. To his horror, the burnt and disfigured skeletal remains were of no animal he recognized – they were human.

Enguer took a step back and emptied the contents of his stomach on the ground.

"What is the matter?" Commander Duraunt called from the edge of the clearing.

"Bodies. Human bodies, Commander," Suri called back.

The Commander waved to the company of soldiers crowded behind him who immediately surged forward and spaced themselves evenly around the perimeter of the clearing while the Bayles and Fire Priestesses moved to the alter.

"You alright, boy?" Suri was beside him.

Enguer nodded and took a long sip from his waterskin. "I'll be fine."

Commander Duraunt dismounted and strode over to them. "I've heard something of this before and markings similar to those have been popping up on walls in the city over the last few weeks."

After a few minutes one of the Bayles and a Fire Priestess strode over. They wore bleak, featureless expressions that forewarned that the news they would impart was not good.

"This is the work of a Death Cult, Commander," the Priestess nearly growled. "They sacrifice human innocents as part of their blasphemous rituals."

"Can you identify any of the remains?"

The Bayle took the question. "The bodies are too incinerated to recognize; however, we found another pit not far away in the forest that contains discarded clothing. Many of them match descriptions of the nightclothes worn by at least three of the citizens abducted."

"There have been four abductions reported in Courth, but it appears that there are many more bodies than that in the pit." The Commander's eyes held barely restrained rage.

"There are at least a dozen," the Bayle confirmed.

Commander Duraunt's voice softened, "How did they die?"

"Sacrificed to their demon god under a blade upon the altar during a new moon," the Priestess was nearly in a rage herself. "The bodies were then burned in representation of them being cast into the Infernal Planes."

"Horrendous," the Commander whispered nearly inaudible. Then he glanced up at the High Priestess, "Open a portal. I need to speak to the Arch Priest."

Stepping to the side, the High Priestess drew symbols in the air accompanied by low intonation. Seconds later, a line of bright light split the air in front of her before popping into an oval plane that shimmered spectrally chest-high above the ground.

"Your Holiness," the High Priestess called through the portal. "Are you there?"

The image in the portal shifted and then cleared. Through it, Enguer could see the Arch Priest sitting at what appeared to be a desk.

"I am here," he replied.

"Your Holiness, this is Commander Duraunt speaking. I have some distressing news."

"I can see you Commander. What do you have to say?"

Commander Durant and the High Priestess repeated everything they had found in the clearing, including the Bayles discovery of the abductees clothing in the forest. The Arch Priest remained quiet and never interrupted the entire time. When they were done, Tanais leaned in closer to the portal magnifying his stern features. "There is a new moon in two days. If my priestess is correct there will be more abductions and another ritual. Stay there and capture as many as you can, then bring them to me."

The portal winked out.

Enguer, Suri, the Commander, the High Priestess and the Bayle were left staring awkwardly into empty space for a moment before anyone spoke.

"That's it then," the Commander spoke with renewed purpose. "Suri, you and the Priestesses set to work creating a blind that we can hide behind and send a pair of your rangers to clear our tracks and watch for anyone that approaches." With quick nods Suri and the priestess hurried away to begin their work.

The Commander set his gaze on the Bayle. "Find out everything you can about what happened here and who the victims are. We need to be certain before we notify their families."

Finally, he turned to Enguer. "Search the forest beyond the perimeter as well as you can and report anything unusual."

Enguer wasted no time fleeing into the forest. He was glad to be away from the death pit and the awful things that had happened there. He didn't know any of the victims, he didn't need to. Anger welled up in him at the thought of what they must have gone through and the pain it would cause their families. Retribution was not a thing of nature and it felt strange burning inside of him, but it burned all the same and he would seek it gladly on those who had done this.

~~~

Tanais sat in the plush chair before his desk staring into nothing. He had not suspected the possibility of a Death Cult in his city, slavers maybe, but never this. He needed to know more about them and he knew just the two men who might have the answers.

Pulling a large rat from a nearby cage, he inserted a tiny rolled parchment into a small tube on its back. It bore a symbol only the two men would understand. Then he projected his will in the form of a geas upon the poor creature's feeble mind and set it free through a small hole in the base of the wall to his study. The rat knew exactly where to go and would die before it wavered from its course. Tanias disliked using rats for carrying messages, but considering to whom he was sending to it made poetic sense.

Two hours later Tanais was casually walking through the lower sewers of Courth. He carried a light-globe in one hand and held his robes above his ankles in the other to avoid the fetid muck below his feet. The narrow dark corridor he followed opened into an expansive arched cavern over a canal of slow-moving waste with walkways on each side. To his relief, torches lined the cavern at short enough intervals that he could put away his light-globe and place a damp cloth over his face and mouth. The air was foul and dank relieved only by a slight breeze that occasionally drifted through from some unseen source far above.

In spite of the discomfort of the setting, the unpleasant location was the perfect meeting place for those who should never been seen together in public. Guild Masters disguised as merchants were not the most convenient associates even if it was a reasonable thing for the Arch Priest to have the two most successful merchants in Courth as members of the special commission. Especially considering that secret meetings with no staff, scribes or pretense would certainly come under scrutiny by those in the know and risk unraveling his complex and decidedly improper relationship with the Guild Masters. So, they met here, among the filth and putrid decay, to discuss important matters of the city.

Tanais continued on his way, he didn't have far to go and rationalized his judgement for the thousandth time doing business with thieves and assassins. He told himself that it was better that he could exert some influence and temper their most extreme activities than to be at war with them. Over the years they had worked together to enrich Courth, the Guilds and the Temple in ways that would have otherwise been impossible. It wasn't the best of means, but it was a means to a better end.

Turning down another narrow corridor, he came to what appeared to be a dead end. Reaching up into a dark corner, he pulled a small lever and a section of the wall the size of a doorway swung open to reveal a dimly lit hallway that ended in a stairway leading further down a short distance away. Tanais left the door behind him open and carefully descended. At the bottom another short hallway opened into a sizeable grotto with a large pool of fresh water at its center and multiple entries along its perimeter. Torches set into sconces on the rough-hewn walls produced flickering shadows that danced sporadically around the chamber even though the air here was still.

Too many shadows . . . Tanais thought to himself.

Stepping further into the cavern, he was not surprised to see two men standing next to a small wooden table set with a pitcher and three cups. One man was thin, the other a little heavier, both about the same height and neither as tall as Tanais. To look at them in plain tunics and breeches under unassuming wool cloaks one would never have guessed that they were two of the wealthiest men in the Western Kingdoms. Only he knew that they were fraternal twins.

"Greetings Priest," the heavier one spoke without a smile. He never seemed to smile. The thinner brother smiled, but said nothing.

"Hello Dyzig," Tanais nodded to the first one and then the second, "Gigot."

Gigot picked up the pitcher and poured a translucent burgundy liquid into the three cups on the table and handed one to Tanais and then Dyzig. Tanais took a short sip and then a longer one of the chilled wine. "Mekali, my favorite."

"We know you better than yourself," Gigot's smile broadened.

Tanais studied the brothers. Of the two, Gigot was the brains of the guild while Dyzig was brutish and streetwise. Throughout their entire career the two had managed to keep their relationship a secret and now they ran the most powerful Guild in Courth. Although no one knew they were brothers, some suspected they were lovers, given their close association over the years. It was a rumor they shrugged off preferring the fantasy of others to the truth considering their parentage.

Always direct to the point, Dyzig set down his empty cup. "Why have you called this meeting?"

Tanais didn't want to spend any more time in the depths of stink than necessary and was happy to dispense with idle chit-chat. "I need information."

He told them about the discovery of the Death Cult and the sacrificial rituals taking place in The Wilds. Neither of the brothers appeared shocked or surprised by the news, but then again, Tanais doubted they would show it if they were. Rather, they kept their gazes steady on him soaking in every word.

When he was done, Tanais drained his cup of the last drops of wine and asked, "What do you know of this Death Cult?"

The brothers looked at each other briefly before Gigot answered, "We know little of them other than their symbols and that they have been quietly recruiting followers for the past two years. So far, they have done nothing to concern us."

Tanais pondered the man's answer a moment before he responded. Often there were clues in the way they spoke that intimated the truth of their concerns. "Perhaps it would be beneficial to us all if you reconsidered your position on the matter bearing in mind what we saw today."

"Perhaps," Dyzig replied. "But a few dead villagers and one or two from the city interests us very little. This seems like a temple matter to us. You know how we feel about getting mixed up in political or religious affairs unless we are being paid to gather information or blackmail by a client."

"Am I not your client? Even your best client?" Tanais was growing irritated. It was bad enough that he was colluding with these two let alone paying them temple money for information to do work he could not possibly be associated with.

"Yes, you're Holiness." Gigot quickly interrupted what Tanais was sure to be his brother's sharp retort. "We will set our people to the task right away." As if by some silent signal, the two men bowed deeply and slipped away into a darkened tunnel close behind them.

Tanais stared after them into the darkness while he considered what he had learned today. Then a man's voice spoke from the blackness outside the rings of light provided by the dim torches, "You play a dangerous game with those two Tanais."

The Arch Priest was not startled, he knew who was there, "That's why I have Assassins for bodyguards," he shot back.

"They must know you would not meet with them here alone. Otherwise, they could abduct you themselves and hold you for ransom. The fact that you don't have a number of Fire Priests standing behind you was probably quite perplexing." The voice laughed, still well back in the dark. "They had at least twenty of their thugs only a couple of turns back down the tunnel."

"And I can trust you and your shadows more?" Tanais snorted.

The voice replied in a mocking, hurt tone, "I am your *brother* after all. Besides, how could I ever explain to mother that I allowed anything to happen to you?"

Tanais spat on the wet cobblestones, "She's been dead twenty years."

"True," the voice replied. "I guess I just owe you for keeping me alive long enough after she died to stand on my own, so I return the favor."

Tanais quietly nodded his head and walked back through the dark passage toward the secret entrance to the temple, "Well, thank the Fat Man for me anyway." There was no response from the darkness.

He knew that he waded through a crowd of men around him but he never saw nor heard a single one of them. There was no doubt in his mind that had the Guild Masters tried to harm him, they and their men would have never left the tunnels alive. He felt a shiver go up his spine as he realized how good these men were at their deadly profession and was glad they were on his side.

Chapter 3

Sacrifice

Enguer watched silently from a position high up in a tree as the Arch Priest Tanais walked among the encampment reassuring the soldiers with words meant to lend confidence to their endeavor. It was nearly an hour before sunset, yet the forest was already as dark as night and growing colder. The Arch Priest had arrived earlier in the day with a dozen Fire Priests and two rangers to add to their small company. It was a shock to everyone when he showed up so unexpectedly with his entourage from out of the forest, a welcome surprise to be sure, and it reinforced the urgent nature of what they planned to do there tonight.

He climbed down from his watch post, there was no point in staying up there after dark, and soon they would all be trekking back to the clearing with the altar to set up their ambush. Tonight, it would be a new moon and the Fire Priestesses were sure that the Death Cult would be stretching another body over their bloody stone to sacrifice. The thought of it sent shivers down Enguer's spine.

"Enguer, it is good to see you." The Arch Priest met him at the base of the tree.

"Greetings, Your Holiness."

"Where are Suri and the other rangers?"

Enguer gestured to the surrounding forest, "Out there, Your Holiness, keeping watch."

"I should have expected that," the Arch Priest laughed. "It has been some time since I mounted a proper adventure."

"Is that what this is, Your Holiness, an adventure?"

The Arch Priest's set his gaze hard on Enguer and his smile disappeared. "A sad adventure of the darkest kind, I'm afraid. Prepare yourself for the worst." He lay a hand on Enguer's shoulder and walked into the night.

Although they were nearly a quarter league from the clearing with the altar, Commander Duraunt had not allowed any campfires for fear that the scent of smoke and cooked food would be noticed by anyone within a league of their encampment. It didn't bother Enguer. Often, he and his father would camp without fire to avoid attracting the attention of certain predators that stalked The Wilds.

A low whistle interrupted his thoughts. It was the signal from Commander Duraunt to break camp. The dim glow of a light-globe blinked between the trees nearby that served as the gathering point for the soldiers and priests. When Enguer arrived, the Commander gave him a quick nod that they were ready to go and Enguer led them into the dark forest. The plan was for Enguer to lead company back to the clearing with the altar while the other rangers shadowed their movements from the concealment of the forest. It was an important responsibility considering that without a ranger to guide them through the dense tangles of The Wilds the soldiers and priests would likely become hopelessly lost.

Enguer had no trouble finding the way while the two rangers the Arch Priest brought with him stayed near the rear to make sure everyone stayed together. In almost total darkness, they covered the distance to the clearing in a little over an hour and quickly found their places behind the natural blinds the rangers had created earlier to keep them hidden.

In the dark and the cold, they all waited quietly over the long hours of the night until the luminescent moon was nearly straight overhead, dimly visible between the tips of the trees and their encroaching limbs. The men and women stirred and shifted, numb from sitting still for so long and the unspoken worry that their quarry might not show up. Then from the west came the call of a night owl out of the depths of The Wilds and a moment later another. It was the call they were hoping for alerting them that someone was approaching. Enguer felt the tension rising. He repositioned his bow and loosely nocked an arrow.

Through the trees on the west side of the clearing a flicker of light bobbed in the distance. Soon he could see that there were many more that followed in a line behind it along the same trail that led back to the edge of the forest near Courth. Whoever these people were, they were confident in where they were going as if they had travelled the path many times before.

Minutes passed before a column of hooded shapes carrying torches and lanterns emerged from the forest into the clearing. *These must be the cultists*, he thought, His palms were sweaty and his breathing had increased. Never had he felt this way on a hunt before, but then again, he had never been hunting another human with deadly intent. Silently, the sinister figures formed a circle around the altar and began to intone a low chant.

Enguer counted twenty of them.

Slowly he altered his position to a low crouch that would allow him the use of his bow, if needed, and waited. He was expecting the order to attack at any moment, but it had not come. *What was the Commander waiting for?*

He listened closely. From the pitch of the chanting, Enguer was able to discern that the hooded figures were both men and women. He had never killed a person before, much less a woman, and he lamented the possibility that he might have to do so tonight. They all looked so weak and vulnerable standing in the open circle with their backs toward the forest where Enguer's comrades lay hiding. It was too easy. Enguer began to hope that maybe the Commander would just take them all prisoner and leave the bloodshed for another day.

A sharp cry rent the air abruptly drawing his attention back to the forest where a lone man, hood down, entered the clearing with an infant swaddled in his arms. He carried it carefully, as if it were his own child, and placed it gently upon the stone altar. There, the man stood over it and joined in the rhythmic chanting. The bundle wiggled suddenly, enough to loosen the swaddle and extend a tiny hand into the air, before erupting in another high-pitched cry that pierced the silence of the forest. None of the cultists reacted or seemed bothered by the uneasy child.

Enguer stared in horror. Were they going to sacrifice the small child?

A torch was set into a sconce attached to the side of the altar by a cultist from the circle. The flickering light illuminated the face of the man who had brought the baby. Enguer gasped. He was the hawk-nosed priest that had prepared his father's body for burial only weeks before. Rochette was his name, a good and holy priest by anyone's account. Enguer could not believe that this man could be involved in such an evil thing.

Rochette raised his arms high in the air and the cultists responded by gradually increasing the pace and volume of their chant. It was growing toward a crescendo that could mean only one thing. *Commander!* Enguer urged silently. The presence of the infant had removed all thoughts of uncertainty about killing these monsters.

As if the Commander had somehow heard his desperate plea, a thunderclap shook the ground around the clearing sending the cultists stumbling in shock. That was the signal. The soldiers broke through the leafy blinds with swords in hand from three directions. Behind them, the Fire Priests followed close by a step. Enguer barely got a shot off, impacting the closest cultist in the gut, when the clearing erupted in flames.

Standing with his back to the infant, Rochette's outstretched hands sent waves of fire into soldiers, Fire Priests and cultists indiscriminately. Enguer, partially shielded by trees and foliage fell back from the intense heat, dodging behind the low rise that surrounded the clearing. When he regained his footing enough to peer back through the burning mass of branches and vines, he was sickened by the scene before him.

Scorched and twisted bodies lay everywhere in the clearing. The corpses were burned so badly it was nearly impossible to tell one from another. The once lush greenery that surrounded the open space was blackened and burning. The fresh earthy scent of forest was overcome by smoke and the charred odor of death. At the center of it all stood one man, and besides the bawling infant, the only living thing in the clearing – Rochette.

Enguer watched the Arch Priest Tanais step into the clearing to face the death priest. He appeared to take little notice of the ruin that surrounded him, despite the fact that many of the blackened and smoldering corpses where the same men and women he had blessed earlier at the camp. The Arch Priest must be a brave man, indeed, to confront the man with the power to wreak such awful devastation on human life. Enguer had to trust that Tanais knew what he was doing, but just in case kept his bow ready in case Rochette raised his arms to unleash more fiery death upon them.

"Good of you to come, Tanais," Rochette nearly spat his old master's name. "Care to join me for one last dance?"

Anger lit inside the Arch Priest's eyes and his response was low and steady like a snake about to strike. "What has happened to you Rochette? How could you have turned from the light of Sunna?"

"The light!" Rochette laughed almost hysterically. "The light trembles at the power of the dark, waiting to consume it, extinguish its final illumination!"

"Those are the words of a mad man. Come quietly with me and we shall seek salvation together. You were content once. I remember how you took comfort among us after your dear wife died." Tanais held out a hand toward the priest. "Even after all of this, Sunna may offer redemption because of your lifetime of service. I believe there must be a spark of light left in you still."

"You will not take me alive," Rochette sneered at Tanais. "My death will only please my god all the more. How many more of you will enter the land of the dead with me?"

"Rochette . . ." Enguer could see genuine sadness cross the Arch Priest's features. The two men must have been great friends at one time.

"The Lord of Death has opened my eyes to a new reality, Holiness! He promised to reunite me with my poor Siva and give me power for us to live forever…and rule. What does Sunna offer? Light! The fantasy of a blissful afterlife?" Rochette was defiant, even proud.

Tanais looked around in mock surprise, "And where is your beloved Siva? I do not see her? What sort of deranged promise did you believe?"

"You fool! Idiot! My Lord would have given her to me tonight after this last sacrifice! And you ruined it! Ruined everything! Except vengeance. There will be awful vengeance upon you and those you love!" Rochette began to laugh again.

Tanais whispered sadly, "Your Lord has no hold on Siva, she was a good and pious woman. She lives in the light of Sunna now. You have sacrificed your life for a false promise."

Rochette smiled. It was an evil smile full of mockery and disdain. "Perhaps you are correct, Tanais. I do have a spark of light left inside of me. Come closer, let me show you . . ."

In the blink of an eye, the death priest's hands were in the air again alight with flames. Enguer barely loosed his arrow when the fire sprang forth. Tanais never moved, he didn't even flinch and Enguer feared the Arch Priest would die where he stood.

Impossibly, Enguer's arrow bounced harmlessly away just before it impacted the death priest in the chest. To his surprise, several other arrows had streaked from the protection of the forest at the same time and they too were deflected by some unseen force. The fire pouring from Rochette's hands abruptly stopped it's advance a span in front of him, curling in every direction around him, making it plain that he was surrounded by some kind of protective barrier. Rochette screamed as the flames of his own making filled the invisible bubble and then disappeared altogether, leaving the death priest seething with anger and singed all over.

"You cannot keep me long in here, Tanais! Soon you will grow tired while I rest and then you . . ." Rochette tried to gasp. His mouth flapping and eyes bulging like a fish pulled from the water.

Cautiously, Enguer made his way over to stand next to the Arch Priest. The remaining rangers, soldiers, and priests came out as well. None of the Bayles had survived.

"What is wrong with him?" Enguer whispered.

Tanais glanced over at him, clearly upset at the situation. "He is right. I would have eventually tired holding the barrier in place. But he did not count on the flames consuming the air inside and I have sealed it tight. When he passes out the men will subdue him and we will take him back to Courth to stand trial in the light of Sunna and under the judgment of the King."

Rochette was beating on the edge of the barrier, desperate for release, his face purple and veiny with no hope for a breath. It didn't last long and soon he had no more strength to put up a fight. He slid slowly down the edge of the barrier to lay twitching and helpless on the ground. It was a grotesque sight that immediately conjured images from Enguer's childhood when he had witnessed a man nearly drowned in the Esmee River.

"Bind him and put a linen in his mouth once he is revived," Tanais ordered. "The barrier is away now."

The priests and priestesses immediately rushed over to resuscitate the death priest while the soldiers prepared leather straps to bind him. After only a few moments Rochette was breathing once again although he had not yet regained consciousness. The soldiers strapped him unceremoniously over the back of a horse, shoved a cloth into his mouth and lashed it tight with a leather thong. Enguer was impressed by their efficiency and wondered if they had done this before. It was an odd skill for a soldier to possess.

~~~

Tanais sat at the small wooden table sipping from a cup of fine Mekali wine in the cool air of the grotto where he awaited the arrival of the Guild Masters of Courth. It was late in the evening after a sleepless night and a long day riding back to the city from The Wilds. They did not stay long at the ritual site where they had captured Rochette. Only long enough to bury the dead and send the rangers into the surrounds to track down any of the cultists that had escaped into the forest. To his disappointment, they didn't find any nearby and Tanais didn't want to risk sending the rangers deeper into The Wilds to find them. He wasn't too worried about the cultists return. The Wilds had a way of dealing with lost men.

He had considered asking Reskalin, to bring men to the forest that night to make sure none of the cultists escaped alive. However, Tanais discarded the idea almost as quickly as he had thought it. Reskalin's men were likely not as skilled in the wilderness as they were in the cities and might have disrupted their entire mission. Although he suspected the rogue had managed to plant a few as soldiers anyway.

"Are you praying or sleeping, priest?" a voice asked with some humor.

Tanais was startled but tried not to show it. He had not realized he was dozing. "I was content until you broke the silence. Why have you summoned me at this hour?"

Dyzig and Gigot walked out of the darkness to take seats with him at the table. Gigot filled their cups with wine and smiled, "We just wanted to let you know that Reskalin returned to Arre today."

The Arch Priest was glad of the near-darkness for concealing the look of shock that must have sprung upon his face. *How could this man know about Reskalin and that he had left Courth?* Tanais responded with a noncommittal grunt.

"He told us that The Fat Man would be grateful if we took you under our protection for the foreseeable future," Dyzig sighed heavily. "Looks like you are stuck with us for a while."

"Can I assume that all of your people are aware of this instruction?"

"They are, most surely," Gigot confirmed. "And as long as we are alive and in masters of our guild, you are as safe as a new-born babe at its mother's tit while you are within the confines of any city in the kingdom. Walk the street day or night draped in gold and jewels, no one will trouble you. However, we cannot guarantee your safety outside of the city, I'm sure you understand."

Tanais sat in silence again. *Why did Reskalin go without telling him?* It was true that they were mostly estranged and almost never corresponded; but they had gotten on well enough over the last few days that he thought maybe there was a chance of reconciling. Now Reskalin was gone without a word leaving him with these two to look after his safety? He and Reskalin may not have been the best of friends but they were blood and with it came a certain level of trust. The Fat Man had long arms, indeed, if he had the power to influence the Guild Masters of Courth. Tanais was genuinely impressed. The old fella had done well for himself over the years.

Tanais changed the subject. "I assume you have heard of the events in The Wilds last night?"

Dyzig nodded. "A few of our men did not return from your little escapade"

For the second time that night Tanais was surprised, if a little less so. He did a quick calculation in his head and came up with the answer. "You've managed to infiltrate the city guard?" It couldn't have been the Bayles or the rangers. Certainly not the priests. At least he hoped not.

Dyzig shrugged.

"Then you know we have Rochette." Tanais leaned forward. "A few of his priest got away into The Wilds. I'll need you to keep an eye out in case their dark arts manage to return them safely to Courth or one of the nearby villages. Here is a list of names of those we identified."

Gigot took the list and placed it in his pocket without looking at it. "It is unlikely that any of them will make it out of The Wilds alive."

"If they have power like Rochette, how can you be so sure?"

"When we last met, you asked us to look into them." Gigot glanced at Dyzig. "We did."

"They were all unexceptional. Low-level tradesmen, farmers, a blacksmith." Dyzig took a swig of wine from his cup. "Seems the only one of note was the priest Rochette."

"Yeah," Gigot agreed. "He was said to have a magnetic charisma, people liked him and his crazy ideas made an impression on a few of the dim-witted."

"So, are we done with the death cult?" Tanais was skeptical but hopeful.

Dyzig waved a hand. "As long as you have Rochette, it looks like it."

"If they pop up again anywhere in the kingdom, even if it's just a rumor or gut feeling, I expect you will inform me immediately."

"We will." The way Gigot said it couldn't have been more non-committal. "Now, about the foreign merchants in Port Francik."

Tanais didn't want to talk business. "Let's discuss that in a few days after I have rested and the trial of Rochette is over."

"Very well, priest." Gigot rose to his feet, Dyzig followed. "We will speak again in a few days."

The pair walked into the darkness together, but before their footsteps receded into the distance Gigot called back, "You are safe now priest, but beware, the rats down here can be viscous!"

Tanais almost laughed out loud. *Was it a warning or a threat?* He was too tired to worry about that now. They had no idea the relationship he shared with the Fat Man. He didn't want to think about that right now, his mind was preoccupied with Reskalin. He poured himself another cup of Mekali wine. If he drank much more his 'watchers' might have to carry him up to his bed.

He leaned back in the small wooden chair and closed his eyes. Twenty years. It had been over twenty years since he had made the decision to leave Reskalin in Arre. It seemed the right thing to do at the time with so much at stake and the lives and power structures that hung in the balance. Reskalin was too young and didn't see it that way. Reskalin must have felt abandoned, eventually leading the poor wretch down a most unexpected road. Tanais should have known.

At the time, Tanais thought he had done well to look after Reskalin. He provided a fair home and education, until the child was old enough to do well enough without his supervision. It was in those early years that the Order of the FIVE needed him more than ever. It was the same for The FatMan, Enguer's father – Gaurin Rand, and two others. Already a powerful influence in the Western Kingdoms, The Fat Man assured Tanais that his people would look after Reskalin while they were away. Tanais was very appreciative not realizing the deep involvement Reskalin would eventually delve into The Fat Man's 'Business'. It wasn't The Fat Man's fault. Neither he nor Tanais realized what they were in for when they joined the Order of the FIVE, or the magnitude of the sacrifices that would come with it.

To his great sadness, his friend Gaurin Rand left the Order for reasons of his own. He was replaced and only years later did Tanais learn the reasons for Gaurin's sudden departure. The ranger had somehow found the time to take a wife and sire a small child a year or two older than Reskalin. His name was Enguer.

The FIVE departed Arre on what they thought would be a short adventure of only a few months. Those months stretched into the better part of a decade and when they finally returned, Tanais found everything had changed. Reskalin was secretive and elusive teenager; barely acknowledging Tanais return as if he was an inconvenience to be avoided. Just speaking with him was an endeavor of fortitude. Tanais pursued Reskalin for weeks in an effort to revive their relationship but Reskalin would have nothing to do with it. Finally, he returned home to Courth and resumed his duties in the temple.

Over the years he kept correspondence with the Fat Man and learned that Reskalin had achieved a very high position within the organization and doing well. Reskalin never replied to Tanais letters. Only recently had Tanais been surprised when Reskalin showed up out of nowhere with a few highly skilled henchmen to protect him, compliments of the Fat Man. This had afforded them the unexpected chance to speak again and express their differences. It had been an encouraging conversation and Reskalin appeared to accept Tanais's reasons for what had happened in Arre so many years before. The Order of the FIVE had evicted much evil from many lands, saved countless lives and built the promise of bright futures where there had been none before. He hoped Reskalin understood that now too. Tanais wished he could have spent more time with Reskalin while in Courth, but that was not to be.

Perhaps he would go to Arre when the trial was over. He could count on a fond reunion with the Fat Man and perhaps this time, Reskalin as well. Tanais rose from his chair and muttered a small prayer to Sunna for guidance. Whether it was for his relationship with Reskalin or back to the warmth and comfort of his own bed he was not sure.

Chapter 4

Something Evil Inside

"Look at him, standing there like an imbecile," the Duke compulsively stroked his long mustaches between his words. "We should just remove his head and be done with it."

"What is wrong with him?" The Earl of Berci leaned forward, his long-curled locks disrupting the short stack of parchment on the tabletop where he sat.

Tanais rose from his chair on the side of the room closer to where the Rochette was restrained by shackles and held upright between two of the king's guard. "He is in a trance. I don't believe he has gone mad." The Arch Priest shot a dark glance at the Duke. "It will be up to King Francik to decide his fate. Before then, I hope to extract more information from him."

Enguer watched the scene play out from the shadows in a far corner. From his vantage he could clearly see the members of the special commission seated at a long table facing the unresponsive stare of the Death Priest. The chamber was illuminated by two braziers set on pedestals between them that did nothing to alleviate the cold dampness that hung thick in the air. They were assembled in what Enguer would describe as a dungeon two levels under the Temple of Sunna not far from the room or cell, he wasn't sure which it might be, where Rochette had been confined since his capture. On their return from The Wilds, Tanais insisted that the Death Priest remain under the supervision of the priests rather than the city guard because of the unique danger that he posed. Enguer had no idea that the temple had facilities for detention. Nor did he have the courage to ask Tanais why. He supposed they had their reasons. One was standing before them now.

"How long has he been this way?" the magistrate sat between the Duke and the merchants Dyzig and Gigot. He appeared almost bored as if he had better things to do elsewhere.

"Only since last night," Commander Duraunt replied. "Which is odd considering he was quite furious when he first awoke in his cell.

He was unconscious the whole way back from where we captured him, thank Sunna."

"What has he told you?" the magistrate directed his question to Tanais.

"Not much, so far." Tanais spread his hands wide. "He goes on about serving his dark god, but will not reveal the deity's name or the reason for the sacrifices demanded to appease him. I will need time to find out more."

"What more do we need?" the Duke sneered. "He admits to murder and coercing others to do the same to some made up god that has no name. Take him before the king and be done with it."

A low, throaty growl rumbled from Rochette startling everyone in the chamber, but his features remained still and impassive. The Duke, whose words seemed to illicit the unexpected response, looked on wild-eyed and fearful, but kept his tongue quiet. Under any other circumstance, Enguer might have thought it amusing.

"Careful your words, my lord Duke," Tanais quietly cautioned.

Silence reigned throughout the room for a long moment before the Earl's words broke the stillness, "What do we do now, Tanais? Are there others like him that endanger our citizens? Commander Duraunt's report spoke of several cultists that fled into The Wilds that the rangers were not permitted to run down. What of them?"

"I believe that the surviving cultists, if any could have survived a night in The Wilds, were unremarkable. Those that died to Rochette's fire and our arrows were common tradesmen, farmers and low-level priests that once served Sunna. None of them could pose a significant threat on their own." The Arch Priests eyes flickered briefly over the two merchants on the council. It was so quick that Enguer was sure it wasn't deliberate. "In any case, I have given Commander Duraunt a list of those we recognized in case they re-appear in the city."

The Council appeared to breath a collective sigh of relief at that and the tension in the room subsided remarkably. Even Enguer, from a distance of ten paces and purely an observer in this matter felt his anxiety slipping away. There were others standing not far from him, mostly guards and priests, that shifted quietly in the shadows with the respite. It reminded Enguer that he was the only ranger in the room and he wondered again why it was that Tanais had requested his attendance.

"Now, if there are no more questions, we will return Rochette to his cell and continue our interrogation." Tanais flashed a hand at the guards holding the Death Priest. "We will plan to convene the council again tomorrow to discuss the results. And in case you're wondering," he looked squarely at the duke, "I am personally keeping the king fully informed of every detail along the way."

The Duke hardly noticed. His attention was on the back of Rochette as he was dragged out of the room by his guards with a line of fire-priests following close behind.

"If we find out anything urgent I will, of course, inform you immediately." Sounding much like a dismissal, the council rose from their seats casually chatting with each other when a shout echoed from the hallway Rochette had just been take.

"Death awaits you all!"

The light banter went dead silent. In panic or fear, perhaps a good measure of both, the Duke bolted out of the room and up the toward temple exit.

Tanais pat the air in front of him to calm the rest of them, "He does that sometimes."

Nervous laughter reverberated through the stone chamber, but not a one of the council members slowed their steps as they crowded the stairwell out. Enguer wanted to follow but it was his place to stay with the Arch Priest until he was dismissed.

Once they had all gone, Tanais motioned for Enguer to join him in the center of the room. "I fear that there is something more than simply madness that has infected Rochette."

Enguer was taken aback by the Arch Priest's candor. For starts, he could offer no advice on the matter of a man's sanity. He was a simple ranger more suited to a solitary life in The Wilds rather than the populace of city-dwellers and he certainly had no experience with the complex intrigue of politics. One again, it begged the question, and he had to ask, "Why have you summoned me here, your Holiness? I don't see how I can be helpful now that Rochette has been captured."

Tanais regarded him thoughtfully for a long moment before he spoke, "In the decades that your father and I adventured together and even later after I was selected as the Arch Priest of Sunna in Courth, I always relied on his advice. His extraordinary perception and understanding of human nature were an invaluable resource. You knew him as a skilled authority on animal behavior, but what you did not know was that he was just as skilled at interpreting human behavior." The Arch Priest barked a quick laugh, "I'm not sure he made a distinction between the two."

"That is something I did not know about my father, but what does that have to do with me?"

"Because I see much of the same in you." As if to emphasize his point, the Arch Priest poked Enguer in the chest with his knobby index finger causing him to flinch. It was a characteristic of his father that he had nearly forgotten. He would often poke Enguer in the same way to make sure he had his attention.

The Arch Priest smiled and continued, "I would like you to watch Rochette closely during the interrogations and report to me your observations. If you have half the talent of your father, you might see something I miss."

Enguer nodded. His father would have wanted him to help if he could. "Yes, your Holiness. I will stay and tell you what I can. When will you speak with Rochette next?"

"Right now."

~~~

Rochette sat in small room constructed of white stone, just like the rest of the temple, with no windows and a single door formed entirely by thick iron bars. There was no furniture, a wash bin, nor even a chamber pot in the room – it was completely empty leaving the Death Priest no choice but to sit on the dusty floor. It did not bother Rochette, or at least it did not bother the physical body that was once the man Rochette. His cognizance, understanding and awareness of who he once was, was long gone. Behind his half-open eyes there was a new sentience that gazed out into the world and those orbs burned with hate and pride.

Yalal rejoiced when he first dominated the high priest. The man had power and influence that he could manipulate to his advantage. He did so very effectively, at least in the beginning. His plan was simple – revitalize a long-extinct death cult and gather a following until he was powerful enough to take control of Courth. Then, with the power of a kingdom, he could spread his influence far beyond its borders. Yalal knew it would take time, perhaps many years, but unlike others like him he was patient. He could live forever moving from one body to the next with no disruption in the line of succession if he was careful enough.

To his dismay, that plan didn't work out very well. He had to suffer fools for followers that eventually brought Tanais and the king's guard down upon their heads. And now he found himself here, bound and gagged in a tiny stone room, waiting for some idiot to try and pull the truth from him. He was hardly concerned. They could question and torture this body all they pleased without doing any harm to him. Unless they killed it. Yalal didn't believe it would come to that. At least not in the short time before his new plan would take effect.

Already, the feeble-minded duke would be running to the king with words that would convince him to do as Yalal instructed. It was an ambitious scheme that he was entirely unsure would work, but if it did, he would usher in a new breed of terror to unleash on the world. Despite the gag, a thin line of drool ran down Rochette's chin. Remarkable how the body reacted to his desires.

Yalal was pleased.

~~~

"How is our guest?"

The fire-priest bowed before he replied, "Unchanged, your Holiness. Quiet since we brought him back to his cell."

"Let us in."

The fire-priest bowed again and gestured to one of four king's guards near the entrance to open up the cell. Enguer studied Rochette through the bars of the door while the guard worked the key in the heavy latch. The Death Priest sat cross-legged with hands bound behind his back, his eyes were nearly closed and he held the damp rag of the gag between his teeth breathing easily through his nose. The strong scent of urine pervaded the space with the obvious source a small puddle underneath Rochette's right leg.

"Douse him," Tanais ordered one of the guards. "He smells like a chamber-pot."

The guard picked up a bucket of water stationed nearby and dumped the cold contents over Rochette's head. He didn't even flinch. Nor did his slow and even breathing change one bit. Enguer knew from his own frequent meditation that what he was witnessing was nearly impossible.

The Arch Priest appeared to pay little heed and marched in as soon as the guard was out of the way. The fire-priest followed to stand next to him in front of their prisoner. Enguer stayed where he was, at the edge of the doorway, he could see and hear everything fine from there.

"Wake up, Rochette," Tanais commanded.

No response.

There was a long moment of silence before Tanais spoke again, "His mind is closed to me, touch him with your power."

The fire-priest reached down, right hand glowing red and briefly grasped Rochette's arm. When he removed his hand, the skin where he had touched the Death Priest appeared bright red and blistered. Still, Rochette never moved a muscle or showed any outward sign of pain.

Tanais grunted. "We may be forced to ask one of the 'Enlightened Ones' to assist us. They have more experience dealing with matters of the mind."

Enguer wasn't sure, but he thought he noticed a slight twitch from Rochette's right eye.

"Very well," the Arch Priest sighed. "We will return tomorrow."

Enguer stood away for the two priests to exit before the guard closed and locked the iron-bar door.

"Keep him clean," Tanais addressed the fire-priest, "and if anything changes send for me immediately."

With a quick nod to Enguer, the Arch Priest strode back along the dimly lit hallway toward the stairs that would take them back up to the temple proper. He remained silent the whole way, giving away no sign of his emotions other than the clear lines of frustration on his face. Enguer was sure the silence was deliberate and dared not speak of anything until he was prompted to do so. They walked through the forest of white pillars that stretched into the shadows of the vaulted ceiling high above and over the smooth grey marble that paved the massive floor of the cella where the masses would congregate during ritual days. The priests and priestesses they passed bowed respectfully to the Arch Priest without losing a step in their travels to one part of the temple or another. To Enguer it all looked chaotic and devoid of order like a disturbed anthill.

Turning down a wide hallway, it wasn't long before they came to a set of ornately carved double doors flanked by a pair of fire-priestesses. When they noticed the Arch Priest's approach, the women immediately opened both doors and bowed formally. Striding through without pause, Enguer thought for a moment he might be stopped and questioned, instead, the priestesses simply closed the door behind them.

"Sit, sit," Tanais motioned to a chair facing a massive wooden desk carved with the same intricate symbols of Sunna as the double doors. The Arch Priest fell into a larger chair opposite Enguer on the other side of the desk.

"So?"

Enguer didn't need to ask what he was talking about. There was only one reason Tanais had brought him back to his office to speak privately.

"I believe Rochette heard every word you said." Enguer paused.

The Arch Priest leaned forward a little. "There is something else, isn't there?"

Enguer hoped he didn't ask how he knew the things he was saying since he wasn't sure how to explain it to himself. "Yes. At the end when you mentioned the 'Enlightened Ones' . . . there was a hint of fear."

"Now *that* is interesting." Tanais leaned back in his chair and looked up at the patterned ceiling. "Perhaps I can use that information to get something out of him tomorrow."

"Rochette displayed an amazing level of control during the interview. Are all of your high priests so highly trained in meditation?"

"Hardly," the Arch Priest sniffed. "He appeared to be in more of a trance than a state of meditation. Except that if what you say is true and he could understand everything I was saying and even react to it, then it was no trance."

Enguer was surprised to hear this. "Rochette didn't even flinch when the fire-priest burned him."

Tanais shook his head, "That surprised me as well. It was no hollow threat to bring an 'Enlightened One' to . . ."

There was a sudden and urgent knock at the door.

"Come!" Tanais responded.

One-half of the double doors opened and a priestess stepped in and bowed. "You're Holiness. The king has summoned the special council. He will arrive at the temple within minutes."

"King Francik is coming to the temple?" The Arch Priest appeared shocked. "Do we know why?"

"No Holiness. We have only just been informed that the king and the special council will convene in the temple immediately."

"Very well," Tanais gestured wildly to her. "Make preparations. Quickly!"

The door closed behind the priestess before he finished his sentence.

The Arch Priest stood and smoothed his white robes. "Why is he so impatient? I have not yet had the chance to brief him on today's interrogations." He threw his hands in the air. "Let's go."

"You want me to attend you with the king?"

Tanais leveled a very serious gaze on him. "Especially with the king."

~~~

"Your Highness, we have not had an opportunity to properly interrogate Rochette. There could be more . . ."

The king slammed his fist on the table, causing the council members to jump. The duke, sitting immediately to the king's right, nearly fell out of his chair in shock. "Have you been outside of the temple since you returned with Rochette? I would guess no. The people are shouting for his head! What else could he have to say of any consequence? The duke is right, we have the head of the snake we might as well cut it off!"

"There may be more that we don't know about . . ."

"Like the ones we do know about? Farmers and tradesmen?" The king shook his head vigorously, "I will not have unrest in Courth when we have the leader of the cult in chains right here under this very roof!"

Rochette was brought into the room held between two of the king's guards. He was dripping wet as if he had been doused with a bucket of water just moments earlier. Otherwise, from Enguer's usual place in the far corner of the room, he did not notice anything different from the last time he saw the Death Priest.

"Put him in the cage," the king gestured to a square structure constructed entirely of iron bars that had been brought into the room. It was easily large enough to accommodate Rochette's slight frame with room to spare once the guards gracelessly thrust him inside, closing the barred door behind him.

"Is it safe to remove his gag?" The king looked over at Tanais uncertainly.

"Yes, Your Highness," Tanais gave a nod. "As long as his hands are bound, he will not be able to cast a spell that would harm us."

Tanais motioned to one of the guards standing near the cage. Without hesitation he reached between the bars and pulled down the gag in Rochette's mouth leaving it to dangle around his neck. The Death Priest made no move to resist or assist, instead, he continued to stare blankly into the distance.

It struck Enguer as odd that Rochette would put himself into an unresponsive trance-like state whenever he was brought before the commission. Although he was hardly much more talkative in his private cell except for the occasional rant or threat aimed at those that imprisoned him. Whatever the purpose of this meeting, Enguer doubted that it would produce any further gains with the defiant prisoner.

King Francik leaned forward over the long table he shared with the members of the commission. He sat centermost facing Rochette two or three strides away with only the thin iron bars him. From his position, Enguer noticed a remarkable dichotomy between the two – whereas the king was tall and powerfully built with long dark locks and sun-tanned skin, Rochette was pale by comparison, short and frail-looking with a clean-shaven pate. Somehow, he looked older than the king even though Enguer knew it not to be true.

"You can stare at me with those dead, black eyes of yours all you wish Death Priest," the king snarled showing the whites of his teeth. "You're fortunate that I have not had those orbs of yours pushed into your head. Sunna knows what wicked images have passed through them."

Rochette did not respond. Not a muscle nor an eyelash at the threat the king was no-doubt fully capable of carrying out. Enguer had never been in the same room as the king before today and certainly not had the opportunity to speak with him. Yet it was the general opinion of the populace that he was a fair judge regardless of the position and influence of offenders brought before him, even if a little heavy-handed in the punishments he doled out. It was said that the king believed harsh penance served as the best deterrent to other would-be criminals. Enguer had no idea if any of it were true.

"That's fine, Rochette," the king continued, "you do not need to speak. I do not require your confession. Under the light of Sunna as her highest authority by birthright in the Kingdom of Courth, I condemn your actions and judge you guilty."

Nothing. The king might as well have been speaking to a stone wall. Enguer suspected Rochette might not react until he was swinging from the gallows. If then.

King Francik leaned back in the intricately carved wooden chair sewn with thick red upholstery on the seat, back and arms for His Majesty's comfort. It was not there earlier and must have been brought into the temple just for his use. "It's well that you stay your tongue and refrain from spewing hate and vitriol at the verdict I have pronounced. Do you believe in doing so that I might have mercy and decide that you are insane and unfit? Perhaps spare you from the hangman's noose?"

Enguer had the strong impression that Rochette's lack of response or the barest acknowledgement of his words infuriated the king more than anything else.

"There will be no mercy!" The king sprang to his feet bringing his meaty fists down on the heavy wooden table with such force that it wanted to break. The thunderous sound resounded through the room causing everyone to jump in shock – except Rochette – and one glance at the Duke's pale countenance, Enguer was almost certain he would take flight again.

Red faced, rage mounting, the king's powerful voice was deafening, "What mercy did you show the innocents that you murdered on a dark alter with sharp knives? Did they cry out for mercy? You and your vile god! You had no right! They were *my* people!"

Just when Enguer was sure he was about to hop over the table and strangle Rochette right there in his cage, the king seemed to calm with almost no effort. Still, the tension was palpable. He stood glaring at Rochette for a long time. No one moved nor dared to sniff. Silence ruled and Enguer wondered if the whole place would scatter if so much as a coin dropped to break the quiet stillness.

When the king spoke again, it was barely above a whisper, but the venom it conveyed, the underlying anger and hatred, carried as much weight as the fiercest roar, "There will be no mercy for you Rochette. And there will be no death, at least not a swift one."

Still silent, everyone sitting at the table exchanged uncertain glances while deliberately averting their gazes away from the king. Of course, there was no reaction from Rochette. A portrait of his likeness hanging in the cell would have been just as animated. The pause lingered awkwardly for a moment elevating the tension even higher. Not a soul knew what to expect, Enguer certainly did not. What could be worse than death?

The king's grey eyes never left those of Rochette black orbs, rewarded only by a hazy stare, and his dangerous tone carried not a hint of waver when he spoke once more. "Animal. That is what you are and thus you shall end your days. The form of a wretched dog shall be your final prison, doomed to confinement in the very cage you stand now, you will be placed in the center of the marketplace forced to beg for meager scraps to survive. Your unwashed body will be tortured by scurvy and canine disease. Most importantly, you will retain your intellect and suffer with the knowledge that you can never change your circumstance as the jowls of a dog cannot form words to talk or speak the dark spells that have served you so well."

King Francik's gaze swept over the dumbfounded expressions of those around him as he raised a tightly held fist over his head. "There will be no swift end for this dog priest, for I decree in front of you all, to be proclaimed throughout the realm, that no hand shall harm this wretched thing or poison the crumbs it is allowed to eat. Let it be known that it is my wish for it to live a very long life and serve as a reminder of those whose lives were cut short."

Tanais stepped forward and spoke in a nearly hoarse voice, "Your Highness, who has the power to do such a thing? Transmutation is not a study that I am familiar with."

'Don't worry yourself, Tanais," the king smiled weakly. "Rauf is very knowledgeable on the subject and he already has everything prepared." He turned to a guard standing against the wall behind him. "Summon the wizard."

Watching the dark priest closely, Enguer's heart nearly leapt from his chest – he was sure Rochette's eyes widened just a hair when the king spoke Rauf's name. Oddly, he had the impression that it was not an expression of fear, rather, an expression of delight.

The guard slammed his fist to steel-plated chest in salute and disappeared up the stairs at a jog.

"Tanais, I will leave it to you to carry out the sentence upon this evil man." King Francik started toward the stairs followed by a pair of guards when he abruptly stopped and turned his gaze back upon Rochette once more. "Next time we meet you will know what it is to despair."

Chapter 5

The Children

What a curious thing it is that any idiot capable of slinging about a bit of magic also comes with an ego the size of the Emerald Isle! And it hardly matters whether they be priest, shaman, holy man or wizard. Especially the wizards in my personal opinion. Take my brother, Myrllin. He's a 'special one'! A legend in his own mind that one is. But that's a story for another time . . .

Wodanaz the Wanderer

The wizard Rauf stood tall in his flowing red robes trimmed with rich ermine and fox fur and decorated all over with silver arcane symbols embroidered into the fabric. His ensemble reflected the perpetually haughty expression he wore like a wet rag upon his face. Tanais knew Rauf, he knew that he was an extraordinarily talented wizard with an infuriating ego to match. Whatever he was going to do to Rochette would be another self-aggrandizing tale that the wizard would be sure everyone in Courth knew about before the end of the day.

Tanais sighed. He might as well get things going. Even if he did not like Rauf, the king trusted him and would expect the Arch Priest to do whatever was required to carry out the sentence to a successful conclusion. He looked around the room to make sure everyone was present. There were the members of the commission sitting in quiet anticipation, four of the king's guards next to the cage, two Fire Priestesses nearby and Enguer Rand standing casually in the far corner of the room. Rauf stood a pace in front of the barred door facing Rochette holding an open tome. His lips moved slightly as he read, apparently preparing the complex spells that he would soon be casting upon the evil priest. Nothing had changed with Rochette and

66

for once Tanais was glad they would not be forced to endure the death priest's rants and curses.

"All is ready when you are, Rauf." Tanais spoke formally and with an air of authority. They were standing in his temple after all.

The wizard did not speak a word, instead he raised his hand in a gesture for everyone to remain quiet. Tanais glanced over at Enguer and rolled his eyes receiving an appreciative smile in return. He liked that boy.

Enguer was almost a mirror image of his father with a spark of impetuousness that had to be inherited from his light-hearted mother. With proper guidance, Tanais was sure the young ranger would easily live up to his father's reputation. Perhaps even surpass it. The problem was that it might be difficult to convince Enguer to stay in Courth for at least a few more years. Tanais had no doubt he could convince the king to add the boy to the roster of rangers serving the crown where he could benefit from the experience of the older men. Enguer had already earned their respect during the deadly foray into The Wilds to capture Rochette and would likely be accepted into their tight-knit group right away. The boy had a grand future ahead of him if Tanais could keep him on the right track. Just the night before he had expressed as much in a letter he sent to Reskalin. He didn't expect a response and never received one when he wrote, but he felt compelled to write often in hopes that Reskalin might get to know him a little better through his words and reach out to him one day.

"I am ready now," Rauf's deep voice echoed through the chamber jolting Tanais out of his tired reflections. Why did the infuriating man have to sound like he was announcing some grave edict every time he spoke? So dramatic. Tanais almost rolled his eyes again in the wizard's face.

"The prisoner is at your disposal," Tanais responded blandly, "you may begin."

Rauf cleared his throat almost theatrically and raised on hand in the air once again. In the other hand he still held the open tome, but when he began to speak his eyes were on Rochette never glancing back down to the pages. The words he used where familiar to Tanais. Although he did not understand them, he recognized them as the arcane language wizards spoke to invoke their spells. He was glad that priests were not required to do the same. All that was required for them to cast a spell was to frame their intentions in their minds, silently beseech Sunna, and by her grace their spell would be cast. Of course, priests did not have the same breadth of options available to them as wizards since they could only cast what they were sure their deity would approve of. So many times had a priest reached too far only to have their spell fizzle at the most inopportune moment leading to either an embarrassing result or a disastrous one.

The wizard droned on and on. The spell he was weaving must have been a complex combination of a curse and a transmutation. If he actually pulled it off Tanais would be impressed, albeit begrudgingly, but impressed nonetheless. He glanced again at Enguer. The Ranger had an intense look on his face as he watched Rochette. Tanais wished he was closer so he could ask him about it. Had the boy noticed something new? He shifted his gaze to Rochette. He looked the same as he had since he was placed in the cage – his eyes nearly closed, hands bound behind his back, his rigid stance had not changed. Then he noticed something new. A small pile of what appeared to be ash on the ground between his feet. Was it new or had it been there the whole time? Tanais watched Rochette's face closely. Was there an ever so slight movement of his lips? He began to regret removing the death priest's gag even though the king had commanded it. Tanais supposed his Highness was expecting to get some kind of a response when brought before him – even if Rochette only begged for his life.

Something hit the floor with a thud and a flutter of parchment. Tanais snapped his eyes onto Rauf. The wizard was standing as he was before, one hand in the air and the other still in the position of holding the book. He had an odd look on his face, as if afraid, and he had taken no notice of the fallen tome.

"Dooaip oiad iadpil bvfd idoigo aqlo mahorela tia butmon de zonrensg cnoqod hoath." Rauf spoke as if in a dream, or a nightmare, his lips moving as if not of his own will. Tanais noticed a change in the words. These were not from the wizard's arcanery. They conveyed feeling as much as sound, at least to him, everyone else appeared wholly unaffected. He stole a quick glance over to the two Fire Priestesses, they stood rigid and unnatural, staring unblinking straight ahead at Rochette. Something was wrong. Terribly wrong. Rauf must have reached too far in his arrogance, made some mistake and uttered

the wrong word or missed a passage. Couldn't the wizard understand what he had done or was this part of it? Yet Rochette's lips still barely moved as if to reflect those spoken by Rauf. Or was it the reverse? Tanais did not know.

The Arch Priest moved toward him as more inexplicable words burst from the wizard, this time gaining volume and pitch as he spoke them, *"Oi amma de homtoh vorsg malpirgi sa teloch sa oln tia levithmong gmilcalzo ioiad!"* With a final terrified scream, Rauf collapsed on the floor in a heap.

Tanais' first thought was to shake him out of the trance he was in, but he never got the chance, something astonishing was happening in the cage and the sight of it froze Tanais in place to watch with mouth agape. Rochette was double over, his limbs somehow freed and contorted, while the dirty robes that once hung loose over his gaunt frame stretched taunt at the point of ripping in a dozen places. Thick dark-brown hair seemed to sprout from every opening and although Tanais could not see the death priest's face, he could see the top of his shaggy head appearing to expand and double in size with long pointed ears forming on each side. Hands palm down on the floor in front of him had transformed into claws with long talons under powerfully built arms covered in fur. It went on for a timeless moment more, the fabric of Rochette's robes finally shredding and falling to the floor. Tanais marveled at the size of the crouching thing that had replaced the death priest. The beast raised its massive head in a sudden, terrifying movement and growled revealing a long snout filled with dagger-like teeth below dead eyes shining with internal light that made the orbs appear to glow red. Tanais could not tear his own eyes away from the vile creature and when it howled it filled his soul with dread.

Stumbling close to where Rauf lay unmoving, Tanais shook him vigorously. "Rauf, wake up!" He turned the wizard over to get a look at his face, glassy eyes stared into eternity, and he knew right away the spell-weaver was dead.

"The Dark Lord has spoken to me." A deep, rumbling voice spoke from the cage punctuated by intermittent snapping. Tanais was surprised the thing could speak at all.

He peered up at the great beast in awe. It stood erect now, glaring at him with those red eyes. It was horrifying blend of a man and a wolf and something more. Its massive form filled the cage and despite the thick iron bars that separated them, the Arch Priest found little comfort in it.

"What are you?" Tanais was certain that this thing was not what Rauf intended.

A rolling growl that Tanais took as a laugh reverberated from deep within the creature's chest. "I am the father of a new breed, a species that will feed upon yours and eventually replace you with multitudes of my kind."

Tanais couldn't believe what he was hearing. How could this have gone so wrong? "No, you are Rochette. Rochette was a good man once!"

The beast snarled, showing the whites of its deadly fangs. "Rochette is no more. He has served his purpose and I have cast him into oblivion as I will do to any who oppose me."

Tanais stood slowly on unsteady legs, the initial shock of the creature dulling enough that he could think more clearly. He quickly surveyed the room. The four king's guards had backed away from the cage and stood ready to draw their swords, the pair of Fire Priestesses still stood motionless, he didn't know what was wrong with them, the members of the commission were bolted to their seats gaping in astonishment – except for the two merchants who had somehow departed without him noticing – and Enguer Rand against the wall with an arrow nocked on his bow. Tanais decided that the odds must be in their favor.

"Whatever you are, there will be no 'multitudes.' You will die in the obscurity of that cage where you stand!" Thrusting his hands forward, lightning crackled from them sending bright blue bolts spiderwebbing over the cage and the beast within.

The creature howled in pain and anger before ripping the iron-bar door from its hinges to cast it aside uselessly. It emerged from its cell with smoke rising from patches of fur touched by the lightning and the look of fury on its face. It charged straight for Tanais.

Thinking quickly, the Arch Priest spun a barrier of air between them, but the thing was too quick and in the flutter of a moths wing it had powerful, hairy claws wrapped around his neck. The beast's maw, thick with sharp teeth and spittle, seemed to smile down at him in triumph, "We know you priest." The creature did not speak the words aloud, they came from *inside* his head! Long strands of sputum hung down elastically brushing the edges of his face. He hardly noticed. "Remember the children you murdered." The grip around his neck tightened.

Tanais head swam. He did remember – it was something he could never forget. But what did this thing know of it? That was over fifty years ago when he and the others of the FIVE were young and early in their enterprise to destroy evil wherever they might find it. He moaned at the memory of that terrible occasion, barely on the edge of consciousness, the iron hands around his throat cutting off his air entirely.

The beast's smile appeared to widen. It knew.

Through haze and delusion, the scene from so many years ago played back in his mind as if he were living it again. A remote village tucked away in a mountain range known as The Spine of Cel, named after the Rasna people's goddess of the earth, a four day walk from the city of Lindium. There they found something very strange. Children. Nearly a hundred children between the ages of three and nine and not a soul older. No adults, no infants, not even a single goat. Only these odd children. In his mind, Tanais shuddered. They had the palest skin, where most people of Rasna enjoyed a smooth-olive complexion, features devoid of emotion, unwashed bodies and the blackest of eyes. Eyes dead of life like bottomless voids that consumed the light and life around them. Eyes like those that bore into him now.

For days the FIVE questioned the children, who barely spoke, and when they did would only claim ignorance of their circumstance. They stayed indoors most of the day sleeping only to emerge after dark to rush ferally into the forested peaks that surrounded the village. Tanais and his companions tried to follow them, but the children were unnaturally swift and agile over the rough terrain leaving the FIVE lost and disoriented in the wilderness.

For nearly a week this went on before they discovered the truth of the children's nightly foray. Purely by happenstance the FIVE stumbled upon a clearing illuminated by the pale radiance of the moon.

The eerie light reflected off a huddle of pale bodies bent low to the ground intent on something beneath them. Approaching closer, the FIVE were horrified to realize that the children were feasting on a massive Nightstalker. Tanais remembered one of the children looking up from the ghastly kill, a boy about six years old with his face and bare chest bathed in the creature's blood and smiled before returning to his grisly feast. It was the first time any of the companions of the FIVE had witnessed the slightest emotion from any of them.

Tanais recalled silently watching the horrifying scene for several long moments. None of the children had weapons or armor to protect themselves. None of them had ever displayed magical ability and Tanais would have sensed it if they had. Yet, the mass of these tiny, half-clothed juveniles had managed to take down one of the fiercest beasts in The Wilds. Nightstalker's were nocturnal feline-like predators nearly the size of a horse, with a double row of dagger-like teeth in their over-sized head, two long horns that protruded above their brow and a hide as black as the night they stalked. It would have been a tough fight for the FIVE to take on one of these creatures let alone a few dozen un-armed children.

Cautiously Tanais and his companions withdrew from the area and returned to the safety of their warded camp near the village. The companions agreed to tread carefully around the children for fear that they might soon turn on them. Based on what they had witnessed that night the nippers were far more capable than they appeared.

The next afternoon a man arrived in their camp. His name was Myrllin, one of the FIVE's mysterious benefactors that often steered them toward their quests and missions. This man, whom they knew only by reputation as a great wizard, led them on a search of the village while the children were sleeping. Tanais had no idea what they were looking for at the time and he suspected Myrllin was nearly as uncertain. They spent hours quietly combing through the village and its immediate surrounds until they came upon a small opening in a rocky tumble of boulders. Squeezing through the narrow space Myrllin cast a light spell revealing a vast cavern filled with ancient crystalized stalagmites and stalactites that connected to form massive columns that linked floor to ceiling from far beyond where the light could reach above.

Most of the cavern was filled with water except for a broad natural walkway that extended to a wide island in the center where stood the crafted stone-work of an elaborate altar. Demonic symbols that seemed to glow dimly red of their own accord covered every surface of the stone from top to bottom. But it was what floated liquidly a hand-span above the altar that was the focus of their collective attention.

A black void, somewhat circular with the occasional disruption of its shape by what appeared to be a pushing, or stretching action around the edges as if something were trying to break through. To look at it directly filled one with the urge to touch it while at the same time an unreasonable fear that verged on panic. Tanais was sure that if any of them possessed anything less than a strong will, the void would have compelled their embrace. The memory sent a series of shivers up Tanais spine. Or were they convulsions?

"Don't go near it," Myrllin had warned. "As I feared, this is the work of the Death Cult."

It was the first time Tanais had ever heard anything about a Death Cult. Certainly, there were many cultures that worshipped a deity that oversaw death and the afterlife – famed Anapa, the jackal-headed Protector of Graves worshipped by the people of TaMehu and TaShemau, came to mind. This was different. He could see the concern, perhaps even fear in the wizard's face and hear it in his voice.

"I must stitch it up, so that no more may escape," Strange words from Myrllin that Tanais did not understand at the time.

Tracing symbols of light in the air, Myrllin intoned low, arcane verses. While he spoke, the light trails formed into thick glowing tendrils that slowly surrounded the black void, restricting slightly after every pause. Tanais watched the void tug at the light, attempting to pull it in and destroy the formation Myrllin struggled to maintain. Sweat coated his brow, his voice wavered almost imperceptibly and there was a slight wobble in his stance, yet the wizard pressed on. Tanais moved up close in case he faltered, not having any idea the scale of the fight Myrllin waged against the void. The Arch Priest would become all too familiar just a few years later when he put it into practice himself.

"They are here." It was one of his companions, the FatMan, who hissed urgently.

Tanais followed his gaze to the edge of the light on the stone walkway fifty paces out. There they stood, silently watching, more of their number arriving every second. Little pale bodies crowding the walkway from edge to edge at least six ranks deep cast their dead gaze upon them. Not a twinkle of light reflected from those dark orbs as if they were miniature versions of the void Myrllin battle behind them.

It was a surreal moment in the seconds that it lasted. A proud moment standing heroically with his four companions in the strange cavern. On his left, the FatMan, who would later become the most prolific Guild Master in the Western Kingdoms and beyond controlling a vast criminal organization that spanned everything from extortion to smuggling. Next to him crouched Gaurin Rand, Enguer's father, who would become a legend in his profession as a ranger. To his right stood Borath Mecrulican, a bear of a man with equal strength clad head to foot in metal armor and the largest war axe he had ever seen. Borath would become the Commanding General of the Rasna city of Arre and later an elder and advisor to the Zilach and his council. Finally, there was the most unusual member of their group, ArteliThalozin, an elf from Avalon with almost god-like mastery of the bow and duel-wielding curved swords.

Tanais felt a brief flicker of pleasure at their memory.

The FIVE stood watching the spooky children staring back at them, when Myrllin uttered words that would change their lives forever, "Kill them. Kill them all." His voice was strained from the effort against the void, but the words were unmistakable.

Tanais and his companions looked to each other in disbelief. How could they kill children? They were strange, feral things that needed to be brought back into the fold of civilization, yes, but to murder them? So many children left on their own without parents who, no doubt, had succumbed to the void were lucky to have survived at all.

"Myrllin, we can't kill innocent children. They need our help," Tanais tried to convince the wizard with sound reason.

The wizard slowly turned his head to face Tanais squarely. There was no uncertainty in his eyes, no regret or sadness. Only determination. "Those children have no life in them. They have touched the void, consumed their parents and everything else alive in their village. They are less than animals now, but if they grow to adults, the demons that inhabit their bodies will become powerful and spread death and chaos across the land the likes of which have never been seen."

Tanais was unsure of what was more spine-chilling – what Myrllin had just said or the act of killing these children. Any decision they might have made, however terrible it might have been, was taken from them the next instant.

With a collective savage scream, the children charged toward them almost as one.

They were unnaturally quick, crossing the fifty paces between them in seconds, tiny teeth and little claws bared to rip the companions to pieces. Tanais remembered fire and lightning flung from his hands scorching and burning pale skin, Borath charging in among them swinging his massive axe rending limbs from small bodies while ArteliThalozin danced behind him curved swords flashing, shredding young flesh. Gaurin loosed volleys of arrows with enough force to lift little feet from the ground and the FatMan, heavy as his name implied, smoothly glided around the edges expertly planting his knives in the unprotected vital areas of their anatomy.

Despite their, size, weapons, armor and magic, the FIVE were nearly overwhelmed by the ferocious children. Outnumbered twenty to one, the children would cling to legs and arms, dragging their larger quarry down. Where their diminutive hands and mouths found flesh, they would claw, bite and chew tenaciously until forcefully dislodged or dismembered. They appeared impervious to pain, crawling forward when they lost a leg or attempting to entangle when they could barely move at all.

And then Myrllin was done, the void was compressed into a tiny point of light until it was gone and he joined the fray.

As exhausted as the wizard must have been, he set about summoning vines from the solid stone to entangle the fallen forms and hold them still while casting fire from one hand and lightning from the other. How Myrllin missed hitting Borath and ArteliThalozin who were right in the thick of it, Tanais would never know. It seemed to go on forever but must have lasted only seconds and then it was over. None of the pale bodies moved, nor would they ever again.

A sharp pain shot through Tanais gut. That had been the worst part. After he and his companions collapsed to the floor physically exhausted, there was nothing left but to survey what they had done.

Once beautiful children lay burned and disfigured all around them. No one would ever see their sweet smiles or hear their infectious laughter again. Even knowing what they had become and that they would have eagerly torn his friends to shreds, the emotion was too much to bear. For a long time, in the dank cave surrounded by one-hundred small bodies in the shadow of an altar of evil, the companions wept like mad men, even the elf. Every one of them would carry scars for the rest of their lives both on their bodies and in their hearts. And for some, it would harden them irrevocably.

Tanais opened his hate-filled eyes, the beast was still there, hands around his throat, yet it somehow seemed farther away. In his mind it snarled and spoke, "You and your friends spoiled the efforts of my minions to gain a foothold in this world many times over the years, each time delaying release from the hateful pithos that was my prison. Despite your efforts I am free again thanks to the folly of what you humans call a goddess." Mocking laughter echoed through his head.

From somewhere in the distance Tanais heard a vague thump and then another. The beast's hands flinched with each sound and a flash of pain crossed its features. Tanais felt nothing. Except hatred. He was floating on a sea of hatred. Beyond help, he felt his consciousness slipping away, darkness creeping around the edges of his vision. He focused all his effort to project one last thought, "I will find my salvation with Sunna and forgiveness for what I have done in her name." Tanais returned the mocking laughter. "What is left for you when the final darkness comes? Nothing! Oblivion!"

Enraged, the beast railed inside Tanais mind, "I am Yalal, greatest of the seven named demons! All will serve me! All will worship at my feet!"

Tanais was falling. There was darkness all around him. The sounds from the chamber receding into silence. The iron grip of the creature's claws around his throat evaporating like mist on a pond. He felt at peace, no fear, no worries, no pain. Then there was a pin prick of light and as it grew it welcomed him. More than anything else he had ever wanted in life, Tanais wanted to go to it . . .

Chapter 6

Chasing a Shadow

Enguer watched in horror as Rochette, turned wolf-creature, tore through the bars of its cage and sprang onto the Arch Priest in a fluid blur of motion that defied the eye. It happened so suddenly, even before the last strands of lightning faded from its coarse hair, that Enguer hadn't the time to raise his bow for a shot. He raised it now and sent first one and then another arrow streaking through the air in rapid succession. The beast flinched with the impact of each barbed shaft into the thick hide of its chest, but it was plain to see that not even the razor-sharp heads penetrated fully.

"Kill it now!" Enguer shouted at the guards. The shock at what their eyes revealed evident as his plea sent them into hesitant motion.

Gazing past them he saw the two Fire Priestesses swaying on their feet with blood running from their mouth, nose and ears. They would be no help. Further to his right the duke and the magistrate were fighting with each other to get through the doorway that led to the stairwell, while the High Priestess stood calmly chanting behind the long table where the commission had been seated. Enguer observed all of this in the time it took to nock another arrow, sending it into the tender space under the monster's right arm, with a second right behind it that lodged in the creature's muscular neck.

Those must have been more painful as the beast reacted with a growl, dropped the Arch Priest's limp body to the ground and leaped forward to grab the High Priestess. She released her spell just as the beast fell upon her, turning the fur on his chest and shoulders white as if the hair had frozen under a snowfall. Enguer struck the thing with two more arrows in the back resulting in barely a twitch of annoyance before it slammed a clawed fist into the priestess' forehead knocking her unconscious. The wolf-creature immediately scooped up her wilted form in one arm and turned to face the approaching guards. One vicious snarl froze them in place as if rooted to the floor.

Enguer paused as well for fear that he might inadvertently strike the High Priestess. Not hesitating an instant longer, the creature bound through the open door and up the stairwell beyond. The screams of men, no doubt the duke and the magistrate, echoed back down into the room from above. The guards, suddenly released from their paralysis, renewed their pursuit, but far too cautiously to hope to catch up.

Enguer rushed over to the fallen Arch Priest. He lay still, glazed eyes open to eternity, with his head at such an angle that it was clear that his neck had been violently broken. Reaching down to close the priest's eyes with his hand, Enguer muttered a silent prayer to Sunna, then stood to survey the rest of the room.

Whatever afflicted the Fire Priestesses earlier had apparently run its course. They lay unmoving in a bloody heap as still as the stone beneath them. No one else was in the room. Enguer looked again into the cage noting the ashes that were now scattered about. He should have been more observant, recognized the ash as the burnt remains of the ropes that held Rochette's hands fast behind him. In this he had failed and Tanais had died, his father's closest friend. *Wouldn't he be proud of his son now?*

Enguer was sickened. This whole thing must have been planned by Rochette. How he managed to pull it off Enguer had no clue. Maybe the death priest had accomplices in high places, an advisor or councilor adept enough at persuasion to encourage the king to proclaim the ludicrous sentence of transmogrification upon Rochette rather than simply hanging him by the neck. It was clear that Tanais was just as surprised by the king's judgement as anyone and he was the one man that would have been able to get to the bottom of it. Now he was dead and no help to anyone. Enguer considered the events of the last few days. There was one man that had the king's ear from the time he rode into Courth to join the commission and that was the Duke of Toulliou. Enguer thought the duke a fool based on his limited observations of the man, but it was also possible that his behavior was part of the ploy to cast scrutiny away from him. It was also likely that the duke was now dead on the stairwell if Rochette had thought to tie up loose ends.

Four others were missing. He knew one was sick in bed but two others had been present when the wizard Rauf had arrived. Enguer had accompanied the Arch Priest when he checked in on the Earl of Berci before going to the temple. He gave the Earl a magic imbued salve to rub on his chest that would clear his congestion. Surely the Arch Priest would have known if the sickness was a ploy. To Enguer's eyes the man looked ill and genuinely grateful for the medication.

The merchants Dyzig and Gigot were at the sentencing at the start, but must have slipped away during the early stages of the transformation. Enguer was surprised he had not noticed. Maybe they didn't have the stomach to watch more. Maybe they knew what was coming.

And what about Commander Duraunt? Why hadn't he attended the sentencing? He was a skilled swordsman that might have interrupted the attack on the Arch Priest, perhaps saving his life and preventing the creature's escape. Enguer would have to find out why he was missing.

Taking one last cursory scan of the room, Enguer cautiously mounted the steps leading up to the main temple. Almost at the top he found the mutilated corpses of the duke and the magistrate. He shook his head in disgust. If they hadn't been so desperate fighting each other to be the first into the stairwell they both might have escaped and survived, even if by the barest margin.

Enguer stepped over their bodies and into the temple proper. There was not a soul in sight. An eerie silence hung in the vast space that was normally teeming with priests and worshipers at that time of day. At least there were no more bodies. He doubted that the creature had any other ambition than to escape the city once he was out of the cage. Picking up his pace, Enguer jogged over the stone pavers of the wide hallway that terminated at the temple's vaulted entrance. As usual, the high double doors stood open inviting a fresh steady breeze to cool the interior and evacuate the smoke from the numerous torches that lined the way. Approaching the doors, Enguer could hear frantic shouts and screams coming from the streets some distance away. He increased his stride to a run, tightening the strap around his quiver to keep the arrows in place after removing two in case he needed them right away.

Outside, the dim light of the setting sun cast its final rays on a city in chaos. Tradesmen, merchants, priests and common folk alike huddled together around corners, behind carts, between statues and under shrubbery. Two wagons once laden with fruits and vegetable lay overturned with their contents scattered in the street. Four farmers crouched behind one of the wagons and a fifth lay unmoving in the open, blood pooling around his head. Everyone was staring intently eastward down the expansive paved thoroughfare that was considered the main street of Courth with terrified expressions on their faces. Before Enguer could fully descend the two-dozen white-stone steps that wrapped around the front of the temple, a squad of at least thirty of the king's cavalry charged down the center of the street obliterating the produce that littered the pavers in front of them.

Enguer hurried the rest of the way down to the street and peered far over the quarter-league length of the boulevard. For as far as his sharp eyes could see, people crowded fearfully in small clusters behind anything that could provide cover while dozens of soldiers, mounted and unmounted, flowed rapidly toward the eastern gate. There was no trace of the wolf-creature anywhere.

Quickly mounting his Lambei tied to a rail nearby, Enguer spurred it into a fast gallop. The beast must have been fast indeed to cover so much distance in such a short time, even encumbered with the body of the High Priestess. He fervently hoped that the creature would be tested by the city guard and forced to drop the priestess if they couldn't manage to stop it from leaving the city. Enguer shuddered at the thought of her fate if it was allowed to escape with her to wherever it was going.

The street was mostly clear of civilians and none of the soldiers he passed made any attempt to stop him allowing his Lambei to sprint unhindered as if traversing a race course. He assumed the guards identified him as a ranger with his bow across his back and earth-toned garb suited for the woodlands. They were all part of the wild chase to overtake the savage beast that had so suddenly appeared in the heart of the crowded city with the body of a High Priestess in tow.

Minutes later Enguer arrived at the eastern gate to a solemn scene. At least a dozen guards lay dead or dying with horrible claw marks ripped across their metal cuirasses or through fabric and flesh. The survivors were attended by their comrades who did what they could to stave off the terrible injuries with tourniquets and bandages before loading them into a wagon that would take them to the healing priests at the temple. The less fortunate were simply lined up in a row next to the high city wall where they would await a covered cart and a final blessing from Sunna. On the road outside the gate at least a hundred cavalry stood in formation with more joining their ranks by the minute while archers and foot soldiers lined the crenelated parapets and packed the towers on the wall above him, the pounding of boots on stone stairs giving away a steady stream of reinforcements.

Making his was slowly through the armed assembly, Enguer spied Commander Duraunt astride his horse addressing several military officers, a few Bayles and the ranger known to him as Suri. Several more rangers sat their mounts quietly nearby apparently awaiting their instructions.

Heat rose inside Enguer at the sight of the Commander. He didn't exactly blame the man for what happened at the temple, but how might things have been different if he had been there. Would Tanais be alive? What about the Fire Priestesses and the magistrate? To hell with the duke. Enguer made an effort to calm himself. His father had taught him that nothing good ever came from rushing to anger, a good ranger controlled his rage and used it to his advantage. Fully composed, he rode over to join them.

"Enguer!" the Commander greeted him with obvious relief. "I feared everyone at the sentencing lost. Where is Rauf and Tanais?" He peered over Enguer's head and through the gate as if expecting to see them. "Are they attending the wounded?"

Enguer slowly shook his head speaking hardly above a whisper, "They are both dead by the hands of the beast."

Shock and disbelief erupted over Commander Duraunt's features, "That can't be . . ."

"The magistrate, two Fire Priestesses and the duke are also dead," Enguer went on. "The two merchants on the commission, Dyzig and Gigot, left at the start so they must live, the Earl is safely sick in his bed and four of the king's guard chased after the beast when it escaped the temple. I do not know their fate."

"They would have rushed back to the king," the Commander replied absently. "I should have been there."

Enguer suppressed the heat once again, "Why were you not?"

"After I went to fetch the wizard, I was met by the duke outside the temple. He told me that the king required my immediate attendance so I returned to the palace." Commander Duraunt sighed deeply. "On my way back to the temple that, monster, rushed by me toward the east gate and I gave chase. My horse is as swift as any, yet I never came close to catching it." His eyes widened with the recollection. "It carried someone over its shoulder, do you know who it was?"

"It was the High Priestess, Rhalia," Enguer dropped his gaze to the ground, "and it may have taken her alive."

"Then we must mount a rescue!" the Commander declared and immediately began barking orders to his officers.

Enguer was about to interrupt when Suri caught his eye with a gesture for him to back off. Then the elder ranger moved his mount a little closer to the Commander drawing his attention.

"Commander," Suri's voice was strong with the confidence of decades of experience that naturally commanded authority.

"Yes, Suri."

"It is nearly dark and we have no way of knowing where, or how far that beast will retreat into The Wilds tonight."

"Be that as it may, we must try, Suri." The Commander's eyes were almost pleading.

Suri shook his grizzled head, "If the beast is intent on harming the priestess, we will never find it in time to save her."

His face flush red with anger, the Commander managed to keep his tone under control, "She is a *High Priestess*, Suri, and Tanais would have burned down The Wilds to save her from that evil thing!"

"Think of your men, Commander. Look at them," Suri motioned to the soldiers still forming ranks around them clad in heavy metal breast plates, grieves and bracers. "They are not fit for this chase. How many of them are you prepared to lose trying to rescue a single priestess? Even a High one?"

For a moment the Commander sputtered on the edge of rage. Enguer could tell that he begrudgingly accepted the ranger's logic but his emotions were making it hard for him to admit it. Finally, he calmed enough to respond through gritted teeth, "Then what should we do?"

Suri did not hesitate, it was clear he knew the answer all along, "I will lead the rangers into The Wilds at first light and track the beast. Once we know where it is, you can send in your troops, but only after we make a plan."

"Very well, we will do it your way." There was no animosity in the Commander's response. Enguer knew he highly respected Suri. Just like Enguer, he was probably blaming himself for not doing more. "However, I am ordering an immediate curfew and all gates closed dusk to dawn until this creature's head adorns a pike on the temple steps." Swinging his mount away, the Commander rode through the ranks of his men sending the Bayles and officers that followed in every direction with his orders.

"Commander's a good man," Suri had his eyes on the dim outline of trees a league to the east, barely visible in the failing light.

Enguer was alone with the elder ranger. He reminded him a lot of his father. "Agreed."

Suri turned his liquidly brown eyes on Enguer, they were intense and serious under a heavy dark brow. "Now tell me about this creature. The people are already calling it a Demon Beast, because of its red eyes and savage nature. I want to know everything."

~~~

Enguer was pleased that Suri had invited him to accompany the Royal Order of Rangers in their search for the Demon Beast. He and the others sat quietly on their mounts just outside the city walls awaiting the first hint of dawn. The moment the distant tree-line was visible, they would get underway. He was anxious to go.

"You hold your ale well for a cub." Suri's voice seemed to blend naturally with the sound of dry leaves skittering across the short grass and the chirping of the morning birds.

Enguer barked a quiet laugh, "During the winters when my father and I would hunt for days in The Wilds he brought along a few waterskins full of a strong drink he called "Ranger's Nectar" to keep us warm at night. It had a much stronger kick than what we shared last night."

Suri grunted, "I know your father's "Ranger's Nectar". He brewed it himself, yes?"

Enguer nodded.

"Well, it has been the cause of many a ranger losing their wits and running off naked and howling into the wilderness." Suri's low chuckle rippled through the air between them. "I can't tell you what trouble we went through tracking them down. If you grew up drinking that stuff then not a one of us can stand up against your constitution."

Enguer returned Suri's infectious chuckle, "It has been awhile. I'm sure I'm out of practice."

"We'll see, my boy. Ah, there's the trees, let's get moving." With a quick gesture in the darkness, Suri led Enguer and five Rangers he had hand-picked from his company eastward.

They travelled slowly at first, not pushing their mounts faster than they could safely navigate the terrain in front of them. It wouldn't do to have one of them step in a furrow and come up lame for lack of patience. Even though Enguer knew they all felt an urgency to track down the Demon Beast as quickly as possible, none of them held out any hope of recovering the High Priestess alive. The only reason that Commander Durant was not with them that morning was thanks to Suri getting him so hopelessly drunk that he would sleep until noon. Whatever the reason, Suri didn't want the commander with them. He said the commander would endanger them all because he was too emotionally involved, but wouldn't say why. It was none of Enguer's affair and he trusted that Suri knew what he was doing.

Sunna marked their slowly increasing pace with the benefit of her warm illuminating rays and by the time they arrived at the edge of the thickly forested boundary that separated civilization from the wilderness they called The Wilds, the sun was fully above the horizon. Suri brought them to a halt there and instructed his rangers to fan out north and south until they found the place where the beast had crossed over.

They were searching only a few minutes when one of the rangers whistled the sharp trill of a local bird to alert the others to his find. The tracks were deeply imprinted in the moist grass growing from soft soil and unmistakable. Easily twice the size of any human, elongated and vaguely wolf-like near the front, they all agreed they had found the trail of the beast.

"We are on foot from here on. Send back the horses," Suri handed the reigns of his horse to one of the Rangers.

It was a remarkable thing how well trained their horses were. The ranger who took Suri's horse, tied a short lead to Enguer's Lambei and then slapped its butt commanding it to "Go Home!" The remaining horses fell in line behind Suri's and they headed back to Courth at a quick trot.

"Won't they get lost?" He asked the ranger.

"Never," he smiled. "They will trot right through the gates of Courth and not stop until they reach the doors to our Order."

It seemed to Enguer that every ranger he met was like his father – short on words and deliberate in their actions, as if they were all cast from the same mold. Enguer supposed that he was much the same way, except that he enjoyed a bit of chatter rather than the doldrums of staring into a campfire mired in one's own thoughts. His father used to tell him it was a flaw inherited from his mother, but he always said it with a slight smile, telling Enguer in his own way that it was OK.

Suri gathered them all together, "I will take the lead, Enguer you take the rear. If any of us miss anything speak up. Keep one eye on me and one on the ground, low talk is fine until I give the signal to go silent."

His eyes touched each one of them for just a moment before he continued, "We may be out here for a number of days. You know the drill – cold camps and cold tac. Hope you all filled your bellies with something warm this morning, it may be a while before we're warm again."

Suri nodded once, then strode quietly into the forest. One ranger followed directly behind him at ten paces and two others flanked them on each side at about the same distance. Enguer followed just far enough behind to keep Suri in sight.

The small group moved at a fast pace considering how easy the tracks were to follow. The Demon Beast had made no effort to conceal its trail either because it did not think anyone would follow it into The Wilds or it didn't care if they did. The latter worried Enguer the most. He had planted six arrows in its hide at point-blank range and it hadn't even slowed down. Suri knew the dangers they faced as did the other rangers, but none except for Enguer had been there. It was the telling and retelling of what happened in the temple that led to the drinking, yet they chose to take on this mission anyway.

His mind wandered while his eyes focused on the forest floor and surrounding flora. So much had happened in the days since the day Tanais first urged him to leave the seclusion of the empty house he grew up in. At the time, Enguer was eager to leave Courth and all the memories behind. He wanted to travel the world, see new places and learn new things. It was an escape plan that would take him away from the familiar places that reminded him of everything he had lost. Lately though, he was considering different options. He was enjoying the fellowship of the Royal Order of Rangers and could envision settling down, making more friends like Suri and maybe having a family of his own one day. It might not even be too late to ask after one of Mrs. Eibhlin's fair daughters, he chuckled to himself. Enguer put those thoughts away and focused on the job at hand. He had to make a good impression on his companions if he were ever going to be considered as a serious candidate for the Royal Order of Rangers.

The morning passed to afternoon and on to evening before the small group stopped to make camp. As Suri promised, it was a cold camp with no fire and no tents. They made lean-tos from branches and wrapped themselves in stout wool blankets they carried in a roll on their backs. This was no hardship for Enguer, he and his father had camped like this hundreds of nights in this same wilderness. He knew these parts of The Wilds like the back of his hand. Tomorrow the terrain would become rockier, the incline sharper and become more difficult to follow tracks the closer they came to the mountains. Enguer suspected that was exactly where they were going if the Demon Beast was looking for a cave to hole up in.

The next morning, they left before dawn. Suri was an impressive ranger. He never missing anything and kept them churning over the leagues stopping only when it was necessary. None of the rangers appeared to mind the exhaustive march, in fact, Enguer thought they might take it as a matter of pride that they could do it.

He did.

On the third day out, Suri slowed their pace by almost half. Although still heavily wooded, they were approaching the first sills and ridges of the mountain range. Smaller rocks turned to moss-covered boulders, the air became crisper and foxes wore a heavier coat the higher they hiked. If they continued another day along the same route Enguer knew they would be climbing as much as walking in the rough terrain. The Wilds were like a second home to him. He loved the serenity of the forest, the wildlife that lived there and the purity of nature that did not define survival in terms of good or evil. The strongest, the cleverest and the luckiest survived longest in The Wilds while the weaker often fell prey to them. It was the cycle of life, constantly renewing, constantly changing, yet staying the same. Most people didn't understand or appreciate the beauty of it. Ranger's did. His father said the elves did as well. Enguer hoped he would meet an elf one day. He met an 'Enlightened One' once. There were a handful of them in Courth that lived in a tall tower capped by a floating crystal in the shape of a pyramid that cast a red glow in the sky at night. Sometimes he and his father would navigate by that light when they explored the mountains not far from where he stood now. He recalled falling asleep, shivering under furs and blankets when they camped at a high altitude, watching the far-off glow of the crystal. It was beautiful.

Those were the times his father opened up to him the most. They were alone together in some remote location with only each other to depend on. He told him stories about the 'Enlightened Ones', who were known in different places by different names. They called themselves Atlanteans. He told Enguer about the elves that lived in harmony with the Atlanteans on a massive island in the Primal Sea. The Emerald Isle, it was called. And how for a time his father had known an elf well enough to call him a friend. He also told Enguer about some of the most dangerous creatures said to inhabit The Wilds. Creatures twisted and unnatural, bred by a strange race of people called the Tuatha De many hundreds of years ago. He said the Tuatha De fought a bitter civil war because of these creatures and that the side that won understood the dangers of corrupting nature and in the end banished the monstrosities to a place called Fomoire. Enguer learned that over the centuries many of the creatures escaped their confinement and found a home deep inside The Wilds. His father named them as giants, trolls, ogres, dragons and orks, plus many others Enguer couldn't remember and hardly wanted to believe. It wasn't that he didn't trust what his father said, but he assumed they must be far, far away since, until now, he had never seen anything in The Wilds other than the usual predators. Bears, wolves, snakes and especially the long-toothed mountain lion were dangerous enough!

Suri raised his hand signaling complete silence. All the rangers stopped dead in their tracks. He had only done this once before when they had nearly crossed paths with a huge brown bear shepherding her cubs to a nearby stream. Enguer felt no anxiety then. He felt it now.

Slowly, carefully, Suri back-tracked to the ranger that follow immediately behind him and beckoned for the rest of them to come to him. "There is an opening to a cave ahead, very well concealed, I almost missed it." Suri squatted on the ground and cleared the sticks and leaves in front of him to reveal the loose soil beneath. "It is below a ridge, here," he drew lines in the dirt indicating the feature he spoke of, "and roughly in the center of a cluster of boulders, here. The entrance is almost completely covered with vines and vegetation. The opening is large enough for the Demon Beast you described, Enguer, if barely."

"Are you certain it is there?" One of the rangers asked.

"I'm sure of it."

Enguer had to ask, "How can you be sure?" and then felt immediately embarrassed that he did.

Suri smiled; his sharp eyes must have noticed the flush that came to Enguer's cheeks. "The Scat."

The other rangers nodded.

Enguer was confused, "The Scat?"

Still smiling, Suri nodded, "As you know, most animals relieve themselves away from their lairs, burrows and bedding, and rarely in the same spot. Scat evacuated in one place over and over, especially in a hole or ditch, is uniquely telling of higher intelligence, like people."

Enguer understood the logic and regretted that he had not made the connection himself. He had spent so many years learning the habits of the wild that he completely disregarded those of the people all around him every day. He would have to rectify that when he returned to Courth. His father would have chided him for closing his eyes to the obvious.

"If as you say this Demon Beast is the corrupted transformation of the High Priest . . . What was his name?"

"Rochette," Enguer replied.

Suri blinked, "Rochette, right. Well anyway, it may have retained some of Rochette's human intellect."

"Which makes it even more dangerous," suggested the ranger crouching next to Enguer.

"Yes, more dangerous," Suri agreed. "Much more dangerous."

Chapter 7

Lost Souls

It was raining. Cold wet drizzle that invaded every unprotected pathway through cloak and tunic eager to touch bare skin and extract every ounce of warmth. It was the kind of rain that left even the heartiest soul a miserable shell shivering and defeated.

Those were not the souls of rangers.

When the rain came with the dark of night and icy chill of the altitude, the rangers put their backs against tree or rock and pulled their knees up to their chest in a tight ball to preserve their heat. Wrapped in oiled cloaks to repel the moisture, they passed the dark hours flexing and stretching their muscles at regular intervals to avoid stiffness and cramping all the while keeping their focus intently on the cave they knew held the Demon Beast they hunted.

Enguer, positioned above and to the left of the opening, frequently cast his gaze to the six dark spots dispersed in various locations nearby. Suri had skillfully arranged his rangers in places where they could view the cave from every angle so not to chance missing the slightest movement in or out. If Enguer had learned anything about Suri in the brief time that he had known him, he was sure that the elder ranger hated surprises. In their profession, surprises often did not end well.

Leading up to the space around the cave, the trees thinned out to be replaced by thick brush and boulders affording Enguer a glimpse of the star-studded sky through the twisted branches. The moon was far across its nightly arc indicating that it was well past midnight. It was too cold and wet to sleep, but even if the weather had been perfect, he would have been hard pressed to catch a few winks anyway. Enguer was on high alert, adrenalin coursing through every vein and fiber of his being, waiting and watching.

The long dark hours passed slowly until just before dawn the rain frittered away and the morning birds began to sing. For the first time all night, Enguer felt the fatigue of the watch and he slid into a light dose on the edge of sleep. It was a numbingly comfortable state where he no longer felt the tightness in his muscles or the bone-chilling wetness of his soaked clothing and it was in this state that he vaguely realized that the morning birds had abruptly paused their serenade. Enguer struggled to break the malaise. It was like swimming in a sea of honey. His body desperately wanted to sleep while his mind urgently cried out for vigilance.

A man's scream rent the misty morning air, just as quickly ending.

Enguer's eyes popped open in a panic. Who was it? Which position? It seemed far away but was it close? His gaze quickly scanned the dark spots that his trained eye knew to be his companions forms and counted five. The one directly above the cave entrance was gone. Nothing moved, no one moved. Enguer's eyes darted from place to place looking for some sign of where he had gone, but the morning birds remained silent and he realized with a start that it was now the rangers who were being hunted.

As if the thought had occurred to Suri in the same moment, a quick, piercing whistle split the air. The signal to abandon the watch and immediately retreat to safety. It was the worst possible signal. It meant that it was imperative that one of them had to survive long enough to recount what they had found to Commander Duraunt. Until then they were on their own.

The first light of dawn filtered through the trees when Suri sent the desperate signal. It was enough light for Enguer to notice the dark shadows of the rangers stealing away into the obscurity of the forest. They were fleeing just as instructed. Enguer was about to skulk away as well when movement caught his eye and he saw it. The Demon Beast. It was climbing down from the ridge above the cave entrance dragging a limp form close behind.

One of the rangers.

The creature dumped his prize on the ground and quickly rushed over to the spot Suri had identified as the place where the scat was accumulated. Enguer would have departed then, but for the shock of what happened next – another Demon Beast emerged from the cave.

Absolutely stunned, Enguer looked on in disbelief. This one was smaller than the first, not by much but noticeably so, and its hair was finer, more delicate. It sniffed the air, then sniffed the body of the ranger, releasing an audible growl. His mind finally working once again, Enguer noticed something very different about the new Demon Beast – this one had breasts! It was hard to tell with all the fur, but when it shifted and turned it was undeniable that this Demon Beast was female.

The large male returned, having completed its business, and they both stood erect sniffing the air around them. A light breeze ran off the mountains and through the trees to wisp around Enguer's face. The two Demon Beasts howled excitedly and crawled up the side of the ridge, disappearing into the darkness of the forest. Filled with dread, he quickly guessed that the beasts must have caught the scent of the rangers that had been on the east side of the cave opening and it pained Enguer that there was nothing he could do for them other than survive to tell their tale. He skulked away as quickly as he dared, fleeing into The Wilds in the direction of Courth.

Enguer hardly took ten strides when a blood-curdling scream echoed through the tangle of trees somewhere not far behind lending him the motivation to abandon any pretense of stealth and run for everything he was worth. It was a treacherous getaway, the footing was slick due to the long night of rain, causing him to frequently stumble and fall. Yet, each time he pulled himself up and resumed his reckless flight. This was not how he imagined this mission to end. The rangers were simply tasked with locating the Demon Beast's lair and returning to Courth with their findings. Suri wanted to be sure and decided to wait for visual confirmation before they went back. Now they ran for their lives. Still, Enguer placed no blame on Suri's judgment. It was the right thing to do. Otherwise, Commander Duraunt would return with a force to kill the creatures based on a near-certainty. And none of the rangers, especially Suri, would ever put lives at stake based on a near certainty. The Demon Beasts were swift runners. He learned that pursuing the one that was once Rochette out of the temple. Enguer knew that his only chance to make it out of The Wilds alive was assuming the creatures would have more trouble than he running through the dark forest. Or they found more of the fleeing rangers. That last thought he pushed quickly out of his mind.

When the sun came up, Enguer paused to catch his breath and listen for pursuit. His ears detected nothing, but his higher senses screamed that the Beasts were there and he ran until the afternoon. Once he heard thrashing through the brush somewhere off to his left, so he angled further north to get away from it. For all he knew it was nothing more than a boar rummaging for roots or a deer tangled in low-hanging vines. It didn't matter, all he knew was that he had to be away from it.

Night returned to The Wilds oppressive, cold and dark. Enguer, exhausted and bloodied from dozens of scrapes and falls, fell upon the soft grass of an open glade. He rested fitfully until a distant shriek brought him alert. At first, he wasn't sure if he had dreamed the terrible cry until another, closer, had him on his feet again sprinting west. He ran for hours through the night and by the time dawn broke he was drained of strength and barely coherent. Not letting up his body ran on, somehow, while his hazy mind struggled to navigate around the next tree or over the next fallen log. He was on his feet as much as he was picking himself up again and still, he ran on.

The next several hours were an agonizing blur of motion. Enguer thought he might have heard another scream far behind, but he wasn't sure of anything anymore. It was only by sheer will that he stayed on his feet and there were still many leagues to go. He thought of Suri, he thought of his father, he thought of the rangers falling behind him and they, more than anything else, kept him going through the next night. The moon high above, seemed to laugh at him and he cursed it. Faces appeared out of the dark forest mocking him, laughing before receding into the gloom. Some he knew and others he didn't. Whatever the hallucination he tried to ignore them knowing that they could not possibly be real. Enguer recognized that his mind was slipping but there was no choice but to keep running forward until his legs would no longer carry him.

More hours passed, punctuated at irregular intervals by dreadful screams from deep in the forest. The sounds echoed in his head as much as they carried from a distance and he couldn't be sure if they were real or imagined. Barely running anymore, his mind weighed down by delusions and exhaustion, Enguer staggered over roots and branches. He had to keep pressing forward. He willed himself not to stop. No matter what he had to endure he must make it back to Courth if to die in the arms of Commander Duraunt. But even that wasn't enough. He had to live to tell the tale of seven rangers that braved The Wilds to hunt down the elusive and dangerous Demon Beast, to slay it where it lived and save the kingdom from its ravages.

Even through the haze of his rattled mind, Enguer knew it was a fairy tale. They had lost the battle from the start. Died in the misery of icy rain, fled in the face of overwhelming terror. None would survive to tell the tale. Screams of the dead echoed relentlessly through his head. Rain pelted down upon him, soaking him through to the bone followed by a chill that made his heart ache. Enguer imagined that he ran and ran. Was it true? Nothing mattered, only that he ran. It was a fool's mission they embarked upon, doomed from the start. He ran. Thin branches lashed across his face, or were they the claws of the Beasts? Was he dead already and didn't know it, living out an eternity of torment in purgatory? Where was his goddess? Where was Sunna? He desperately yearned for her warm embrace. Why had she forsaken him? How could his father have left him alone?

Sunna rose from the edge of the world bringing light unto darkness. All across the sky she travelled bestowing her life-giving warmth upon the land below. She reigned the heavens above until her sister, Eriu brought forth the moon and with a loving kiss replaced her sister's voyage to reign for a time over the night until Sunna brought forth the glow of her radiance once again....

Enguer awoke to the light of a new day thawing the frost that had settled over him. He opened his eyes to see first the long needles of green grass abundant all around and next the warmth of the sun upon one cheek. Still, he did not test a muscle to move. It must be a dream that he lived after all the horror of.... days? He did not know. He could only revel in the contrast of the ice-touched grass and the warmth from above. If there was a nirvana this must be it.

Long minutes stretched into hours while he lay still and unmoving. Strength was returning slowly, but Enguer wasn't confident he could stand yet, let alone run. His delusional mind urged him to get moving before nightfall. That it was a matter of survival. Paranoia and worry shrieked that he had lay there far too long already. The Demon

Beasts were coming. They would find him soon if he didn't find the strength to run. Enguer tried to move his exhausted legs, press the wet grass with his hands to raise his weary head and collapsed on the ground again for all his effort. Shadows crowded his vision turning the world around him black. His conscious spiraled down a dark shaft into nothing.

Enguer awoke briefly late in the afternoon, maybe the same day, he had no way to be sure and he hardly cared. The warmth from Sunna was tempered by the chilly wind rolling of the frozen peaks to the north. He could move his legs, fingers and arms. His limbs barely twitched but it was enough to know that he could move them again, if only a little. Still, he felt helpless and completely vulnerable. Unable to keep them open, his eyes closed again and he drifted into an uneasy slumber, his dreams plagued by strange visions, panic and running.

It was dusk when Enguer opened his eyes and sat up. He was a hundred spans from the gloomy silhouette of the tree-line that marked the edge of The Wilds. Were there rangers in there still? If he had the strength, he would have gone back to find them. Except that he was supposed to do something. What was it? Hunger and thirst suddenly ruled his body compelling him to drink gingerly from his waterskin and nibble sparingly on the dried meat in his pack as he watched the final glow from the sun dip below the western horizon. Enguer unrolled the wool blanket strapped to his pack and settled himself for a fitful sleep. There was no point in trying to go anywhere until he was rested.

Once again Sunna brought warmth to the grasslands that separated the Kingdom of Courth from The Wilds. Enguer awoke feeling halfway lucid. Pain wracked his body from a hundred cuts and bruises he had no account for. His memory of the past few days and hours was hardly reliable, He had no idea how much time had passed since he had stumbled out of The Wilds. The only thing he knew for sure was that he had to return to Courth and report to Commander Duraunt everything that had transpired.

His weary eyes were drawn to a furtive movement at the edge of the forest. Enguer raised his bow and marked the dark figure emerging from under the shadows of the trees. If it was a Demon Beast, he intended to launch a dozen arrows into it before it ever came close. He waited for the image to form completely before he let loose the first arrow. Just a few moments more....

The image that formed took the shape of a man. Wiping his eyes to make sure that what he was seeing was true, Enguer watched sharply over the shaft of his arrow at the familiar shape emerging from The Wilds. He smiled.

Suri.

Enguer lowered his bow. Suri had called forth the signal to escape by any means necessary and survive to warn the officials of Courth. The dark memories flooded back in an unrelenting wave. He recalled a second Demon Beast, one with breasts...a female. Tears rolled down Enguer's cheeks as he relived the moments before his flight. Two Beasts. Screams in the night. Running. Cold.

Dropping the bow to the side, Enguer held himself fast rocking back and forth in the supple grass. Everything was coming back in a rush, every detail of the terror and hopelessness. How had he survived? And then there was a hand on the back of his head and a warm embrace. He was no longer alone and no longer afraid. Still the tears kept coming and he buried his face in the chest of the man he admired more than anyone alive and he felt the warmth returned without judgment. He felt like he was home again.

He was home.

~~~

"My Lord General, I present to you Commander Suri Privou and Enguer Rand," Commander Duraunt stood at attention facing the general who was sitting at a small table casual enjoying a breakfast of porridge and sliced fruits.

Almost as if the commander's announcement was no more than a distraction from his meal, he waved for the rangers to step closer. The commander stepped up with them until they were all standing quietly two paces from the breakfast table.

"These men are the only survivors of the rangers that tracked the Demon Beast to its lair in The Wilds . . ." the Commander paused while a pretty servant-girl walked over to place a cup of steaming honey ale on the table. She waited until the general gestured for her to leave, giggling playfully when he lightly tapped her on the buttocks.

Clearing his throat, the commander continued his introduction, "They have important information that you need to hear and urgently pass along to the king as it may well effect the security of the kingdom."

Not even looking up from his porridge, the general scoffed, "I've read the reports, Commander. We are talking about a mentally defective priest turned into a rabid wolf by that pompous fool wizard. Rauf got what was coming to him. I don't know what His Majesty ever saw in him."

The commander's faced reddened several shades and through a heroic effort managed to keep his voice under control, "What about His Holiness, the Arch Priest? Did he have it coming to him as well, Lord General?"

The general flashed a quick glare at the commander before returning his gaze to his porridge, "No, Tanais was a good man and my friend. So, the rangers chased it into The Wilds, is it dead and forgotten?"

"No, my Lord General," Suri spoke up. "We found it's lair and took positions to watch the entrance. Despite our precautions, it somehow sniffed us out and ambushed one of my men."

"Did your man kill it?" the general pierced a piece of fruit with a small breakfast knife and shoved it in his mouth.

"I don't think you understand what we are dealing with, Lord General," Enguer could see that Suri was becoming irritated. The old ranger didn't take well to ignorance or neglect and he would make plain his aggravation no matter the station of the man or woman he chastised for it.

Stabbing another fruit wedge, still the general didn't bother to look up. "So, explain it to me, I have little time to dally."

Suri glanced over at Commander Duraunt, standing stiff and red faced and sighed. By now Enguer knew Suri well enough to know that he was about to lose his temper. Having been through what they had been experienced the days before and the terrible losses they had suffered, Enguer felt much the same and would have gladly defended the elder ranger if he had walked over and slapped the fruit right out of the insufferable general's hand.

"It is no rabid wolf, this thing. Rauf created some kind of monster nearly twice a man's height and at least four times heavier. It killed a skilled wizard, a more than talented Arch Priest, two fire priests, a duke, the minister and several of the king's guards on its way out of the city." Suri paused for a breath.

Not waiting for Suri to finish, the general pounded a fist on the table and turned a fierce gaze on the three of them for the first time. "I know all this," he shouted. "What is your point?"

Suri's voice dropped to a low growl, veins throbbing the length of his neck, "My point is that this monster tracked down five of my best men in The Wilds and dragged them off. I pray Sunna will watch over their lost souls. And do you recall that it stole away with the High Priestess Rhalia?"

The general nodded curtly.

"It appears to have changed her into one of its kind somehow. Now there are two of them." Suri's unwavering gaze was locked with the general's as if in some test of wills.

The general shifted his gaze to the commander. "Is what this man says true, Duraunt?"

"Suri has been the Commander of the Royal Order of Rangers for more than a decade. If he says it is true, I believe him," Commander Duraunt stuck out his chin in what Enguer interpreted as a subconscious act of defiance toward his commanding officer, "and so will the king."

That last part had the effect on the general like a slap on the face and he stood suddenly, sending his chair tumbling behind him along with the cup of still steaming honey ale to splash across the floor. If he wore a sword, Enguer imagined he might have drawn it. The general stood staring at the three of them for a long moment before he finally appeared to relax. Then he marched forward, Enguer and Suri moving to get out of his way.

When the general reached the door, he turned back to them and spoke as if he were addressing common soldiers, "I will inform the king of your news and come up with a suitable plan to deal with this threat." Casting one last dark glare Commander Duraunt's way, he turned on his heel and marched down the sunlit corridor.

Commander Duraunt breathed a long sigh of relief and looked over at Enguer with a slight smile on his face. "Well, now you have met Lord General Bufont."

Enguer didn't know what to say. He assumed by the man's nature he was a noble of some sort, maybe a duke, that had been appointed to the position by the king. He also had a strong suspicion that anything of consequence that was accomplished by the military was almost entirely due to the competent leadership of Commander Duraunt.

"So, what do we do now?"

Commander Duraunt barked a laugh that held no humor in it, "The Lord General would have us wait on his command. That may not come for days. In the meantime, I will work with Suri to prepare a force to kill these things for good."

Enguer was eager to do something as well. "What can I do to help?"

Suri squeezed his shoulder and smiled sadly, "Stick with me boy. There are a lot fewer of us now and I'm going to need you more than ever."

They walked out of the general's breakfast chamber and along the corridor toward the front gates of the palace. Servants rushed in every direction doing their masters biding while housemaids polished silver and crystal or dragged armfuls of linens to be laundered. The nobles of the kingdom lived in the palace when they were in the city, but Enguer had no idea if it was a political calculation or they were required to by the king. Of course, they all had estates on their own lands where they oversaw whatever industry they were responsible for to generate income and taxes. Courth was known for its logging production more than anything else, although Enguer was aware that Port Francik, in the south, thrived on tanning and fishing. He and his father had made a decent living selling hides to the merchants from that part of the kingdom for many years.

Enguer was suddenly reminded of something Commander Durant had said earlier to the general, "Suri, do you have the rank of Commander like Commander Duraunt?"

Commander Duraunt had a knowing smile on his face, but Suri's reply struck Enguer as one of begrudging acceptance, "I'm a ranger. I don't need no fancy titles to impress my men. They follow me 'cause they choose to."

Enguer kept his smile in check, but he couldn't restrain the spontaneous humor inherited from his mother, "As do I, Commander. As do I."

Chapter 8

Broken Towers

The sound of hooves on cobblestones echoed through the quiet haze of the early morning. A rider was fast approaching almost heedless of his mount's exhausted condition. Enguer's sharp ears could pick-up the distressed huffs of puffs of the horse even from a distance.

Mouth open at the point of intoning Sunna's Blessing of Dawn, the High Priest standing at the top of the stairs paused to stare in the direction of the clamor when the rider rounded the corner of the temple and skidded to a halt on the slick cobblestones still wet with dew. Flanks heaving and hot breath steaming in the cold air, the horse nearly stumbled from fatigue. The rider, a soldier from the look of what was left of his tattered uniform, was in no better condition. He practically fell from his horse in his haste to dismount, taking only a few steps before he collapsed in a heap on the ground.

"Bring that man to me!" Commander Duraunt shouted to two of the king's elite guards standing nearby, but they were already in motion.

The High Priest quickly descended the temple stairs two at a time to stand next to the commander. Enguer was surprised at how nimble the old man was in his long white robes. Half-carrying, half-dragging the ragged soldier, the guards brought the barely lucid man to sit on the stairs before the commander and the High Priest. A low murmur rippled through the crowd of soldiers and rangers. The condition of the battered man was shocking. His uniform was not threadbare and unkempt from wear, it was ripped and torn, stained with blood from deep gashes in his flesh underneath. Likewise, his hair was matted with more blood that left streaks down his face and neck. Most disturbing were the man's eyes, brown orbs blood-shot and wide with crazed fear. He tried to speak, but his voice was cracked and hoarse, resulting in a desperate gibberish.

"Give him water!" Commander Duraunt ordered to no one in particular.

Almost immediately one of the rangers was kneeling next to the soldier helping him to take short sips from a waterskin while the two guards held him steady. Enguer felt the tension as everyone fell silent in anticipation of what the soldier was about to say.

Finally shoving the waterskin away, the soldier's eyes focused on the commander. "Commander Duraunt," he croaked, "the Demon Beasts . . ." He faltered and hung his head low with obvious exhaustion.

"Take a moment," the commander whispered.

The High Priest placed his hands on the soldier's head and seconds later a soft-blue glow appeared under his fingers. The soldier's body twitched with spasms. It only lasted a few seconds and as quickly as the High Priest withdrew his hands, the soldier looked up and stood on his own, much recovered.

"Commander," the soldier's voice was clear if still a little unsteady. "The Demon Beasts have over-run at least three watch towers on the borderlands. Dozens of soldiers have been killed or carried away into the forest."

"Two Demon Beasts were able to over-run three towers?" The commander sounded incredulous.

The soldier vigorously shook his head, "Two no, there were many, I don't know their numbers. At least a score, maybe more. I was barely able to escape with my life."

"We are glad that you did," Commander Duraunt assured him with a calming smile. "What is your name, soldier?"

The soldier blinked for a moment as if he couldn't remember. "E . . . Erol, sir."

Commander Duraunt put a hand on his shoulder. "Erol, you are a Foot Soldier, yes? I cannot see the rank on your uniform."

Erol pounded his fist to his chest in salute. "Yes, Commander. Please excuse the state of my uniform."

The Commander waved the comment away. "I am more concerned with the state of your health and that of your comrades. Which unit are you from?

"Borderland Watch Group Four, Commander."

"The northern towers? That's fifteen leagues north of here. You must have ridden half the night to get here."

"Yes, Commander, as quickly as I could without killing my horse."

The commander pat Erol on the shoulder. "Your bravery will be rewarded. Now off to the barracks and get some rest, but first have a healer take a look at those wounds."

"Yes, Commander!" Erol saluted and took the reins of his horse. Slowly, he walked toward the military district, with a slight spring in his step born of his recent heroism.

Enguer followed Suri to stand next to Commander Duraunt. "Looks like a change of plans?"

Nodding, the Commander addressed the assembled group. "King Francik has designated this troop as the 'First Expeditionary Force' with the mission of tracking down the Demon Beasts and killing them by any means at our disposal. But first we must find them." His dark brows furrowed sharply. "The sad news we just received gives us a new starting point and hopefully the opportunity to recover survivors. Mount up!"

One hundred mounted soldiers, several fire priests and a dozen rangers rode north out of Courth. They had all expected to be in The Wilds retracing Enguer and Suri's footsteps back to the Demon Beasts lair, but the attack on the northern towers meant they were not at the lair and may have moved since the rangers had found it. Worse still, the creatures number had grown and Enguer feared that they were marching more men to their deaths.

~~~

By mid-afternoon the company arrived at the first watchtower only to find it completely abandoned. Enguer studied the ground around the tower while the more experienced rangers fanned out beyond the immediate grounds to determine which way the Demon Beasts had retreated.

There were obvious signs of a battle – the main door of the tower was shattered and broken, sections of armor, tattered clothing and weapons were strewn about and there were small pools and spatters of blood everywhere. But not a single body.

Why would the Demon Beasts carry off the bodies of their adversaries? Enguer wondered. Would they take them away to devour them later or might they have a way of bringing them back to life as more Demon Beasts?

He studied the array of boot marks interspersed with evidence of dragging and the strange claw-like tracks. Enguer studied them closer – they were wolf-like at the front and stretched into the semblance of a human heel in the back. They were nearly twice the size as the boot marks and the depression they made indicated that the creatures stood on their hind legs the same as a man. Exactly like the tracks they found in The Wilds. There was no doubt in his mind that it was Demon Beasts that had attacked the towers.

Enguer glanced around. No horses had been left behind. Their tracks showed panic and wild flight in several directions. Where ever they were now, the Demon Beasts did not bother to kill them nor did they take any with them.

Returning to Commander Duraunt to report what he had found, Enguer joined Suri and another ranger discussing what they had discovered.

"The Demon Beasts dispersed into the forest in several directions," Suri was saying. "They may converge again later on, but to follow them all we would have to split our force into several smaller groups."

Commander Duraunt shook his head in frustration. "Any idea as to how many of the Demon Beasts there were?"

Suri looked at the other ranger and nodded, "At least nine," he replied

"Nine?" Commander Duraunt's face flushed. "Nine of these creatures overcame twenty of our soldiers?"

"We believed so, Commander."

Enguer agreed with their assessment. He too had seen only nine unique sets of tracks. "They are quite large, Commander," he rejoined.

A grave expression overcame the commander's features. "I remember well enough – a head taller, heavier by a quarter and far stronger." He glanced over at the splintered doorway of the watchtower. "Any idea if they carry weapons or wear armor?"

Suri shrugged, "Sharp claws and teeth appear to be their only weapons. It is unclear if they wear armor or even clothing. The ones we found in The Wilds wore nothing.'"

Commander Duraunt glanced at Enguer.

He nodded his agreement and then added, "I doubt they have a need for it. The arrows I sunk into the thick hide of the one that was Rochette never slowed. Besides, I think they use their speed to their advantage."

"Agreed," the commander nodded slowly, "the one that passed me in Courth ran as fast as a horse can gallop."

"They have a strange loping gait the way they grip the ground and push off with their foreclaws. Very efficient for their frame, I suppose." Suri confirmed.

Commander Duraunt called over a pair of his captains and laid out his orders, "Take a third of our force to each of the other watchtowers and tend to the survivors if you find any. I doubt you can return before nightfall, so make camp and set defenses. We will regroup here in the morning."

"Yes, Commander." The captains thumped their chests and strode away barking orders to their men.

"We will need to set up a perimeter watch in the forest tonight," he told Suri. "I want to know if anything comes within two-hundred yards of the tower." There was a clearing of about a hundred yards between the forest and the tower and with the rangers in the forest not even a possum should be able to approach without being seen.

Suri nodded and turned to Enguer before departing. "Stay with the commander, Enguer. You will keep watch for our signals from atop the tower.

Enguer was crestfallen, he wanted to be in the forest with the other rangers and although he knew that one of them would have to stay behind on watch, why did it have to be him? After everything he and Suri had endured a few weeks earlier when just the two of them escaped from the Demon Beasts, the rangers still saw him as the youngest and least experienced of the group. So, of course, the watch duty fell to him.

He followed the commander back to the watchtower. Soldiers worked hard to reinforce the door and clean up the interior. Enguer decided to find a spot at the top of the tower to rest until nightfall and keep out of the soldiers' way. He would be up all night watching and waiting while he worried about Suri and the others positioned at the edge of The Wilds. The Demon Beasts had sniffed them out once before.

Sometime later, Enguer opened his eyes to a star filled sky and the smell of cooking fires. He stood and looked over the crenelated wall of the watchtower to the camp fifty-feet below. The soldiers and fire priests sat together in clusters around low campfires to ward off the frigid cold of the night. Around them stood small tents and lean-tos inside a perimeter of a rudimentary log wall with sharpened spikes facing outward. The men and women spoke quietly among themselves. It was nothing like the typical soldiers' camp with bawdy conversation and laughter. Enguer doubted the commander was allowing a single drop of mead or wine on this night.

Settling himself into a comfortable sitting position to keep an eye on the forest, he pulled a piece of jerky from his pack. One of Mrs. Eibhlin's hot spring-berry pies would have been nice right now. He doubted he would be seeing any of that again any time soon.

Enguer watched the forest diligently, his mind on the rangers that were out there in the darkness keeping them safe. For at least the hundredth time he wished he were one of them. Hours passed and soon the conversations from below tailed off into loud snores and the pop of the campfire. The forest was dark and quiet, aside from the occasional hoot of an owl or call of a night bird. Those were always good signs that nature slept undisturbed. As calm as the night was, Enguer did not feel the tug of fatigue often brought on by extended periods of boredom. His father had trained him how to stay clear-headed and alert for hours at a time with mental exercises and stretching techniques. Enguer put them to good use as the night lengthened.

Until the forest became disturbingly silent.

This was how it had started before. Enguer's anxiety heightened while his attention was focused sharply, almost desperately, on the tree-line looking for any visual or audible signal from the rangers. It could come in many forms – directed light from a light-globe, an animal call out of place in the local environment or a series of thumps on a log – every ranger was trained to recognize them all. He hoped that the silence was nothing more than a natural predator in the area that had spooked the wildlife.

Minutes stretched by like hours, Enguer felt the blood and adrenaline pumping through his temples like the low beat of drums. It was going on too long. Something was happening out there that he couldn't see. Alarm bells were screaming in his head.

Without warning, a shadow burst from the black outline of trees into the clearing. It was the size of a man and appeared to be moving at a full sprint. Seconds later, Enguer could hear him screaming something over and over, and although he couldn't make out the words, there was no doubt he was in distress.

Taking no chances, Enguer shouted down to the camp below, "Make ready! Make ready! Eyes to the forest!"

Soldiers and priests stumbled from their tents and bedrolls, fully armed and armored and rushed toward the log wall. From the depths of the tower he heard soldiers pounding up the stairs to take positions at the top of the tower with him and the distinct ring of Commander Duraunt's voice bellowing orders repeated down the line by his officers.

Enguer steadily watched the man running toward them. It was hard to tell in the light of the stars, but he appeared to be one of the rangers. There was no one else it could be. But which one? A second form burst from the forest about fifty yards behind the first. He too desperately ran across the open field. Halfway to the tower, Enguer could finally understand the words the first man was screaming. It was nearly a shriek, full of fear and panic, so unlike the demeanor he would expect from the normally reserved and composed nature of a ranger. This one had seen something that terrified him.

"The Demon Beast!" the ranger screamed. "They are coming!"

There was a sudden flurry of voices and movement from the soldiers below. They had heard him too. Enguer looked hard at the forest wall for any hint of movement.

Nothing.

The second ranger was only a quarter of the way into the field when much larger shadows emerged from the trees in pursuit. At such a distance, the details were sparse, yet there was no doubt the figures were moving very fast and on all fours in the fashion that Suri had described earlier in the day. The soldiers and priests below shouted encouragement to the rangers to run faster as if they were part of some sadistic sporting competition. Enguer had to concede that his comrades *were* in a race – a race for their lives.

Four archers joined him from below and nervously readied their bows. They all wore round-eyed expressions of fear. Enguer doubted that any of them had ever experienced combat of any sort, let alone against creatures born of a nightmare. They would all be veterans after tonight if they survived.

Finally, the first ranger ran through a break in the log wall and collapsed huffing and puffing on the ground to the cheers of everyone defending the towers. The second ranger was still fifty yards behind and running for his life. Enguer counted a dozen large creatures in pursuit with the ones in the lead only about twenty yards behind the ranger and closing fast.

He was never going to make it.

Enguer nocked and arrow and shouted to the archers next to him, "If you can make the distance, fire on the large dark shapes. Take care not to hit our man!"

His first arrow impacted a Demon Beast when it was only a few yards behind the terrified ranger, the force of it knocking the creature from its feet and off to the side in a wild roll. The soldiers below let out a loud cheer. Still, the ranger was forty yards away, with more of the creatures on his heels.

The next Demon Beast closed in and Enguer nailed it squarely in the hind leg causing it to slide sprawling on the wet grass.

Thirty yards.

The archers to Enguer's left and right were doing their best to help, but their shots were all over the place, some landing dangerously close to the fleeing ranger. These men needed training, he thought absently, nocking another arrow.

The danger was far from over. A pair of Demon Beasts were hard on the ranger's heels and would soon be within reach of the poor soul. The first ranger, having recovered enough to add his voice to the disharmony of shouts calling for the second ranger to hurry, was no help. To Enguer's disappointment he had lost his bow and could be nothing more than a spectator until the beasts came within striking distance of the blade he held high in the air.

All alone, the spring ranger's life was in Enguer's hands with the Demon Beasts nearly on him. It had to be now. He pulled his bow up and looked down the shaft of the arrow allowing his mind to shut out the noise around him and control his breathing. Just like his father had taught him.

He let the arrow fly and another followed a second later.

The first arrow sprouted from the chest of the closest Demon Beast and it tumbled away knocked off balance, in not dead. The second shot impaled its companion in the shoulder causing it to slow considerably, falling several steps behind. Cheers rose from all around Enguer as the archers slapped him on the back praising the two impossible shots.

The ranger, realizing he had been saved, raised his arms high and shouted in triumph. He was only fifteen yards away and the closest Demon Beast had an arrow in its shoulder with no hope of catching him before he reached the camp.

And then he stumbled.

Enguer watched horrified as time slowed to a crawl. The ranger fell hard on the grass, but almost immediately popped back up on one knee preparing to launch himself into a final sprint. It was too late. The Demon Beast, slowed by his injury, had gained the ground it needed to leap off its hind legs over the final distance. Spinning around, the ranger slashed desperately at the Demon Beast with his sword, only to have it slapped away. He let out one final scream before his body was ripped apart.

Enguer, the soldiers, the Fire-Priests, the archers and even Commander Duraunt watched in silence and disbelief. Then there was a fierce shout from someone down below and a collective rage took hold of the defenders. Enguer felt it as well, and he began reigning down arrows with deadly effect upon the charging Demon Beasts.

It wasn't enough.

Of the four he had hit, only the one impaled through the chest lay unmoving. Luck had found a soft spot. The rest bounded over the log wall or crashed through it. Bolts of fire launched from the hands of the Fire-Priests scorched fur hides, yet appeared to only enrage them more. The soldiers stood valiantly forming ranks and locking shields at the command of their Captain while Enguer and the archers fired into the monsters from atop the tower at almost point-blank range. Still, the Demon Beasts ripped the shields away and brushed off the arrows.

They were unstoppable.

A scream from below alerted Enguer to a new danger as he realized one of the Demon Beasts was in the tower. These were not ignorant creatures. They understood the threat from above and one of them was on its way up to deal with them.

The trap door sprang open and a Fire-Priestess scrambled up. "It's coming up the stairs! It will be here any moment!"

"Stand with us," Enguer ordered the terrified priestess. The rest of the archers joined him facing the trapdoor in a tight semi-circle. "We will only have one chance. When it comes through hit it with everything you've got."

They waited in silence for what they knew would come. Below, the battle raged on, yet Enguer felt somehow detached from what was happening down there, even with the screams of man and beast terrified and dying.

"Don't fire until you can see it's whole body," Enguer cautioned. "We can't afford to miss."

With stunning violence, a Demon Beast burst through the trap door, shattering it into a thousand pieces and bound onto the landing. There was a terrible pause. Maybe it was paralyzing fear or shock at what stood before them, Enguer couldn't say, but it lasted only a second before a dozen arrows and a cone of fire exploded onto the creature's body.

The Demon Beast stumbled backward from the impact to the edge of the tower wall and a second volley sent it shrieking over the side fully ablaze. Enguer and the others rushed over ready to hurl down more arrows and fire, but it lay unmoving and burning at the base of the tower.

Enguer grabbed the fire priestess. "Watch the stairs in case any more of those things decide to come up here. Don't hesitate to fill it with your fire!"

The priestess nodded and climbed back down through the opening vacated by the trap door. Enguer turned and rushed back to the edge of the tower to support the soldiers fighting below. The battle wasn't going well. Two Fire-Priests lay still and bloodied along with at least half-a-dozen soldiers with chunks of their armor practically torn off their wrecked bodies. Only two of the Demon Beasts were down as far as he could see. Worse still, there were less than a dozen arrows left in his quiver. A few more shots and he would go down and fight alongside those brave souls no matter what the outcome.

One by one the archers spent the last of their arrows to good effect felling one more of the Demon Beasts. When they had none left between them, Enguer drew his sword and faced the men he had come to think of as his to command. So far, they had accepted his leadership but it was a responsibility he did not enjoy.

"We have nothing left to offer but our swords. Follow me if you have the courage. Sell your lives dearly." Enguer headed down the stairs with the archers-turned-swordsmen close behind.

When they passed the surprised Fire-Priestess keeping watch on the stairwell she yelled, "What's happening?"

Enguer did not stop. "We are out of arrows!" he called back to the priestess. He was not surprised that she joined them.

Nearly tumbling out of the watchtower Enguer and his men immediately came upon a Demon Beast attempting to peel one of the soldiers out of his armor. Unnoticed by the creature, Enguer crouched low and slid his blade across its hamstring. The beast collapsed to the ground screaming in rage and agony. The archers did not let the suffering go on long, although they might have wanted to, stabbing deeply with their short swords to ensure it did not rise again.

It was a quick victory unlikely to be repeated. Nevertheless, it gave them all the confidence to keep going. Enguer led them around the bend of the tower and stopped dead in his tracks. Two Demon Beasts, thick wisps of smoke rising from scorched patches of fur, had just ripped a Fire-Priest in half. They stood staring at the small groups sudden appearance. Not wanting to lose the advantage, Enguer charged.

For a moment he recognized the glint of intellect in their eyes and an almost sad inevitability that he too was about to be ripped and slashed like some worthless garment. Enguer did not hesitate. The priestesses fire engulfed the pair of Demon Beasts setting their fur ablaze, forcing them back a step. Enguer did not falter. Anger flared in the eyes of his adversaries and the intellect he saw earlier was replaced by primal fury unaffected by the agony inflicted by the flames.

If these were to be Enguer's final moments he planned to spend them savagely and to the credit of the four archers that followed closely behind, he would not greet Sunna alone. Nearly upon them, the Demon Beasts braced for the impact of his charge. Sword held low, Enguer was determined to take at least one of them with him before he was done.

From out of nowhere, something crashed into him from his flank with such force that he was sent spinning to the ground. The shriek of horses and pounding of hooves compounded his disorientation, but he focused his eyes in time to see the final death throes of the two Demon Beasts trampled under the weight of heavy warhorses. Mounted on the lead horse was Commander Duraunt.

He reared his horse around and called down to him, "Are you alright, Enguer?"

Enguer waved a hand at the commander indicating that he was okay and then hurriedly cast his gaze around to find his men and the priestess. The four archers stumbling toward him, narrowly missed by the commander's charge and the priestess was picking herself off the ground bruised but unharmed. They all stood gasping for breath exhausted from fear and exertion. Enguer was relieved they were all safe and when he looked back the Commander was leading his small cavalry of three toward the remaining sounds of battle.

His head still spinning from nearly being crushed by the Commander's massive warhorse, Enguer struggled to his feet and stumbled to follow. The four archers and the fire priestess quickly joined him and soon they rounded the watchtower to an unexpected scene.

Commander Duraunt was dismounting and although the carnage of battle lay everywhere, the fighting had ceased and there were no Demon Beasts anywhere in sight.

Enguer released a huge sigh, "Have they gone?"

"They have," the Commander confirmed, "and we are in no condition to pursue them."

"We will pick up their trail tomorrow when the rest of our troop returns. I'm sure I can show you the way . . ."

"No Enguer," Commander Duraunt was shaking his head. "Look at what only a dozen of those creatures did to us. What if there are more? We will return to Courth tomorrow and report this incident to General Bufont. I have misjudged these monsters terribly. Only the king can mobilize the forces we will need to face the horror of what awaits us in that forest."

Enguer knew the Commander was right. They had barely survived the night in a fortified watchtower. How could they expect to survive a single day unprotected in The Wilds? He had always considered The Wilds his natural home, but tonight had shown him how naïve he was outside of the shelter of his father. It was time he grew up.

Thinking of his father reminded him of Suri. He had taken the balance of the rangers to watch the forest facing the other two towers north of this one. Enguer prayed to Sunna they were all unharmed. If there were enough Demon Beasts to attack those towers as well, then the Commander might be right and it could take an army to destroy them all.

Chapter 9

Unto The Wilds

"I apologize, Your Majesty," General Bufont puffed with rage when he arrived in the king's private meeting room. "I was unaware that Commander Duraunt had pushed himself into see you without my leave."

Enguer was sitting in a high-backed hardwood chair carved from the finest oak cut by the loggers along the Esmee River in the northern part of the Kingdom. He sat against the wall behind Commander Duraunt and Suri who were sitting at a large oak table situated in the center of a room sizeable enough to host a ball. King Francik sat at the head of the table facing a large map of the Kingdom of Courth laid out in front of him. Several servants stood nearby at the king's beck and call and otherwise attempted to blend into the background.

The king did not immediately reply to his general, rather he waited for the chunky man to make the long walk from the door to where they sat. By the time he arrived, sweat covered his brow and he was out of breath. Looking at the general in his fine leather boots, wool trousers and blue silk tunic under a long fox-fur lined coat, Enguer wondered how anyone could become a general without ever serving as a soldier. Not even his clothing held any semblance of a uniform.

Graciously, the king motioned for him to sit. "Thank you for joining us, General Bufont. I truly appreciate your prompt response to my summon."

"Thank you…. Your Majesty." He plopped down into a chair opposite Suri and Commander Duraunt, still breathing heavy and dabbing his forehead with a silken handkerchief.

"Commander Duraunt and Commander Suri have advised me of some troubling news," Enguer almost laughed out loud watching

Suri's back straighten at the use of his official title and he was sure that if it hadn't been the king that uttered it Suri might have spat some choice and unsuitable remarks.

"It seems that you have not been entirely clear about where we stand with these Demon Beasts," The king's eyes were boring into the general like daggers causing more sweat to appear over his brow.

A few days earlier Suri had given Enguer quite an education about the king on their way back to Courth from the watchtowers. Apparently, the king's father, King Francik III, refused to allow his children to lead the pampered lives of royalty. In addition to their formal tutelage, they were sent to live and work on farms, learn the merchant trade and enter military service. The current king, Francik IV had been a fisherman, a soldier, a cavalry commander and a general himself before his father passed away and he was crowned king. His two sons, the eldest of which would become King Francik V one day, were even now working at a logging camp deep in the northern forests. Enguer knew well how much Suri and Commander Duraunt admired the king and their misgivings regarding His Majesties judgement appointing his wife's brother as the general of his armies.

"Your...Your Majesty," General Bufont stammered, rapidly dabbing his forehead, "it's a complex matter. The Demon Beasts could be anywhere. Where should we go to find them? I reinforced the norther towers and tripled the forces stationed there. And...and I have patrols of a hundred men or more with Fire-Priests and rangers frequenting the villages and farmsteads in the north. What else can we do?"

"Yet, in just the last month a dozen or more of my people have disappeared from their homes and fields. Duraunt tells me of reports of dark shapes outside the walls at night and howls that echo out of the darkness. The people are terrified to leave the city. They won't farm or hunt or trade with the local villages!" The king stood from his chair and forcefully pressed his finger onto a spot on the map in front of him. "And why should they? Yesterday morning an entire family was found missing from their farm house not a league from the city! Every man, woman and child that they take could be adding to their numbers. If we keep with your plan we could well be facing an army of Demon Beasts soon!" Leaving the table, King Francik paced along the wall in silence until he came upon a bust of his father displayed regally in a high alcove.

"'What a fine king he will make'. That's what he used to tell my mother." The king gently pat the base that held his father's image. "They were both very proud of me. It is some relief that they are no longer here to witness their son's shame."

"Shame?" the general began. "There is no shame . . ."

"Silence, you fool!" the king spun around to face the terrified general. "It is because I allowed myself to listen to your advice that death and worse, has come to Courth. You and that idiot duke! If only that beast had ripped the tongue from his head, rather than a quick merciful death!"

Perhaps not realizing it, General Bufont held both his hands over his mouth, under eyes as wide as saucers.

"Even Rauf was too blind in his arrogance to see the folly in what was done to Rochette," the king raged. "The three of you made your king a fool. A proper fool indeed!"

King Francik stepped back to the table and leaned heavily on his outstretch fists exhaling his anger into the air between them. "I am done with two of you," he spoke calmly, staring at the beautiful pattern of the wood grain that ran the length of the heavy table. "Now, I will be done with the third."

"No, Your Majesty," the general blubbered. "Please, I will fix everything. Call up the army. I will lead them myself into the . . ."

The king's laughter drowned out the rest of whatever General Bufont was about to say. "You lead? No, you will lead your horse back to your estate and endeavor to actually generate some taxable revenue for the kingdom. I better not see you again until you do."

The former general stumbled to his feet, his face flush with anger and humiliation, "My sister will be very angry with you for this! She will not allow you to dismiss me so easily!"

The king stepped quickly and grabbed Bufont by the shoulders pulling him within inches of his deadly serious countenance, "Hear me well," the king hissed. "Your sister is not the king of this realm. Take care you never forget that."

Visibly shrinking under the king's gaze, Bufont rushed from the room as soon as the king released him. Enguer and the Commanders remained silent while the king strode back to the head of the table to reclaim his seat.

"Gentlemen, I have been the real fool in this tragic Drama." King Francik placed his palms flat on the maps in front of him. "I should have been listening to seasoned veterans rather than patronizing nobles with political agendas." He slid the map across the table until it was in front of Suri and Commander Duraunt. "Now tell me, what do we need to do to kill every one of those bastards?"

His mother's humor once again playing in his mind, Enguer took delight in the irony that the king had not been specific about whether he was talking about the nobles or Demon Beasts.

~~~

"I was given a fascinating book last night," Commander Duraunt was telling Suri. "It is a translation from an ancient language from Hellas that details the requirements for casting a spell that transforms a person into a 'Wolf-Man' or 'Lukánthropos', as they call it."

"Where would anyone find such a book?" Suri asked, never taking his keen eyes off the forest less than a half-league ahead of the column of men and women they lead.

Once again, they were headed into The Wilds. This time, they were trailed by five-hundred hardened veterans from the king's guard, a dozen experienced rangers and two dozen Fire-Priests and priestesses. Their plan was to return to the lair where they found the Demon Beasts a few weeks before and if they were still there, slaughter them all.

"It was the one Rauf was using to turn Rochette," Commander Duraunt shrugged. "Where he got it, we will never know. A High Priest from the temple brought it to me. He thought it might be helpful."

"Does it tell you how will kill them?" Enguer guided his mount closer to the other two.

"I have it with me here for reference," the Commander turned in his saddle and pulled the familiar-looking book from a saddle bag, "and yes, it lists the dangers for one of their kind to avoid. One moment, I will find the page and read from it directly." He flipped through several pages until he found the passages he was looking for. "Here it is. It says, *'The body once transformed into the state of Lukánthropos has special endurance against true death. Except under specific conditions of injury will the Lukánthropos regenerate after some time, returning life in a renewed physical form.'* Here are some exceptions. *'If the body becomes dismembered, burned or submerged in water for a long period, there will be no regeneration and true and final death will occur.'*" Commander Duraunt closed the book with a sharp clap. "Therefore, it seems that although they are extremely powerful physically, once they are overcome, we can apply one of these three methods to keep them dead."

"Yet, can we incapacitate them in the normal course of battle and then kill them in a more permanent fashion as you described?" Suri asked uncertainly.

"That is what the book says," the Commander nodded. "It's a good thing that we happened to burn the bodies of the ones we killed at the north tower Otherwise, they might have crawled from their graves fully functioning Lukánthropos again."

Suri looked at Commander Duraunt with shocked relief, "Thank Sunna for our fortune that you found that book. I doubt we would have burned any we killed in the forest."

"The book also details how they grow their numbers," the Commander frowned. "They produce an infection when they bite an otherwise normal person causing severe illness until the corruption is activated by the next full moon, at which point they complete their transform into a Lukánthropos. During this time, they are extremely vulnerable and can be killed by the usual means." The Commander's frown deepened, "One thing I am not clear on is why their strength increases significantly during the three days of a full moon. It has something to do with an obscure Moon Goddess from Hellas's ancient past, but that is all I have been able to gather about that so far."

Suri raised his left eyebrow high on his forehead, "Well, that explains why there are not many more of them already,"

"Do you know how soon we can expect another full moon?" concern painted Commander Duraunt's features.

Suri blew a sharp whistle of relief, "Not for another two weeks, praise Sunna."

"Is that it then? Is there nothing else in that book that can help us?" Enguer wanted to know.

"There is one last thing," The Commander replied, "We must arrive at the cave during daylight when the Lukánthropos are weak and lethargic and unlikely to be anywhere except in their enclave resting. Apparently, they are nocturnal beasts that take strength from the moon regardless of phase it is in."

"Then let's get to it," Suri spurred his mount ahead toward the looming forest. "Rangers!" he called to his men. "We must chart the way for the fine host that follows! 'A hunting we will go', children of The Wilds, 'A hunting we will go!'"

~~~

For three days and three nights the brave men and women of Courth traversed the foreboding wood under the watchful care of Suri's rangers. When night fell, they camped around the glow of cooking fires and shared yarns spun with laughter and comradery. There was no need to cold camp and creep through The Wilds with five-hundred souls, it wouldn't have helped if they tried. Enguer knew and Suri knew, that if the Demon Beasts, the Lukánthropos, were out there keeping watch, then they would know they were coming no matter how carefully they tread.

The area where the small army camped was drier than the previous days, the ground was rocky and the trees gave way to as much thick brush. They were close. A brief gust off the nearby mountain range sent a cold shudder through Enguer. The last time he and Suri had crossed this terrain they were running for their lives. This part he remembered vividly, since he had passed this way only a few hours after Suri sent out the signal to run away. It was the hours and days after that became a blur.

"You know, if they are there, we're going to kill them all this time."

Enguer nearly jumped. He had not heard the stealthy ranger walk up on him. He smiled at the older man. "I have no doubt, Suri. There can't be so many of them yet."

Suri nodded in the dark.

"What if they aren't there?" Enguer worried more about that possibility.

"Then we will burn down The Wilds until we find them." Suri stared into the tangled darkness as if it were daylight. "What choice do we have?"

"And if we miss any?"

"Then we will find them. Looks like the king will have us on steady coin for a while," Suri chuckled.

Enguer stretch his tired back from the days long hike. It was nothing, he could have continued through the night if he had to. "I heard that the king disbanded the Commission."

Suri grunted, "Most of them dead and gone, there was no need of it. Besides, the king doesn't want to trust any more decisions to others in this matter. He will see it through himself." Suri chuckled again. "It took half a day to convince him to stay in Courth after we made our plan. He was hell-bent on coming with us."

"Would that have been so bad?"

"King Francik is a good king. Good for the kingdom and the people. We need to keep him king for a while yet."

Enguer agreed. There was no reason to risk the life of the king for no real purpose when he had men like Commander Duraunt and Suri that the crown could count on to keep the kingdom safe. At least, Enguer hoped they could.

"You think we can get to the cave before noon tomorrow?" Enguer was unimpressed with the speed their force travelled in a day.

"If we leave at dawn, we will," Suri assured him.

"I better get a few hours of sleep then," Enguer yawned. "I think I've been spending too much time in the city enjoying the comfort of soft beds lately."

Suri laughed and slapped him on the back. "I'm betting that if we survive tomorrow, we'll both be looking for a warm bed soon enough!"

~~~

Enguer was frustrated.

Commander Duraunt and Suri had decided that it was best not to simply assume the Lukánthropos still occupied the cave and the only way to do that without camping it – for Sunna knew how long – was to send a force inside to find out. Enguer did not disagree. The Lukánthropos would certainly know a force the size the king had sent were outside their door and they might be prepared to hole up for weeks. The Commander was not willing to wait in case they were wrong and the Lukánthropos had indeed moved their lair to some other location.

None of that bothered Enguer.

Before entering the cave, Commander Duraunt had sent groups of twenty soldiers, led by a couple of rangers and two Fire-Priests to scour the land within half a league in every direction. They were looking for any openings in the earth that could potentially connect with the one they knew about and provide the Lukánthropos with an escape route. Aside from a shallow cave where one group roused an angry bear, they found six openings into the ground that the Fire Priests had 'sewn up'. What that meant, Enguer had no idea, but the Commander was sure they were sealed tight.

Enguer was fine with all that as well.

He was frustrated because, when the fifty soldiers and four Fire-Priests were at last sent into the cave, he was ordered to bring up the rear. Suri and two other rangers lead the group inside. It seemed to Enguer that Commander Duraunt and Suri were still playing safe with him and he supposed that's the way it would be until he was officially accepted into the Royal Order of Rangers. At least he was not stuck outside waiting . . .

The entry to the cave was wide enough for three men to walk abreast. Knowing they would likely be in close quarters and without the benefit of formation, the soldiers had discarded their spears in favor of short swords and shields. A few carried short bows as well and all of them were clad in bronze-tinted metal armor adorned with a long cape at the back with the emblem of Courth embroidered into it. These were the king's guard – an elite group of warriors tasked with protecting the king's person, his family and the palace. They were the best of the best, proficient in both melee and ranged weapons, almost fanatical in their loyalty and willing to give their lives in the king's service. Enguer knew them by reputation and as fierce a warrior as any of them might be, he was unsure if they would be enough against the terrible Lukánthropos.

Enguer held a short sword in his right hand and a long dagger in his left. Ahead, he watched the tight mass of shiny helmets reflecting the light from the torches they carried. He wished he could see Suri and the pair of rangers at the front, but there were too many bodies between them and the corridor twisted and turned, widened and narrowed, every few paces and always descending. After a short while, the corridor opened up into a large cavern that stretched beyond the light they carried into the darkness. The troop came to a halt just inside.

Visible now, Enguer watched Suri and the other two rangers scout ahead a few strides. It was eerily silent, except for the occasional drip of water into a pool somewhere nearby. Above, the light barely reached the ceiling, reflecting off glistening moisture and droplets that coated the smooth rock. Around the edges of the room, as far as they could see, jagged ledges jutted out from the walls at random elevations with some connected at steep angles by natural ramps. There were dark voids behind some of the ledges that could easily be deep depressions or corridors leading away from the cavern. Enguer and his father had never spent much time in caves deeper than a few paces, but Suri had mentioned that he enjoyed exploring their depths when he was younger. It was a revelation to Enguer that caves could be more complex and vaster than a city with multiple levels, a maze of corridors and numerous entrances spanning across leagues. He wondered if the Fire-Priests could have possibly 'sewn up' all the openings to this one.

In the deafening silence, the soft rustle of small stones from somewhere above sounded like an avalanche. Suri must have heard it as well and he made a quick gesture with his upraised hand. Slowly and deliberately the soldiers moved forward until they formed a defensive arc in front of the opening from where they had emerged. The Fire-Priests were tucked protectively in the center of the formation with Enguer only a step behind. Suri and the rangers were still moving carefully through the cavern, one following the line of the wall on each side and Suri right down the center.

Again, something shifted in the dark. Sound travelled in an unusual way underground and Enguer couldn't be sure if it came from above or in front of them. Maybe it was a rat or some other small animal. So far there was no sign that the Lukánthropos had ever been here. He pushed his way to the front of the soldiers' line and scanned the walls and ledges more carefully. They appeared natural and unaltered. To his left, a thick leafless vine ran down from the edge of one ledge to another below it. This seemed to be a common feature among most of ledges that he could see nearby. The closest vine appeared to have regular bulges along its length that could have been mistaken for knots. Enguer was sure he could use them to climb to the ledges above if he wanted to.

Knotted vines...Why would there be vines deep in a dark cavern in the first place? A chill swept down Enguer's spine. In a panic he cried out, breaking the unholy silence that enshrouded them, "Suri, above us!"

Suri spun around and immediately cast his gaze around at the ledges above them. One by one, a pair of red orbs vaguely framed in a massive figure darker than the darkness around it, appeared on the ledges. The soldiers noticed the creatures as well and compacted their formation even further. Enguer could almost smell the fear, he was terrified himself knowing what these monsters could do.

Movement caught his attention on the ground as he watched Suri and the rangers sprinting back toward the group. Before they were close, startled shouts erupted from the soldiers and Enguer watched in disbelief as the Lukánthropos vaulted from the ledges. It was a reckless plunge of a dozen heavy fur-clad bodies into the tightly packed midst of the soldiers. The crush of metal and snap of bone combined with barks of pain, vicious snarls and roars of fury made for a scene worse than madness and chaos. Lukánthropos, impaled on sharp blades as they landed, never faltered a step, ripping into fleshy thighs and shredding through bronze breast plates. It was a close-quarters brawl that brought beast and man eye to eye in a struggle, not to survive, but to savagely slaughter the other.

Outnumbering the beasts four to one, the soldiers skillfully maneuvered around each Lukánthropos until the creatures were spinning and swiping in every direction. Suddenly a bright light abruptly appeared all around them with no discernable source causing the beasts to cover their eyes with one massive limb and swing blindly with another. Blades flashed in rapid stabbing and slashing motions causing deep, bloody wounds where they landed, sometimes driving deep into the creatures' thick hide and other times cast away as if striking stone. Still, the Lukánthropos did not falter or attempt to flee.

Enguer, too far away to help, even his bow of no use in the crowded ruckus, kept one eye on the ledges above in case more of the creatures appeared. Not far from him, a Fire-Priestess, with no room to cast from a distance, placed hands roiling in flame on the back of one of the Lukánthropos. Its fur ignited with the magical fire sending it screaming in a desperate flurry. To Enguer's horror, the Priestess, with no room to escape in the press, found herself holding in her innards after the creature split her up the middle with a purely random rake from its hind claw.

So it went all around him.

Men died to be dragged away by their comrades and replaced by the next in line. The light dimmed and was renewed by another cast from a Fire-Priest or Priestess while the Lukánthropos continued their frenzied assault. Enguer spied Suri at the far end of the battle fluidly slicing through a creature's forearm sending a spray of blood into the air. It was a battle of seconds that seemed to stretch into eternity, but with every second the Lukánthropos were pin cushioned by a dozen sharp strikes and a few well-placed blows. Soon, one of the beasts went down and then another. Thanks to Commander Duraunt and Rauf's book, the soldiers were all well versed on what it would take to kill the Lukánthropos and they put their knowledge to constructive use hacking the beasts to bits.

When all the creatures were nothing but a mash of fur, flesh and fluid under the boots of exhausted soldiers Suri crossed over the expanse of death to grasp Enguer by the shoulder. "Are you OK, boy?"

Enguer snorted, "I couldn't get near one I was so far back."

"Count yourself lucky," Suri motioned to the numerous armored corpses that littered the cavern floor. "You could have been among these poor souls."

Enguer cast his eyes downward. "How many have we lost?"

"Around thirty dead and wounded soldiers, two Fire-Priests and the ranger Geoff."

Enguer knew that one. "I'm sorry about Geoff, he was a good man. I'm sorry about all of them."

He stood quietly with Suri watching the surviving priests tend to the wounded while the soldiers piled up the remains of the Lukánthropos under the direction of their captain. Causing a brief stir, the magical light suddenly winked out prompting the restart of torches with a little help from the Fire-Priests. None of them wanted to be cast back into the darkness in this sinister underworld.

"Do you think we finished off the Lukánthropos?"

Suri looked around critically. "I would guess we killed around a dozen, maybe more. I don't think there were more that attacked the watch tower, but it has been a few weeks."

Once the remains of all the Lukánthropos had been collected, one of the Fire-Priests propelled a stream of flame into the gory mass causing a thick oily smoke to rise up toward the cavern's ceiling. The smell of burning sinew and greasy fur along with the sound of popping fat turned Enguer's stomach. From the looks of everyone around him, it did for everyone else as well.

"Grab an arm or a leg and get the injured out!" Suri ordered the soldiers. "Quickly now!" They did not need to be prompted in the least and soon the last of their torchers were moving down the corridor toward the exit.

"You two can follow them out," Suri told Enguer and the remaining ranger. "I'm going to stay a few moments to make sure these bastards burn thoroughly, don't want any of them finding their way back together again."

The ranger nodded and jogged to catch up with the others, but Enguer hesitated. "We will leave together," he spoke softly.

Suri nodded and they both stared at the grotesque bonfire in silence.

Enguer looked up at the cavernous ceiling and noticed that the smoke was slowly expanding over ledges and into corridors running further into the earth. If there were any other openings from this complex Commander Duraunt would know soon enough with smoke billowing out, Enguer thought dryly. And if not, any Lukánthropos left alive would soon be suffocating from the smoke . . .

A ravenous howl echoed from somewhere overhead deeper inside the cavern. It was followed by another and another, with several more in angry response.

Suri looked at him with a fearful look that reminded him of the last time they ran this place.

"Run!" he said.

It was enough.

Chapter 10

Lukánthropos

An ancient creature of darkness, born of an evil curse most vile with an insatiable hunger for power. This nearly immortal shape-changer lives among men, feeding upon them, changing them, waiting with indelible patience and determination. Named Lukánthropos by the people of Hellas, the foul beast is a stain upon history that will inspire nightmares until the end of ages.

Wodanaz the Wanderer

Enguer and Suri broke through the leafy vines covering the entrance to the cave moments after the last of the soldiers carrying their wounded. It was a relief to shed the oppressive weight of the earth, see trees and sky again, inhale the clean chill air. Even if it wasn't very warm, the natural light brought forth by Sunna was a gift to the earth and all who lived there, liberating life from the darkness.

"Hold!" Commander Duraunt cried when they burst forth from the cave. Heedless, a nervous bowman released an arrow, breaking on the rocks next to Enguer's foot.

"Hold, damn you!" the Commander cried again.

Given that more than a hundred skilled archers trained their aim on the entrance to the cave and the tension that hung heavy in the air, Enguer was happy that he and Suri had not been immediately shot through by the lot of them.

"The beasts are coming!" Suri bellowed, lurching forward.

Almost on their heels two Lukánthropos burst from the cave and this time the Commander did not hold back. "Fire!"

They threw themselves flat upon the stone threshold of the cavern to avoid the cloud of projectiles that flew like an angry hoard of wasps inches above their heads. Enguer twisted his neck rearward in time to watch the two beasts, peppered with arrows, fall to the ground. It wasn't enough. Bleeding from a dozen or more mortal wounds, the creatures clawed their way forward snatching at Suri and Enguer's legs and feet quick to kick and get away.

In seconds, a dozen soldiers rushed forward and pinned the beasts to the ground with spears while the others hacked body and limbs into bloody parcels of unrecognizable lumps. One more emerged to be greeted by jets of flames from the hands of a pair of Fire-Priestesses plus a few dozen arrows for good measure. This one's fate was to writhe on the ground engulfed in fire until the blaze died down sufficiently for the soldiers to complete their bloody task. The prodigious stench of seared hair and burning flesh combined with the oily-black smoke their bodies produced was enough to motivate more than a few soldiers to empty the contents of their stomachs and Enguer, who had not eaten at all, thought he might never want to again.

Several wild-eyed soldiers came forward and dragged Suri and Enguer to their feet. They knew there were more inside, many more. The beasts howls and snarls resonated from inside the shadowed hollow of the cave entrance, but none of them attempted to break the cover of darkness where they hid. Enguer looked toward the Commander, worried that he might order an attack that would send scores of men to their deaths. Instead, he waved to a lone man standing near the top of the cave.

With no little enthusiasm, the soldier stationed there pulled on a long rope tied to a stand and when he did, the supports gave way sending enough trees and brush tumbling down the incline to block-up the cavern's entrance with heaps of debris. Seconds later, the entire bit erupted in flames from jets of fire cast from several directions nearly at once.

'Well played," Enguer complimented the Commander who was too far away to hear. It was a part of the plan he had apparently missed while he was with Suri preparing to enter the cave the first time.

Furious howls accompanied by savage growls erupted from inside the cavern. The Lukánthropos must have known they were trapped and with no avenue of escape would soon succumb to asphyxiation from the billowing smoke and lack of air. A few grew so desperate that they braved the barrier of fire and broke through only to be met with more fire and a deadly rain of arrows that put a tragic finish on their ruthless lives. Enguer was sure it was fitting if not pretty and he greeted it all with a smile.

"Why are you smiling?" Suri asked.

"I am happy to see an end to these wicked creatures," Enguer couldn't take his eyes off the slaughter.

Suri eyebrows furrowed. "Be careful boy, finding joy in taking life, no matter how wicked, will stain your soul. Remember, every one of them was a father, brother, husband or wife before they became those things."

Enguer was embarrassed. Suri was right. Rangers believed in the sanctity of life for all creatures. But did that include the corrupted, unnatural ones as well? His father was never clear on that subject. Maybe Suri's point was deeper than . . .

A roar unlike any other echoed from the cave followed seconds later by the bulk of a Lukánthropos, twice that of any other, bursting from the cave and onto the forward ranks of soldiers four deep. It moved with impossible strength and speed for its size, tossing soldiers and priests around like rag dolls abused by an angry child. This was no child.

Enguer was not far from where the thing landed. He drew his blades and charged toward it with Suri on his heels. Before they could cover half the distance to the great beast a commotion broke out behind at the cave entrance.

Cleared of much of the burning lumber and branches by the larger beast, the Lukánthropos he recognized as the female strode out of the cave followed by a dozen more. Enguer shouted to get the soldiers attention, but they were so distracted by the massive Lukánthropos that they were caught completely by surprise when the new arrival hurled themselves into the disjointed line creating a din of chaos.

Commander Duraunt, mounted on his tall black stallion, shouted orders and called for formations. His captains repeated the orders as best they could and the footmen made a valiant attempt to organize in the face of terror and death that was so suddenly upon them. Enguer ran, horrified, to their aide.

Five hundred men, swarmed in one direction and then another, their ranks fragmented by stands of trees and a broken, rocky landscape. Where they could form up, they were too few and the beast rolled through them. Where they were many, the soldiers could not organize and the beast rolled through them. Each time the Lukánthropos, that was once Rochette, left a trail of dead and dying it its wake.

The ancillary was as effective and no less devastating. The female Lukánthropos and her companions viciously attacked smaller groups of soldiers, quickly overwhelming them before charging into another. A group of Fire-Priestesses made a stand behind a natural wall of boulders and trees. They hurled fire in jets and streams into the group of Lukánthropos driving two of them away reeling in flames. But the female Lukánthropos was clever, she avoided the blaze with a series of swift feints and circled around to rip them all apart from behind.

Enguer watched it all unfold in the battle that surrounded him. It was a nightmare that he could never have imagined. How could five hundred highly trained soldiers and a dozen Fire-Priests be so impotent against these creatures? Were they all destined to die in this dark wood?

"We must kill the female," Suri grabbed Enguer by the shoulder and pulled him toward the edge of the combatants. "She is the first the Demon Beast abducted as his own. If we kill her, he will come to us."

Enguer understood the logic but his mind screamed, *And then what?*

They followed the female and her entourage to a cluster of soldiers arranged in three ranks in a shield formation. She recklessly threw herself against them and was thrown back bleeding from punctures in her thick hide. With redoubled effort she assaulted the line again with her followers that now numbered eight. Somehow the line held and she was forced back again. Enguer, led by Suri, took this moment to make their move.

Slashing at hamstrings and thighs from behind, four of the Lukánthropos were quickly reduced to crawling, their howls of pain lost in the clang and clatter of battle. The next four and the female were intent on dismantling the human wall when Enguer and Suri approached from behind. As if she had eyes in the back of her head, the female spun to face them with a fierce growl. Enguer did not hesitate, he thrust his short sword forward while slashing with his long dagger. Both made contact drawing streams of blood, but he miscalculated the reach of her deadly claws and as she lunged for him Suri appeared, sliding over a moss-covered boulder, to impale her through the abdomen with an up-cutting thrust with his two blades.

The female Lukánthropos screamed in rage and she screamed in pain. It was a howl that rang across the whole of the battle and gained the immediate attention of the massive Lukánthropos piling up the dead by the dozen. Enguer watched with trepidation the heavy mass cross the haggard terrain as if it were a field of soft grass and daisies, bracing himself for what was to come. This would be it, the final confrontation while the remaining Lukánthropos died in pieces and flames around him. Suri saw it coming too and took a position beside Enguer to absorb the blow. In seconds they would be on the receiving end of a force likely as not to kill them both. Likely they were dead already and didn't know it. Whatever happened, Enguer knew one thing – if he died beside Suri, he died proud and unremorseful.

The last Lukánthropos, the high priest once known as Rochette, bound toward them ignoring every petty arrow and spear point, seemingly unrestrained by the inconvenience of mortality, until it landed in front of Enguer and Suri.

"This will not end," the beast hissed, jaws snapping. A shudder wracked the Lukánthropos body from a score of arrows impacting the thick hide on its back. It did not waver, it did not falter. "Your descendants will suffer your audacity to challenge the Lord of a new species that will one day test the power of the Tuatha de!"

Enguer did not understand what it spoke of, merely its danger, and he lashed out reflexively thrusting his long dagger aimed at skewering the great beast's eye. Instead, the slim blade punctured the creature's upraised claw, impaled it through, allowing only the bare tip to pierce the red-glowing orb. The Lukánthropos did not flinch a muscle, nor did it cry out in pain as any natural thing would have. Rather, it smiled and closed its long talons over the blade, slowly pushing it away. A slow trickle of blood descended from the injured eye, yet the glow from deep inside remained unchanged.

Enguer and the Lukánthropos stood eye to eye for a long moment. The young ranger powerless to force his dagger forward or even remove it from the beast's iron grip. Fear gripped him only a second before he decided he would not try to run or beg for his life. He was ready to die in the face of this thing confident that his distraction would allow Suri and the others to finish it off.

The twang of a hundred bows sent a cloud of deadly missiles whistling toward their mark and the flash of a sword expertly angled to cleave with deadly effect played through Enguer's mind in slow motion. It was an odd sensation, almost numb and unfeeling. There was no fear, no pain, no anger or regret, only a strange curiosity. He watched in fascination as another crimson droplet slowly fell through space from the Lukánthropos eye, smelled as much as tasted the haze of dust kicked into the air and the oily sweat of smoldering torches . . .and death. Everywhere death.

And then the world went black.

~~~

"Enguer, Enguer!" A voice called from somewhere far away. Was it his father? No, the timbre was off. He opened his eyes to a blur of greys. His head hurt and he thought there might be a gash on his hand.

"Enguer, wake up!" The voice was insistent, hovering just above him, blocking out the light. Was that light?

There was a rush of movement followed by disorientation and nausea, then a cup was pressed to his lips spilling as much of the cold water down his chin as touched his parched tongue. He tried to speak, resulting in a low grunt and more of the chilly liquid trickling down his throat before the cup was moved away.

"Enguer, can you see me boy?" Enguer recognized that voice. It was Suri. He blinked hard and shook his head to clear his vision. Soon, the distinct features of Suri's face resolved in front of him as if out of a grey mist and there were others too. Commander Duraunt and a priestess he didn't know. He was startled to realize that her hands were on his head and he was sitting up. The cracking pain in his skull slowly slipped away and he realized it was night-time.

"I am alive," Enguer was surprised. He expected to next open his eyes to the eternal light of Sunna, if she would have him, but this was better. He wasn't done with this world yet.

"Yes, you are," Suri laughed. "We thought you were dead when that Lukánthropos barreled through you. It was a good thing he knocked you flat, otherwise the arrows meant for him would have done you in."

"He's dead then?"

Suri shook his head sadly. "That fella is fast. After he knocked you over, he bounded back into the cave and disappeared."

"Then let's finish this." Enguer attempted to stand, but fell back on woozy legs.

"Stay put, young Ranger." Commander Duraunt steadied him from behind. "There is no need to go back in there for anything. In fact, we can't. We cut more trees and set the entrance to the cave ablaze over an hour ago. Soon, the priests are going to collapse the entrance, sealing that monster inside if it yet lives."

"There may be another way out," Enguer protested weakly.

The Commander disagreed, "We've blown so much smoke up into that cave that if there was an exit that we missed earlier then we would have seen the smoke by now."

Enguer relaxed. It made sense what the Commander said. It was over. The Lukánthropos that was once Rochette would be dead soon if not already. He would just rather have had a body to be sure of it. Enguer suspected they all felt the same way. "So, what now?"

The Commander smiled wide enough to show his perfect white teeth, "We take the good news back to our king."

"Clear away!" Someone shouted from a distance behind him. Enguer twisted painfully and watched as the top rim of the cave collapsed in on itself trapping the burning conflagration of branches inside leaving a pile of smoldering rubble and debris outside.

"That's it then," the commander appeared satisfied with the priests work. "We leave in the morning." He turned and called out orders to set camp for the night, his long strides taking him through the resting ranks of soldiers and priests.

Enguer, still sitting, looked up at Suri. "Will the Lukánthropos ever really die trapped in there with all that smoke and nothing to eat?"

"Don't know," Suri's eyes thoroughly surveyed the crumbled entrance of the cave. "I think the book only mentioned what could kill it for sure. We can only hope that no one is fool enough to open up that cave again one day."

Enguer sighed. "We can only hope."

~~~

There was no sleep for Enguer, no matter how exhausted his body had become during the return to Courth. For three days he swayed in his saddle on the verge of delirium, mechanically going through the motions of setting up camp only to lay starring through the branches at the stars above. In the blessed moments when he would finally doze off, terrifying dreams of the Lukánthropos brought him sweating and awake again. Even during the day, he could not shake the nightmares, they would always return with new shocks of what the beast might do if it escaped.

Suri tried to help, but he appeared in nearly as rough a state as himself. They both lay awake at night envious of the men and women camped around them who slept ignorant of the danger that still must live, trapped beneath the earth, far into The Wilds. It was a tomb Enguer prayed would never again receive the light of day.

When they rode through the city gates, the people of Courth cheered their return. It was a distant echo in Enguer's mind. He should have been proud, waving gallantly to the crowds they passed. Everyone knew that if they returned then they must have been successful in clearing the land of the terrible scourge that had plagued them for so long. Enguer cared for none of it. Quietly he followed Suri down a side street where they didn't get a second look from the shoppers and tradesmen rushing past them to have a look at the returning heroes marching down the main boulevard.

They stopped in front of a two-level grey-stone building with a set of massive antlers mounted above a pair of heavy oak doors. From the corner ran a young man dressed in casual earth tones and sturdy leather boots who took the reins of their horses when they dismounted. This was Enguer's new home since the day he left his father's house. It was the lodge dedicated to the Royal Order of Rangers where he had been fortunate enough to enjoy a small room at the bequest of Tanais.

Tanais. The thought of the Arch Priest still pained him deeply.

Several rangers looked up at their entrance, a few raised their hands to hail them and then just as quickly settled themselves back to sharpening blades and mending leather armor. They knew from the looks on Enguer and Suri's faces that it was no time for idle chat. Rangers respected one another in that way, not that they spoke much anyway even to each other, unless there was a fair supply of ale to limber up their tongues. Those moments were reserved for evenings around the massive stone fireplace.

Enguer separated from Suri at the top of the stairs and found his room at the end of the hallway. He closed the wooden shudders leaving only a few cracks for the light to invade, then slowly removed his boots and cloak and rest his head on the feather pillow. At first, Enguer watched the slivers of light play across the ceiling, his fog-enshrouded mind envisioning fairies and sprites from tales his mother used to tell him as a small child. It was comforting thinking about his mother, recalling her warm embrace and bright smile. He wished he could re-live that time again, do it over, better. His muscles relaxed, heavy eyelids fell shut and he drifted to a place in his memory that was safe and reassuring . . .

There was a sharp tap at his door, then another. Damned if it's Sunna herself, he was just falling asleep! Enguer opened his eyes, the light looked different in the room, earlier somehow. That damn tapping!

"What is it?" he called angrily.

The door opened hesitantly and a headed popped through the breach. It was one of the young house servants. Enguer thought his name was Twig. At least that's what the other rangers called him. Probably a silly nickname.

"I'm sorry to disturb you," Twig's eyes were wide as they tried to adjust to the dim light. "Suri asked that I fetch you to the common room. He has just received a summons from the king himself!"

"So soon?" Enguer didn't want to stir a muscle. "We have only just returned. Was Suri insistent?"

"He was," Twig regarded him curiously. "But you returned two days ago, Enguer. I had to practically drag Suri from his bed to receive the messenger."

Two days? Enguer could hardly wrap his brain around it. He was sure he scarcely lay his head on his pillow. Closing his eyes, Enguer attempted to summon the strength to stand up. His body was in full revolt.

"Enguer?"

"Tell Suri I will be right down."

Quietly, Twig closed the door behind him.

With what felt like titanic effort, Enguer rolled his legs off the bed and sat up. His head hurt a little, but at least the fog was gone. Slowly he flexed his muscles going through a pattern of exercises he used when sitting in one place for long hours. At first, his limbs tingled, then gradually his heart rate increased and he felt renewed circulation bringing life back to his muscular frame. He was feeling much better after all.

After a quick wash and a change of clothes. Enguer strode down to the common room with renewed vigor. There, Suri sat staring into the blaze of the wide fireplace with a parchment hanging from one hand and a mug in the other. When he saw Enguer descending the last of the stairs he looked up and smiled.

"I hear you received an important message?" Enguer smiled back.

"Yes, the king wants to put a medal on our chests or some such." Suri took a long swig of ale.

Enguer's stomach growled reminding him he had not eaten in two days. He motioned to Twig cleaning a table nearby. "May I have a crust of bread and a mug of ale, please?"

Twig smiled broadly, "I'll have a plate of steaming venison and leeks coming from the kitchen and fetch the ale."

Nodding appreciatively, Enguer sat at the edge of a long-table cattycorner to where Suri lounged in his chair. "Will everyone receive a medal?"

"Commander Duraunt's men received theirs yesterday, as did the priests and my rangers. I should have been there." Anger tinted Suri's tone, "That thing drew half the life out of me."

"Same as I," Enguer agreed. "Except for the last two nights, it has tortured my dreams."

"It had powers we will never understand."

Twig arrived with a bowl of venison cubes and leeks swimming in a dark broth along with a tall mug of ale. He set them in front of Enguer and returned again with a dozen thick slices of crusty bread and a slab of butter. "Anything else for ya?"

Enguer's stomach rumbled louder from the aroma of the food. He couldn't remember anything smelling so delicious before in his life. Forgetting that Twig had spoken, Enguer attacked the vessel with gusto.

"I'll take another cup," Suri chimed.

"I'll bring two," Twig laughed. "This one will be ready for another before I return."

After two bowls of venison, a loaf of bread and three cups of ale, Enguer and Suri were mounting up to go meet the king. It was late morning with clear skies and a hint of chill on the light breeze that cascaded down from the mountains. Enguer loved mornings like this. If not for the most recent events, he would have been eager to spend a few days in The Wilds hunting and trapping. As it stood, he needed a few more days of rest and the passage of time to dull his memories before he found the enthusiasm to resume his regular life. He muffled a laugh, drawing a side-long look from Suri. *What was regular life for him anymore? For that matter, what was he going to do with himself after today?* Maybe the king would invite him to join the order. *Did he still want that?* It was an attractive prospect assuming they were done with the Lukánthropos. *What about travelling the world as his father had done?* By Sunna, he was so tired. All he really wanted was a bed.

Turning down a shadow-filled alley, a woman's scream split the sedate calm from around a curve in the alley, "Help! Robbers in my house! Help!"

Reacting instantly, Suri kicked his mount into a fast sprint. Enguer followed quickly a horse-length behind. She couldn't be far ahead.

"Don't touch me!" The woman's cry became more desperate.

Approaching the bend in the alley, Suri glided around it smoothly, his horse familiar with the uneven stone that paved city streets. A little more cautious, Enguer's horse fell another length behind Suri. He was unconcerned, it was only a matter of a couple of seconds. Then in his peripheral there was a blur of sudden movement on his right and left, the narrow pressure of a rope pushing on his chest and his horse riding on without him. When he landed on the ground Enguer was immediately set upon from all sides. Shadows of men held his arms and legs down against his struggling and a bag was thrust over his head. The last thing he heard before something hard crashed into his skull, was the amused laughter of a woman.

Chapter 11

Truth and Lies

Drip, drip, drip.

The subtle sound of droplets falling into a pool of water was the first sensation Enguer awoke to. The second was his splitting headache. He opened his eyes to see what appeared to be the cavernous ceiling of an underground cave or grotto. Immediately he was struck by the terrifying aspect that the Lukánthropos had somehow escaped and dragged him back to its lair.

"He's awake." The gruff voice was human. Little comfort.

"Well, help him up then." This voice was more refined and oddly familiar.

Two big ruffians lifted Enguer by the arms and sat him forcibly upon a wooden chair. He wanted to fight and run, but he didn't have the strength. There was a small table within arm's length with a cup upon it.

"Drink," the refined voice spoke again. "You will need your strength."

Enguer look up to see who it was and nearly fell out of his chair. Standing a pace beyond the other end of the table stood the two merchants he knew from the Council – Dyzig and Gigot.

Despite his weakness Enguer shot to his feet and was immediately pressed back into his chair by the two ruffians standing behind him. "What is this?" Enguer's voice cracked dryly. "Why have you taken me?"

"Driiiink," Gigot drawled.

Figuring the cup wasn't filled with poison – they could have slit his neck at any time – and his throat was stone dry, he took a long draft. To his surprise, it wasn't ale, it was red wine. A very particular red wine that his father had been given as a reward from some noble for finding his son lost in The Wilds. His parents told him it was a very expensive wine from an Atlantean vinery far across the Primal Sea on the Emerald Isle. A slight smile bent his lips after he drained the cup.

"I see you have an appreciation for fine wine," Gigot walked over smiling with a bottle in his hands and refilled the cup. When he was close, the ruffians placed their hands firmly on Enguer's shoulders to prevent him from jumping up again.

"It's called Mekali wine." Gigot sat in the empty chair on the opposite side of the table. "Dyzig and I are their biggest customer," he shot a glance at the other merchant and laughed. "Of course, they don't know it."

Feeling better, Enguer tried to lean forward, but the ruffians held him in place. "Why am I here?"

"We need to send an important message, one that should be delivered in person by someone familiar with all the details." Gigot motioned for his men to release Enguer. "You see, Tanais was a significant partner of ours and his younger brother works directly for our patron."

Enguer was dumbfounded, "You want me to deliver the news of the Arch Priest's death to his brother?"

"Precisely," Gigot's smile widened. "He should hear it from someone close to the Arch Priest and I'm sure he will have so many questions we couldn't properly answer or convey in writing even if we wanted to." Gigot shifted another glance to Dyzig. "Isn't that true, Dyzig?"

The merchant grunted in response. He seemed in a mood to bash Enguer's head in again rather than carry on a pleasant conversation. If that's what this was.

"I don't recall the Arch Priest ever mentioning a brother," Enguer lied. His headache was fading and he could think more clearly. "Why can't one of you go speak to him."

Gigot tapped his fingers one by one on the table, "Oh no, that wouldn't do at all. As I said, his brother, Reskalin is his name, will want every little detail. Perhaps our patron will as well and you were a keen witness to the Arch Priest's sad demise and the final resolution with those Lukan…Demon Beasts, better than anyone."

Enguer sighed, "Where is this . . . Reskalin?"

"Not terribly far," Gigot perked up. "Just the next kingdom over. The city of Arre in Tarre."

"Tarre!" Enguer was shoved down in his seat again. "That's over five-hundred leagues away and across the Spine of Cel!"

"You are Enguer Rand, the son of the famed ranger Gaurin Rand, yes?" Gigot spread his hands apart as if that said everything. "And from what we have ascertained, you are nearly his equal."

"I am not my father," Enguer spat back.

Gigot stood fluidly from the table. He reminded Enguer of the way duelists moved with their thin rapiers, prancing around their adversaries in a deceptively deadly dance. "No, you are, or will be better than he. Anyway, go to Tarre, deliver the news to the Arch Priest's brother and return to Courth if you wish. I'm sure Tanais would have been very grateful to you and we will be grateful to you."

"Why would I need your gratitude?"

"Dear boy," Gogot tittered, "a man of The Wilds could always use friends in the stone jungles of Courth. Wouldn't he Dyzig?"

"Why don't I just tell Suri or Commander Duraunt how you have treated me today and let you tell your story to the Bayles?" Enguer had enough of this. "Besides, I don't know if I'm going to stay in Courth much longer anyway."

Gigot strode a little closer to Enguer, "Careful child, you don't want to involve friends in our personal conferences. They can become such a liability very quickly."

"You wouldn't . . ."

"That's up to you," Gigot spun, his long green coat flaring around him dramatically and gestured to Dyzig. "My partner has a bad temper when it comes to disloyalty and sometimes others have to get hurt to bring one back into our smiling graces."

With one quick stride Gigot was kneeling at eye level only inches from Enguer's face. "And our patron, he has reach and influence within every city of the Western Kingdoms. Isn't that right, Dyzig?"

Another grunt from the ham-fisted merchant.

Carefully, almost hesitantly, Gigot reached up and gently stroked the left side of Enguer's face. "Such a pretty boy." He jerked his hand away as if surprised at himself for what he was doing and smiled. "Wouldn't it be better to have the gratitude of powerful people rather than their ire? It's just a small favor we are asking for someone you respected and admired. Am I wrong?"

Enguer groaned deeply. He had a feeling he would never leave this room alive if he refused them. "You are not wrong."

Gigot stood and danced backward a step; fists planted on his hips. "Then we are in agreement?"

"One question first," Enguer rubbed the swollen knot that had formed on the back of his head. "Why didn't you just asked me straight out without hitting me over the head and dragging me down to... wherever this is?"

Another awkward giggle from Gigot, "Our business is in the shadows. Haven't you figured that out yet? There would be far too many questions if people found us all conversating in a local tavern over a round of ale!" Gigot spat on the rough rock floor. "And I detest ale!" Gigot leaned in toward Enguer once more, his long dark hair falling around his face, "We both know that you would not have taken our little chat quite as seriously under any other circumstance. I ask one last time, are we in agreement?"

Enguer nodded reluctantly.

"Wonderful!" Gigot clapped his hands and nearly sprang into the air. This would be a meeting Enguer was sure he would never forget. "Now, let's get you back to Suri so the king can plant that pretty medal on your chest."

Dyzig produced a cudgel from inside his burgundy coat and stepped forward while a sack was thrust over Enguer's head from behind.

Wait, wait!" Enguer shouted. "You don't have to hit me again!"

Gigot lifted the front of the sack to reveal Enguer's face. The bizarre man had a very concerned look on his face. "Perhaps not. We wouldn't want you meeting the king with two lumps on your head."

Relief flooded through Enguer.

From inside his coat pocket, Gigot produced a small vial and emptied it into an empty wine cup. "Drink this. You will be out for less than an hour."

"Why can't your men just lead me out with this hood on?" Enguer didn't like the idea of being unconscious in the hands of these madmen regardless of how it was done.

"It's the only way we can be certain you don't know how to lead anyone back here." Gigot pushed the cup to Enguer's lips. "Take it now, time is up."

Enguer pulled his head away from the cup. "Wrap my ears in heavy cloth! I'll keep the bag over my head! It will be easier for you if I walk... '

"Time's up," Dyzig's feral grunts had somehow formed words and then the world went black again.

~~~

The lump on his head was larger. Somehow the stupid oaf of a man had managed to club him in the same spot twice. Rising unsteadily to his feet, Enguer thrust his hand into the darkness and found the support of a stone wall. Wherever he was, it smelled rancid like the inside of a rarely cleaned privy and was as quiet as a tomb. Carefully he moved around the room hugging the wall. He was looking for a door or shuttered window that he might be able to force open.

What an ordeal this day had become, he thought bitterly. The merchants, or whatever they really were, said they were sending him off to Tarre. So why was he here? Did they decide to imprison him in some kind of dungeon to teach him a lesson? Maybe they had changed their mind and threw him in a hole under the city. Fury rose within him. If he ever got out, he was going to kill them both, especially that fella with the club.

Stone changed to wood underneath his blindly guided hands. He followed the grain up and down and then over to the other side where it changed to stone again. A door! There was not a pinch of light shining through a crack or keyhole or anywhere around its edges. Enguer was disheartened. If he got through the door, would it simply lead to another part of the dungeon? He had to try. Feeling around the center left, he had no trouble finding the heavy iron latch. Next, he ran his hands up and down the door seam – no bolts or locks, at least not on this side. Gripping the latch tightly, Enguer put his shoulder against the door preparing to exert as much force against it as his body was capable. He held his breath and turned the handle. The door popped open easily sending him stumbling into the street.

It was dark.

Enguer spun around looking in every direction at once. The alley was deserted. Far down one end of it he spied the warm glow of lanterns and the sounds of merriment. The other way was pitch black and devoid of any life other than the skittering of rats. He had enough of the dark. He set out toward what he guessed must be a tavern. He just needed to find out where he was so he could get back to the lodge.

The tavern was crowded with people spilling out the open doorway singing bawdy tunes or pressed up against one another in passionate embraces. One was using nearby doorways as his own private toilet while others pissed openly on the wall on both sides of the alley. Enguer had never seen depravity on this scale. He wanted to run as much as throw up. These people were worse than animals.

Cautiously, he pushed his way inside trying hard not to step on toes and bump elbows. The last thing he needed was to get into a fight because he pushed too roughly past some drunkard looking for an excuse to hit something. Finally, he came to what he thought must serve as the bar. Looking down its length, he could see a number of patrons passed out with their heads in pools of ale and vomit while all around them busy barkeeps passed patrons wooden mugs of ale and cheap wine. Enguer raised his hand and called for a barkeep and found himself quickly rewarded with a mug of ale. Only then did he realize how thirsty he was so he drank deeply to quench his dire thirst. And very nearly spewed it back over the bar. The swill was awful. How it could remotely pass as ale he had no idea. Worse still, the people in the tavern appeared to love it.

After several attempts to talk to a barkeep, Enguer got fed-up and took leave of the bar. It was too loud to understand anything inside and the patrons outside were too drunk or belligerent to be helpful. He would have to find his own way. Fortunately, he knew Courth well enough to know that the alleys generally dumped onto a main thoroughfare or to the perimeter lane that ran around the inside of the fortified wall. Either way, he would be able to find his way back to the Ranger's Lodge.

Briefly, Enguer felt a pang of worry for Suri. He had no idea what had happened to the elder ranger. He imagined all kinds of scenarios that did not end well for his friend until finally he had to push his fears away and end the speculations. Suri was a competent ranger who knew how the seedy side of Courth worked. If anyone could survive it, Suri would.

Peering through the cold fog of pre-dawn morning, the only thing Enguer was sure of was that he was somewhere in the old town. The alleys twisted and turned, ran into dead ends or doubled back on each other. He trotted through them for an hour before he finally arrived on a wide boulevard that ran east and west. Some distance to the east there were well lit streets and closer in the other direction he could spy the looming outline of the high curtain wall. He ran east.

Tired and aching all over, Enguer jogged for another hour before he had to stop for breath. He never realized how large the city was since he had spent most of his time in one small section of it. The palace appeared to the north, but he wouldn't be going there now. It was grandly lit by torches, lanterns and light globes along its walls and up its spiraling towers. East of the palace stood another great tower with the glowing red crystal at its apex. He knew it to be tended by the 'Enlightened Ones', as the people of Courth called them. Enguer also knew them as Atlanteans. Recently he had watched a group of them riding a wheel-less cart on their way to the palace. Through some mysterious means it floated above the ground without horses or hydruntin to pull it. And although he had seen them once many years before, he was still struck by their beauty. He recalled how slender they all were, with long hair of yellow or black that hung past their broad shoulders, their sharp angular features, large almond-shaped eyes and ears that came to a point at the top. They might have been mistaken as elves if it weren't for their most notable and slightly disturbing feature – blue-tinted skin over strange elongated skulls.

Enguer ran on.

A few blocks further, he trotted past the Temple of Sunna, then turned north up an alley before he reached the eastern gate. Two more turns and he was bent over with hands on knees huffing and puffing in front of the Ranger's Lodge. Hesitating before the entrance, he feared what he might find out inside about Suri as much as he feared not knowing. He braced himself for whatever came and pushed through the door.

Inside, a score of rangers stopped what they were doing and stared in his direction. They were preparing for battle, all of them armed and armored in leather cuirass, greaves and vambraces. No one spoke a word.

"I can't believe my eyes." The rangers separated to let the man who spoke through to the front. It was Suri.

Relief flooded through Enguer. The old ranger lived! And appeared no worse for wear.

Striding forward, Enguer embraced his friend. "I was worried about you."

Suri laughed, "You were worried about me? I was never in any danger!" He gestured to the men around him, "Me and the boys were about tear old town apart looking for you. Commander Duraunt is on his way now with a hundred of his own!"

Enguer slapped the ranger on his padded shoulder. "I guess I just figured they took you as well."

Turning sharply, Suri raised his voice for all to hear, "Enguer is back and unharmed! We won't be invading old town tonight!"

Cheers filled the room followed by trays of fine ale brought out by Twig and the kitchen staff. Suri pulled Enguer over to a table, but before they could sit Commander Duraunt strode through the door with one of his captains. "Suri!" he called above the din. "We are ready to . . .Enguer? Is that you?"

Suri waved him over. "I don't have the story yet, but he is here with all his limbs as far as I can see."

The Commander leaned over to his captain, "Relieve the men," and then joined them at their table. "We feared we had lost you."

Enguer, still overwhelmed by the lengths his friends were ready to go to save him, steadied himself for the questions he knew would come. "Did you save the woman?"

"The woman . . .?" Suri's face reddened. "That wench laughed at me and ran off. I might have caught her if I hadn't gone back to find you."

"Tell us what happened, Enguer," Commander Duraunt prompted.

Twig set mugs of ale in front of them and pat Enguer on the back before he went back to the kitchen. Enguer took a long draught of the cool liquid. It didn't compare in the slightest to the warm piss they served at the tavern in the old town.

"I was about two lengths behind Suri in the ally," Enguer began slowly. "When we came to the bend, I was pulled off my horse by a rope. They had a hood over my head, pressing me to the ground before I could move and then one of them cracked me with a cudgel."

"We'll have a priest look you over," Suri offered.

Enguer took another long draft of ale emptying the cup. Twig was there in an instant to fill it back up. He drained that one just as quick. Everything he said so far was true, but this next part would be where the facts would diverge. Enguer had thought about it a lot on his run back to the lodge. He couldn't tell them the truth without putting them in danger. Nor would they allow him to do what he had promised Gigot and the other one. It went against everything he believed in to lie to these good men, but he had been left with no choice.

"They took me to a basement somewhere and forced me into a chair. When they removed the hood, I could see four of them – two in front and two big ones behind me making sure I stayed put," Enguer ran his hand through his hair. "I think they were all as surprised to see me as I them."

Confusion painted Commander Duraunt's features, "What do you mean?"

Enguer shrugged, "It took me a while to work it out while they were arguing with each other, but I believe they meant to nab someone else."

"Who might that be?" Suri was sitting back in his chair studying him closely.

"I don't know. Maybe a noble's son. I couldn't catch a name," Enguer felt Suri's eyes burrowing into him. The old ranger knew he was holding back. "All I can be sure of, is that they were expecting someone else under the hood. Someone that would fetch a tidy ransom."

"So, they let you walk away?" the Commander appeared incredulous. He was certainly a man of many emotions, while Suri remained still, watching and listening.

"Hardly," Enguer emptied a third cup of ale. "I told them I was a ranger and that if I came to any harm, my brothers would not rest until they avenged me." Enguer couldn't bear to look in Suri's direction. "I never dreamed that what I said could be true." At least he was back to the truth again.

"What happened next?" Suri's cold stare never wavered.

"They cracked me on the head again and when I woke up, I was down an alley in old town." Enguer wanted to tell Suri everything, but the lie was out already and he could never take it back.

Commander Duraunt stood up and pat Enguer on the shoulder. "I'm glad you're OK. More than glad. Now get some rest. I'll send a Bayle in the morning to gather descriptions of the men and a healer to see to your head."

Suri stood as well. "The Commander is right, boy. Get yourself to bed. We'll talk more in the morning."

Enguer climbed the stairs that led to his room with the feeling that every eye was on his back burning with accusation. He was sure that Suri had worked out a tell that confirmed his lie. It was one of the saddest moments in his life to realize the great ranger might never trust him again.

The next morning, Enguer awoke when the sun was high and the city bustled with the usual activity that came with the approach of the noon hour. He recalled that during the night Suri had come to check on him and found him delirious and on the edge of sleep, sweating profusely with a fever. The memories were hazy, but a priest arrived at some point and soon after he slept fitfully the remainder of the night. It felt as if he had slept for a week, the bump on his head was gone and for the first time in a long time all felt right with the world again.

But it wasn't

He was compelled to take a journey to Arre for reasons he didn't completely understand and he had lied about it to his friends. Laying there, staring at the cracked plaster on the ceiling, he supposed he would make preparations that day and leave first thing the next morning. How would he explain his hasty departure to Suri? Enguer didn't like the idea of parting with him that way, especially since it could be a while, if ever, before they saw each other again.

There was a light knock at his door.

"Come in," Enguer called out. He hoped it was Twig bringing him something to eat.

The door opened and Suri popped in with his usual half-smile on his face. "Don't look so disappointed."

"I'm not," Enguer flung his legs over the side of the bed and sat up. "In truth, I was hoping it was Twig with a bowl of warm stew."

"Ah," Suri laughed. "I left orders for you not to be bothered. You had a rough night and I figured you needed your rest."

Enguer found clean clothes to dress. "I did," his reply muffled through the tunic he cast over his head. "Now I am hungry as a wolf."

"Then come down when you are ready. I will have Twig prepare something and we can eat while we wait for Commander Duraunt to arrive."

"You are expecting the Commander?" Enguer was a little alarmed.

"Yes," Suri paused before going out the door. "He and a few of his men are going to escort us to the palace. The king was more than a little put off that we never made it to his little award ceremony and decided to make sure we made it this time. See you downstairs."

Now Enguer was truly alarmed. What would he say to the king? Surely, he would ask what Enguer's plans were now that they had dispensed with the Lukánthropos. He had to think of something that would satisfy the king and ease Suri's suspicions at the same time. He had to think fast, Commander Duraunt would be there soon and this time he wagered they would make it to the palace.

Suddenly Enguer wasn't so hungry anymore.

~~~

Fifty nobles, dressed in their most pompous finery of feather, fur and lace, watched Enguer and Suri accepting Courth's highest honor – the Medal of Admiration. Receiving it conferred the title of Lord, if only in name and the everlasting admiration of the nobles and citizens of Courth. The king placed the first medal on Suri and then moved on to Enguer.

"I'm sorry you and Commander Suri missed the official ceremony because of your wounds. It is a relief to us all that the Demon Beasts, Lukánthropos I believe you call them, will not trouble us again." King Francik pulled a thick metal medallion attached to a long gold chain from a box held by Commander Duraunt. "And that business the other day. Waylaid by bandits? Right here in the city? What is our world coming to?" He carefully placed the chain over Enguer's head and set it to rest on his shoulders, the heavy medallion weighing against his chest. It matched the one Suri was wearing. "I trust the two of you are fit and healthy again?"

"We are, your majesty," Suri assured him.

Taking a step forward to face the nobles, King Francik cleared his throat and announced for all to hear, "By the grace of Sunna and by my right as King, I award the Medal of Admiration to Lord Suri and Lord Enguer for their heroic risk of life and limb in service to the crown. Their fearless bravery to go forward into the dark unknown and vanquish the terrible evil that came rampant upon our fair kingdom, shall stand as an inspiration to all through the ages. They are recognized with honor and shall be recognized with honor by every citizen of Courth for their brave sacrifice. Go now in the light of Sunna and spread the word of their deeds to all you meet."

The nobles rose and cheered vigorously for a few moments before politely departing through the main entrance of the throne room.

"Good, that should satisfy them. Now won't you join me for refreshments?" The king did not wait for an answer. He turned and strode toward a door visible only because of a small gap showing its outline among the heavily embellished ornamentation decorating the walls from floor to ceiling.

Enguer followed dutifully behind Suri and Commander Duraunt. Inside, they found themselves in a small room with a simple table and four chairs. The king sat heavily in one and gestured to everyone else to follow suit. With hardly a pause, servants entered with a plate of cheeses and hams and tall mugs of Mekali red wine.

"The only fool in this kingdom is me playing to a troupe of other fools that allow my family to retain power," King Francik muttered irritably. "If not for the blessing of Sunna bestowing the gift of sovereignty upon my family generations ago would I give it all up for a simple life."

Enguer nearly laughed out loud, successfully covering his rudeness by a cough. Or so he thought. The king scrutinized him over the cup of wine while he drank from it and rather than an unapproving glare, Enguer was sure he caught hints of a smile. Only a few years ago his father had jested that all nobles bemoaned the heavy burdens they bore on behalf of the realms they served and often stated their wish to lead more germane lives, but seldom meant it.

As if reading his thoughts, the king addressed him, his face the manifestation of appreciation, "You are much like your father, Enguer."

Enguer smiled and glanced at Suri. "That seems to be a common perception, Your Majesty, although I strive every day to earn the resemblance."

"Well said, young man," the king raised his cup in a gesture of honor to the ranger's memory. "He and I were travelling companions for a while before I was ensnared by duties of the crown when my own father passed. That was a long time ago, but in that time, we became fast friends and over the years I relied heavily upon his wise council nearly up until his death."

Enguer was surprised by that. "I mean no offense, Your Majesty, but I had no idea that my father knew you at all."

King Francik laughed amicably. "None taken, dear boy. Your father was a well of mysteries to all of us. Those who knew him will always love him and cherish the memories of the many ways he touched our lives."

Suri and Commander Duraunt both added their jovial, yet solemn agreement to the king's sentiment. It was a strange thing to know men who knew his father so well, yet knew so little of him. The man they often described was very different from the father Enguer knew growing up. To these men, even the king, Gaurin Rand was an epic adventurer, a distinguished ranger without equal – a living legend. To Enguer, he was a loving father crushed by the tragic death of his loving wife, coping to raise a young boy on his own the best way he knew how.

"Enguer, I want you to join the Royal Order of Rangers and continue the service to Courth your father accorded us in the twilight of his life!" The king slapped the table loudly. "It would honor us all if you would carry on his legacy."

Enguer had prepared for this, only because Suri told him to expect it while they waited for Commander Duraunt to retrieves them from the Order's common room. The old ranger admitted that he was not surprised Enguer had plans to travel, Tanais had told him as much early on. Suri still seemed skeptical about the reasons, but Enguer thought he had repaired much of the damage from the previous night and they would part as friends.

Before he could reply, Suri interjected, "Your Majesty, Enguer is young and like his father, wishes to spend a few years exploring The Wilds and the world at large. Perhaps it is too soon to expect him to settle when he has barely left the nest?"

The king frowned, "Is that how you feel Enguer? Are you, indeed, drawn to travel and adventure like your father?"

154

"I am, Your Majesty," Enguer dropped his eyes to the table. "Perhaps it is the curse in our bloodline that we must wander for a time before we 'set aside our weary boots for a warm blanket'."

King Francik roared with laughter accompanied by Suri and Commander Duraunt. "Spoken as if from your father's own lips!" The king wiped the tears of glee from his cheeks. "I think we have all endured the pleasure of Gaurin's famous, and often infamous, sayings!"

Enguer took advantage of the light moment. "I am honored by Your Majesty's offer. It is far more generous than I deserve."

Suddenly dead serious, the king held Enguer's gaze with his own. "It is not."

Enguer let his gaze slip once more to the oak grain on the table that was becoming far too familiar and worried he had miscalculated. They were all well aware of the price so many had paid at the hands of Rochette and the Lukánthropos. Enguer didn't intend to belittle their sacrifice.

"Look at me boy." Enguer raised his gaze back to the king. "Never sell yourself short. I know your father has told you that. The men in this room respect you, as do I and every soul in Courth."

From the corner of his eye he glimpsed Suri and the Commander gravely nodding in agreement and his cheeks reddened with embarrassment. He was such a fool. How many in the kingdom could say they sat in the presence of these men and felt for a moment their peer?

The king's eyes softened. "I will not withdraw my offer. It will stand as long as I am king. When you decide to 'set aside those boots' it is my wish that it will be here, among your countryfolk and friends, if that is what you desire."

Still feeling the heat beneath his collar, Enguer bent his neck in a sincere bow, "Thank you, Your Majesty."

"So, tell me young Ranger, where will you go?" The king had an amazing ability to command the emotion in the room. The tension dispelled; the strain of the previous moments faded away.

At least this was not a lie, Enguer thought with some relief, "I am going to Arre, Your Majesty. Arch Priest Tanais has a younger brother there that I wish to personally inform of His Grace's passing."

King Francik appeared puzzled. "Won't he know by now? Surely pigeons have been sent to the winds with that news among others."

"The Arch Priest confided in me his contentious relationship with his brother and his fervent wish to reconcile." Enguer held fast to the truth like a drowning man to a log. Sunna might forgive him for not revealing everything to her earthly representative, but perhaps not a bold-faced lie. "I believe this is what His Grace would wish that I do since I can disclose so much more than a few sad words carried on the leg of mindless bird."

"You honor our late Arch Priest, Enguer." The king stood, quickly followed by Enguer and the others. "Tanais and I fought about what was best for Courth, bitterly at times, but his heart was always in the right place, where mine may have been swayed by politics. Despite that, he was a friend, and in the end, together we would do what was best for Courth even if it did not appear the best for everyone. I will miss our battles, the late-night debates, but mostly I will miss my friend." While he spoke, King Francik made his way around the table and lay a hand on Enguer's shoulder. "You make your king proud by what you do, Enguer."

Enguer felt a pang of guilt run through his gut. If the king only knew the truth of it would he be so proud? Would any of them?

Not waiting for a response, the king made a quick step toward the door held open for his anticipated departure by an attentive servant. "Suri, give the boy a tenth from my account," he called over his shoulder on the way out.

"Yes, Your Majesty," Suri replied, but the king was already gone.

Enguer turned to face Suri and Commander Duraunt, both displayed wide smiles that caught him off guard. "What?"

"You made an important friend today," the Commander replied, all the while Suri nodded knowingly beside him.

Chapter 12

Hunted

The dark figure curled in a split of rock was seething with rage. Rain water seeped through tiny fissures forming thick, cold droplets that matted coarse hair over a thick hide leaving it wet, cold and miserable. The Lukánthropos noticed none of it, the heat of anger warmed its soulless form and defied the slightest shiver.

For days its lifeless body, burned and broken, lay where it had landed just inside the collapsed entrance to the cave. If any eyes could have witnessed, they would not have detected the smallest sign of life. Yet, inside, Yalal stirred. The demon might inhabit a corpse, but he had not been compelled to leave it as would normally be the circumstance. This one was different; life would come again soon.

And it did.

First came the timid flutter of a heartbeat that vigorously multiplied forcing black blood to circulate through cracked bones and open wounds. Those healed quickly. The body felt pain, intense pain, but there was no consciousness to suffer it. Yalal simply chose to block the unwanted sensations away and for the time being he was an observer, watching the mangled body heal itself, feeling it grow stronger day after day.

That was the nature of the Lukánthropos.

Those humans, the sun-worshippers from Courth, had almost defeated him. In fact, he was once again the lone representative of his kind. The sole survivor in this dank subterranean prison, no longer worshiped by his followers, no longer feared by thousands. That would soon change when its body healed and he was free again.

His first wild inclination was to return to Courth, rebuild his pack and destroy them all. *Had he learned nothing?* He would never be able to grow his followers fast enough before they were set upon again by soldiers, fire-priests and those vexing rangers. The humans

157

had somehow discovered how to kill the Lukánthropos and next time he might not be so lucky to escape them. Even now, Yalal felt vulnerable trapped inside an undead corpse, weak and starved, entombed in the dark depths of a cold lifeless cavern. The thought enraged him anew. He had only recently escaped from the Pithos that had imprisoned he and his brethren for more than a millennium. To be trapped again so soon with the taste of freedom still new and so many plans ahead and power to be had – even the demon could not bear the thought of it.

Yalal hated flesh for its weakness. It was vulnerable and spent too much time resting and healing only to emerge a fragile and delicate thing that had to be jealously guarded against a never-ending stream of dangers. Even the immortal Lukánthropos faced its own mortality under catastrophic circumstances. It was the ultimate irony that demons in this world would be so closely tied to corporeality for their own survival.

Days passed before the Lukánthropos was strong enough to explore the winding corridors in search of a way out. Yalal could feel its hunger. Yet there was nothing to eat, not even a rat or one of its own kind to sacrifice. They had all escaped the cavern to be burned by the priests' fire.

Through eyes magically altered to see clearly in the dark, Yalal guided the beast to all the back outlets. It would have no trouble finding flesh to rip with its claws and bones to grind between its teeth once it was back on the surface. But dark luck could not find him a way out. The vile rangers had been diligent in their reconnaissance and found every escape route from the cavern. There were only a few. Yalal chided himself for not locating a den that was more expansive, with a larger network of caverns and tunnels. One that stretched for leagues, not just a few hundred spans and offered a number of exits. It would not be a mistake he would repeat if he ever found a way out.

There were four exits aside from the main entrance and all were sealed tight by the Fire-Priests. Their magic had reformed the rock, infused it into one solid mass that covered the openings so completely that there was little hope of breaking through. Yalal could see their work clearly and not a one had the slightest flaw for him to exploit.

For weeks Yalal drove the starving Lukánthropos over every inch of the cavern searching in vain for the smallest hint of escape. In desperation he compelled the Lukánthropos to physically attack the barriers and force its way through. The test of strength shattered claws and fractured bones, leaving its body exhausted and broken once more. It was a dark time for Yalal, certainty dawning on him that he could be trapped there for centuries, or forever. And already the madness started creeping in again. If it had ever left. Yalal was surprised how quickly it returned. All the demons had been touched by it to one extent or another during their stay in the Pithos. It had made them weak, stripped them of their physical forms and left them relying on the strength of mortal bodies that they could possess and compel to do their bidding.

Yalal knew that time would bring despair and that despair would hasten the madness. He was trapped in a body that would never die and without death there would be no escape for the demon. It was just like the Pithos. Not even dreams of rising again as the god of Lukánthropos and reigning over nations to the end of ages would sustain him through another millennium of darkness. Yalal howled his rage through the Lukánthropos. The sound of it echoed through the lonely dark caverns of his prison.

~~~

A swirling pillar of flame rose from the base of the mushroom cloud and quickly engulfed it entirely. The thick clouds of pulverized earth it had disgorged into the atmosphere churned with whirling gusts of red-hot flames that produced several burning funnels that slowly lengthened toward the ground like the divine fingers of an angry god. At the center of it all rose the Phoenix. Its wings stretched out to the far edges of the raging clouds of fire as if holding the blazing funnels in a protective embrace. And no different than suckling hens, they drew strength from the Phoenix and grew larger and larger.

"Micma nanaeel! Solpeth bien ialpor a ivonpovnph. Toatar a ciaofi! Ol iolcam croodzi. Zirenaiad. Zorge sa noas hoath. Q adoian teloch aaf ialpvrg!" the demon spoke with words like thunder from the blistering maw of the Phoenix.

"So, it fancies itself a god," Wodanaz mused. "I don't feel much like praying today, how about you?"

Myrllin discharged a grunted laugh, "Why does every demon we meet have a god-complex?"

"I've got the perfect cure for that," Wodaniz snapped his fingers bringing forth a fine spear with a smooth oaken shaft capped by a mithril blade inscribed with glowing runes.

Myrllin knew this spear as 'Gungnir' and it was his brother's favorite weapon. The Dwarfs forged it for Wodanaz as a gift in return for something he had done for them at one time, but Myrllin couldn't recall exactly what that was at the moment. The Dwarfs were always fawning over his brother and the Vikja were practically worshiping him. Sometimes Myrllin wondered why no one flattered him with attention, although he would probably become annoyed by all the fuss if they did.

Making a great show of tossing a spear astride his horse. Sleipnir reared on his back hooves and thrust the other six forward like the rampaging Lyons on the banners of Lyonesse, while Wodanaz struck a heroic pose and thrust his arm forward releasing Gungnir in what should have been a high arc. Myrllin knew it didn't matter how Wodanaz threw it. As soon as the shaft left his finger-tips the spear shot forward in a blur of motion propelled by magic and in the blink of an eye crossed the span that separated man from beast.

If the demon saw the spear coming it had no time to avoid it. Gungnir struck somewhere near the center of the creature and disappeared through its burning chest shaft and all. For a second everything was quiet, Gungnir appeared once more in Wodanaz's hand and he pulled back for a second toss, when a shriek pierced the hot air with such a pitch that Myrllin was forced to cover his ears with his hands. Gungnir sped forward a second time, but Wodanaz was left swaying in his saddle from the terrible noise.

Myrllin felt only a fraction of his brother's pain through the link that they shared, but he knew Wodanaz was in trouble. "Sleipnir, take your master away!" he shouted urgently.

"No!" Wodanaz steadied himself.

The Phoenix screeched a second time forcing them both to cover their ears again to block out the disorienting sound. Myrllin noticed Wodanaz was covering one side of his face while holding

Gungnir. The shaft steamed and sizzled against his brother's skin causing scorching blisters on his face and hand. Myrllin realized the spear was returning so rapidly that it hardly had a chance to cool.

"Look at what you are doing to yourself!" Myrllin yelled at his brother when the screeching ended. "Get away from here, I will deal with this!"

"I'm not leaving," Wodanaz hollered back. He pulled a candle from his pocket and tore off two large chunks then tossed the candle to Myrllin. "Do what you must, Gungnir is taking its toll. I can feel it!"

There was no point arguing. Wodanaz would do as he wished and there was no changing his mind once it had been set. Myrllin deftly snatched the candle from the air and shoved a piece of tallow in each ear before urging Dergo forward. They would need to get a lot closer for his spells to be effective. Gungnir streaked past again, followed by another terrible screech. This time it was bearable with the tallow in place.

OK, Dergo, Myrllin sent the mental thought to the dragon. Come in high from under those clouds. A few quick passes should do it.

As you wish. Dergo's response in his head was imprinted with doubt. Myrllin paid it little mind. The dour dragon always sounded doubtful.

The swirling funnels around the Phoenix appeared to swell in size the closer they approached. The rotation of their fiery winds stretched from the earth to the heavens and the whole thing pulsed with restrained energy. Myrllin quickly recognized that feeding these flaring tornados had to be the only reason the Phoenix was suffering strike after strike from Wodanaz's Gungnir. There was something powerful happening. An elemental change that was growing stronger by the second. Still more than half the distance from the terrible bird, Myrllin watched the Phoenix pull back its mighty plumage and with one beat of its powerful wings, the force of a thousand-thousand winds drove the spinning funnels of fire forward.

Heat rushed over Myrllin's face. When his vision cleared, his eyes counted a dozen burning tornados tearing toward him in a sporadic jittering hop that swayed dangerously from side to side forming an unavoidable canvas of fire. There could be no getting around them, they were too close and coming on too fast, even for the swift dragon. Dergo dove left and then right, up and to the side, every direction unexpected and desperate with the barrels of fire burning down upon them. The twisters shifted violently like thrashing snakes forcing Dergo to lift and dive, turn and evade in a heinous dance of death. The heat was so intense that the dragon's scales steamed and tiny flames ignited at the end of his wingtips. Myrllin too felt the heat, safe within his bubble, but for how long he could not say. If the demon's magic overcame them the bubble would be stripped away and he would be dead in an instant.

The blazing whirlwinds surged all around them, careening into each other then recoiling unpredictably in a new direction. Somehow the great dragon stayed one step ahead, dodging through the smallest gaps and spinning away just out of reach. Only once did Dergo roar fiercely with rage when the tip of his spiked tail was briefly ingested by one of the broiling columns before they emerged from the test of fire unto the other side.

To face the Phoenix.

The massive creature towered above them dwarfing even the red dragon. Horrid red blotches encircled searing rifts that exuded thick molten fluid like bleeding wounds where the spear Gungnir impacted its flaming breast over and over. Even as Myrllin and Dergo arrived, another streak of light passed over their heads and struck the Phoenix causing it to screech intensely.

Myrllin could feel the pain through the bond with his brother each time Gungnir returned to his hand. It would soon become unbearable. But Myrllin and Dergo focused by necessity upon the fiery bird whose attention was now fully upon them with the intent to reduce them to ashes.

"*Kures gi biab*," the demon spoke through the Phoenix as if he expected them.

"*Zin Kures*," Myrllin replied.

Myrllin knew the ancient dialect well. It was the native tongue of the Tuatha De Blood. The language attributed to gods and demons. It was a vernacular beyond the structure called the Tower of Tongues created by the Atlanteans to make trade and peace more efficient throughout the domains of men. Maybe a score of souls on this terra-forma understood the words spoken, he and his brother included. It pained him to hear the beautiful speech corrupted by a demon's wicked tongue.

~~~

Enguer rode along the edge of the mountain range known as the Spine of Cell that ran down the southern coast from Courth through Tarre, the length of Rasna and all the way into the land of the Sicans where the monstrous volcano known as Etna was said to belch its noxious gasses. At least that's what the merchants claimed. True or no, it didn't matter to Enguer, he was only going as far as the series of passes that led north to Coni. There were shorter ways to go if he took the direct route through The Wilds, but that meant travelling on foot and he would want a mount when he arrived in Tarre. Taking the coastal road would take a few more days, but he would be on his own horse and enjoy the warm breeze that pushed inland over the tepid waters of the Great Sea this time of year.

Caravans of tradesfolk from cities in the east passed him on their way to Port Francik where the Esmee terminated into the Great Sea. Many of them would continue up the river north to the city of Courth and return east with wagons full of lumber. The Tarre people were a common sight in the kingdom peddling bronze tools and implements skillfully crafted in molds of stone and clay, crates full of grapes, barrels of wine and flax for linens. The traders from Rasna were particularly skilled in the manufacture of jewelry made of copper or tin and often set with precious gems. They almost always travelled in caravans guarded by scores of mounted spearmen to protect their valuable cargo. Enguer was aware that the Kingdom of Courth was considered among the wealthiest on the Great Sea and conveyed a brisk trade with nations as far north as Lyonesse and as far east as the mysterious sister kingdoms of TaMehu and TaShemau. He also knew that made citizens of his homeland a juicy target for the pirates from Tartessos and raiders from at least half a dozen small realms situated around the Great Sea. It was a good reason to keep to himself and the gold he carried hidden from discerning eyes.

Gold.

Having never possessed a single gold coin in his lifetime, now he carried a bag of ten crowns in a pocket under his cloak, compliments of King Francik. It was a fine gift, but Enguer was all the more anxious with the press of it against his breast as a constant reminder that he had something of value to lose other than his life. Enguer tried not to concern himself. He had a swift horse and a strong sword arm if any bandits thought to accost him.

Travelling over the leagues of well-worn roads, Enguer took refuge at inns and waystations that frequently populated the roadside and nearby villages. With the fine weather, he could have easily set a camp every evening, hunted down a rabbit and camped under the stars. A sack full of gold convinced him that a warm bed and hot meal for only a few coppers was the better way to go. Besides, he would be spending more than a few nights next to a camp fire soon enough, so he thought to indulge himself while he could. It was also a good opportunity to share a drink with a local farmer or roving merchant, practice his social banter that he always felt deficient due to his mostly solitary lifestyle, and enjoy the musical talents of a travelling minstrel. Enguer was having such fun that he almost forgot the reason he was making this journey in the first place. He didn't think about it much. Allowing his thoughts to take him to a dark place would serve nothing. His mother often teased his father about being an implacable brooder. He was still not sure what the word 'implacable' meant, his mother had a way with words, but it was true. His father would often drift off into a bottomless pit of gloom, particularly late in the night, and refuse to speak about it. The occasions increased after his mother's death, leaving Enguer feeling alone even when they were together. Fortunately, the new light of dawn would always bring his father around and their life would go on. Blessed Sunna.

Trekking through the last mountain pass into Tarre, Enguer expected to arrive in the city of Coni before evening. The road was thick with trees on each side, not as heavily forested as The Wilds that bordered Courth, but thick enough that their branches filtered much of the morning light and cast shifting shadows over the underbrush. It was an illusion that reminded him of his childhood with similar images playing on the walls of his room through cracks in the shutters, the smell of cooking eggs and ham from the kitchen and his mother's blissful singing. It made Enguer smile.

All thoughts were abruptly cast aside as the tranquil morning deteriorated into chaos. Men and women dressed in the garb of villagers, some clutching small children to their beasts, came crashing through the thick underbrush of the forest. Many more of them ran wildly around a bend in the road screaming. Enguer's horse reared in panic, nearly throwing him to the ground. Recovering quickly, he realized that they were not attacking him, they were running by him. Many shouted a warning, mostly they cried for him to run, yet it was unclear why they were running. Kicking the flanks of his horse with his heels, Enguer spurred it forward into a fast gallop careful not to trample anyone fleeing in the opposite direction.

Within seconds Enguer was around the bend cresting a low rise. The trees thinned and a secondary road trailed into a green field surrounding a sprawling village larger than most he had seen since he left Courth. This one was marked by a substantial difference – black smoke rose from several structures engulfed in fire. It was a conflagration of flames that consumed huge swaths in strange linear patterns. People and animals ran in panic every direction and no one was doing anything to combat the blaze.

At first Enguer feared the village was under attack, but there was no fighting, no combatants chasing down the villagers and there didn't appear to be any logic in the route the villagers were dashing away. A group of several ran toward him and then they stopped, eyes wide with fear at something beyond him, before darting left and right in terror. Enguer pulled his mount up short and twisted in his saddle just in time to catch the swift movement of a vast, dark shape fly fast overhead. Snapping his eyes back toward the village, he watched in horror as fire shot forth from the creature's massive black head incinerating everything along its path.

It was a beast from legends, tales told in books and around campfires, too dreadful a thing to imagine it could be anything more than a story. Yet there it was, like the shadow of death it sailed across the sky on great wings spread wide and leathery like a bat trailing a long tail from the mass of a great muscular body with thick limbs that terminated with lethal talons the length of a man standing. More frightening was the massive horned head with glowing red eyes and a great maw lined with sharp teeth longer than a broadsword through which a stream of flaming death assaulted the village. Tip to tip it was black as night and for all the terror it awoke within the deepest depths of his soul, Enguer admired its subtle grace. He remembered this creature well, soaked up and delighted in the fairytales from his youth, how he was inspired by the excitement and glory of the contest with metal-clad warriors. Penhallow wrote page-turning narratives about the thing and Vyvyan captured it in beautiful lines of prose. They called them Dragons, an invention of the Tuatha De freed upon the world after The Breaking over three-thousand years ago. To look upon it now inspired fear and awe.

Enguer watched the dragon burn a deadly line through the village. Everything it touched, from huts raised a span above the ground by wooden piles to public buildings built of stone with wooden rooftops, all succumbed to the flames. And people. Only then did Enguer realize that the scorch marks on the ground, littered with lumpy ash, were the sad remains of unfortunate villagers. Circling low, the dragon landed heavily near the center of the village where it lingered over a pen of petrified sheep. These did not die by fire. One by one the dragon tore into their flesh ripping with claws and teeth. The frightened animals made hardly a bleat when it was their turn so overcome with shock they must have been. Enguer too could only stare in morbid fascination.

Apparently satisfied with the meal, the dragon stretched its wings and propelled its great bulk into the air once more. Fearing it might notice him, Enguer jumped from his horse and crouched a few paces away in a copse of bushes. He loved his horse, but he was not about to sacrifice himself with it if the dragon came their way. Watching the dragon's slow spiral to gain altitude, Enguer was relieved when the great beast altered its course and sped away to the south over the snow-covered peaks of the Spine of Cel.

Adrenalin fading from his body, Enguer stumbled over to retrieve his horse. It greeted him with wild eyes and sharp stomps, but it didn't take long to calm it now that the dragon was gone. His senses less fixed, the world suddenly expanded around him and he could hear the pop and crackle of burning wood, the cries of the dying and the vitriolic stench of sulfur and burning flesh.

Enguer rode down the rest of the way to the village. Others were slowly, cautiously climbing out from under cover that would not have saved them and huts that were lucky enough not to be caught in the line of fire. The carnage was indiscriminate and without purpose. Had the dragon just wanted to eat the sheep, no one could have stopped it. No one would have tried. Instead, the beast murdered countless innocents out of what could have only been a lust born of pure evil. Such a creature was appalling in Enguer's mind and like all unnatural abominations' courtesy of the Tuatha De, they had to be destroyed. Sunna only knew how a massive black dragon would meet its end, but it had to be done somehow.

At the outskirts of the village, Enguer dismounted and approached the first burned-out hut that he came to. Two figures were stretched out before it. He surmised that the pair had been shielded by the flames well enough to escape the structure only to die of burns and asphyxiation in the street. The lead form was burned and blackened all over with the toe of a work boot the only clue that he was looking at the remains of a man. A pace behind, the smaller form, must have been a woman as evidenced by a thin length of sandy-blonde hair that poked up from beneath where she lay face down in the mud.

He was turning to leave when he thought he noticed a slight twitch from the body of the woman. It was not unusual for remains to spasm after a traumatic death, he had seen that many times hunting, but he had to be sure. Crouching down next to the scorched figure, Enguer gingerly rolled it over and received the shock of his life.

The face and upper torso of the woman was almost completely unharmed except for severe blisters and scorching at the edges. Even the front part of her linen tunic looked clean and well-kept around the neck and chest. More wisps of blonde hair stirred in the light breeze, gently caressing her checks and forehead. Enguer watched her closely, fascinated and revolted at the same time, looking for some small sign of life. A moment later, her body shuddered weakly and spittle slowly bubbled between her lips. Her eyes, covered with mud, opened wide enough for Enguer to notice they were a beautiful shade of grey and she released a low moan that bespoke of the intense pain she must be experiencing from the disfiguring burns.

Leaning close, Enguer spoke so she could see his lips. He had no idea if she could hear through what remained of her ears. "I will get help. Do not worry, I will return soon."

Before he could stand, the woman's moaning turned insistent and her body shook as if she were attempting to move her limbs. Enguer had the distinct impression that she was trying desperately to reach out to him, to stop him from going.

Enguer leaned close again, "I must find a priest that can heal. Surely you must have one here?"

Her eyes fluttered in the direction of the man that died beside her and Enguer realized that the man must have been the priest. He knew it was highly unlikely for there to be another in the village and his heart sank knowing that all he could do was try and comfort her through a very painful death. Her body shook once more drawing his attention and her eyes drifted to the long handle of the dagger poking up from his belt. Her sorrowful moaning escaped from lungs no longer capable of producing the screams of pain her mind frantically desired.

Enguer's eyes welled with tears. It was plain to a blind man what she wanted. How could he deny her? Wouldn't he want the same? Slowly he drew his long-dagger and the woman calmed. Her eyes pleaded for an end, an acceptance of her fate, escape from her suffering. He wanted to cradle her in his arms, say prayers to Sunna, speak words of comfort. But there would be no comfort for her and moving her in the slightest would only cause more pain. There was nothing left to ponder as each second of deliberation was an eternity of torture for the woman. It had to be done.

He plunged the dagger through the linen tunic into the flesh between the space of two ribs and through the heart of the woman stopping it forever. It was an expert thrust, precise in its execution that Enguer had barely given thought. His attention was on the woman, their eyes locked. Enguer forced a kindly smile upon his face. It was all he could give her in the form of condolence and in the final moment of life, she rewarded him with a gift. A gift of gratitude in her eyes before they glazed over in the eternal stare into the beyond. It was the purest moment he had ever experienced in his life and he would remember it vividly until the last of his days. He was sure of it.

"Murderer!" A woman's scream split the air.

Startled, Enguer jerked his head around to see a young woman standing twenty paces away looking at him in stark horror.

"Murderer!" She screamed again. "You killed my sister!"

Enguer jumped to his feet and plucked his dagger from the woman's chest, realizing almost immediately how bad that must have looked. "No, no!" Enguer pleaded. "She was dying, she begged me . . ."

An explosive sob erupted from the young woman and she turned and ran into the smoke-filled village shouting "Murder!" and calling for help.

Enguer, standing with a bloody dagger in his hand over the corpse of the lovely woman he had just put out of her misery was not in a strong position to explain his actions. An angry rabble of voices was heeding the young woman's call and soon he would be faced with a mob intent on exacting revenge on something or someone for the hell they had all been put through. He surmised that the dragon would be a distant thought, or at least an inconvenient one, while they were busy stringing him up by the neck.

Not willing to take a chance on their sympathy, Enguer pressed his lips to the woman's forehead then hastily mounted his horse. He rode hard through the smoke and chaos of screams and mourning never looking back. He knew they could not catch him, but in his mind, he felt hunted all the same.

Chapter 13

River Boats

There are few cultures as compulsively organized as the peoples of Tarre. They arrange their streets in straight rows, line them with nearly identical houses built on stilts and light the way with precisely placed lanterns brought to life at the same time every evening. To travel between their high-walled cities one finds them almost indistinguishable one from the next prompting the unsuspecting foreigner to often seek a reminder as to which one they were in. From their tribal days of freely wandering the vast grasslands as hunter/gatherers, they have embraced civilization and all it has to offer in a most extreme fashion verging on the ridiculous. If I do say so myself.

Wodanaz the Wanderer

The leagues churned under the thundering hooves of Enguer's Lambei. He was pushing the beast hard, he knew it, but he needed to stretch the distance between him and the terrible actions he had performed in the village. Anyone who witnessed the events would not have called it murder, on the contrary, it was an act of mercy. But there were no witnesses, except at the end, and the woman's cry haunted him relentlessly in the hours since. It may not have been murder, yet Enguer felt the stain of murder upon him all the same.

That morning had begun so beautiful before it was shattered by a chain of horrors and a desperate flight to Coni. And finally, there it stood before him, built upon an expansive embankment surrounded by a moat and a double-walled palisade. It was an impressive city if primitive by the standards of Courth. Outside the walls stretched a league of farmsteads in every direction, one of which Enguer passed through now. The farmers sometimes waved at his passing and inevitably stalled their greeting given the grim stare he returned and the hurried pace he kept. It was not in his nature to act this way toward descent folk, especially farmers since they reminded him so much of the Eibhlins, but his heart felt cold with sadness and anger.

Enguer approached Coni from the south where the River Bodin flowed down from the highest ice-shrouded peaks of the Spine of Cell and ran toward Anzi a few leagues east. A small, but bustling port hosted the dockage of a dozen riverboats loading and off-loading their cargo on the city side of the river. Further west, several ferry boats transported travelers and merchants from the southern bank to a separate dock adjacent to Coni's south gate. There, people and carts streamed into the city in clamorous groups herding livestock or calling for local laborers who lingered nearby waiting to attend the merchants to their destination where they would offload volumes of cargo. All were under the watchful gaze of spear-wielding city guards posted atop the walls and standing idle near the gate.

The next ferry bore him quickly across the Bodin. When it landed, Enguer stayed ahead of the throng, crossing over the moat of fast-moving water supplied by the river and through the city gates without a second look. Coni was the closest city in Tarre to the Kingdom of Courth and the two nations were allies in trade if nothing else. From the many stories his father had told him over the years, Enguer knew Tarre as a peaceful kingdom ruled by a benevolent king from their capital, Povigi, a few leagues west of the Travini Pass which led through the Asinippi Mountains and into the Eastern Kingdoms. Although Enguer never had the opportunity to travel outside of Courth, his father's words lent him a familiarity with Coni, and Tarre as a whole, that he was only now appreciating as he crossed the city's threshold.

Enguer moved with the crowd down the main thoroughfare and quickly recognized that the streets were arranged in a quadrangular pattern around various taverns, inns, temples, public buildings, and gardens. Most of the buildings were constructed of wood with thatched rooftops no taller than a single story. Open courtyards revealed tradesfolk skilled in metallurgy casting various bronze implements in molds of stone and clay or carpenters creating works of art out of everyday items like chairs and wooden doors that were in evidence everywhere Enguer passed. Almost immediately he realized that every tradesmen's door was beautifully engraved with symbols identifying their shop and the type of work they did inside. From what Enguer recalled from his father's teaching, the people of Tarre used many of the same symbols for words as their neighbors in Rasna to the south, however few of the common citizens could read them and instead were dependent upon imagery to find their way around. Tarre was still very much tribal at heart having advanced from their ancestral roots roaming the vast Grass Basin north of the Bodin that they called the Plains of Tarre, to developing settlements, cities and agriculture just a few hundred years previous. Enguer acknowledged that they lived crudely compared to Courth, but he admired their cheerful disposition and welcoming nature.

In the distance, Enguer glimpsed an elevated fortress on the northern edge of the city. That would be where the wealthiest citizens lived and most of the city guard barracked. It afforded its own moat and a massive embankment with a wooden double-walled palisade on top. Stone-constructs two or three stories high could be seen over the wall, but the most impressive feature was the tall tower on the east side of the compound that rose higher than any other. It featured dozens of open-air balconies adorned with plants and leafy vines and at its apex rotated a red crystal that cast a crimson light into the sky. Enguer was not sure what the Tarre citizen called the inhabitants of that tower, he knew them as the Enlightened Ones and more accurately, according to his father, Atlanteans. In the open space that occupied the ground in front of the fortress stood hundreds of shaded carts and kiosks selling all manner of goods and produce. Already, Enguer could make out the calls of hawkers selling the 'finest flax' for textile fiber or 'grapes so plump they must have been touched by the gods'. Enguer smiled to himself – the markets must be the same no matter where one travelled.

Down the side streets several residences came into view. Enguer was startled that they were not unlike the ones in the village he encountered earlier. Most were elevated upon thick wood stilts with deep pits underneath for sewage and refuse. They were clustered around wells and large cooking pits only a few streets off the main. Once in a while the breeze pushed in foul odors from their direction barely covered by the heavier mask of smoke from the cooking fires. Enguer supposed the Tarre people had not completely cast off their heritage now that they could build walls even though it was unlikely the city was prone to flooding as the outlying villages might be.

Not wishing to get caught up in the congestion of the market, Enguer guided his horse to a nearby inn. As fortune would have it, there was a mat available in the common sleeping room where he could lay his head for the night and room enough in the outdoor pens for his horse. If not as private and comfortable as his room at the Rangers Lodge, the mat was clean, the inn was warm and the fare included a steaming plate of bean stew with grilled flat bread. Enguer would not complain, he had endured much worse in The Wilds.

The next morning, Enguer rose with the light of Sunna and rode down to the port of Coni to find a river boat headed east toward Rasna. The dock was busy with activity as crews prepared to disembark once there was light enough to navigate. Making haste, Enguer inquired with one after another, but none were going further than Anzi. By the time he got to the end of the dock most of the boats were cast off and he barely made one whose captain would agree to take him and his horse.

At a crewman's direction, Enguer tied his Lambei in a pen holding a pair of oxen, several goats and hydruntin adjacent to the boat's single mast then found a spot upwind near the bow where he could sit and watch the landscape roll by. A good night's rest had revived his humor as long as he avoided thinking too much on the previous days' events. The bustling city and the changing landscape offered a good number of distractions.

"You found a good spot," a cheerful voice from behind startled Enguer from his thoughts. He turned to see an older man dressed in an open tunic and linen breeches tucked into worn leather boots. He was Tarre by the look of him and probably a member of the crew. He settled himself on a barrel lashed to a dozen others on the centerline of the deck. He wore an infectious smile on his weather-beaten bearded face.

Enguer grinned and thrust a thumb back toward the penned animals. "Any spot outside of their wind is good, I think."

The man laughed good-naturedly at Enguer's observation. "That is as true as the sun coming up in the morning. I am Kratu, captain of this old bucket."

"Well met, Kratu. My thanks to you and your first mate for allowing me passage to Anzi. Do you know how long it will take?"

The captain licked his palm and held it up in the air. "If this breeze keeps up, you're in luck and I'll be lifting the sail. That should get us there inside two days. It takes longer on the return since we are under oar most of the way."

"That's good news," Enguer pat his stomach. "I'm not used to travelling over water."

"You from Courth, I expect?"

"The city," Enguer nodded. "I've taken a ride down the Esmee to Port Francik a few times as a boy, but I prefer a horse under me to the shifting planks of a boat."

Captain Kratu laughed displaying a number of gaps for missing teeth, "You must not be a logger then. I hear they ride their logs down the river in the summertime. A woodsman, maybe?"

It was Enguer's turn to laugh, "It's true, some do ride them down from the logging camps. Sometimes the river is so thick with timber you can walk from one shore to the other without getting wet!"

For a moment they both laughed together. Enguer was sure the captain thought he was joking, but there was more truth in his statement than most would believe. Courth was a wealthy kingdom because of its logging trade and it cut and shipped untold numbers throughout the Western Kingdoms.

"I'm something close to what you might call a woodsman, I suppose. My name is Enguer Rand, ranger and traveler."

"A ranger!" the captain's grey eyebrows shot up on his forehead. "You must know all about trapping and hunting and living among the beasts in The Wilds. You see, I've heard something of the rangers from Courth."

"My father was a ranger before me, so I naturally followed in his footsteps."

"Ha!" The captain barked. "My sons want nothing to do with the river trade. One is a soldier, another cuts stone and the youngest is an apprentice to a tool-maker." He shook his head sadly. "I don't see them much, never did. Maybe that was the problem, plus the fact that each of them has a different mother!"

The captain cackled at that and Enguer joined in, but inside he thought it was sad. It was a rare thing in Courth for a man to have children with more than one woman unless his first wife had passed away. Funny, Enguer didn't think his father ever had a thought for another after his mother died.

"I'm glad to have a ranger on board," the captain went on. "You're the first I have met, anyway. If you don't mind, what is taking you to Anzi"

"I'm only going to Anzi to find another boat," Enguer saw no reason to hide where he was going. "From there I hope to find transport to Arre. I am bringing sad news of the passing of a friend to his brother."

"That's a long way to go to carry such a message. He must have been a good friend."

"He was," Enguer sighed. "But it's more than that. I wish to travel a bit before I settle down. Can you tell me something of Arre?"

"Sure I can. Arre is the northern most city in Rasna. In fact, once we get to Anzi all the land south of the Bodin River is Rasna territory." Captain Kratu bit his lip in thought for a moment before he spoke again. "It is said that the people of Rasna and Tarre came from the same tribes that once roamed the Plains of Tarre. Hundreds of years ago one group went south and the other west to scrape out a life, That's where it stands up to now, I suppose. Only in Rasna the cities they settled fought one another for supremacy until just a few decades ago when they got together and formed what they call the League of Free Peoples. Now, the Lauchme, their word for King, is elected from the Zilach, or governors, of the cities to reign for life." The captain coughed a laugh, "Or until they depose him for neglect or abusing his power."

"You know quite a bit about their history, captain." Enguer had heard all this before from his father, but he hoped the captain might add something new.

"I've spent all my life on this river, trading as far as Pluthi. You hear a lot of stories on a boat with nothing else to do but talk to the passengers for entertainment." The captain winked. "You'll find the cities in Rasna far less simple than the ones in Tarre and far more dangerous if you're not careful." Captain Kratu leaned forward and slapped Enguer on the knee. "Don't get me wrong, the citizens of Rasna are a fine people with a strong military and religious tradition. They just haven't quite found their way yet."

Enguer had heard how warlike Rasna was. Fortunately for the Western Kingdoms they had turned their phalanx and mounted warriors against the Enchele tribes that settle the lowlands between the Spine of Cel and the Asinippi Mountains, according to the latest news in Courth. "Any advice?"

The captain shrugged, "Respect their beliefs, don't criticize their government and don't steal." He smiled broadly, "Pretty much a good rule to follow anywhere."

"You're a wise man, captain."

"Pffft," Captain Kratu spat on the deck and laughed, "I heard that from a travelling story-teller a few years back and stole his line!" His laughter abruptly trailed off and the expression on his face turned serious. "One more thing, and this is important, be warry of their women."

Enguer was unsure where the captain was going with this. "I would show no disrespect."

"Stay with that attitude. You see, unlike much of the Western Kingdoms, men and women in Rasna are considered equal under the law and their society emphasizes pairing." The captain rolled his eyes, "Monogamy! For life, if you can believe it!"

Enguer's sides nearly split from laughter.

~~~

The towering city of Arre was perched high on a series of hills overlooking the mouth of the Bodin River where it emptied into the vast expanse of Lake Teluron. Stone buildings, most two or three stories high, crawled over the gradients for at least a league astride wide streets that zig-zagged up and down the entire elevation of the hillside. At the top stood what appeared to be a grand palace that lorded over the wealthy estates and government buildings immediately below its lofty inner wall and all the rest of Arre down to the crowded port far below at the water's edge. Surrounding the entire city stood an impressive defensive stone wall with intimidating images of Gorgons carved into them under each watch tower along its length. The frequent flash of metal from crimson caped soldiers in polished bronze armor stood out among rows of red banners rising high like long sails above the walls. Arre was considered by many the jewel of the Rasna Confederation, especially by those who lived there.

Enguer first caught sight of Arre soon after the noon hour on the last leg of his river-born journey from Anzi. Most of the voyage had been tolerable, except for a few cold summer showers brought by bitter winds from the north, skirting along the southern edge of Lake Teluron in the shadow of the snow-capped peaks of the Spine of Cel. Two hours later the river boat was only just beginning to glide up to a mooring at the dock. He didn't mind. The port was located on the lake side of Arre which afforded him the opportunity to study nearly the entire city as they drifted down the last length of the river. To him, Arre was the most picturesque city he had ever seen. Constructed up the steep slope of a high hill, it was like the gods had tilted Arre on its side affording him an unrestricted view like an eagle flying high above. The brisk movement of people in colorful garments that contrasted starkly against the beige and grey stone structures broken by regular intervals of green trees, vibrant gardens and sparkling water fountains. There was a certain beautiful artistry to the strict patterns of architecture against the offsetting wild and then manicured landscaping in Arre that Enguer had not seen before.

When the boat was secured to the dock, Enguer retrieved his mount, and bid farewell to the captain and crew of the river boat and walked along the crowded pier toward the city gates. The crew on this boat were from Rasna and far less talkative than the Tarre boat he traversed from Coni. Captain Kratu had been entertaining and informative, whereas his most recent hosts kept to themselves and their work. It didn't change his impression about the people from Rasna from the few he had observed in Courth. They were courteous enough in their own way, venerating a conservative, idealistic morality that rivaled the Temple Knight culture in Lyonesse.

Two weighty timber doors reinforced with iron strapping stood open to the port allowing an unimpeded flow of goods and people in and out of Arre. Soldiers with short cropped hair under bronze helmets and breastplates, wearing heavy leather sandals that laced around the ankles and long flowing red capes, stood vigilant with spears in hand and a short sword at their waist. They did not hinder anyone's passage, barely giving Enguer a sideways glance with his earth-toned cloak, longbow strapped over his right shoulder and hard-worn leather boots. He doubted they knew much about rangers and imagined he was viewed as little more than a foreign traveler that lived off the land. One thing was clear – he definitely stuck out from the locals. Most of the local men wore robes that gave way to a tunica, cinched at the waist by a leather belt, with a colorful cape draped over one shoulder that scarcely concealed the hilt of a short sword or long dagger and sturdy leather ankle-high boots. Their complexions ranged from a ruddy olive-tan to a milky pale that rivaled the skin-tone of many in Courth and long raven-black hair woven into braids.

But it was the women that Enguer could hardly keep his eyes from. They were astonishingly beautiful modeling a great variety of hairstyles above airy robes with decorated edges down to their feet where they most often wore high-laced sandals. His perceptive eye quickly discerned that the women displayed their social rank by the degree of decoration and fearlessly walked the streets wearing robes adorned with exquisite jewelry sometimes accented by a heavier colorful mantle. To Enguer's shock, many of these aristocrats displayed a single naked breast for all the world to see. He found himself red-cheeked averting his gaze from the spectacle of bared flesh rather than openly gawk. No one else appeared to pay them any mind.

Tearing his gaze from the women, Enguer realized that the buildings in the lower part of the city were constructed of dried bricks on a heavy frame of timbers and heavily plastered to look as if they were stone. Carved and painted reliefs decorated the walls with what Enguer guessed had to be scenes of religious significance, especially the afterlife. The only thing he knew about the Rasna people's religious beliefs was that the mountain range that ran the length of Rasna, the Spine of Cel, was named after their Earth Goddess.

Along with the painted reliefs, sculptures of bronze and clay, also painted with great care, were often arranged in front of the public buildings and gardens he passed. They appeared almost life-like in their coloring and pose leaving Enguer with the impression that they must have been the work of master sculptors. One recurring symbol that was present from the moment he entered the city gates was the motif of the mythological Gorgon. Nary a building or wall was not inscribed with its likeness. From what little Enguer remembered from his father's tales of Rasna, the Gorgon was the ancient symbol of power over life and death. Not so much a god, but as a symbol of government. The only reason he remembered any of that was because he was so enamored with the striking appearance of the Gorgon – the face of a beautiful woman surrounded by long locks of sinuous snakes in place of her hair. His father's spooky descriptions alone gave Enguer nightmares for a week when he was a child.

Wandering aimlessly, the sights and sounds and smells nearly overwhelmed his senses. He wondered if people walking through the streets of Courth for the first time felt the same. Enguer gathered his wits and focused his attention on finding a suitable inn. He had no idea what to look for as the shops and public houses used a block-style script above their doors to announce their trade or purpose that he could not read. Enguer realized that, unlike Tarre, Rasna's population must be educated with the lowest born literate enough to read the symbols. He decided to walk with the crowd a little while longer before he stopped to ask for directions.

Enguer expected an exhausting walk the further he climbed in elevation considering the entire city sat exposed on a series of increasing elevations, but the zig-zag design of the streets cut the incline to a subtle slope that was almost unnoticeable. However, from what he could see, most of the side allies off the main thoroughfare seemed to climb almost straight up and employed lengthy stairways between buildings that had to be daunting to ascend. Enguer hoped he would find an Inn closer to the bottom of the stairs than at the top.

Less than a quarter of the way through the city, Enguer's ears perked up at the sound of music drifting from the open doorway of a three-story building. The sun was bright outside making it difficult to see inside the darkened room beyond the door. He had passed several like it since he first walked through the gates of Arre, but this was the first that had music playing from it. If it was a tavern, then there might be rooms for rent.

With some hesitance, Enguer approached the door and immediately found himself eyeball to eyeball with a young man wearing a simple tunic and trousers.

"May I take your horse, sir?"

Enguer was unsure, "Is this an inn?"

The boy gestured to the symbols above the open door and smiled, "A fine inn, sir. Your horse?"

Enguer removed his travel bag and handed the boy the reigns. "Thank you."

Stepping inside, the smell of roasted duck and barley stew reminded him that he had not eaten since the early hours on the river boat. It took a moment for Enguer's eyes to adjust to the dim lighting but once he could see, he was impressed by the elegance of the room before him. Bronze fittings flashed from the hinges of dark wood cabinets against the walls surrounding a large open space filled with stuffed matts and pillows arranged in half hazard circles. Several patrons lounged upon them with one arm propped over a pillow to support their weight or sitting upright and cross-legged while they conversed quietly and feasted on small plates of fruit and shredded duck meat passed between them. Oil-burning lanterns flickered with life all around, producing dim illumination and dancing shadows on sheer white fabric that hung from the ceiling at odd angles obscuring the far end of the chamber.

Two musicians, one playing a subtle tune on an alabaster pipe while the other accompanied on a percussion instrument, sat in the far corner by themselves seemingly entertaining only themselves. Enguer thought it strange for the common room of an inn to be so quiet. In Courth, a common room was always filled with laughter, bawdy tales and upbeat music, not to mention at least a couple of fights before the end of the night. This place was sedate in comparison.

"May I help you?" A slim man with short-cropped hair wearing beige linen robes under a fine red tunica fastened at the waist with a corded belt emerged from the forest of hanging fabric.

Enguer assumed he must be the innkeeper. "I would like a room if one is available."

The man looked him up and down curiously. "A simple room?"

"I suppose that would be fine." Enguer had no idea what a simple room entailed.

"Very well, ten coppers per night. Fifteen if you would like a meal. Paid in advance." The man held out his hand, palm up.

Enguer produced the required copper from a small pouch and handed it to the innkeeper. Captain Kratu had been kind enough to exchange coppers and silvers for gold as well as wise advice to keep what he had to himself.

The innkeeper's shifty eyes flickered over the small bag from which Enguer had removed the copper, accepted the money and handed him an iron key. "You can take the Epsilon room."

Enguer stared at the key and then spoke quickly before the man turned away, "How will I find this room?"

The innkeeper's eyebrows shot up and he made a tsk sound with his lips, "I suppose you can't read?"

Enguer felt a little insulted. "Of course I can read, just not your language."

Taking the key from Enguer's open hand, the innkeeper flipped it over and pointed to a symbol carved into it. "That is the symbol of the Epsilon. Match it with the one over the door to the room and you have found it."

"I see, thank you."

Nodding curtly, the innkeeper gestured for Enguer to follow him through the sheer fabric to the opposite side of the room. There, he pointed out a narrow stair case leading up to the second floor before he disappeared through a doorway that smelled of the kitchen when it opened.

Shrugging to himself, Enguer followed the stairs up to a connecting hallway with several wooden doors along its length. Only a few doors down he located the Epsilon mark above one and used the key to let himself in. The latched clicked easily and the door swung inward revealing a small windowless room furnished with a thick mat for sleeping and a small wooden table with a black bucchero pottery bowl and matching pitcher. In the corner a hole in the floor served as the privy. Enguer found himself surprised at the idea that the Rasna would have sewage. His whole life he had thought of them, and Tarre, as little more than civilized tribal people. That may yet be true of Tarre, but Rasna was turning out to be just as advanced in their civilization as Courth or any of the other kingdoms in the west. Suffice to say, he wasn't disappointed with his 'simple room'.

Enguer dropped his bag on the floor and lit the small lantern hanging from a hook on the wall with the flame from another in the hallway. It was not yet late afternoon, but he was tired and decided he would take a quick nap before going back down for super. The mat was comfortable and clean with an extra blanket underneath in case he got cold. Laying still, he could still feel the rock of the river boat and found himself relieved to be back on dry land again. He thought about what it must have been like when his father first began his travels. He imagined it was not so different, except that Enguer would have to find this Reskalin fellow soon. Whatever the reasons that led them both to begin their wandering, Enguer felt the strength of the bond they had shared and prayed to Sunna that his father would somehow know the path he had set upon and smile down at him for it.

Chapter 14

Danger in Arre

From the outside looking in, Rasna is a powerful coalition of city-states with a strong military tradition and a deep distrust of outsiders. Yet, hiding behind the austere nature of their population one finds a warm, rich culture built on the foundation of family units where joy and laughter are a constant presence within the walls of their colorfully decorated homes. It is no surprise to me that these are the ancestors of a people, in another age, that would one day rule half the known world. Just as an aside, I am particularly fond of their women's fashion. Inspirational. Yes, that's the word for it.

Wodanaz the Wanderer

Enguer opened his eyes to a small room lit by a single lamp hanging on the wall and for a moment he forgot where he was. Panic gripped his heart before he realized he was in the Rasna city of Arre laying on a mat in a rented room on the second floor of an inn he didn't even know the name of. Slowly rising to his feet, he poured water from a pitcher into a bowl and washed his face vigorously all the while wondering what time of day or night it was. He still felt tired, but hunger would keep him from sleeping again until he found something to eat. Hanging his cloak from a peg on the door, Enguer donned a fresh shirt from his pack and walked into the hallway.

Sounds of music and merriment drifted up from the stairway that led to the common room. From the sound of it, Enguer guessed that it was quite crowded. He decided to go down and bother the innkeeper for a bowl of stew and whatever they claimed for drink even if he had to bring it back to the room.

He descended the stairway and stopped at the entrance to the common room to gawk at the scene before him – the sheer fabric remained as it was before, but through the wind sweeps from the open front door everything else had changed. The mats and pillows were pushed into a massive bunch on one side of the room around a huge open hearth that filled the room with a comfortable warmth while people lounged in far more casual and revealing robes and gowns than he had seen during the day. To a man or woman, they all held cups that they drank from liberally while a servant stood ready close by to fill it back up. Laughter filled the room as easily as the up-tempo music played by a half dozen musicians with lyre, flute and instruments Enguer had never seen before. Between them and the lounging patrons, men and women danced to the aggressive tune while hired dancers wearing sheer gowns that left nothing to the imagination, jiggled bells, clacked castanets and twirled in rotating circles around them.

The cheer of victorious voices from a side room Enguer had not seen before drew his attention. Through a wide opening he could see a dozen patrons engaged in board games and gambling with dice. Skirting around the dancing, he peeked in for a closer look, but none of the games were familiar to him. Cards were the draw in Courth. Dice were just beginning to catch on and typically they were crudely fashioned from animal bones. The ones he observed here were well-crafted, white in color and polished to a glossy sheen. If a set of these were brought to Courth, Enguer could imagine every noble and possibly even the king taking them up.

"Join us, friend." A jubilant call came from the room and others echoed the friendly invitation.

Enguer didn't know much about gambling except that it always served as an allure to his curiosity. Unexpectedly, a cup was shoved into his hand full of a red liquid as smooth as satin followed by another as quickly as he emptied it.

The man who called out to him, tall and handsome with long braided dark hair and a scar over his right eye, joined him cup for cup and explained how the game worked. "Each participant tosses three dice. Triples with the highest number on its face wins over pairs and any face showing a single digit is removed from the game even if all three are the same." The man pulled a set of smoothly finished dice from his pocket and handed them to Enguer. "Wagers are made on every toss. You can bet on a high or low, winner and loser, even the number of singles thrown in a turn."

Enguer was feeling flush from the wine and a little heady. "Sounds simple enough. What is the wager?"

"The players set the minimum, but anyone can buy in." He pointed to columns of silver coins neatly stacked in front of the two players rolling dice and several uneven stacks of silver on a narrow shelf along the wall. A man marked symbols in front of each of them with chalk and kept up with all the side bets.

"Would you like to try once?" The friendly man's good nature and easy smile set Enguer at ease.

"I suppose . . ."

Before long Enguer was tossing those beautiful dice into the corner of the shadowy room against men he didn't know. Sometimes the crowd cheered and other times they bemoaned his loss, but every time he found his cup full of wine and dice in his hand.

"Where are you from, my friend?" the affable man asked between rolls of the dice.

Enguer couldn't figure a reason not to be truthful. "The city of Courth. Do you know it?"

The man responded with a jocund slap on his back, "Do I know Courth? Of course, I do! Been a few years since my last visit, but it left me with memories I will cherish forever!"

A sarcastic laugh burst from someone close by in the crowd and a dark look briefly crossed the man's face before it was quickly replaced by his charismatic smile once more. "Cheers to my friend from Courth!" the man announced holding his cup in the air. Everyone in the crowded room responded with lively hails and applause.

Hours later, it was impossible to tell, Enguer's head swam and his vision was blurred to the point that he was nearly blind. He was singing a local song, some vulgar thing, shoulder to shoulder in a tuneless harmony with several others. A spill of wine sloshed over hand reminding him that he still held a cup, but the dice were gone and the games continued without him.

Then the vague outline of a familiar figure appeared in front of him and the voice he recognized as his new companion spoke gruffly to someone nearby, "Take him to his room, there is nothing left to take."

How strange, Enguer thought from the fog of obscurity. The friendly man that had encouraged him all night, commiserated with him when he was down and encouraged when he was up, would now order his retirement. Enguer didn't even know his name. He had drunk so much that he barely knew his own name for that matter.

Rough hands dragged him up the stairs and to his room where he was unceremoniously dumped upon his mat. There was a brief rustling afterward and the quiet click of the latch on the door. Then the heavy haze of drink and adrenalin faded into darkness.

~~~

The room was pitch black except for a sliver of flickering light that cut its way through the space between the base of the wooden door and the cold stone floor. Enguer hated waking up with no certainty whether it was day or night. The next time he rented a room he would make sure it included a window. He rose from his mat and blindly searched for the oil lamp hanging on the wall. Along the way his booted toe caught something small on the floor that skittered away with the distinct clink that he recognized as a coin of some sort. Odd that he would have dropped it, he thought as his hands closed around the invisible shape of the lamp. To his dismay, the lamp was empty of oil, so he propped open the door to the hall to allow enough light for him to wash and change clothes.

Immediately he knew there was something wrong. His pack lay emptied of its contents and his clothing and other personals were scatter all over the room. On the floor next to the small table he caught the glimmer of the coin he had kicked earlier and picked it up. A single copper.

Enguer suddenly realized that the weight of coins against his breast was missing and when he reached inside his tunic, he found the pocket empty that had held the pouch. Panic rose within him as he feverously rifled through his pack and his cloak that had been pulled from the door peg and flung on the floor. All the pouches of coin were gone. Every one. He was penniless, except for the lone copper.

Repacking his bag, Enguer searched everything one last time before he descended to the common room. It was early morning with only a few patrons in quiet conversation lingering over plates of fruit and cheese. The room was nothing like he left it the prior evening. All of the mats and pillows were placed in neat circles around the room exactly as he had seen them when he first arrived at the inn. There was no evidence of the dancing, drinking and gambling that had taken place the night before. It was almost as if it had never happened.

"Did you enjoy your evening, sir?" the innkeeper approached him from a group of patrons he had just served.

"Is it like that every night?"

The innkeeper shrugged, "Most nights, unless it's a holy week. We are a pious people in the day to please our gods and satisfy our vices at night while they sleep."

That was a striking statement where the gods were concerned and Enguer would have liked to understand it better if he didn't have more pressing matters on his mind. "Did you see the men that brought me to my room last night? I believe they robbed me of every coin I possessed while I was . . ." Enguer didn't want to admit the rest, even to himself.

"Every coin?" the innkeeper raised one eyebrow.

Abashed, Enguer nodded.

The innkeeper held up his palm expectantly, "Then I suppose you will not be spending another night here."

Enguer silently lay the iron key to his room in the innkeeper's hand.

Snapping his fingers shut around it, he dropped the key in an open pouch attached to his belt and snorted, "Wait here a moment."

Enguer watched him stride casually through the hanging fabric in the direction of the kitchen. While he waited, for what he hadn't a clue, anger built inside of him. Not at the innkeeper, maybe for the men that robbed him, but mostly at himself. How could he have been so stupid? The first night in Arre and he had lost all his money and duped like the fool that he was. *Had he not been cautioned by Suri and Commander Duraunt to watch out for himself?* Captain Kratu went even further to warn him about flashing his coin about, yet a few drinks and the beguiling smile of a stranger and Enguer had been transformed into the Count of Aquita. At least in the children's story it was a witch that cursed the count with the inability to say 'no'. What was his excuse? There were no witches in his story to blame.

The innkeeper returned with a package wrapped tightly in leather and tied with twine. He shoved it into Enguer's arms and sniffed again as if he were annoyed with himself. "If you have a skill, there is work to be had in the trade district. It doesn't pay well, not enough to stay here, but it pays enough at the end of the day to live a meager existence."

"And this?" Enguer shook the solid package.

Eyelids fluttering nervously, the innkeeper took a small step back. "Enough cheese, bread and smoked meat to keep you from starving for a few days while you find work. Now I must go." Spinning on his heel, the innkeeper swiftly moved off to tend to a group of patrons at the far end of the common room.

Enguer was left standing stunned. He had not expected charity from this man and wanted to express his appreciation; however, the moment had passed and he suspected any further conversation would be awkward and unwelcome. Placing the package of food in his pack, Enguer walked out of the inn and summoned the stable boy.

"Are you leaving, sir?"

"For a time," Enguer hoped he could take a chance with this boy. "I need to leave my horse in your care for a few days. When I return, I will pay you double the rate. If I am not back within five days, you may sell it to recover your costs. Will you agree?"

The boy shuffled uncertainly, wiping sweaty hands on the front of his tunic. "I will have to check with my pa."

Enguer displayed his best smile, placing a gentle hand on the stable boy's shoulder. "I'm in a hurry and it would be better if this pact was just between us two men."

Puffing out his chest, the boy took on airs of maturity and spoke in a slightly deeper tone, "Then we are agreed, sir." Deflating slightly and lowering his voice to a whisper, he quickly added, "But please return. I don't want to have to explain to my pa how we came to own a horse."

Enguer almost laughed. 'Not to worry, good man. I will see you again in five days or sooner."

It was a relief that he wouldn't have to drag his horse around the city with nowhere to stay at night. He needed to find Reskalin but had no idea where to start. Perhaps he could ask around for the Fat Man, but that seemed silly. Although most of the people he had seen in Arre were slender, there were bound to be any number of fat men in the city. He decided that, while his food lasted, he would explore the shops, markets, inns and taverns, discretely asking after Reskalin in case anyone knew him. After that, he would be forced to retreat into The Wilds, hunt for more food and collect a few furs and pelts that might be worth a few coppers. He conceded to himself that it wasn't a good plan, but at least it was a plan.

The only thing Enguer really knew about the Arch Priest's brother was that he was somehow associated with the export of goods from Arre. He had no idea what kind of goods they were, but it was enough for him to determine that he should start by asking questions of the local merchants. Maybe one of them would give him more to go on, if not the actual shop or trade office that he worked in.

From what he had observed so far, Arre was a large city with markets of various sizes throughout. Initial inquiries pointed him to the ones located near the north, east and west gates, particularly the one at the east gate closest to the port, as the largest of them. He thought it made sense to start there considering that whatever Reskalin exported would have to go through one of them to exit the city.

Standing at the edge of the east gate market, Enguer was disheartened by the sheer size of it. Rows upon rows of stalls lined broad streets in every direction, clustered in open courts that served as hubs and continued again down narrower alleyways. The ground was level at the lowest level of the city formed by a natural shelf inside the walls where the large crowds could move about freely. If the other markets were anywhere near this size, it could take him weeks to find Reskalin. If he ever could.

Beginning on the south side, Enguer took a deep breath and started his search. He found it easier to go with the flow of the crowd on one side of the street rather than attempting to crisscross and speak to every vendor. He could catch the other side of the street on his way back. Enguer also decided to approach only the local merchants since they were more likely to know Reskalin than the foreign ones. At least he hoped that was the case.

As fast as he could, Enguer weaved through the crowd making brief inquiries with the merchants as he went. Not a one said they knew anyone by the name he sought and it seemed that nearly all of them dabbled in some bit of import and export. By the end of the day Enguer was feeling exhausted and discouraged. It was like looking for a double-capped acorn in the forest. *How long would the men in Courth give him to find Reskalin, anyway? A few days, weeks?* They were not clear on that point. The only thing he had gained in his first day of searching was that the merchants reacted unfavorably to his inquiries. They were all polite in the beginning until he mentioned Reskalin's name. Most appeared unsettled, perhaps even fearful, while others grew angry. Maybe they didn't like the idea of a foreigner asking questions about their fellow citizen. He would ask some of them about a different name the next day to see if there was a different reaction.

That night, Enguer spent the dark hours in a secluded area of a public garden away from the ever-present city patrols. Other than the occasional drunkard or young couple looking for a moment of privacy, Enguer was the only one in the garden with nowhere to go. He guessed that there must be an area of the city where the homeless slept, but he had not come across one yet. The patrols quickly shooed away anyone they found lingering in the garden too long never guessing they were being watched from concealment in the foliage only a few spans away. Enguer had never imagined he would find a use for his skills as a ranger surrounded by a city of thousands.

The next day, Enguer rose before dawn to wash in one of the garden fountains before the city came to life. Even in that early hour he had to pause once to avoid a patrol and then again when an old fellow, probably a baker, strode through the garden whistling on his way to work. Enguer wasn't sure how long this could go on and put his mind to finding a place where he could sleep and wash without running into the bushes every time someone came near.

When the sun came up and the shops began to open for the day, Enguer decided to change the venue of his search. Rather than continue at the vast market near the port, he would try the one near the west gate. It was at least half the size serving travelers that came by road from Anzi up the river and Fela deep in the mountains. It would be easy for Enguer to leave Arre an hour or so before dark and set a camp in the wilderness that he could return to every night without fear of patrols and passersby. It would also be an ideal opportunity to hunt and fish, wash in a stream and set fur traps in the mornings before the markets opened. In a few days he might make enough money to pay the stable boy and in a week maybe treat himself to a soft mat and a little bread and cheese if the traps produced.

Although smaller in scale, the west gate market was much like the one near the port. The reaction of the merchants to Reskalin's name was no different either. Although, oddly, other local names he tried elicited far more natural responses. The only conclusion he could come to was that Reskalin was known to the merchants and either hated or feared by them. Either way, it would only make it all the more difficult to find him.

With the approach of evening, Enguer found himself on the opposite side of the market from the west gate. Initially, he thought it might be faster to traverse the tangle of streets around the market to get to the other side. Unfortunately, shoppers by the hundred were also beginning to flow out of the market and back to their residences in ever-increasing numbers. By the time he reached the west gate it was well after dark and the reinforced double doors where shut tight for the night. Enguer would have to spend another night in the city.

Rather than walk the hour it would take to the garden he slept in the night before, Enguer found another, smaller garden, near the high wall that surrounded Arre. This one had no fountains, but it was not far from the western gate and Enguer had already determined that he would skip the markets the next day and set a proper camp and traps outside the city. He was getting better at understanding how Arre worked which gave him high hopes that he would soon become far more efficient in his search for Reskalin. Getting his horse back would help as well by speeding up the time it took to get from camp to market and back. His plans were improving every day. At least there was that.

Sometime late in the night, Enguer's light slumber was interrupted by the loud clanging of bells from the direction of the west gate. These were not the finely tuned bells often rung from temple towers. These were meant to get one's immediate attention. They had to be gongs of alarm. In short order the bells were swiftly answered by others further away until the entire city was abuzz with bells and lights burning in every window.

Enguer jumped to his feet and carefully replaced the branches concealing his hiding place in case he returned soon. He stopped to watch a man running down the street carrying a spear followed almost immediately by several more. They were all headed in the direction of the western gate. Whatever was happening was happening there. Strapping on his weapon belt, Enguer grabbed his bow and quiver of arrows and used the remaining branches to quickly hide his pack.

In the street, armed men and women were running in increasing numbers. They carried all manner of weapons, mostly spears and short bows, sometimes wearing a bronze helmet and breastplate for protection. Enguer joined them. Closer to the gate soldiers and armed citizens were filling the towers and lining the wall side-by-side, sometimes two ranks deep. There didn't appear to be any effort on the officers' part to dissuade the citizens from joining in the defense, in fact, they marshalled them into positions as if they were regular soldiers. Images flashed across his mind from the burning village. He feared the dragon was attacking Arre and worried that so many men lined up on the wall would be burned to ash where they stood. Enguer ran on toward the gate.

Arriving at the gate, the open space behind it was a study in organized chaos. Men streamed up to the walls or lined up in ranks on either side of the iron-strapped doors leaving a wide space in between. Further back, cavalry units were forming in preparation to charge through the gate. These were professional soldiers fully protected by bronze armor and round shields that glistened in the flicker of torchlight, with short swords at their hip and long iron-tipped spears held at the ready. They looked every bit as impressive and capable as the heavy cavalry that defended Courth.

Unsure of what to do, Enguer followed a group of soldiers up to the wall astride the gate all the while gauging his chances of jumping off again if the dragon appeared. The soldiers moved further down the wall leaving an open space against the crenellations that he quickly filled. Behind him men were yelling and running – a beehive of activity – that contrasted sharply to what lay beyond the wall. The wide-open space in front of the western gate was completely clear. Nothing moved in the circles of light cast by iron braziers set high in the stone towers on each side. Dozens of flaming arrows littered the ground creating their own small circles of illumination thirty paces out and still nothing moved. Enguer glanced over at the man standing next to him, he was an officer, perhaps a captain, and he stood desperately peering into the darkness as if expecting . . .something.

"What is it?" Enguer whispered.

The captain kept his gaze outward, lifting a hand for quiet. "Orks."

For a moment Enguer was relieved. Not a dragon. But orks? Another creature from legend that his father had long ago recounted stories about. They were an invention of the Tuatha De, designed to serve as laborers in their mines. Like so many others, the orks were banished to Fomoire after The Breaking, but they were an intelligent species with a talent for hiding. Like rats they scurried into the depths of the Underdark disappearing in the leagues of tunnels and caverns that they knew so well. Out of reach of the Tuatha De, the orks eventually formed small tribal communities in the mountainous regions scattered throughout The Wilds, developed their own language and it is said; their own gods.

"There!" the captain shouted to his men urgently. He was pointing to a circle of flickering light cast by a fire arrow less than a stone's throw from the wall.

Enguer strained to detect what the captain had seen and seconds later was rewarded by sight of a faint shadow of movement at the edge of the dim illumination. The captain must have had exceptional eyes to catch it. Fire arrows shot overhead from the gate tower and landed in the spot where Enguer had seen the mysterious activity. They lit-up the area revealing a cluster of the most revolting creatures he had ever set his eyes upon.

For what felt like an eternity there was a collective pause as the shock of what the dim illumination revealed out of the silent darkness. The creatures stood erect like men, walked like men, wore dirty leather armor and boots like men, carried shield and spear like men – but that is where the similarities ended. Enguer's heart jumped. They looked too much like the Lukánthropos and for a wild second he thought maybe the captain was mistaken. Their lean, muscular forms were covered in short bristly brown fur interrupted by pink snouts and ears that poked out from under bronze and leather open-faced helms where black eyes reflected the light from the fires. Four of them stood in awkward throwing stances, their claw-like hands releasing well-crafted iron-tipped spears into the air that appeared to Enguer far too short and heavy to be effective range weapons. They clattered harmlessly against the stone wall, never achieving an appropriate arc to bring them anywhere near the height required to pose a threat.

It was enough to break the spell.

Immediately, the spears were answered by a hail of arrows from across the long span of the wall. Dozens found their mark, peppering the orks with a rain of deadly shafts that left them convulsing in the mud. A roar of cheers rose from hundreds of citizens and soldiers, men and women slapped each other's backs in congratulations and laughter steeped in mockery echoed over the wall.

"Something is not right," the captain muttered worriedly. "We have never been so boldly attacked by the orks. A merchant caravan or outlying village is rare enough. Why would they attack the city walls?"

Enguer didn't know anything about ork battle tactics, he could only relate how pack animals hunted in The Wilds. Not the typical pack of dogs or gangs of giant rodents. They overwhelmed their prey by force of numbers. It was the more intelligent pack predators like dire wolves and the reclusive goblins and faery folk that used strategy and tactics to overcome their quarry.

The entire area within fifty spans of the west gate was suddenly flooded with magical light globes hanging in the air revealing dozens of small clusters of spear-wielding orks slowly approaching the wall.

"Tivr protect us," the captain hissed at the sight of them. "This is nothing more than a distraction." Turning to look at Enguer for the first time, the captain's eyes were wide with fear. "The real attack is somewhere else."

Chapter 15

Orks

Clouds of arrows flew from the walls of Arre leaving guttural cries of death and barks of injury in their wake. The orks retreated to the edge of the magical light where the darkness would shield them, abandoning their wounded comrades to crawl through the sludge or die on their own. The few spears they managed to launch in their hasty withdrawal fell hopelessly short of the wall.

"How can you be sure the attack is a distraction?" Enguer was troubled by what he witnessed as much as the idea that the orks would sacrifice themselves like this.

The captain gestured across the field of carnage beyond the wall. "How many ladders do you see? How many battering rams to force open our doors? And those spears they carry were never designed for throwing."

It was so obvious, Enguer was almost embarrassed. A horn blared from the courtyard behind him and the colossal iron-strapped doors that hung between the towers of the west gate opened outward with a bang. Without hesitation, a long column of cavalry, five across, charged through with their long spears level and thirsting for blood. Cloaked figures bearing no weapons that Enguer could see, rode in the center of the column holding raised fists in the air bathed with light. When they neared the edge of illumination, light burst forth to illuminate several spans further into the darkness that camouflaged the waiting groups of orks. Barely through the gate, the cavalry skillfully separated into two groups ten deep and stampeded into orks on the right and left.

The waves of horse and men broke over the smaller groups of orks sending them scattering to one side or the other if not trampled under the sharp hooves and piercing spears of the charging cavalry. At first, it appeared as if the orks would run away, but they quickly regrouped around the edges of the magical light flicking out their heavy spears from the shadows impaling horse and man indiscriminately. Within moments the cavalry formations collapsed into small knots of mounted soldiers skirmishing with shield and sword against the longer reach of the orks heavy spears.

"This is exactly what they wanted," the captain looked on horrified.

Then a powerful bellow reached Enguer's ears from the inner courtyard, "Swords and spears to me!"

Straightaway soldiers and armed citizens came off the wall to assemble around an impressive-looking officer wearing bronze armor from head to toe with a high red plume of feathers sprouting from the top of his open-faced helm. Officers under his command hastily formed the men and women into ranks with those carrying shields placed along the outside of the formation and the professional soldiers up front. After only a matter of moments the plumed officer was leading his company at double-time out the gate to support the cavalry.

Enguer raised his bow and took aim at an ork across the field, but before he could put his arrow in flight, the captain grabbed his arm. "Careful boy," he growled. "You might miss and hit one of our own."

Not lowering his bow, Enguer looked the captain dead in the eye, "I won't miss."

After a moment of hesitation, the captain nodded and then shouted to the remaining bowmen on the wall, "Choose your shots carefully!"

Enguer sent his first shot screaming toward an unaware ork and dropped him dead at one-hundred paces.

"Nice shot," the captain praised

Slowly, the archers followed his lead, most taking safe shots at orks in plain view and close by with little chance of injuring their own countryman. Enguer held no such hesitation. The bow was an extension of his arms and the arrows an extension of his eye. Everywhere he found orks threatening to overwhelm a cavalry unit, he left the beasts drowning in their own blood even if he had to thread the shot between his flailing allies to save them.

A roar erupted from the field below and Enguer watched the plumed officer charge into the heaviest concentration of orks on the north side of the main road. Another group charged to the south side while a third group charged straight ahead. Pretty soon, mounted and unmounted men and women fought side-by side against the orks who had dropped their spears to fight savagely with swords and axes of their own. The swirl of bodies made the shots harder and less frequent, still Enguer found the throat or eye socket of an ork as often as the opportunity presented.

Once the melee entered the fray the battle crumbled quickly for the orks and soon they were retreating into the forested hills that backed-up to the higher elevations of the Spine of Cell. Cheers rippled through the Arre combatants. Enguer had no qualms about skewering the creatures through the back when they ran knowing well that they would have held no mercy for him or the innocents in Arre. The soldiers, in their bloodlust, would have chased the orks into the forest if not held back by their commanders leaving Enguer to wonder what would have become of him had he set up his camp in the wilderness outside the city as he planned.

"What's your name, boy?" the captain sagged wearily against the side of the tower.

"I am Enguer Rand, from Courth."

The captain nodded. "My name is Captain Tineus, commander of the west gate guard. Is your skill with a bow common in Courth?"

Enguer laughed. "Actually, Captain Tineus, we are known for our heavy cavalry. It's mostly the rangers who favor the bow."

"So, you're a ranger then?"

"I am, sir."

"Never met a ranger before," the captain held out his hand. "Never knew anyone that could shoot the way you do either."

Enguer clasped Captain Tineus' forearm in the traditional Rasna greeting. "Thank you, captain."

"Where are you staying?"

Enguer hesitated and then decided to tell the captain the truth. They were brothers in arms now and it didn't feel right to lie. "A bush in a garden a few blocks south of here."

The captain laughed and shook his head, "I'll leave word at the barracks on the west side to give you a mat and hot meals for as long as you are in Arre. It's the least I can do for all the lives you saved out there."

"Thank you, captain," Enguer smiled appreciatively. "Will the orks return tonight?"

"Not likely, but I believe the dark truth of why they were here will be revealed by tomorrow morning."

~~~

Enguer hardly had the chance to sleep the rest of the night. As promised, the captain arranged a mat for him at the barracks and apparently mentioned how Enguer had saved the lives of several soldiers by killing a score of orks from a distance. Enguer hadn't kept count. Somehow, the soldiers returning to the barracks during the night all heard the tale and kept him up swapping stories of the battle over several cups of ale. Those he had not counted either and before long his head was pounding for it.

Rising with the call to break the fast with the other soldiers, Enguer sat with many of them at one of the long tables where they dined. Like himself, the soldiers were exhausted from the night before and a heavy pall loomed over their quiet conversations often invoking the name of a friend or fellow who had lost their life in the battle. It reminded Enguer of the Courth soldiers in the aftermath of the battles with the Lukánthropos.

"You are here." Captain Tineus sat opposite of Enguer with a plate of cheese and fruit.

"Good morning, Captain." Enguer supplied a quick nod. "Thank you again for the accommodations, it was a relief to enjoy the camaraderie with your men rather than hiding from them in the garden."

The captain chuckled, "Well, let's not let it get out that you are an outlaw."

"Have you heard anything more about what you suspected with the orks?"

Captain Tineus countenance turned serious and he punched the cheese wedge on his plate with his knife, "We lost thirty soldiers and civilians last night. Mostly cavalry. A few horses."

"That's regrettable," Enguer tried to sympathize. He understood the bond between warriors and all that but his views had been shaped from an early age on the survival of the fittest, the balance of nature . . . death as a natural occurrence in life. Of course, he was a hypocrite. It was easy to apply those high ideals to others. Not so easy to himself and the memories of the ones he loved.

"It is not for them I ply this somber tone. They were soldiers and soldiers know the risks and gladly accepted them. It is for the others that I mourn."

Enguer didn't understand. Something else had happened. "The others?"

Captain Tineus push his plate aside untouched and rubbed his blood-shot eyes. "The orks destroyed three villages along the Bodin River last night. Burned them to the ground killing everyone, every innocent life they came upon. Only a handful escaped to tell the tell. Over seven-hundred souls between them lost in a single night."

Enguer could hardly believe it. The number was shocking.

The captain slammed his fist on the table, knocking the plate with fruit and cheese on the floor. No one was surprised as he already had every one's rapt attention. "This climbs to the level of war!"

Soldiers around the room shouted their agreement, anger filling their hearts with hatred and the desire for retribution. The look was plain on every face. If an ork walked into the room right then, the creature would have been torn to bits. It was a dark turn their conversation had taken and although Enguer liked the captain and the soldiers he had met, he had no desire to be dragged into someone else's war.

Angry cries for vengeance filled the room nearly drowning out the sharp resonance of a horn from the courtyard outside. Reluctantly, the soldiers picked up their shields, buckled on their sword belts and filed outside grumbling the whole way. The captain didn't flinch.

"What will happen next?" Enguer gently prodded. The last thing he wanted was to turn the captain's anger on himself.

Surprisingly, Captain Tineus' reply was calm and controlled, "The Zilach will announce today that the city is committed to eradicating the ork threat once and for all. To that end he is calling on any person or group, citizen or no, to track down the source of these foul beasts. In the meantime, he is sending adversaries to Pluthi to request support from the Lauchme and an army to march on the orks lair once it is found." The captain looked up from where the plate once sat and deliberately held Enguer's eyes with his. "Sounds like a good job for a ranger. The first part, I mean."

This was what Enguer feared as soon as the captain started speaking. How could he tell Captain Tineus he was in the city for another reason and that the lives of his friends depended upon him completing his task. How did their lives compare to the villagers that died the night before or those that would die in the future if the orks were not found? Enguer felt confident he could find them. It would be easy for a ranger to follow the tracks of a hundred or more orks anywhere. Would it be so easy for anyone in Arre?

Maybe he could do both. "Where would I sign up for such an expedition?"

~~~

Enguer stood staring over a wide white marble stairway that terminated at a massive platform where tall columns flanked the entry to the expansive government building set only a few paces outside the palace complex. This was where Captain Tineus had directed him to find out how to join the expedition to track down the orks. He scaled the steps two at a time, enthusiasm at the prospect for a new adventure coursing through his veins. When he reached the top, he stopped short. Through the open iron-studded wooden doors that reached nearly the height of the columns a mass of humanity swirled around white-haired balding men dressed in long beige robes with wide sachets hanging from their necks. Each of the sachets differed in color and style, with block-like symbols running their length that Enguer could only guess indicated rank, position or academic specialty. These would be the city Elders, according to Tineus's description, the closest advisors to the Zilach and tasked with the challenge of forming the expedition.

Many of the men and women that surrounded the Elders looked familiar to Enguer. Not that he knew any of them, but their dress and mannerisms easily identified them as hunters, trackers, soldiers and explorers. He expected that he looked much the same to them.

Entering the building, Enguer was further amazed that he was standing at the threshold of a wide, open-air courtyard filled with fountains, statuary, trees and hedges surrounded by three stories of columned hallways lined with doors. Had there not been so many people filling the space, Enguer was sure he would have appreciated the beauty of it all. However, he was not here to admire the Rasna architecture and landscaping; he needed to find a way to speak with one of the Elders.

He strode through the room making an effort to push through the crowd without offending anyone, but he couldn't get close enough to hear what the Elders were saying over the din of voices. After a few curses and rough elbows, Enguer made his way to the edge of the courtyard where he could breathe and found an empty bench to rest. Perhaps after a while the crowd would diminish and he would find an opening. It was turning out to be a frustrating experience that he worried he might regret. Still, he had to admire the passion the people of Arre demonstrated to defend their city and avenge their countrymen that had fallen to the ork raid. The people of Courth would be no less incensed, as he had witnessed during the hateful days the Lukánthropos had terrorized them, but they expected King Francik and his soldiers to deal with them rather than take up arms themselves. Watching the stern faces of men and women, noble and commoner standing side by side in the press around the Elders, there was no doubt in Enguer's mind that Rasna was a true warrior society. He was glad that Courth was named among their friends if this was the excitement and fervor with which they pursued their enemies.

From somewhere down a narrow hallway behind him, Enguer detected the sound of children laughing. It was an innocent, delightful sound that gave him pause. Listening closer, the laughter was accompanied by the deep, steady intonation of a man, as if he were telling a story. Intrigued, Enguer followed the sound down the hall and into a small courtyard occupied by a grey-haired Elder sitting on a bench surrounded by a clutch of a dozen small children.

"… pointy ears, slanted eyes blue as the waters of the Bodin and hair the color of icicles glistening in the sunlight!"

The children laughed.

"It's true, I say! He was an elf from Avalon on the Emerald Isle a long way away and no truer friend did I ever have!" The Elder's tone lowered to almost a whisper and he leaned in closer to the children, "Do you want to know a secret about the elves?"

"Yes!" the children shouted.

"They live a long time. Two hundred years and more!"

Wide eyed and excited, the children responded with 'oooh's and aaah's'

"And I bet you would never guess his name."

"Tree-face!' a little girl shouted from the front.

"Ha-ha!" the Elder laughed. "I will have to tell him that the next time we meet! The elves have very unusual names. My friend is called ArteliThalozin, can you say it?"

The jumble of words that the young voices tried to repeat made Enguer laugh, drawing a quick glance from the Elder. The man did not appear annoyed at Enguer's presence, but there was something that lingered on his face that might have been sadness or regret. Feeling as if he had intruded, Enguer turned to leave.

Maintaining his gaze on his audience, the Elder thrust a hand out in his direction, "Wait," he commanded sternly and then spoke again to the children in a kindly tone, "Practice the name, I know it's difficult, and we will meet again tomorrow. I have a story about an ugly dwarf with warts on his nose you will not want to miss!"

The children erupted in cheers and ran down another side corridor leaving the echo of laughter in their wake. Enguer watched them go and then returned his attention to the Elder. To his surprise, the old man was staring back at him intently. The sachet he wore was somehow different than the other Elders. It was blood red with the image of a clenched fist holding a sword enveloped with fire on one side and a tree on the other with only a few of the blocky symbols the Rasna use in their writing.

"I didn't mean to interrupt . . ." Enguer began.

"I knew your father."

Enguer's stared in disbelief. How could this man know anything about him? "What?"

"Gaurin Rand, your father. I was saddened to hear of his passing."

"How . . . How could you possibly know he was my father?"

The Elder smiled and waved for Enguer to sit with him on the bench. "You are obviously from Courth and the spitting image of Gaurin when he was your age. When I first saw you, I thought I might be seeing his spirit or becoming delusional in my old age. But then I realized that you have your mother's eyes." He laughed and tapped the side of his head. "It takes a little longer to puzzle things out than it used to."

Amazing. All that had gone on in the Elder's head in the space of a brief glance? Enguer doubted his was nearly as quick witted at less than half the Elder's age. "How did you know my father?"

"My name is Borath Mecrulican. Your father and I, among others, travelled together for some time. We became close friends."

Enguer sat on the bench with Borath leaving a wide space between. Only then did he realize how much larger than he the Elder was. The layers of his robes and the sachet did well to conceal his broad chest and thick neck revealing just his heavily muscled forearms to hint at the rest. "I'm sorry, I don't recall that he ever mentioned you."

"It's not surprising," Borath frowned slightly. "We all did our best to put our past behind us when we finally settled. I knew about you," his features brightened. "Gaurin was so happy when you were born. I came to visit once soon after. Sadly, we lost contact after your mother passed."

"Our lives change quite a bit after mother died," Enguer nodded. "My father spent the last of his days training me in the only craft he knew."

"A ranger, then? Be glad for that. Gaurin was the best. You couldn't have asked for a better mentor."

"So I have heard," Enguer chuckled.

"What brings you to Arre, young Enguer? Did you inherit Gaurin's yearning to wander?"

"In part," Enguer had just met Borath, yet he felt like he could trust him and if anyone could help find Tanais brother . . . it was worth a shot. "But I have an obligation to perform first. An old friend of my father's, the Arch Priest Tanais of Courth, recently died . . ."

"Tanais is dead?" the Elder looked shocked.

"You knew of him?"

Borath sighed deeply, "He was another that travelled with your father and I. How did he die?"

Enguer told the Elder about the Lukánthropos and all the events leading up to their defeat. "Now I am here in Arre to track down his brother, Reskalin, and inform him of Arch Priest Tanais passing."

Confusion washed over Borath's features, "His *brother*, Reskalin?"

"Yes, do you know him?" Enguer didn't understand the Elder's reaction. Had he not been clear with the details of his story?

"Reskalin works for a notorious figure here in Arre known as The Fat Man. Their business activities are what most would consider questionable. Forget Reskalin. Reskalin is a dangerous person to be associated with in Arre. I have no doubt that Reskalin has already been informed of Tanais death by the Fat Man."

"You don't understand," Enguer tried to be careful not to come off as pleading. "The Arch Priest entrusted me with personal information he wanted his brother to know in case he died. It is urgent that I speak with Reskalin myself."

"Urgent, you say?" Borath held him with a skeptical gaze. "I will see what I can do. Where are you staying?"

"The west gate barracks. I was of some assistance to Captain Tineus when the orks attacked and he has been most gracious to offer me a bed and meals while I am in Arre."

A smile cracked the Elder's face shifting the dark mood. "Captain Tineus. A very competent soldier that cares for his men. Is that how you came to find me here? Are you planning to sign up for this fool expedition to search for the orks?"

"I had considered the idea," Enguer was hesitant in his reply. "A ranger might be helpful in this endeavor don't you think?"

"Just this morning I counselled the Zilach against issuing a decree offering one-thousand gold coins to anyone that could find the ork's lair." Borath stood and paced to the other side of the courtyard. "My advice was not to endanger the lives of hundreds of good men and women by sending them into The Wilds with no practical experience with what they would be getting into. My people are proud and resourceful under command. I would pit them against any standing army in the Western Kingdoms! But The Wilds?" He flung his hands in the air. "The Wilds would eat them alive before they ever found an ork. And even if they had the talent or dumb luck to find the orks lair then what?"

Borath sat down heavily on the bench, exasperated. "The Zilach thinks he can send an army into The Wilds and wipe them out. Orks live in vast subterranean complexes with defenses we cannot begin to imagine. Do we invade or siege? How many exits does it have? How many orks for that matter? It would be better for Arre if we strengthen our defenses, triple the patrols and outposts making it so costly for the orks to attack us that they move on."

"Haven't the orks always been a problem?" Enguer was familiar with tales of orks raiding villages and fighting with goblin tribes in The Wilds. They were faraway events that he hadn't thought much about. As far as he knew, no ork had ever been seen near Courth.

The Elder shrugged, "Here and there. Nothing like the raid last night on the villages and never against Arre. Something is driving them to attack us far more vigorously lately. Almost as if they were probing our strengths and weaknesses, how fast we react, preparing for something much bigger to come. I hear that the city of Provigi, in northern Tarre, is experiencing much the same."

"I've lived most of my life in The Wilds," Enguer spoke quietly. "I know how to survive the worst it has to offer. If I can help by locating the orks lair and perhaps gain some idea about why they are attacking human settlements, perhaps that will reveal more options for the Zilach to consider. Pushing them off of Rasna will only send them north to Tarre or somewhere else and more people will die."

Sniffing loudly, Borath stood and placed a hand on Enguer's shoulder. "Just like your father, always trying to save the world. If you are determined, then I will tell the Zilach we have a ranger from Courth willing to take up the charge. That should be enough for him to postpone the expedition if only for a few weeks. At least it's a chance."

Enguer stood to face Borath eye to eye. "I would like to speak to Reskalin before I leave. Will you arrange it?"

Closing his eyes a moment as if seeking inner guidance, the Elder nodded slightly. "I will promise to make sure Reskalin is aware you wish to speak about Tanais, but I cannot promise Reskalin will reach out to you."

"Fair enough," Enguer agreed.

"One more thing," Borath searched the folds of his robes and produced a bland metal ring. "Take this, it will improve your chances out there."

"What is it?"

Smiling slyly, Borath placed the ring on his finger and immediately vanished. Enguer couldn't believe his eyes. Where had he gone? There was movement from behind and a quick tap on his shoulder causing Enguer to spin around swiftly. There stood Borath, ring in hand, a big smile on his face.

"The ring will hide your form but not your sound or scent. It has come in handy from time to time. I suggest you practice with it a bit before you bet your life on it."

Enguer carefully took the ring and looked it over closely. There was nothing remarkable about it at all. He pushed it over his finger and gasped when his physical form disappeared. He took it off and he was there again.

"Understand, I am loaning this bauble to you. I expect that you will return it to me when you get back. It is a debt you owe me and I will not accept your death as excuse for default." Borath was still smiling but his eyes were deadly serious.

Enguer shuddered. In that moment he had no doubt Borath Mecrulican would drag him from the depths of hell to repay his debt.

Chapter 16

Reskalin

A crisp chill flowed off the Spine of Cell whipping lines hung with clothing that dried on balconies, buffeting ladies' long decorated robes sometimes baring fine legs lean from walking and tossing the colorful capes of the men that accompanied them under a canvas of stars. It was the time of evening when couples, families and lovers strode the shops and taverns meeting friends for a meal or speaking intimately in the darker shadows of the public gardens. Occasionally, a mounted patrol casually swept by, red caps fluttering dramatically in their wake, bronze armor clinking in time with the cadence of their hooves. Enguer was beginning to appreciate the passionate nature of the Rasna people. Whether in love or at war, their ardent loyalty to family and fellow citizen where virtues to be admired.

A cart rumbled through a small crowd of people sending Enguer scurrying out of the way. He accidentally brushed by a man close enough to put him off balance resulting in a confused glare directed at no one in particular. Enguer ducked into an alley to get off the street. Maybe it wasn't such a good idea to try out his new ring during the peak of the evening. Moving down the narrow backstreet, he stepped into a niche next to a doorway. Before he could remove the ring, the door slammed open and a heavy brute of a man dressed in fine robes embellished by gold necklaces and rings on thick fingers stumbled into the alley and turned to face the niche where Enguer was hiding. The man fumbled with the layers beneath the belt that cinched his robes and exposed the length of his manhood held loosely in one hand. Enguer was so stunned by the action that he scarcely dodged the stream of urine that splattered on the wall where he had been standing. The sound of Enguer's quick movement interrupted the man's steady concentration and he cast his wobbly gaze up and down the lane with only a minor disruption to the task at hand.

Enguer wanted to slap the man in the back of his balding head. Why was this fool pissing on the side of the wall in a city that boasted a fully modern sewer system? He stood silently against the opposite wall fuming while he moderated his breathing all the while hopeful that the distant commotion from the street might help conceal his presence. Enguer found moving quietly in the city far more challenging than when he was in The Wilds. There, he knew the sounds that attracted attention, how to move through the foliage and over branches and leaves without leaving a trace or causing a stir.

The man completed his business and staggered back through the door. The faint sounds of music and conversation from somewhere deep inside cut short with the slam of the door. Enguer exhaled a breath of relief and was just about to remove the ring a second time when a soft noise up the alley caught his attention. It sounded something like the sweep of fabric or scuff of a boot. He couldn't be sure. Rats and cats were common in cities, although he couldn't recall seeing either in Arre since he arrived. The lane was dark with only the faintest illumination from the narrow stretch of stars visible between the buildings for light. It was barely enough to make out the dark outlines of crates and barrels against the walls and the dim outline of doorways on brief landings between short flights of stairs.

Another faint scuff broke the silence of the darkness. Enguer was sure it had to be a footfall this time. As quietly as he could manage, he crept along the wall to the first short set of steps and peered into the shallow alcoves that held the doors on each side of the landing. Both were closed tight with not a glimmer of light escaping the space above the doorstep. Slowly, he climbed the stairs and crossed the landing to the next short stairway. The landing was similar to the one where he stood except there was a crate next to the door with something draped over or on it. It was too dark to tell. He paused to listen. Nothing.

"You must be daft," a throaty voice, smooth and soothing could have been a man or a woman and it was stained with amusement making no effort to remain faithful to the quiet stillness. It spoke from nowhere, out of the darkness only steps in front of him.

Enguer froze. Could it be addressing him? Enguer glanced down at the first step that held his foot, but his foot, nor any other part of him was visible. The ring had not failed. He waited to find out who the voice was speaking to. There had to be someone else further up.

"I know you are there," the voice taunted him. "Have no fear, whatever device you use to conceal yourself works, but you stomp around loud enough to keep the dead from eternal sleep."

The form on the crate slowly rose until it took the vague outline of a cloaked figure standing almost close enough for him to touch. Enguer sprang backward down the steps nearly falling in the process and drew his sword. What was this creature that spoke with a human voice and could hear with the acuteness of a bat? Or was it magic? Enguer had already experience far too much not to believe that this thing was something other than a creature of dark legends. Perhaps a ghoul that roamed the streets at night feeding on lonely passersby or a doppelganger that could take the form of another, collecting their dead victim's organs to revitalize their own. Children's stories. They were all children's stories until they became real.

And that had been happening all too often of late.

"Put your sword away, Enguer. It is *you* that has been looking for *me*." The figure spread hands apart that appeared human enough, as well as he could see them anyhow. "I am here."

It knew his name. Enguer decided it must be a man, short and slight by the shape of his form. "How do you know me? How is it possible for you to see me? Are you a sorcerer?"

Soft laughter trickled down the stairway to tickle Enguer's ears. This was a professional that knew how to speak in a way that didn't carry farther than intended. It was a skill that he too was adept at in the wilderness.

"First, I am not a sorcerer. Far from it. And in my line of business, you are careful not to trust your eyes at the expense of all your other senses." The man took a step down the short stair way. Cautiously, as if approaching a wild animal. "For example, I can smell the smoke that lingers in your hair. Have you been sleeping next to a campfire or hearth? And the way you move is unusual for a city dweller. You seem to know instinctively how to step softly without the benefit of experience on cobbled pavers and gravel typical of an urban environment. There are other things as well, but I won't bore you with the details."

Extraordinary, thought Enguer. If this fellow was not a sorcerer, then he was as skilled in the city as Enguer was in The Wilds. Maybe that was it. The city was his wilderness. He must be footpad or assassin.

"Have you been sent by Gigot and Dyzig?" Enguer growled. "Have they run out of patience so soon?"

The laugh came again, more forceful this time as if what he had said was truly comical, and then it abruptly stopped. "Those fools can barely run the underground of a city as docile as Courth. You know what their secret is, yes?"

"Secret?" Enguer let himself relax a little bit.

"They call themselves brothers, but the truth is they are lovers. Everyone knows it, even their own. I don't know why they pretend otherwise. Anyway, they care far more about their own comfortable lifestyle than a gullible ranger."

"Gullible! I *am not* gullible." Enguer was becoming irritated by this little man. "They threatened to hurt my friends if I didn't come to Arre with a message for someone. I assure you; they were very serious about it."

"Gigot is quite the actor. Or is it Dyzig? I can never get the two straight." Enguer had the distinct impression that the man was smiling at him. "I assure *you*; the threat was an empty one. King Francik would have turned Courth upside down if anything untoward would have happened to his precious Commanders Suri and Durant." The man took another slow step down. "Gigot and Dyzig compelled you to come because I asked them to."

This was a baffling turn of events. Who was this man that wanted Enguer to personally come to Arre? "Then you know the man I am looking for? You know Reskalin?"

"Did you miss the part earlier when I said 'I am here'?"

"*You* are Reskalin?"

"You are not turning out to be the clever ranger I was led to believe you were." Reskalin's voice dripped with sarcasm.

Enguer had enough. He sheathed his sword and removed the ring from his finger. "You have no idea what I have gone through since I was sent on this folly! I've been nearly roasted by a dragon and then chased out of a village by a mob for murder, had all my money swindled from me the first night in Arre and battled orks defending your city!" Enguer tried to calm himself. "Now here you are. Do you even care to know anything about your brother or was that just a preface to something else as well?"

"Quite the adventure," Reskalin took the last step to the landing bringing him within a stride of Enguer. His face was obscured in the shadow of a hood that revealed only his thin lips and narrow chin. "And no, it was not a pretense. I loved Tanais. And I hated him. It's a long story. In any case, why don't you come with me, there is someone else that wishes to hear your tale and I'm sure you would prefer not to tell it twice."

"Where are we going?" Enguer felt a little trepidation at the idea of going anywhere with Reskalin considering everything he had learned.

"To see someone who knew Tanais even better than I. He will be very grateful if you came with me and in this city his gratitude is worth his weight in gold."

The smile on Reskalin's face appeared genuine as far as appearances went with this man and Enguer decided to take the chance. Although he wondered if he really had a choice in the matter. "Very well, Reskalin, I will go with you."

"I thought you might." Without turning, Reskalin rapped lightly on the door adjacent the landing and in response it opened silently inward to a dark interior with not the slightest source of light for guidance. "Follow me. I will step loud enough for you to keep yourself oriented. There will be precious little light before we find our destination."

Enguer followed Reskalin through the murky entryway doing his best to focus on the sounds around him. It was an exercise he had put into practice on numerous occasions in The Wilds and the challenge of it was diminished further by Reskalin's continual chatter. "So, tell me more about how your money was swindled from you . . ."

~~~

Twists and turns, descending and ascending stairways in the darkness and on occasion the feeling that they were doubling back finally brought them to a dim hall where they stood facing a plain-looking wooden door. Enguer had no idea where they were in the city and he supposed that was the whole point. There was one torch in the short corridor, the first bit of light since they had left the alleyway, and it illuminated dozens of small holes drilled in the walls, the ceiling and even the floor. Enguer had the uneasy feeling that they were being watched and would have bet all he had left in the world that the holes were precisely wide enough to accommodate a bolt from a crossbow. He waited for Reskalin to knock on the door, but he made no move to do so and instead waited patiently for whatever would happen next.

"Waiting a moment for our eyes to adjust," Reskalin must have sensed Enguer's uncertainty. "He hates it when we come in squinting like rats."

A tiny bell rang from somewhere behind the wall and Reskalin immediately opened the door exposing the backside of heavy dark fabric hung over the other side. Not hesitating, Reskalin walked through a split that appeared in the center and Enguer followed. Inside, a large room was awash with illumination from light-globes and candles that flickered upon their entrance. The décor was opulent with lavish furnishings, the finest cut furs on the floor, gilded sconces and hanging tapestries. Enguer's eye was drawn to a long table at the center surrounded by vacant dining chairs and set with elaborate candelabras and a sea of food representing an array of cuisines he could only guess at.

At the far end of the table sat the chamber's lone occupant in a plush chair with one leg flung casually over its padded arm and a jewel encrusted gold goblet held lazily in one hand. The finery of his long tunic and robes adorned with jewels and ermine fur accompanied by a mound of gold necklaces and chunky rings with more jewels must have rivaled the costume of the most flamboyant king. All of it grossly distracted from the elderly man, tall and morbidly obese, that sat amongst all the finery tossing grapes into his mouth, grinning like an idiot.

Wrenching Enguer's attention away from the incredulous scene, he watched as Reskalin addressed the man with a formal bow, "Greetings o' wise and Benevolent Overseer of the Seven Stars Brotherhood, Master of the Sewer Rats and Benefactor of the Sassy Ladies, I present to you our honored guest Enguer Rand, Tracker and Ranger from Courth." Not skipping a breath, Reskalin turned and formally addressed Enguer, "You are now in the presence of the Fat Man."

Enguer somehow managed to withhold the bark of laughter that begged to escape his chest. Surely this was some kind of joke. How could this foolish-looking man be the most powerful guild master in the Western Kingdoms? If his father had ever taught him anything it was never to presume, so Enguer went along and bowed gratefully to the Fat Man. "It is my honor to meet you."

"Likewise, Enguer Rand, son of Gaurin Rand!" the FatMan was jubilant in his greeting, like a drunkard in a tavern. "Sit, sit. Both of you! My table is abundant with many of my personal favorites. Please try them all!" He paused and then pointed one pudgy finger at a bowl of figs, "Except those. Don't touch those! They are reserved for my less-welcome guests."

Reskalin gave Enguer a reassuring nod and they both sat down on opposite sides of the table next to the FatMan. Furtive movement from around the room revealed several servants emerging from behind tapestries with flasks of ale, wine and water. A tall cup of each one was set in front of them along with a stack of large round platters and eating utensils. The servants wore plain long-sleeve tunics, breaches and soft boots that barely made a sound on the expensive rugs and furs that lay half-hazard around the room. Most remarkably, they all carried at least two long daggers at their waists and Enguer was sure he spied shorter blades tucked under their sleeves. If the servants were armed then there was likely a dozen or more guards behind tapestries and shadowy hallways nearby. The Fat Man was certainly taking his security seriously.

Reskalin stood and walked the length of the table filling his plate with delicacies all the while chatting casually with the Fat Man about the weather, what the merchants were selling and the latest gossip. Not a trace of the previous formality remained. Enguer was not very hungry, but he followed Reskalin's lead and placed a few items on his plate that looked promising. When they returned to their seats the light conversation continued while they ate. The food was delicious and after he had cleaned his plate Reskalin motioned for him to take more. Enguer did so gladly. The little that he started with had opened his appetite and he piled the platter high determined not to make the same mistake twice.

When they finished eating, the Fat Man called for a servant to bring the after-dinner wine and a few moments later Enguer was presented with a mug full of a silky red wine. It had a familiar scent and flavor that reminded him of the wine he had enjoyed at King Francik's table a few weeks before.

On their second cup, Reskalin's took on a more serious tone, "Enguer, it is time for us to hear what you have come all this way to tell us about Tanais and the circumstances of his death."

The Fat Man continued with his lazy posture in the chair, but his eyes were focused and intent on what *he* had to say. Enguer held nothing back, describing his encounter with the Arch Priest at his home, how they had captured the dark priest Rochette and his transformation that resulted in the Arch Priest's death. Neither the Fat Man nor Reskalin showed any emotion, even at the end, but Enguer could see the sadness that tinted their eyes. There were deeper connections with these two that he knew nothing about and doubted he ever would.

They asked Enguer several questions about Tanais, some of which he could provide answers and many more he could not. He wasn't sure they realized how short a time he had spent with Tanais before his death and that he was less a confidant than he was an observer of the events that had transpired involving the Arch Priest. Finally, Enguer parlayed how the Lukánthropos were eventually defeated and the commanders concerns over the possibility that one or more may have escaped the burning caverns.

After several hours and a complete retelling that was beginning to feel like an interrogation, the FatMan nodded to Reskalin.

"You have served us well, Enguer, and for that you will be properly rewarded," Reskalin withdrew a pouch from inside his cloak and tossed it over.

Enguer caught it and placed it on the table in front of him, the plate of crumbs long since removed. "Is that it then? May I go about my business without reprisal in Courth or anywhere else?"

"There is one thing," the Fat Man shifted his weight causing the layers of necklaces to ripple across his chest. "We understand that you intend to seek out the orks and that Borath has cleared the way with the Zilach."

"Yes," Enguer was unsure of where this was going. These people seemed to know everything. "I volunteered to help the city and keep the Zilach from encouraging hundreds to go into The Wilds to a certain death."

The Fat Man pat the air in front of him, "That's all fine and well. We won't keep you from your desire to oblige your conscience. But here's the thing; Tanais spoke highly of you, told us how your skills were nearly a match to your father's and would probably far exceed them one day. It would be more than a little impressive if it were true. Your father was exceptional in many ways."

"Did you know him?" Enguer would be surprised if his father knew someone like the Fat Man or Reskalin. Most of what these two men were involved in would likely not align with his principles.

The Fat Man glanced at Reskalin who sat impassively giving no outward sign of his interest in the conversation either way. "That is a story for another time. Perhaps we can pick up on that when you return from your journey."

Enguer rose from his chair and bowed to the Fat Man, "Well, thank you for the grand feast and fine wine," he held up the pouch, "and your generosity."

"Sit down, Enguer, we're not done yet," the Fat Man chided, although there was more humor in the tone than irritation.

Enguer sank back into the chair. He was tired, a little drunk and ready to find a bed.

"Tanais thought that if you ever ventured to this part of the world you and Reskalin might have something to teach each other. I happen to agree. That is the real reason you are here." The Fat Man sunk deeper into his chair as if waiting for the sun to rise on Enguer's head.

Enguer shot a glance at Reskalin. "What can I teach . . . you want me to teach Reskalin to be a ranger?"

"Maybe not all of it," the Fat Man conceded. "Just the important stuff. I don't want him away for years, you see. And I bet he will prove a quick student." The Fat Man smiled at Reskalin who rolled his eyes in response.

Enguer sighed, "I suppose I can spend a few months in Arre when I return."

The Fat Man laughed, "No, no. That won't do at all! Reskalin will be going with you to find these orks. What better opportunity than to learn on the job?"

Alarm bells filled Enguer's head. "No disrespect, but having someone untrained and inexperienced in The Wilds without the added hazard of orks would compromise our chances of survival."

"Nonsense!" The Fat Man struggled to sit up in his chair. "Don't be so dramatic. Reskalin will be an asset to you in short order, I'm sure of it. And when you return, he will reciprocate by teaching you how to get along in a city. Tanais mentioned you had some serious short-comings in that area."

Enguer was feeling more trapped by the moment and was beginning to suspect that there would be no escape without playing this through. Meanwhile, Reskalin was intent on examining the wondrous display of food on the table appearing to pay little attention to the unfolding drama between Enguer and the Fat Man.

"These are perilous times," the Fat Man finally wriggled into a sitting position. "Or perhaps the times are no more perilous than any other time, but these are the times we live in and they are perilous and our need is current. To be clear, our organization is in need of someone with your particular skill set and here you are. Quite precipitous wouldn't you say?"

Enguer leveled a flat stare at the Fat Man. They both knew he had no choice but to agree. Still, he wondered it they would resort to murdering him if he went so far as to defy them. He hoped not, but he wasn't about to push it and find out.

The Fat Man spread his hands apart in a display of innocence. "Ah well, perhaps it's a matter of perspective. In any case, we are quite confident in our influence in the cities and surrounding villages, but the in-betweens and certain interests we have in The Wilds are out of our reach. So, there you have it."

"What time in the morning would you like to leave?" Reskalin had not spoken in so long that Enguer was again taken aback by his soft-spoken, yet direct manner.

"Half-past dawn," then Enguer remembered, "but I have to stop and pickup my horse at the inn where I left it." He hoped there was enough coin in the purse they had given him to pay off the rent.

"Don't worry about your horse," Reskalin stood from his chair and started toward a tapestry hung on the wall. "We already retrieved it for you. Let me show you to your room."

Enguer rose from his chair and cast a dark look at the Fat Man who responded with a wide grin and a shrug. They had him from the beginning and they knew it. This whole night had been nothing more than a nice way of telling him. If nothing else, at least they were polite.

Would they be any less polite sticking a knife between his shoulder blades? He had to wonder.

Chapter 17

New Friends

Enguer's mind was racing. If he had any doubts before, he had none now, that Reskalin's 'business' was nothing more than a criminal organization led by a bizarre personality they called the Fat Man. Was that a name or a description? Maybe both. Enguer didn't know and he didn't care. All he knew was that he had agreed to another scheme that could well end up with him dead doing someone else's bidding. It was enough to keep him up most of the night tossing in the luxurious blankets of a strange bed in a strange house somewhere in a city that had not treated him very well so far. The only consolation was that he would soon be out of Arre and back in The Wilds where he would be in control again. Yet even then, he was under obligation to someone else. He could face the orks, he could deal with the denizens that prowled the dark wilderness, but could he manage Reskalin?

He sat up in bed and ran a hand through his dark curls. Another room with no windows and no idea of the time. The lone candle left for him was down by more than two thirds, the shine of the molten tallow reflecting the weak flame in thick lumps on the table and on the floor. If it wasn't dawn then it was close enough.

Swinging his legs over the low bunk, Enguer found the bowl and pitcher for washing and splashed water over his face. It felt cool and refreshing on his skin with a chilly nip from the cold air in the room. He would have preferred a hearth to all the blankets, although the cold had never really bothered him. All those winter nights in The Wilds with his father had toughened him up, he supposed.

His father.

Heat rushed to his head evaporating the last droplets of moisture and he uttered a low curse. Why had his father been associated with this, this . . .thieves guild? The Fat Man had referred to Gaurin as a friend and apparently admired, perhaps even revered the man. Every notion Enguer ever had about his father was being challenged by something new he found out about him. Prior to the Arch Priest Tanais practically dragging him from his home to chase down Lukánthropos, Enguer was firm in his belief about who his father was and the principles he stood for. Since that time, he had learned so much more about who his father really was and he feared it was just the tip of the mountain waiting for an avalanche. Enguer put it out of his mind. He had to focus on keeping himself and Reskalin alive in The Wilds and distractions would help neither of them.

Dressed in a clean tunic and breeches under studded leather armor freshly oiled against the damp weather, Enguer threw his wolf-hide cloak over his shoulders and strapped the belt holding his short sword and axe around his waist. Only then did he realize how outlandish he must have looked to the citizens of Arre. No wonder he caught every eye he passed. They must have thought him a barbarian. Enguer laughed in spite of his bad humor that morning, grabbed his travel pack and opened the door that led from his room.

"What's so funny?"

Enguer jumped and then cursed again. It was Reskalin standing right outside his door. "Been waiting long?"

Reskalin shrugged his slight shoulders, "I'm ready when you are."

The slim little man turned on his heel and walked down the lightless corridor that ended in another doorway. Enguer followed him through to find a plain table set in the center of a small room lit by a dim light-globe floating in the air above it. Reskalin picked up his travel pack and heavy wool cloak from the table as well as two small bundles wrapped in wax-cloth tied with twine. One he handed to Enguer.

"What is this?" Enguer turned the package over in his hands. It felt heavy.

"Enough cheese and goat jerky to get us by for a few days. Is that ok?"

Enguer was startled to realize that Reskalin barely reached the height of his shoulder. It was the first time they had stood this close together in the light. "That's fine. We will hunt and forage for what we need when it is gone."

"Sounds appetizing," Reskalin muttered to himself as he pushed through another door, but Enguer heard and forced himself to swallow a snicker of amusement. The Wilds might be rougher on Reskalin than the little man anticipated.

The icy chill of the pre-dawn air rushed across Enguer's face like a slap as soon as he went through the door. They were standing in a dark alley outside. Enguer was surprised. It had taken them what seemed like an hour through hallways and corridors to reach the Fat Man and only two doors to get outside. The clop of a hoof and a cold nose pressed into the side of his neck startled him further, but it quickly turned to joy at the sight of his tall buff Lambei. A second horse, somewhat smaller and black as the night, stood quietly nearby. There was not another soul in the street that he could see.

Without hesitation, Reskalin tied on his pack and mounted the black mare. Enguer followed suit and the two trotted through the empty streets and out the north gate just as it was opened by the guards allowing a stream of farmers in to setup in the market. The first rays of Sunna danced across the sky between sodden clouds with the promise of an afternoon rain that Enguer didn't think would last very long, nor would he have to concern himself with if they could get a few leagues behind them.

A short distance later and they were boarding a wide ferry set to transport them to the other side of the Bodin River. A fair group of farmers had disembarked with carts headed to the city, but Enguer and Reskalin were the only ones going back across. He figured it would be the reverse later that day when the farmers returned home for the evening.

"I suppose you have some idea of where we are going?" Enguer knew little of the Asinippi Mountains where the orks were purported to be coming from.

"North," Reskalin gestured. "It's a good forty leagues across the rolling Plains of Tarre before we arrive at the Travini Pass."

"That's where the orks have been crossing over?" Enguer presumed.

"According to our people in Provigi," Reskalin had his arms over the rail at the bow of the boat watching the light from the rising sun sparkle like diamonds over the surface of the water. All the while Enguer sat on a crate a step away trying to keep his stomach settled. The cadence of the rowers behind them would have been lethargic otherwise. "That's the capital of Tarre and only a day away from the pass. Their settlements have seen much worse than ours."

Enguer knew of Provigi and the pass and he had guessed that's where they were headed. Captain Kratu had made reference to tales of orks burning villages near the northern Asinippi, but even he had been dubious about their veracity. Now it all made tragic sense.

Reskalin looked over at Enguer, the sun reflecting off his olive-toned features. "Not doing too well, eh? I though all you people from Courth were log-rollers." He was smiling, baring perfectly aligned rows of white teeth between thin lips on a clean-shaven face. His eyes were brown, glittering with life, below sharp eyebrows and a forehead covered with dark curly locks. A remarkably handsome fellow in the sunlight, Enguer thought.

"Everyone seems to think so," Enguer tore his eyes away and looked out over the water. "I've spent my life in the wilderness rather than on the river."

"The good news for you is that's exactly where we are headed," Reskalin teased.

It *was* good news as far as Enguer was concerned. He would rather be in the city as opposed to a damn boat. Craning his neck to see over the bow, he could see that the northern bank of the river wasn't far away and it would only be a few more minutes before he could put land under his feet again. It gave him a small measure of relief in his misery.

When they were back on their horses, it occurred to Enguer that the orks must have come this way to attack Arre. "Does anyone know how the orks crossed the river?"

Reskalin pointed west to where a few narrow ribbons of black smoke hung lazily in the air far in the distance. "The villages they burned are there. Only a few dozen crossed to keep the patrols close to the city and distract from the object of their raid. They stole fishing boats from the villagers and rowed over, but not many lived to return back across."

"Surely Rasna must keep outposts nearby to protect the villages?"

"They do," Reskalin kicked his mount forward. "Their men were bottled up just like Arre. The Zilach is sure to double or triple those garrisons after what happened."

Enguer spurred his mount to keep up and they followed the unpaved road north into the sprawling plain where Captain Kratu had said the tribes that predated Tarre and Rasna used to roam. It was a fertile land with farmsteads dotting the country side and villages along the roadside every few leagues. The road ended at a military outpost surrounded by a double wooden palisade with regular towers and a moat in between. In the adjacent field cavalry were running drills under the command of an officer wearing a high-plumed helmet and polished bronze armor bellowing orders in a booming voice that carried all the way back to the road. His men must have been well trained as they charged in perfect formation with their long spears thrust forward and red capes fluttering wildly behind. They looked every bit as impressive as the famed cavalry of his homeland if a little smaller in frame and less encumbered by heavier armor.

The pair skirted west around the outpost and out onto the open plain. For the next thirty leagues or so the land would be almost completely devoid of further human habitation and before long, Enguer began to notice the subtle signs of wildlife coming to life fearless and free. To his eyes, nature was in full, unobstructed force with herds of bison and auroch moving slowly over the landscape, a pride of lumbering mammoths further west and a pair of wooly rhinoceros eyeballing each other around a waterhole that showed faint traces of predatory saber-cats, wolves and wild dogs.

Reskalin, clearly out of his element, appeared nervous when they came too close to any of the animals, fingering the short sword at his hip as if expecting attack at any moment. "I never realized how many animals lived on the Plains of Tarre. There must be hundreds!"

"My father once told me about a land across the Great Sea where there is a vast savannah called the Ibhr Rrbi, or 'Sea of Grass' in the native tongue of the Imaziyen tribes that reside there. He said there were countless millions of animals that lived in harmony with the tribal people." Enguer pat his Lambei on the side of the neck. "I don't know why I remember that."

Reskalin flashed him a rare smile that Enguer found oddly attractive for some reason. Maybe it was because the little man's features rarely carried any humor that Enguer could see. "Would you believe this is the first time I have been more than a hundred paces off an unpaved road? I am urban to the core with a soul that desires little else. You may have a difficult challenge if you expect to convert me into a ranger with a love for all of this," he gestured broadly over the plains.

"I have no expectations other than that we survive." It came out far harsher than Enguer intended, although it hit the mark for truth as far as he was concerned. He tried to soften it a bit, "What I mean, is that I will teach you what I can, but I will not try and force you to learn. That will be up to you."

The stern visage had returned to Reskalin's face, "I will not only learn, but I will master everything you offer."

"Well then," Enguer pulled the reigns to halt his mount and pointed at the ground. "See that mark in the patch of mud?"

Reskalin stopped as well and studied the turf, his thin eyebrows contorting in a curious way that made Enguer want to laugh. "I see an impression that looks like a claw. There is the padded ball and above it four toes. The impression is deep, so I would guess it is a large animal and the way the water is pooled at the lowest part tells me it is recent. What animal is this?"

Enguer was impressed. There could be hope for this one after all. "It is the mark of a sabre-cat that passed this way less than an hour ago."

Eyes wide with alarm, Reskalin cast a quick glance in every direction at once, with one hand firmly griping the hilt of his sword. "I have heard stories about these animals and sometimes artists draw their likeness at the market. They look terrifying. What should we do to avoid it?"

"Nothing," Enguer adopted a soothing tone. "Sabre-cats live in the mountains and often come down into the grasslands to hunt. The prefer auroch and deer, a rabbit when food is scarce and will even pilfer a nest for eggs. Sabre-cats almost never attack humans unless they are desperate from starvation or cornered by those foolish enough to hunt them."

"How large do they grow?"

Enguer held out his hand and gauged its size against the print – it was easily half the size. "I would guess that this one is about the size of your horse."

Reskalin's face paled by a few shades and a hunted look passed over his eyes. It was a dangerous look that hinted of desperation and violence. At first Enguer found it comical. Most city dwellers thought of almost any wild predator no different than they did a monster and if he didn't make Reskalin understand the difference from the start, he might never make the distinction in his heart and fully connect with nature.

"In nature, size does not matter," Enguer kicked his horse and they rode on again, "A thousand ants attacking you in your sleep is just as dangerous as that sabre-cat. I fear more the cunning creatures like wolves, goblins and the unnatural creatures that haunt the shadows than I do the solitary predators."

"Goblins? Unnatural creatures?" Reskalin appeared at ease again.

Enguer nodded. "Those creatures that escaped into The Wilds from the Tuatha De, like the orks and dragons. The goblins are something else altogether. According to my father, many years ago an Enlightened One explained to him that goblins were like humans, except that they evolved along different lines. They live in clans deep in the forests and mountains of The Wilds, far away from human settlements. They build huts, hunt, fish and grow small crops much like we do and tend to settle in one place for the majority of their lives. Orks are among their biggest rivals for resources and territory, often fighting with each other until one group moves away."

"You mentioned dragons," Reskalin spoke slowly. "We received a report from Funa recently that something described as a 'lizard-like creature with wings' set fire to the city killing hundreds. We thought little of it until you told us of your encounter south of Coni. Is it possible that this beast can exist?"

"I would not have believed it either had I not seen it with my own eyes, but after the Lukánthropos, I can believe almost anything."

The next few hours churned by slowly with Enguer stopping frequently to point out tracks to Reskalin and tell him more about the animals that made them. By the time they stopped for camp, Reskalin was familiar with over two dozen prints, the approximate size of the animal and the direction in which they travelled. The extraordinary part, was that Reskalin remembered every detail, even if they had come across the track just once.

"You have a mind for detail and eyes for critical observation," Enguer commented as they sat in together next to a small campfire he had built to ward off the chill of the night. "I was concerned you would have a hard time with tracks and prints."

Reskalin smiled ruefully at the fire, "It's not so different than following tracks in the city – looking for every scuff and mark, a print in the mud or dirt road, a spot on the wall. It seems animals leave unintentional traces of their passing as much as people. You'll learn the similarities soon, ranger. Hopefully I won't have to beat it into you like it was for me. Don't get me wrong, I wasn't abused or anything like that, my handlers were just . . . committed . . .to my success."

"You are still angry with your brother for leaving you under the Fat Man's protection?"

"At first I was very angry," Reskalin kicked a stick into the fire with his narrow boot. "I was very little and felt abandoned. I didn't understand that my mother had died and I needed a father . . . figure in my life. Turns out I got dozens of them. It was hard for a while, but after a few years I decided I didn't need Tanais, there were others in my life that meant more to me and I had a life that I had earned on my own. Of course, he tried to reconcile and in the end I was willing to, but it was too late."

Through the floating embers and rising heat, Enguer thought he could see the slight glisten of moisture in Reskalin's eyes, "I'm sorry

Reskalin. I wish you could have gotten to know your brother. He was a good man."

"So I am told," rising to his feet, Reskalin looked into the darkness. "Where can I relieve myself?"

Enguer used a charred stick as a pointer. "Just go a few steps beyond the horses. Not too far. You can dig a hole if you need to cover."

Alone at the campfire, Enguer was glad Reskalin had come along. It surprised him a little to think that way and he would probably change his mind when things got harder, but for now he was enjoying the company. In the near distance the sharp howl of a wolf interrupted the buzz and chirp of bugs and frogs that called from the tall wet grass all around him. Enguer paid it no mind. He looked up at the stars and traced mental lines between them to form the constellations that he knew. The guiding star was there, the one that would orient him to north when needed and . . .

The howl came again, this time from another direction and close by.

Enguer jumped to his feet. If there was one this close, then there were a dozen and Reskalin was out in the darkness away from the protection of the flames. He grabbed a burning stick from the fire and started off in the direction Reskalin had gone only a few minutes before. A chorus of growls sounded from the darkness on the other side of the horses prompting Enguer to break into a run. Wild-eyed and nervous, the Lambei and the mare stomped the ground on the verge of panic. Enguer knew that if they broke their tethers or pulled up the stakes that held them and ran, they would die. Steps past the horses, the growls intensified.

"Reskalin!" Enguer shouted, waving the flaming stick over the ground to find his tracks.

No response.

Another few feet and Enguer found a boot print barely discernable in the flickering light. "Reskalin!"

Nothing.

Suddenly the growling was punctuated by a sharp yelp, then silence.

"Here!" Reskalin's low call cut through the darkness.

The growling started up again, more frenzied, more forceful. It meant only one thing – blood had been drawn.

The last vestiges of flame were dwindling down to nothing when Enguer finally spotted the dim shape of Reskalin, light reflecting from the naked blade of a short sword in one hand and a dagger in the other. He was crouched low and slowly turning one way and then another. A still form, covered in grey fur, lay at his feet while several other grey shapes darted in and out of the light and around Reskalin looking for an opening.

Enguer rushed to his side, sword drawn and positioned himself so they stood back to back as the last of the flame shrank to nothing. "Hope you are good at blind fighting," Enguer huffed.

"I think I can manage. Thanks for coming, by the way."

Enguer felt the push of air from the growling form before he saw its sharp teeth flashing toward him an arms-length away. He was ready. Slicing upward and out, his short blade pierced fur, sinew and bone impaling the beast from underneath the jaw up through and into the base of its skull. Enguer kicked it off just in time to slap away the deadly snapping of a second blur of grey fur going for his thigh. A violent push from behind told him Reskalin had born the brunt of a charging body. He wanted to turn and help, but he was forced to cut a quick arc down on his left over the shoulder of a wolf that had grabbed a hold of the edge of his leather chest piece in an attempt to pull him to the ground. It joined it's packmate in a bloody heap at his feet.

Blood pounded in Enguer's head while he waited for the next attack. He raised his sword at every rush of grey that came near, but none came close and soon the snarling growls and yaps receded into the distant night. For a long moment he rested panting against Reskalin's slender back and felt relief that the man was still standing.

When the cold air no longer burned his dry throat with every intake of breath, Enguer called over his shoulder, "Are you hurt?"

A moment passed and then another before Reskalin replied in a raspy voice that mirrored his own, "A few scratches. Nothing serious."

"Can you stand on your own?"

Reskalin pulled the weight of his body forward nearly causing Enguer to fall flat on his butt. He caught himself at the last second and turned to face his comrade.

"Can *you* stand?" Reskalin's perfect teeth flashed in the darkness. The fool was smiling again.

Enguer took a deep breath and looked back toward the camp. The horses had not run off and the campfire burned bright and welcoming twenty paces away. Livid heat flushed Enguer's face, *what was wrong with this little idiot?*

"Why did you go so far from camp!" he practically shouted. "I said just a few steps. I don't care how clever you are, alone in the dark in The Wilds will get you killed quick!"

Reskalin leveled a heated gaze of his own Enguer's way. "I was close," he hissed. "When the wolves found me, I lead them away from the horses! Do you want to walk the rest of the way to the Travini Pass?"

"You won't need a horse if you're dead!" Enguer countered. "And that's exactly what you would be if I didn't find you."

Reskalin sniffed, "I can handle myself. One of them was already dead before you got here."

"Until the other seven pounced on your back! You have to listen to me. You don't know how things work out here!"

"I've listened enough tonight!" Reskalin turned his back on him and stalked back to the camp leaving Enguer standing in the dark shaking his head with six dead wolves at his feet.

By the time Enguer returned to camp, Reskalin had washed and cleaned the wound on his arm and retrieved a roll of cloth from his saddle pack for a bandage. He didn't say a word upon Enguer's approach, ignoring him as though he wasn't even there. Enguer took one look at the deep wound, went to his own pack and pulled out a small metal container sealed by a waxed lid. He walked over and dropped it in front of Reskalin, "Put this on first. It is from a plant with healing properties that will prevent infection."

Reskalin reluctantly picked it up, unraveled the bandage from his arm and opened the container. Enguer watched with amusement as the stench of the salve permeated the air in the immediate area. Reskalin hesitated, but remained silent, his restless eyebrows the only indication of his irritation. Even the horses shied away to the ends of their ropes to avoid the pungent stink. Finally, Reskalin went all in and scraped a small dollop from the can and rubbed it over the scratches wincing silently at the sting it caused.

Sighing heavily, Enguer sat down next to Reskalin and wrenched the can of salve from his grip almost forcefully. "You have to dab if you want it to work properly."

Taking hold of his arm, Enguer gingerly dabbed the salve on the angry trenches running up Reskalin's arm, then wrapped it tightly with the roll of cloth. When he was done, Enguer looked the little man over, "Do you have any other injuries?"

"No," he replied shortly never shifting his gaze from the campfire.

"Look," Enguer did his best to keep his tone neutral. "I know you tried to do the right thing, but you really have to listen to me out here. For both our sakes."

Reskalin appeared unmoved.

Enguer shook his head and began to stand up, "I'm sorry, but I would prefer to have a dead horse than a dead friend to mourn."

Stopping him midrise, Reskalin put his hand on Enguer's arm pulling him back down beside him. "Apology accepted."

Annoyed as he felt, Enguer chuckled. He had a lot to learn about this unusual man.

Reskalin shifted his body to face him. His large brown eyes twinkled in the firelight. There was a depth of emotion behind them that Enguer had never suspected and something else. "You are right. I have been foolish. You can count on me to listen and learn while we are out here. I won't jeopardize our lives again."

"Thank you. That's all I ask," Enguer couldn't pull his eyes away. "I'm sure the Fat Man will be appreciative if you return in one . . ."

Reskalin put a hand on Enguer's cheek stopping him in mid-sentence. He slowly slid his hand over the unshaved stubble of two days growth on his face. "You're a ruggedly handsome man. I wish I could pull that off."

Enguer didn't know what to say. In fact, he was speechless. Never had he been complimented by another man in this way or touched so intimately. There was something beautiful about Reskalin – his eyes, his smile, the way he moved. It was very confusing and growing more awkward by the moment. He knew of men who loved each other like a man and a woman. They were uncommon in Courth but not unheard of and there were no laws that prevented it. For his part, Enguer never judged them. Feelings, instinct and intuition where a foundational part of nature and he doubted whether or not it mattered if you applied it to human or animal. All he knew was that he didn't share those feelings with Reskalin. At least he didn't think so. Still, there was something about him that Enguer was attracted to and it caused his temples to throb with excitement, anticipation. *Of what?*

Reskalin abruptly pulled his hand away and quickly shifted his gaze back to the fire. He must have felt the unease as well. A moment later he barked a laugh, "You know what? I still have to pee."

Chapter 18

Pursuit

"The Travini Pass."

Enguer peered through the haze that blanketed the lower elevations of the Asinippi Mountains that morning. "I see it."

For the past two days the pair had trekked north over the Plains of Tarre never speaking of the awkward moment they shared the night the wolves attacked. Enguer tried not to think about it and instead focused on rigorously training Reskalin to recognize the subtle signs of animal tracks over various terrains, identifying scat types, discussing the ecology of the various wildlife and how to be resourceful in the wilderness in order to survive. Reskalin proved to be a willing and eager student catching on quickly with an intuition about tracking in particular that was remarkable. Enguer was relieved that they had settled into a relaxed rapport that allowed them to work closely together without discomfiture during the day and laugh together around the fire pit at night.

"Another hour or two and we should be . . ." Enguer let the thought die. "What's this?"

Several spans ahead to their left a black scorch mark made an ugly scar upon the green plain with what appeared to be the remnants of smoldering branches. The wind was at their backs, otherwise Enguer was sure he would have noticed the smell of smoke the from further off. This was the first campsite they had encountered on the plains and from the size of the area trampled around the remnants of the fire a large group must have stayed here.

Enguer swung down from his Lambei and walked slowly around the perimeter of the camp, his sharp eyes darting from stretches of pressed-down grass, to over turned stones and patches of mud. Every detail his mind evaluated and catalogued, compared them to what he knew and what he suspected. After only a few seconds it was obvious to him what they had found. He looked back to find Reskalin right on his heels. The little man tread surprisingly silent over the long, wet grass.

"The ork camp?" Reskalin knelt down to inspect what appeared to be the mark of a large sandaled foot with claws protruding from the front.

Enguer nodded and made his way over to where the campfire had been. It was still very warm. "They only made one fire and it was used for cooking rather than for heat. It doesn't look like any off them slept near it."

Reskalin joined him. "They always attack at night. I wonder if they have some aversion to light? Can you tell how long ago they were here?"

"At least twelve hours ago." Enguer picked up a stick and kneeled down to prod through the ashes. "My guess is that they travel at night and rested during the day."

"Those look like animal bones," Reskalin spoke over Enguer's shoulder.

"Goat and pig mostly." Enguer tossed the stick on top of the heap of cinders and stood up. "The orks must have stolen them from the villages they attacked. What else do you see?" There was no reason not to use the opportunity as a training event.

Reskalin carefully walked through the camp, frequently dropping to one knee to look closer at the ground as he strode in a spiral pattern back to the edge of the camp. Walking a few paces behind, Enguer followed in Reskalin's footsteps. He was once again impressed with his friend's methodology. Whether it was intuitive or learned, Reskalin knew how to conduct a proper search.

"There were at least thirty orks and a half-dozen humans." Reskalin's face darkened as he spoke, "Traitorous dogs. Why would any human ally himself with these monsters?"

"They aren't the orks allies," Enguer motioned for Reskalin to come over to where he was crouched. "See those holes? They held stakes driven deep into the ground. And see these patterns here?" He pointed to what appeared to be linear scuff marks amid human-sized boot and sandal prints. "They are captives."

Fury flashed over Reskalin's features, his dark eyebrows converged sharply over the bridge of his nose and intense brown eyes seethed with internal heat. In sharp contrast, his reply came out low and calm like the hiss of an adder before it strikes, "What will they do with them?"

Enguer stood and started back to his horse. "The trail will be easy to follow until we get into the mountains. If we push through the night, we can gain a few hours on them and perhaps catch them at camp tomorrow morning." Pulling himself up on his mount he looked back to see that Reskalin had not moved. "Reskalin, we are only two and they are over thirty. With a little luck and this ring," Enguer pat the place on his cloak where the ring sat inside a small pocket, "we may be able to free some of them."

"And if not?"

Enguer knew little about orks, but he had heard some things from his father and others and he had a fair idea about what creatures created by the Tuatha De did with the humans they captured. "They will become slaves or worse. Either way, they will be lost to us." He hoped he wouldn't have to explain what the 'or worse' meant.

Reskalin didn't ask. He sprinted toward his horse and sprang upon it's back in one fluid motion. "Let's go then."

They set off at a brisk league-churning trot that would not exhaust the horses over the long hours before they rested again. The Travini Pass was not far ahead and already the soft soil of the grassy plain was becoming harder with larger patches of coarse dirt and rocks. Enguer was confident he could follow the large party of orks no matter what terrain they crossed over, but they might have to slow down to spot their tracks and that could put them beyond their reach. And if they did manage to rescue any of the captives and get away, they simply couldn't send them back to Arre on their own. They would never survive in The Wilds. It would effectively end their search for the orks lair for the time being. Maybe Reskalin could take them back and he would continue on his own. Enguer thought that might be best for everyone.

The Travini Pass was a twisting rock and boulder strewn dirt trail in the shadow of sheer cliff faces on both sides. Low growth and copse of deciduous trees infringed on the little-used path at frequent intervals without hindering their course and provided residence to populations of rabbits that scurried for cover. To Enguer, it looked as if some ancient god had split the mountain cleanly with one earth-shattering swing of his divine blade and then crooked it this way and that just to annoy anyone passing through it. The ground, drier and harder than on the plains, still showed clear signs of the orks passing in the loose dirt. Even without the tracks being so obvious they would not have needed to slow considering that there was no other direction to go.

"Does the Fat Man have a real name?" With little necessity to watch the ground the entire time, Enguer thought he might try and get some answers to his curiosities.

Reskalin responded with a barking laugh, "If he has one, I have never heard it."

"He must not take offense to the obvious implication."

"Hardly," Reskalin smiled slyly. "More than one fool has thought they could take advantage of what they perceive as a weakness."

"Isn't it?"

"He would have everyone think that to keep his enemies off balance," Reskalin displayed that striking smile of his again. "Only a year ago I watched him cross the length of a room and slice a would-be assassin like a mackerel in two blinks of an eye."

Enguer couldn't tell if he was joking. The Fat Man didn't look like a man that could move his bulk in a hurry for anything other than the opportunity to sink his teeth into a greasy leg of pork. "So, what is your relationship to him?"

The smile disappeared and Reskalin looked at him as if he wasn't sure what he was asking. After a moment pause, the little man appeared to decide and cocked one of his slim eyebrows. "The guild is structured like a pyramid. The Fat Man is at the top, under him are a handful of what are called Big Brothers, below them are Little

Brothers and at the bottom are children. Not actual children. Well, we have a few, they make good spies. My position is as a Big Brother."

"Impressive," Enguer really was impressed that Reskalin held such a high position in the guild. "Do you have specific responsibilities?"

"I did before you came along. Now you are it." Reskalin sneezed suddenly. It was a high-pitched sound that sounded strange coming from him.

Enguer cast Reskalin a side-long look. "What did you do before I disrupted your picture?"

"Our guild is called the Seven Stars Brotherhood. Something to do with the seven founding members. I don't know, it was long before me. Anyway, there are several organizations within the guild headed by a Big Brother. For example, prostitution falls under the group called the Sassy Ladies. We also have groups responsible for protection, smuggling, assassination, etc." Reskalin grew excited as he spoke, revealing far more about the guild's business than Enguer thought prudent. "The most lucrative business concern is the trafficking of information. That was my group. I called them the Sewer Rats, but in truth, they were skilled thieves and spies from every walk of life. I even had gaggles of street children on the payroll!" Reskalin sniggered to himself.

Enguer became more alarmed with every word. He never expected Reskalin to be quite so forthcoming. The one thing he knew about thieves guilds was that the less you knew about them the better. "Perhaps you are telling me things I really shouldn't know."

Reskalin shrugged off Enguer's concerns, "Much of what I am telling you is already known by anyone that matters." The sly smile returned to his lips, "Besides, you're one of us now which means that your life depends on not discussing guild business outside the guild."

A chill ran down Enguer's spine with those words. How did this happen? All he was supposed to do was train Reskalin to master a few basic ranger skills and receive reciprocal training in an urban environment. Now he was a member of the Seven Stars Brotherhood guild? He would have to get this worked out with the Fat Man when they returned to Arre.

Hours passed with Reskalin chatting heedlessly about his guild, the nobles, the cities they controlled and story upon story about his nefarious exploits. If it was all true, it was stunning. Enguer didn't want to hear any of it, but what choice did he have? He couldn't get Reskalin to change the subject. So, he kept to himself, refusing to encourage the little rogue with any more questions and just hoped he would eventually shut up.

"You know I'm just popping your daisies, right?"

"What?" The night had overtaken them and Enguer couldn't see Reskalin's face.

"The part about you being in the guild. You think it's that easy?" Reskalin's high-pitched laughter echoed off the rock walls like a torrent of humiliation. "You should have seen your face earlier! And you've been brooding ever sense!" The laughter could have split mirrors.

"I haven't been brooding," Enguer mumbled. Despite his embarrassment, he felt a good measure of relief and silently vowed to reciprocate the gag ten-fold. "How much of that was true?"

He couldn't see it, but Enguer somehow knew that Reskalin was wearing his sly smile again. "Some of it. None of it. All of it."

Enguer decided he would never know and if it amused Reskalin, that was fine with him. He hated to admit it, but Reskalin had got one over on him. Enguer never had friends growing up. He imagined that this must be what it was like to have a friend. He considered his father a friend before he died and Suri was a friend, but that was different. This felt different.

"You know I wouldn't tease you if I didn't like you," Reskalin's tone was soft as silk.

A thrill shot through Enguer, he couldn't deny it, leaving an unexpected grin on his face. He was glad of the night to hide it. He was glad that he had a friend. "I like you too, Reskalin."

Near to dawn Enguer detected the sound of running water further up the canyon. An hour later, the new sun slowly flooded the pass with illumination revealing sheer cliffs that gave way to stone-cluttered slopes with a scattering of trees running up their steep sides, but no sign of water. They pressed onward. The sound of the water grew louder and closer and by the time they reached the base of the first slope and followed the trail around a sharp bend, the source of the running water sounded as if it were coming from somewhere beyond the slope on their right.

Enguer stopped. The trail they followed continued into the densely forested northeastern face of the Asinippi Mountains ahead, but he had spied a disturbance in the mix of dirt and pebbles that were strewn along the incline.

"See the tracks going up the slope?" Enguer pointed out the faint traces on the rock that indicated the orks had changed their course.

"They are difficult to make out," Reskalin was off his horse studying the rocky incline. "You must have the eyes of an eagle."

Enguer shook his head. "Remember that you told me once to use all my senses? Now I am reminding you of the same."

Reskalin stood quietly and closed his eyes. When he opened them a short time later, he had a triumphant look on his face. "It's the water, of course. You think they went toward the water."

"The noise of the water was the main reason I looked more closely at this slope," Enguer prompted his Lambei to climb up the incline a few lengths. "They must have been low on water and if I'm correct, would likely set their camp close to its source."

Dismounting, Enguer tied his horse to a nearby tree and started up the slope on foot. Reskalin hurried to catch up and in a few moments the pair were laying on their bellies looking down into the ravine below. There they could see the source of the water – a river disgorged out of a horizontal fissure in the side of the mountain, flowed down through a ravine and disappeared into the heavily forested elevation beyond. It was a shallow river only about thirty spans across, fast-moving over a bed of smooth sand-pebbles and littered with larger rocks that had found their way down the slope and into the water over the decades. It was the birthplace of whatever they called this river and Enguer knew from others he had seen like it that over the next few leagues it would grow into a powerful serpent cutting through The Wilds bringing its life-giving waters to civilizations in the east.

"Something is moving on the other side of the ravine near the tree line," Enguer pointed to the southeast. "There! I can't tell for sure from this distance but their numbers match the group we are looking for."

"What do we do now?" Reskalin had that dangerous look in his eyes again. A look that could get them both killed if they weren't careful.

"You stay here and keep watch. I'm going to find out how well this ring works in The Wilds." Enguer placed the ring over his finger.

If Reskalin was startled in the least by his sudden disappearance, he didn't show it. Rather, he showed more frustration at being left behind. "Be careful," he grumbled.

Enguer slid down the slope using the trees and brush as hand-holds to keep him from tumbling down the sharp incline. At the edge of the river he removed his boots and rolled up his breeches. The water was frigidly cold, but it never rose higher than his knees and he was safely across in a matter of minutes. On the other side he pulled on his boots and slunk quietly into the scant forest keeping his eyes and ears peeled for patrols and foragers. He wasn't sure if orks made use of either. Still, he preferred to approach their camp cautiously, moving silently from tree to tree, as if he were fully visible.

Not far from the encampment, Enguer detected the putrid scent of burning flesh similar to what he had experienced when bodies of the deceased were sent to Sunna from atop a funeral pyre. The stink was unforgettable from when he was a child after his mother died and later his father. He hated the disgusting odor. And its presence here confirmed his worst fears. For a moment he was tempted to turn back and give Reskalin the bad news about his countryfolk, but he had to be sure.

He had to be certain.

Enguer drew closer and traversed a wide circle around the perimeter of the camp. If the stench of burning flesh was bad, it multiplied with the added stink of unwashed orkish bodies and their less than efficient disposal of their waste. He cursed the Tuatha De for creating these nasty creatures.

Quiet as the still wind, Enguer approached the camp. At first, he could see a large bonfire through the branches eclipsed by shadows passing in front of the light. The entire camp site was situated under the heavy boughs of beech trees whose thick canvas shaded the orks from direct sunlight. How light from the sun versus the campfire might affect the orks differently he had no idea. He made a mental note to ask Borak when, if, he ever made it back to Arre.

A few steps closer and Enguer could make out the outlines of orks moving about or laying in disorganized clusters under the trees and away from the campfire. It was still early morning so only a few must have had the time to eat before they went to sleep. The rest were standing or seated around the fire cooking cuts of red meat.

Enguer crept nearer.

The stench was nearly overwhelming forcing Enguer to breathe through his mouth to avoid gaging. The meat they cooked were nondescript raw chunks stripped of bone and tissue and impaled on a stick, fat dripping to sizzle in the fire, none of it identifiable. He knew what it was. Still, he had to search for the captives, there might be one or two still alive. Enguer orbited the camp further, his eyes searching, his mind cataloging. He would remember ever detail, even the ones he desperately wanted to forget.

And that's exactly what he found next. Circling to his right, the fire light illuminated a scene of pure horror. An ork wearing a leather smock and wielding a blade reserved for butchers stood over the mangled remains of numerous human bodies. To be more accurate, it was a pile of human parts. Male or female there was no distinction. Legs and arms were hacked from torsos, split down the middle and the meat cut from the bone. Some were cracked for the soft marrow inside. The ork was doing his vile work over a wide stump saturated with the blood and carnage of flesh, his knife hacking through a torso to remove organs that he placed in a large bowl with so many other hearts and livers. Only an hour earlier those same hearts must have been beating in terror. Enguer's mind displaced the emotion, the revulsion, the horror, the rage. His father had trained him to think unemotionally. There was no place for it in The Wilds, only instinct.

So crushing was the weight of the moment that Enguer nearly missed the worst of all of it. For, at the orks feet lay six decapitated heads, their faces frozen in terror, eyes and tongue removed leaving bloody hollows and the jagged, unkind cuts to the neck that would have prolonged the suffering of the butcher's victims. He had enjoyed the suffering and the agony inflicted. It was intentional and deliberate.

Enguer was so focused on the macabre scene that he nearly missed the approach of an ork headed in his direction. At first, he thought he had become visible somehow, but the orks expression was passive and his intent became apparent when he sauntered up to the tree Enguer was hiding behind. Hot steam rose from the other side of the tree trunk inspiring Enguer to silently move away. When the ork had completed his business, he turned to march back to the camp.

The sharp crack of a rotten branch halted the ork in his steps. Enguer jerked his head around to identify the source of the commotion just in time to catch a blur of movement

Reskalin, Enguer silently cursed his friend. How had he gotten this far unseen? No doubt he was talented. *A talented fool!*

The ork spun on his heel. "Gorak zal torack!" he called into the forest, striding confidently forward.

Enguer rolled in behind him as he passed and planted his dagger in the base of its thick neck neck at the same time a second blade, not from his hand, sliced into the fleshy part under the orks sternum. The creature stood there, a standing corpse, between the press of the two of them. Enguer stared over the shoulder of the ork into Reskalin's eyes who almost seemed to stare back at him heedless of his invisibility. It was a strangely intimate moment, looking into this man's eyes and recognizing something different that Enguer could not understand. There was a scent, not like the stink of the ork they held upright or the fragrance of the flora and fauna that crowded the space between the trees. His father had always said he had the nose of a wolf and Enguer recognized the smell from the tinge of sweat that glistened dully in the shadows of Reskalin's cloak. I didn't make sense…

The ork dropped to the ground as Reskalin stepped back ending Enguer's contemplation. The sudden movement was a jarring reminder that they were still in danger and that Reskalin, who shouldn't have been there in the first place, had just made their situation more hazardous. If the orks found the body they might suspend their return home and begin a search that could stretch on for days.

Enguer removed his ring and pulled the ork under a heavy thicket. "What are you doing here?" he hissed angrily. "I told you to wait for me."

Reskalin made no apology, "I had to see for myself."

Enguer grabbed his arm and pulled him further away from the ork camp. "You made a promise that you would listen to me."

"I kept my promise," Reskalin shot back. "And then I acted as I felt necessary."

"What if they find the body? Did you think about that?"

Reskalin smirked, "Even if they do, they will most likely think he was killed by a rival. From what I've heard they fight with themselves as much as any other."

"You're going to be the death of me before this is over," Enguer chided, never stopping their silent retreat back to where they left the horses.

Reskalin did not resist, managing an admirable job of not making any noise in their hurry. "This was your own doing. From now on I'm not letting you out of my sight!"

Enguer snapped his head around to glare at the infuriating rogue and nearly lost his footing. It would have been a fitting humiliation to fall flat on his face that underscored his inability to control Reskalin in any manner whatsoever. He might as well try and tame a saber-cat for all the good it would do.

And no less dangerous.

~~~

A ball of fire shot forth from the Phoenix's foul beak and sped through the air like a meteor from amongst the stars. Dergo arched his neck and expulsed a jet of flame intercepting the fire-ball in midflight and sending it off course and away. Two more followed and then a fourth. Each one deflected in the same fashion. The absence of Gungnir's regular flight prompted Myrllin to look behind to see what had become of his brother. To his relief, Wodanaz appeared out of the fiery chaos of the tornados racing toward them on Sleipnir. When he looked back, the Phoenix had dispensed with the fireballs and retreated a short distance away.

At first, Myrllin thought the demon-bird might flee. Instead, the Phoenix spread its wings and fanned out its feathers in a posture similar to a Cormorant sunbathing. It was an odd display . . . and one that left the fool demon vulnerable to attack. Myrllin was ready.

He cupped his hands and thrust them out before him. There was a flash of light, a low compressive pop and the smell of sulfur in the air resulting in a pure bar of energy as bright as the sun discharging from Myrllin's open palms. When the short narrow beam struck the feather chest of flames it made no more sound than light touching the side of a wall, but the effect of that touch was devastating leaving a perfect hole the size of a wagon wheel burned through and through.

Predictably, the Phoenix screeched in pain and rage. Unpredictably, it began to spin. It spun slowly at first, drawing its wings in tight across its body and tucking in its head. Myrllin, sagging from exhaustion, watched in fascination. The bolt had taken an enormous amount of energy to produce. A second one might destroy the Phoenix, but it would likely kill him as well.

"What is happening?" Wodanaz called when he was close. "How could that thing survive one of your death bolts?"

"It's not a 'death bolt'," Myrllin replied wearily. "It's called an 'Energy Bolt'. I'm not some mad sorcerer hermit in The Wilds, ya know."

"Call it what you want. Every time I've seen you use it obliterates whatever it hits." Wodanaz thrust his thumb toward the Phoenix, "Except this time."

The Phoenix was spinning faster. Much faster. It was a blur of motion no longer recognizable as anything more than a luminous object in the sky that throbbed bright and hot. Myrllin could feel the waves of heat it gave off escalating, intensifying, growing stronger. Sweat beaded on his forehead and his robes felt heavy. Aside from the methodical beat of Dergo's wings it was dead silent. Why was there no sound from the Phoenix?

Myrllin looked over at Wodanaz passively drumming his fingers over the square block that formed the head of his Warhammer and felt a hint of panic rising up inside of him. "We need to leave," he shouted.

Wodanaz appeared startled by the urgent call and hefted his hammer. "You think it's healing?"

"I think it's dying . . ." the words left Myrllin's lips but never made it to Wodanaz's ears.

There was a sound like the vibration from the low chord on a lute or the release of the string on a bow, a flash brighter than the sun and a sudden drop in pressure. Time slowed to a crawl and the air rippled with a swell of light and heat surging toward them. The Phoenix rotated slowly again, the blazing feathers on its outstretched wings discharging like fiery bolts in every direction.

The wave crashed into Dergo in mid-turn. Myrllin watched helplessly as he was flung violently up and away from the red dragon through air thick as molasses. It was like floating weightless in a cosmic sea, tumbling end over end, uncontrolled, abandoned. Bright light blocked out the sky, the ground and everything around him and Myrllin worried that he had been cast into another plane of existence.

His liquid thoughts were abruptly shattered by a jarring turbulence that wracked his whole body, time returned and the blinding light faded away. In its place came the sensation of falling and the hot rush of air pressed against his face. Struggling to open his eyes, Myrllin squinted through watery narrow slits at the rapid approach of the jagged rocks below. His mind tried desperately to grasp its meaning. The fog was still heavy over his acuity, hampering his ability to think clearly, preventing him from taking the action he knew he must take.

Chapter 19

Revelations

Enguer and Reskalin lay on their bellies watching the orks camp until nightfall. So far, there had been no sign that they had found their dead comrade. To the contrary, their forms moved slow and sluggish around the fire after sleeping the majority of the daylight hours.

"Why haven't they posted a single guard or sent out a patrol?" Enguer was fascinated by the orks absence of concern or fear. "Don't they know that Tarre and Rasna want their heads?"

Reskalin yawned, apparently tired and bored from watching orks sleep. "Why should they worry? No one has pursued them into The Wilds before."

With the setting sun, the orks moved around more vigorously preparing to vacate their encampment. It didn't take them long since they did nothing to conceal that they had been there, barely taking the time to haul a bucket of sand from the riverbank to put out the fire. Soon after, a coarse bellow erupted from one of their number and they all moved off in a southeasterly direction parallel to the river.

Reskalin stood up and brushed off the front of his cloak. "Ready?"

Sweeping the dirt off his own cloak, Enguer walked down the incline to where the horses were tied and removed a bedroll tied over his travel pack. "The horses need water and a bit of feed," he pulled the remaining packs off his horse, "And we need some rest as well."

"Aren't you worried that we will lose them?" Reskalin had not made a move to remove anything from his own horse. "We can't afford to allow them the chance to get away. What if we can't find them again?"

Enguer wanted to roll his eyes. "Have you learned nothing this whole time? Those creatures are too stupid to care about the trail they leave behind and even if they did there are too many of them for me to miss their tracks." He lowered his tone as he thought about his next words, "Besides, there is no longer any urgency. They have killed all of their captives which means they must not be more than a day or two away from home."

Heat rose to Reskalin's cheeks but he said nothing.

"It's a terrible thing, I know," Enguer placed a hand on his friend's shoulder. "But there will be time and opportunity to avenge their deaths soon enough."

"Very well," Reskalin acceded sadly. "I could use a little rest." He barely stifled a yawn that shook his entire frame.

The next morning the pair concealed their camp and trotted off along the riverbank following the route taken by the orks the night before. The cloudless sky with the bright sun rising through it gave Enguer hope that it might warm up enough to take the bite out of the chill breeze flowing off the snow-covered peaks that paralleled the river. It felt colder on this side of the Asinippi.

"Why did we cover up the camp?" Reskalin's leather armor creaked a little in need of oil. "Nobody is chasing *us*."

"We are in The Wilds. You never know what may be hunting you and it's better not to tempt anything that might if it were to come across our passing."

Reskalin grunted. "You think you're so clever, don't you?"

"No," Enguer had never thought of himself in that way. 'My father and I lived in The Wilds for a few years before he died and I trust in his advice and teaching. You would do well to follow them also as everything that I pass along to you are not my original ideas."

They travelled the next few leagues with Enguer quietly pointing out the tell-tale marking left behind by the orks. It was an easy trail to follow, their heavy bodies leaving deep impressions in the mud and gravel alongside the broadening river. Sometimes the track travelled over rocks or through the forest where Enguer had to pay a little more attention, but always they stayed true to the water's course.

By the time the sun was setting on another chilly day, they found themselves at higher elevation scouring over the remains of another camp.

"They managed to kill a wild hog and a few deer," Enguer sifted through the remains of the campfire. "I doubt it was enough to feed them all."

"Their lair, or burrow, or whatever it's called must be less than a day away?" Reskalin guessed.

Enguer nodded. "I agree. We will be more cautious from here on out in case they take the security of their home any more seriously than that of their camps." He wrinkled his nose at the prevailing stench all around them. "Let's camp up wind. The stink of ork turns my stomach."

Reskalin laughed and almost gauged at the intake of foul air, "Wish I could bottle it," he coughed. "You know what the nobles of Rasna would pay to subject their adversaries to such an unpleasant hoax?"

As expected, Sunna brought forth her golden rays to flood the land with her life-giving radiance and a new day. Enguer noted the increasing absence of many of the larger animals and in particular the predators that should have been stalking The Wilds the further southeast they rode. In his experience, it was a glaring sign that they were getting closer to a settlement that overhunted the region and relied little on agriculture. It could only mean the orks and it hinted at the reason why their raids across the Travini had intensified of late.

"Show me the tracks," Enguer was testing Reskalin's skill. They were ascending a rocky slope with few patches of grass or dirt that would reveal an obvious imprint. It took a combination of patience, skill and experience – mostly patience – to follow tracks over rock.

"I see a scuff here," Reskalin pointed from atop his horse, "and the underside of those stones are exposed," he paused. Enguer watched his eyes follow the elusive signs up the incline. "They went over the ridge."

"Good," Enguer was pleased. Reskalin was turning out to be an excellent tracker when he put his mind to it.

That morning the orks trail had not continued along the riverbank as expected and after a little searching they found tracks on the other side of the river. The orks had crossed over and headed deep into the Asinippi Mountain Range. How deep, they might soon find out.

"Let's go on foot for a while and keep a low profile going over this ridge." Enguer dismounted and led his horse up the steepening incline. Near the top he stopped and forced the end of his mount's reins under the edge of a heavy rock. His horse was trained not to wander off or runaway in fright unless panicked, but on the sharp incline he didn't want the Lambei moving about too much and lose its footing.

Enguer crawled to the edge of the ridge followed closely by Reskalin. When he looked over, he was dismayed at what he saw. Leagues stretched into the distance covered by a rock-strewn landscape of ravines and sharp rises that escalated into snow-capped peaks in the distance. It was cold unforgiving terrain with little to hunt, bare scrub for the horses and few sources of water.

"We will have to leave the horses in the ork camp," Enguer hated the thought of leaving his horse alone in The Wilds, but the animals had little chance of surviving the trek through the mountains.

Reskalin gave him an uncertain look, "Will they be safe?"

"I think so," Enguer tried to sound confident although he wasn't completely sure himself. "I haven't seen signs of many predators in the last day or so and the stench should keep any away that may wander by for at least a few days."

Although he looked unconvinced, Reskalin reluctantly agreed, and they returned to the ork camp where they removed their mounts straps, harnesses and packs and allowed them to graze free. Enguer suggested each of them carry only two days of water and rations so they could travel light anticipating that they could hunt small animals along the way. The mountains might be far more desolate than the forest, even still, there was life in every wilderness and he had survived them many times before. His biggest concern was for his

Lambei and he almost had second thoughts when they were ready to cross back over the river.

"I've never heard you call your horse by name," Reskalin stood next to Enguer staring back at the ork camp. "Does he have one?"

Enguer shook his head. His dark hair had grown nearly to his shoulders in the weeks since he had last had it cut. "I have never understood why people give animals names. They don't want them. What is yours called?"

"I never cared to find out. Maybe she has one, I don't know," Reskalin's light laughter belied his love for the animal. "I rarely ride in the city. I just call her my beauty."

"They are both beautiful animals," Enguer agreed. "May Sunna keep them from harm while we are away." Boots in hand, he turned and started across the river.

"Sunna, eh?" Reskalin was right beside him in the frigid, waist-deep water. "Our sun-god is Usil. Although I pay homage to Tivr, our moon goddess. Most of the work that I do is under her illumination."

"Are you a pious man?" Given what he knew about Reskalin, Enguer said it almost as a joke. He had to be careful though, in Rasna maybe the thieves and assassins were as devout as the priests.

Reskalin made a sound like a scoff between chattering teeth, "Hardly. My people serve many gods. Their teachings are kept in a series of sacred books known only to the priests who tend to interpret them to their best advantage to govern the people."

"The Zilach are all priests?" Enguer cared little for politics, but in Courth the Arch Priest was a close advisor to the king, not the ruler.

"That's right," Reskalin stepped out of the water and dried his feet with the edge of his cloak before putting on his boots. "And our king, the Lauchme, is chosen from them."

They strode up the rocky slope again and crawled over the crumbling top of the ridge to keep their silhouette low against the sun. It wasn't far to the bottom before they were climbing a steeper incline to an elevated plateau that rose like steps to a wall of high crags many leagues in the distance. If it were not for the persistent traces left by the orks, Enguer would seriously doubt that they were going the right way.

The plateau was cut by shallow crevasses that forced them to zigzag over the rugged stone. It was the same path the orks had followed the night before, Enguer was sure of that, and he wondered if this was the only approach to their enclave. The Zilach of Arre would be hard pressed to send an army of infantry over this terrain let alone cavalry and supply wagons. He glanced over at Reskalin. The way the rogue's eyes moved over the landscape gave him the impression that he was thinking the same thing. Regardless of what they found of the orks, Rasna's campaign against them was likely to end right here.

When the sun stood high overhead, they stopped to drink a little water and eat a bite of their goat jerky and cheese. Despite the rock underneath their feet soaking up as much heat as possible, the cold gusts that frequently blew a shock of frosty air under their cloaks sapped the warmth from their skin. And they had scarcely covered half the distance over the plateau.

"This is madness," Reskalin sat close to Enguer with his hood up sharing their collective warmth. He tore off a bite of jerky and spat it out just as quickly onto the dry wind-swept slate rock that stretched unyielding in every direction. "We should just turn around and you can tell Borath about this place and the futility of sending anyone else after the orks."

"I'm inclined to agree, except that unless I find the orks, it will remain a mystery as to why they have become so bold to raid so deeply into human territories." Enguer spat out the jerky he had been chewing for some time in favor of a crumble of slightly less hard cheese. "The Zilach will not stop sending groups out to find the answers as long as the orks keep raiding."

Reskalin peered around the edge of his hood, his brown eyes sparkling from the shadows under long lashes that almost made him appear childlike. "It's not worth our lives, Enguer. Better to let the generals and politicians deal with the orks. Neither of us are soldiers. I am better suited to the shadows of Arre and you are a foreigner with no obligation to do anything for Rasna. This isn't your fight."

Enguer put the hood of his cloak up to shade his eyes from the blaring sun and warm his cold-numbed ears. Reskalin was right. He had no duty to help the Zilach or anyone else in Rasna. Yet he knew he was doing the right thing. What he wanted to do. The reason he had left Courth in the first place and he knew that his father would have done the same.

"I am a Ranger, Reskalin. I have been born and bred to do just this. Who in Arre or even Rasna would be more able than I? If I give up and return as you suggest, others would be sent and they would all die. Dozens, maybe hundreds." He stood and pat Reskalin on the shoulder. "Maybe it would be better for you to return to Arre and tell Borath what we have found. I will fill in the rest when I return."

Reskalin practically jumped to his feet, his forehead and cheeks were red with anger and his thin eyebrows were practically crossed. "I told you I'm not letting you out of my sight. If we go back, we go back together. If we continue then we . . ."

"Shush" Enguer interrupted. His gaze was focused on dark shapes crawling up from a ravine less than fifty paces ahead of them. "Something is moving over there."

Reskalin turned his furious glare toward the figures emerging from the ravine. There were four of them and when they stood, they were easily as tall as a man if not a head taller. Scale and leather armor covered their shoulders and torsos, boots cut open at the toe to reveal curled claws protected their feet and each carried a double-edged axe or sword designed for one purpose. Killing. The lead ork snarled and spoke harsh guttural sounds through wolf-like jaws lined with sharp teeth and capped by a piggish snout. His pointed ears twitched with nervous energy or anticipation, Enguer would never know, to match the rigid fur covering the entirety of its body spiked like a belligerent cat. Only their eyes could he not see as they each wore a black headscarf across their yellow orbs to presumably reduce their sensitivity to the sun's brilliance.

The orks charged.

Instinctively, Enguer and Reskalin pushed off each other to give them space to move freely. Enguer pulled his short sword and long knife and assumed an open fighting stance that would allow him to strike or as easily dodge depending on the opportunity. On his left, Reskalin carried a longer, thinner sword and a needle-like dirk that appeared too fragile for combat and he crouched low as if preparing to jump. Just then it occurred to Enguer that he had never seen the small man fight. Could Reskalin hold one or two of the beasts off long enough for him to finish his own and come to his aide? Dread filled him at the thought of losing his friend to these nasty creatures but he had little time to stew on it with the orks right on top of them.

The lead ork came in hard with his axe raised to swing down on Enguer's head. Stepping out and under it, Enguer let the ork stumble past and steadied himself to face a second one closing fast. He had never fought an ork before and as beastly as he thought of them, their lean frames allowed them to move with surprising agility. A high-pitched squealing bark from behind nearly distracted Enguer from the next orks attack. This one foolishly stopped his charge and swung his sword wildly. Enguer easily avoided the unsteady arcs and slapped the blade from its grasp. He spun around just in time to deflect another swipe of the battle axe with his sword giving him the opening he needed to neatly plunge his long dagger into the soft flesh under the orks jowls and through the back of his skull. Not wasting his time to pull free the dagger, Enguer let it fall with dead ork, dancing away to face the ork frantically trying to retrieve its sword on the ground.

It was too late for him.

To Enguer's astonishment, Reskalin was already on him, smoothly sliding the edge of his long blade across the back of the orks neck at a downward angle that nearly decapitated the beast, save for the tenuous muscle that held its head dangling over its chest before it hit the ground to lay twitching and staining the hard stone with the almost black blood that pulsed out of its body.

Enguer cast around urgently for the other two orks. One was still on the ground with Reskalin's dirk lodged in its eye through the headscarf it wore and the other was squirming nearby desperately trying to keep its guts from sliding through its clawed fingers. Reskalin started toward it, presumably to finish it off, when a sharp screech filled the air and a shadow briefly blotted out the sun.

Falling prone, Enguer rolled to a crouch and searched the sky for the source of the new threat. Not far away, a large creature with scaly legs, lizard like head and sinuous tail turned on leathery wings back in their direction. It screeched again, one long pink tongue split at the end, darting out of a maw filled with razor-sharp teeth.

"Run!" Enguer shouted, waiting long enough to make sure Reskalin knew the danger.

He did.

With no hesitation, his friend followed and the two sprinted toward the nearest ravine. In seconds they came to the edge of one and jumped in not knowing if it was six feet deep or fifty. As luck would have it, the trench was shallow and they landed roughly in a bed of loose rubble littered with sharp edges that left them cut and bruised but alive all the same.

'Was that a dragon?" Reskalin hissed. He had a wild look in his eyes as if he couldn't accept what they were seeing. "The orks have a dragon?"

Enguer took a deep breath to slow down his heart rate and avoid panic. "No, not a dragon." He crawled to the edge of the ravine and looked over. Reskalin cautiously climbed up next to him. "It's called a wyvern – similar to a dragon but not the same. Not the same at all."

The wyvern swooped down and splayed open its wings to slow its descent before landing amongst the dead and dying orks. Its sharp claws clacked on the stone with each step it took while it sniffed at each of the stinking bodies.

"My father drew pictures and made notes about many of the beasts that he encountered in The Wilds to help me learn about them. This is one of them." Enguer couldn't take his eyes off the monster striding around less than a stone's throw away.

"Is it one of the things made by the Tuatha De?" Reskalin's voice was calm and in control again. Enguer was glad. He would need his friend about his wits if they had to fight this thing.

"No. It is a creature of nature, odd as it may be."

The quivering ork began to squeal when the wyvern brought its head down to take a sniff. The shrill sound appeared to startle the beast and it reared up briefly flapping its great wings. Then, with one giant claw it roughly turned the shrieking ork onto it's back and struck at it with the tip of its tail. Enguer would not have believed that the orks animal-like screams could have gotten any more shrill, but they did, and its body shook violently. It only lasted a moment before it fell silent forever.

"What just happened?" Reskalin had his sword and another dirk in his hands.

Enguer realized he still held his sword as well and wished he had retrieved his long-dagger. "The end of its tail is like a scorpion and filled with deadly venom. If it comes for us, one must distract it while the other cuts the end off the tail. It is more dangerous than anything else the wyvern can do to us. One hit from that tail and . . . well, you saw what it does."

"Ok, I'm ready," Reskalin nodded and started to crawl out of the ravine.

Enguer grabbed his leg and pulled him back down, "Are you mad? I said if it comes for us. Those orks have more than enough meat on their bones to fill it. Wyverns hunt during the day and return to their nest at night. We will wait for it to leave and then get as far away from here as possible."

"Got it," Reskalin sounded relieved and leaned back against the side of the ravine as if it was the only thing holding him up.

For all the talk of wanting to abandon their mission and go back to Arre, Reskalin was a courageous fellow, Enguer had to give him that. Who under the light of Sunna would willingly face a wyvern? Only a hero or a fool. Which one were they? A little of both, he suspected.

Moving very slowly, Enguer positioned several rocks at the lip of the ravine so than he could watch the wyvern without fear of attracting unwanted attention with any inadvertent movement. The creature might not need any more flesh to fill its belly, but that wouldn't stop it from eliminating anything nearby that threatened to steal its new-found bounty. From what he remembered about the notes his father had taken, wyverns were primal beasts of limited intelligence that were good at two things – killing and making baby wyverns. Enguer never asked how his father could possibly know the latter.

Reskalin was beside him again watching the wyvern efficiently tear through the tough leather shirts the orks wore and rip open their chest cavities to feast on the tender organs inside. It was a grotesque visual accompanied by the noise of snapping bone and eager, sticky slurping that made Enguer's stomach want to turn inside out. He decided that this part he didn't need to watch so he turned his back and lay flat against the incline doing his best to ignore the awful noise.

"What a terrifying creature that is," Reskalin whispered.

Enguer glanced over to see a face not struck with fear but more of a morbid fascination with what he observed. It wasn't the blood and gore that disturbed Enguer, he had seen enough of that in The Wilds and cleaned his fair share of carcasses he butchered for meat. It was the thought that if the orks had not come along when they did, at that precise moment in time, it could be they watching he and Reskalin get torn apart on the bloody plateau. It was something about fate or luck or divine intervention that always gave him pause, for it always seemed a far too frequent visitation in his life. He wondered if everyone felt the same way.

After a while, the wyvern ate its fill and flew off toward the high crags. Reskalin wanted to leave right then, but Enguer's instinct was to wait. His decision paid off as less than an hour later the wyvern returned to eat more. Had they left their cover, the two men would have been out in the open and clearly visible on the desolate plain.

"Why did it come back?" Reskalin asked nervously. "Can it digest its food so quickly?"

Enguer thought there might be another reason. "It must have a brood somewhere up in those peaks and like many carnivorous birds, it probably feeds on its kill and then regurgitates the partially digested food to sustain its young. It may do this several times before it is done."

They waited for night to fall. Enguer tried to rest, but he felt impatient to depart and prayed that Sunna would pass through the sky with a little more haste. The wyvern came and went three more times before Sunna answered his prayers and finally took her rest beyond the horizon. With the darkness came the cold, but it wasn't enough to keep them huddled in the ravine a minute longer than Enguer felt necessary and they scurried over the edge of the ravine and out onto the plateau to resume their southern trek to find the orks. They travelled lighter this night having each lost a dagger and their travel packs to the mess of stinking ork guts made by the wyvern. At least they stole away with their waterskins and their lives.

Careful not to lose the orks trail, Enguer stopped frequently to check for signs of their passing. Fortunately, their tracks led unwaveringly south until the plateau's seemingly endless arid stone desert eventually broke into a rocky slope with large boulders and even a few stands of trees that could provide a modicum of cover if they needed to hide. To his relief, the trail led to a cold spring that gurgled up from beneath a pile of rocks and flowed down a natural channel to a creek fed by several more springs along its winding path.

Enguer thrust his hand into the water and tasted the tips of his fingers. "Fresh water. Let's fill our waterskins."

"Do you think those orks on the plateau were waiting for us?" Reskalin crouched beside the spring filling both of his waterskins at the same time.

"I doubt it. My guess is that they were a hunting party crossing the plateau in search of big game. The fact that they would have to travel such a distance for food is more proof that their situation is becoming desperate."

Reskalin hung his waterskins across his chest and paced around the spring surveying the area. "The tracks lead down to the creek."

"Good," Enguer nodded. "Let's follow. I have a feeling we are not far now."

The ork tracks ran roughly parallel to the creek for a goodly distance before veering off to crawl up a thickly forested slope. The sun was long beyond its zenith by the time the pair crested the summit, only a couple hours before nightfall, and the cold breeze that pushed its way up the other side swaying the tree tops brought just a hint of a smoldering cook fire. Enguer motioned a warning to Reskalin to keep silent and waved for him to follow. Leaving the trail of ork prints behind, Enguer followed the summit southwest where it met another, sharper gradient that led higher into mountainous elevations sparse with trees and thick with giant boulders and precarious outcroppings.

They climbed up to the first ledge and over its length on their bellies to look over the edge into the valley far below. It was nearly dark, more so in the valley given that it was below the horizon, but what was revealed there was unmistakable.

Like ants slowly emerging from a wide crack in the earth on the opposite side of the valley, dozens of orks made their way into the basin to light cooking fires and prepare the 'morning' meal. The entire vale, one hundred paces up both sides was completely denuded of trees and brush and through its center ran a shallow creek no more than six strides wide. The orks washed there and filled their cooking pots. Several makeshift forges complete with warming hearths, billows and crude anvils stood alongside cauldrons of salt and stretched hides prepared for scudding that must have been tanneries. Stands of hundreds of completed sets of leather shirts were erected in rows, some fitted with iron buckles, others with studs, all in the process of completion like some fiendish farmer's crop. Opposite the field of leather, racks and racks of spears, swords and axes sat waiting leather handles or a final sharpening. The operation was extensive. It was extensive enough to supply an army of thousands.

The trickle of a dozen orks turned into hundreds when the last streamers of light retreated from the heavens. The entire valley was filled with torches, cooking and work fires eclipsed by the constant movement of bodies in a whirl of activity. And there was no sign that the deluge of orks heaving from the great cavernous mouth was anywhere near its end.

"This is not at all what I expected," Enguer was almost breathless in disbelief.

Reskalin's answer was controlled, but tinged with fear, "Nor I. This is not a clan of orks on the verge of starving and running out of resources. This is an army preparing for war."

Chapter 20

The Enclave

Brought to life by a misguided people who thought themselves superior to all others, the orks were creatures meant to toil in the mines digging up precious metals to please their masters. If the Tuatha De Blood were not nearly extinct already I might just strangle the bunch of them for the vanity that led to the creation of such abominations in the first place. It's a hard thing to bear, I tell you, to acknowledge this glaring flaw in my family history. I stand chagrined.

Wodanaz the Wanderer

"Are you mad?"

"How else will we find out what their true purpose is?"

"Even with that ring of yours, how do you expect to get around so many of them? They must be packed like fish in a barrel down there and it's probably worse inside that cave." Reskalin was talking faster and faster. It was an annoying characteristic Enguer had noticed about his friend when he became upset. "And you see those glowing orbs down there? Those are light-globes. That means they have spell-casters, shamans or whatever they call themselves. They might be able to see right through your veil of invisibility."

"Calm down, Reskalin. If I go during the day there will be only a few of them awake. And they have shown no compulsion to set guards or patrols, so they won't be expecting anyone to be sneaking about their enclave." Enguer did his best to sound reassuring, "Don't forget, I know a little something about getting around in caves."

"This is still madness, Enguer," Reskalin was almost pleading. It wasn't like him at all. "We should go back and report this. Tarre and Rasna, the whole of the Western Kingdoms for that matter, need to know about this threat. Those forges and tanneries are shockingly efficient for those brutish creatures and by the looks of it they are only

259

a few months away from arming a massive army. Maybe less if they have more equipment stored inside!"

"You're right, Reskalin."

"Finally! Some sense out of you. As soon as dawn breaks let's get out of here."

Enguer sighed heavily, "I mean you are right that we need to report this as soon as possible. At dawn I am going into that cave and you need to head back to Arre with this news. I will follow tomorrow and might even catch up with you in a few days."

Reskalin's cheeks reddened and his eyebrows looked as if they wanted to trade places. The words that followed were slow and deliberate with a slight pause in between each one for emphasis, "I . . . told . . . you . . . I'm . . . not . . . leaving . . . you . . . alone. Why do you keep trying to send me away? If you are hell bent on going into that cave then I'm going with you."

Now who was talking madness? "Reskalin, how? I have my ring to keep me hidden. You will only endanger us both." Enguer wanted to beat his head against the rock underneath him. "If you don't want to leave, stay here until I return. But if I'm not back by tomorrow night you will have to take word of what we have found to Arre."

Scooting back on his belly away from the edge of the outcropping, Reskalin got to his knees and removed his cloak. Enguer watched as he reversed it and put it back on inside out. The material underneath was strange and shimmery like watching heat rise off heated stones. Enguer felt like scratching his eyes when he looked directly at it.

Reskalin pulled the cloak around him and bent forward in a tight ball. "What do you see?"

To Enguer's amazement, the small man had somehow transformed. "I see a rock," he almost stuttered.

Reskalin sat up and crawled on his knees to the back side of the ledge and stood up against the rock wall. "Now what?"

"Nothing. I see nothing but the rock." It was still dark, but in the starlight, it looked as if the rock had simply swallowed Reskalin up.

A pale pair of hands appeared and then Reskalin's disembodied head seemed to float impossibly in mid-air and he was smiling like an idiot. "You see, I have my own tricks as well."

Enguer scurried away from the ledge and stood up next to Reskalin. Even as close as he was to the rogue, he could not for the life of him see the outline of his body. Just rock. He reached out to touch, expecting to feel a hard surface and instead encountered the silky fabric. It shimmered and blurred when he gently shook it. "Amazing. Why didn't you tell me about this before?"

Reskalin removed his cloak and turned it back the way it was before. "Because you didn't need to know. You think that just because we are friends now, I will tell you all my secrets?"

"I guess not."

Reskalin fixed him with a steadfast gaze that brooked no disagreement, "And I'm going with you. It settled now, right?"

Enguer didn't want to laugh. He tried hard not too, still; a mild chuckle escaped. The little man was so earnest and proud that any further discussion on the subject would have just been a waste of his breath. "Yes, we will go together and die together if we must. Now, let's get a couple of hours rest, tomorrow will be a long day."

At the first light of dawn Enguer was up washing his face in the cold water from the spring. Before he was done, Reskalin was beside him doing the same and then they took their places on the ledge watching the last of the orks crowd into the wide cavern entrance. Not a single ork lingered outside.

"We could probably just walk right up," Reskalin whispered.

"Let's not. However, we will get as close as possible before I put on the ring." Enguer suddenly realized that he would be just as invisible to Reskalin as the orks. "How will you follow me?"

Reskalin flashed a smile, "Remember how I found you in Arre? I will listen."

Enguer shrugged and crawled backwards off the ledge until he was out of sight of any unseen eyes in the valley. There may not be any more orks out, but he wasn't taking any chances. Quietly, they made their way down the forested slope until they came to the tree line, beyond which they would have to cross about two hundred paces of cleared trees, the shallow creek and various ork constructs that reminded him of the shanty town near the docks in Port Francik.

Enguer took the lead, threading his way around stumps, weapon racks, stinking pots still hot from the fire and hastily erected shelters held together with nails and twine. And no orks. He chose a route that approached the cave opening from the west along the side of the slope rather than straight across the vale. If the orks did post guards, they would be deep in the shadows of the cave opening where they couldn't be seen and if they were paying any amount of attention could sound the alarm before Enguer and Reskalin were halfway across. Approaching from the side would at least give them the chance to hear the orks inside if there were any.

In moments, they were standing against the rock at the edge of the cave entrance. Enguer suddenly felt very small. From a distance the opening did not look very large, but from where he stood now, he thought it was wide enough for thirty men to stand side-by-side and at least four times a man's height. Unless they were Reskalin's size, then it might be a few more. Enguer didn't know why that silly thought had popped into his head. Maybe it was his nerves. He had to focus. The sun was already above the edge of the valley and they were short on time as it was. He motioned for Reskalin to listen at the entrance for any noise. Enguer had discovered the hard way how good his friend's hearing was having been caught more than once muttering under his breath at the often-annoying rogue. He had since learned to keep his mouth shut. Most of the time.

Reskalin gestured that the way was clear and removed his cloak to turn it inside out. Enguer avoided looking at the shimmering patch as much as possible while he retrieved his ring and set it on his finger. They were ready.

Enguer took the lead followed closely by Reskalin only an arm's length behind and stepped into the cavern hugging tight to the side wall. There they waited for several minutes while their vision adjusted to the darkness. The entry itself held no light other than the natural light of day outside, but it was enough to see that the cavern was empty save for a rough-hewn corridor at the back leading into darkness. Slowly, they made their way around to the hallway. It was wide, twenty strides at least, and too high to touch the ceiling. Somewhere ahead the passage curved off to the right and out of sight. Maybe it was a trick of his imagination, but Enguer thought he detected a slight green glow from around the corner. His biggest concern before entering the orks enclave, aside from getting himself and Reskalin killed, was how they would see in the darkness.

Moving silently through the dark, the green glow appeared brighter the closer they came to it and the more Enguer's eyes acclimated to their new environment. Cautiously peeking around the corner, everything was quiet. The source of the green glow was an unusual fungus that covered much of the walls and ceiling. It was thick and hairy-looking almost like a worn tapestry with missing parts and irregular in its shape. He had never seen any such thing and was glad for it there now. With any luck it would be a regular feature throughout cave system.

Enguer stayed in the main corridor passing many smaller passages twisting away bathed in the green glow of the fungus. So far, there had been no sound from any of them. It was a strange dichotomy between the thousands he had watched going about their business outside, beating their hammers, squabbling and laughing raucously in contrast to the still, empty feeling of a tomb inside. Where had they all gone?"

Reskalin's hand on his back alerted him to danger before he heard the sound of skittering from a side passage a few paces ahead. Positioned tight against the wall, Enguer held his dagger close and waited. Moments later a small ork, barely waste high, came careening around the corner. It bounced off the opposite wall with such force that Enguer was sure it had injured itself. Instead, it stumbled backward disoriented and fell directly into him before regaining its footing and running happily down another passage at full speed. Enguer felt bullets of sweat running down his face and brushed off the hand on his back jiggling in silent laughter.

Taking a moment to collect himself, Enguer silently crept down to the next bend in the wide corridor. He could clearly hear the jumble of crowded voices that echoed from whatever lay beyond. Finally, he thought, they found them. He peered around its edge. The passage opened into a vast, heart-stopping, cavity covered in wooden framework attached to its walls supporting over a dozen levels of what appeared to be living spaces. Rope and wood bridges spanned the expanses from one end to the other and in between like a vast spider web while sturdy ladders and wide ramping walkways provided easy access to the next level above each one.

And there were orks everywhere.

Big orks, little orks, male and female orks, young and old; they were all represented here. Many walked together in family units, mother's carried infants, children played and ran and laughed. At the base of the cavern large storage alcoves were carved into the walls containing barrels and crates and sacks of all sizes. A complex pully system hauled everything from water to wood planks to baskets of food stuff up to the higher levels where he could see women standing over stone ovens preparing meals for a line of men each holding a wooden bowl. These were the monster's created by the Tuatha De, the raiders that burned down villages and murdered families, the eaters of human flesh. Yet here they were acting nearly as normal and civilized as any human community. A depressed community perhaps, desperate to survive and feed their families. How quickly would the Zilach burn this place to the ground and murder every man, woman and child in it? Were humans the monsters in stories ork mothers told their children at night?

The stink drifting on the warm air escaping the cavern was repugnant at best, turning his stomach and forcing him to breathe through his mouth. It was the most awful thing, but the orks did not appear to be bothered by it in the least. His father told him once that animals detested the smell of humans and that was the reason why people were not often preyed upon. Enguer wasn't sure about that. It might have just been one of his father's jokes. Sometimes it was hard to tell.

A weight pressed up against his shoulder and he could see the blur of Reskalin's form from out of the corner of his eye. "There are passages leading out of the cavern at every level," he whispered in Enguer's ear.

It was true. Looking closely, Enguer could see dozens of passages leading away. Some to other caverns just like this, he guessed. Outside they had seen thousands of orks. In this one room alone, there might be around five-hundred. It could take them weeks of searching to find out anything useful. The task was impossible.

"This place is too vast," he whispered to Reskalin. "We will never find anything here."

"You could be right, but we are here and we have the rest of the day. Let's check some of the lower levels where there are not too many orks around. Maybe we will get lucky."

Enguer proceeded into the cavern, keeping to the wall, until they came upon a vacant passage leading down at a gentle slant. This one was wide enough for two to pass by easily but not more. If they came upon orks walking side by side it would be a problem. They followed the turning, twisting passage lit by the green glow of fungus further into the depths. There were no other intersecting corridors or doorways along their route giving Enguer the impression that this passage was designed for a purpose. Before long, the air became stale and humid, the sides of the passage 'sweat' with moisture and a pungent, musty smell filled their nostrils. The further they descended the stronger it became and Enguer was about to turn around when the passage leveled out and he could see several open doorways lining each side of the long corridor.

Against the wall opposite the first opening, Enguer could clearly see a wide cavern with a low ceiling dripping with perspiration at nearly the frequency of a light rain over organized sections of fungus, mushrooms and molds. Several female orks crawled on hands and knees between the planted sections tending to the plants with care as if they were crops in a field back home. It occurred to Enguer that these women were cultivating the growths to supplement the orks diet. How the orks palates could tolerate such ill-fragrant fare, he had no idea, but it may well explain why they smelled so bad.

"We won't find anything here," Reskalin hissed near his ear. Enguer found himself startled and somewhat alarmed at how close the nimble rogue could get without stumbling into him. Subconsciously he glanced down to where his legs and arms should have been visible to make sure he was still masked by the magic of the ring.

Enguer quietly followed Reskalin's blurred outline back into the main passageway and across to another carved hallway that led in the opposite direction. It was dark here as well, only sparingly lit by the occasional torch at long intervals. It was enough for Enguer to see by, but far too little for him to keep track of his friend's distorted form. Amid the drips and echoes of the sounds behind them, Enguer relied on the infrequent scuff of a boot or brush of fabric against the wall to give him an idea of how far Reskalin was ahead of him. He had a notion that the little man was purposefully making the discreet noise for his benefit and could have been completely silent if he wanted to. It was a skill Enguer had mastered in The Wilds that Reskalin was still adjusting to, yet it was clear that in this environment the shoe was quite literally on the other foot.

An opening appeared a few strides ahead on their left. It was a rough hole large enough for an ork or a man to crawl through and into a larger room on the other side. A faint scraping and skittering accompanied by sharp squeaks of anger drifted from the chamber on stagnant air thick with the stench of rot and decay. Enguer caught a hint of movement against the pale illumination of a torch inside that he guessed was Reskalin's cloak settling into the illusion of the dark stone he was pressed up against on the opposite side of the hole. Enguer crept up and peered inside.

A great stone-worked cavity, easily thirty strides in diameter, held a deep pit surrounded by a wide ledge along the outside edge under a high ceiling that was almost dome-like. Four torches mounted in sconces at equal distance around the room revealed dark patches of dried stains on the stone walkway near a wooden rack holding unusually long spears set with pointed barbs. These too were stained from their iron tips well down the long length of the shafts. Most horribly, three tall baskets held the butchered remains of animal carcasses stripped of their hides, meat and organs and covered by a shifting cloud of large flies.

A smudge in the air indicated that Reskalin had silently moved inside to investigate further. Enguer followed, stepping lightly through the hole, and carefully looked over the side of the pit into the shadows below. Several spans beneath the ledge, plump bodies covered in grey fur with black eyes, pink claws and long slithering tails roiled over each other like boiling water. There had to be hundreds of rats the size of dogs in a frenzy of expectation. Brief flashes of ivory betrayed an impossible depth of bones picked clean and broken for their marrow underneath the animals. The reek of feces and ammonia was nearly overwhelming.

"They sense our presence," Reskalin spoke low from somewhere nearby. "The must expect to be fed."

"What do you suppose they . . ." Enguer cut himself short. There were voices in the passage outside.

"Move to the other side of the pit," Reskalin whispered urgently.

Enguer did not delay and by the time he was around to the opposite side, a pig-like snout on the head of a hairy ork was pushing himself through the hole and into the room followed by another. Each of them carried a bucket of water and rather than armor, they wore leather smocks discolored and streaked with viscera matching the hand axes that hung from a belt at their sides still wet and sticky from their most recent work in whatever passed as a kitchen down there.

The orks poured the contents of the buckets over the rats in the pit and casually walked to the wooden rack, each removing one of the long spears it held. They spoke the whole time in their coarse guttural language that sounded more like a series of barks and heavy consonants between sharp squeals of laughter. It was obvious that these two knew each other well and Enguer didn't need to understand their language to know that this was just another routine day they shared together over countless months. Perhaps years. He wondered if either of them had been part of the raiding party sent to slaughter the humans and if they felt any more remorse for the humans slaughtered than the rats awaiting their fate below.

Reversing his grip on the shaft, the first ork plunged the tip of the spear down into the pit. The swift thrust was immediately answered by an anguished screech and a violent shuddering of the spear held tightly in the orks hands. One more push set the barbs firmly before he pulled his prize hand-over-hand up to the ledge, alive and wriggling desperately to free itself. Undeterred, the ork removed the hand axe from his belt, knelt beside the struggling rat and deftly severed head from body, sending it back down to a flurry of sharp teeth and claws eagerly waiting to fight over the bloody morsel. The second ork made a comment and they both laughed. They were no different than pig farmers in Courth eking out a ghastly living as best they could endure it. There was no cruelty in the butchery of the rats, it was matter of fact and necessary for their survival and despite how much Enguer detested the orks culture, he was forced to appreciate if not admire their perseverance. But Enguer knew that idea was an illusion, he knew them for what they really were, what cruelty they were capable of. He had to keep reminding himself of that no matter how civilized they might appear on the surface.

The ork stepped to the side, still holding the twitching body of the rat on the end of his spear and angled it over the side of the pit allowing the carcass to bleed out in a crimson spray upon its comrades, while the second ork readied his own spear to claim the next victim. Abruptly, a surprised look came over the face of the first ork and he muttered something that sounded like a question, but the second ork paid no attention focused solidly on the rat he planned to skewer.

Shifting the spear with the headless rat to one hand, the ork probed behind him with the other, then his eyes widened with surprise and his mouth opened to speak, but no words came forth. Instead, the flash of metal crossed his throat leaving a red line in its wake while at the same time the tip of a second blade sliced through the front of his smock from the inside. With slow deliberation, the body fell forward and tumbled into the pit still holding the spat rat.

"Ah-ha!" the second ork called out triumphantly impaling his quarry.

His glee turned to confusion and he cried in shock when his coworker plunged past him into the pit and then again to terror when an unseen force pushed him over the edge close behind. The screams that followed were brief if toe-curling to witness as the rats devoured the wretched ork alive, leaving a silence behind that was nearly as unbearable.

"I had to do it," Reskalin dropped his hood to reveal his face slick with sweat. "I should have been more careful. I shouldn't have stayed so close."

Enguer removed his ring revealing himself once more. "What's done is done. As much as they appear to do things as we do them, they have no conscience, no care for the life of others. If they had found us here do you deny that they would have dropped us both down that pit and enjoyed every second of our suffering? Never forget that they are the creation of the Tuatha De, built for a purpose that no longer exists."

Reskalin nodded silently and returned the hood to its place concealing him against the backdrop of the stone wall. A disembodied voice spoke across the void of the pit, "Let's get on with this. I'm ready to leave this place sooner rather than late."

Casting a weary smile in Reskalin's direction, Enguer placed the ring back on his finger. "A few more hours and we will leave here forever."

Stepping back into the passage, Enguer was relieved to leave the sights and sounds and smell of the pit behind, if not the memories that would haunt his dreams for years to come. There was no time to worry about that now. They had to stay alert and focused if they were going to survive this ordeal. He knew Reskalin would leave the orks enclave at any moment, but Enguer needed to satisfy himself that he had learned as much as possible before acquiescing. In his gut he knew there was something they were missing.

The passage turned a corner and ended at a broad wooden door. From outside Enguer could hear the chatter of orks, clinking of metal pots and chopping on wooden boards that indicated they had found the kitchens. Even from the opposite side of the door waves of heat warmed the damp chill from his bones threatening to lull him into lethargy. Then the door opened forcing him to press his back up against the wall to let a female ork pass by in a rush. A slight brush of fabric on his hand told him that Reskalin was right beside him.

Shooting out his arm to catch the door, Enguer held it for just a moment to scrutinize the activity inside. The large cavern was filled with the clamor of at least a hundred orks in the process of preparing meals for the enclave. Some cooked rats on spits, while others chopped them up into bits and combined them in pots with chunks of mushrooms, molds and fungus in a putrid smelling stew that made Enguer want to sick-up everything he had ever eaten in his life. From kettles further away, orks filled buckets with the steaming mash and placed them in a depression on the wall where they attached their handles to a hook at the end of a rope. Seconds later, the bucket was lifted out of sight through a chute that must have ended at a level above. It was another impressive adaptation similar to what he would expect in King Francik's palace, rather than the stinking den of orks.

An ork stopped in his passage across the kitchen and looked squarely to where Enguer was holding the door open. An angry expression darkened the orks features and he turned to stomp deliberately toward them. Enguer gripped his long-dagger, certain the ork was coming for him, but the thing stopped short and with a shout into the passage that sounded like a curse, he slammed the door closed.

Enguer's heart raced and he backed a few steps to check that there were no other orks nearby before he spoke in the direction he supposed Reskalin was standing, "Let's go back to the main passage and down one more side tunnel. If we don't find anything there, we leave."

"Agreed," Reskalin's voiced a simple response from the shadows. To say there was a mountain of relief in that one-word reply would have been a patent understatement that gave Enguer pause for concern that perhaps they had already overstayed their unwelcome.

Chapter 21

One True God

Enguer's mind was set in indecision. The third path off the main they followed led to a series of chambers devised for the care of juvenile orks of various ages under the watchful eye of a host of overseers instructing them in tasks as mundane as wood-carving to viscous hand-to-hand combat. It was startling the level of violence encouraged for the martial training at such a young age. Tiny orks that Enguer guessed could be only two or three years old fought like feral beasts with tooth and claw to the praise and cheers of everyone around them. These creatures were raised almost from the womb to kill with no remorse or regret and from the looks of what they endured, barely a thought for their own suffering. They instilled a mindless devotion in their young, survival of the fittest that was a basic tenant of nature he understood all too well, except that the orks were not creatures of nature, they were unnatural, organized and extremely dangerous. It was a realization that chilled Enguer to his very core.

"It's time to go," Enguer whispered to the blurry figure behind him. "We might not have ascertained the purpose behind their planned invasion, but we have discovered their intent."

"Will your mind be content?" Reskalin sounded skeptical.

Enguer dismissed his concern with a shrug he could not have seen, "I will be content with what we have learned."

Without debate, Reskalin's hazy outline melted into the shadows between the glow of torches in the direction of the main passage. No longer aimlessly wandering unfamiliar corridors, Enguer followed as close as he dared back the way they came toward the cavern opening. They tread as quickly as they could through the twisting ways pausing only when Reskalin's sharp ears picked up the distant step of an ork that passed by blithely ignorant of their presence. Throughout much of their retreat back to daylight, the clatter they

271

heard before had subsided noticeably and Enguer reminded himself that it was the orks 'night' and many of them must have settled down for a few hours of sleep before the toils of their miserable lives continued once again.

Up through the main passage the pair practically ran, as fast as they could without making undue noise that might attract unwanted attention, swiftly passing intersecting hallways and caverns unattended. They would be out in a matter of minutes, back to the relative safety of the forest, rocks and crags, sucking fresh air into their lungs to expulse the vile gases they were forced to draw in among the stinking beasts. Until unexpectedly, Reskalin brought them to a stop nearly causing Enguer to pile on top of him.

"What is it?" Enguer hissed angrily. His mind was set to be far away from this place by sundown.

Reskalin shoved a sharp elbow into his ribs, "Quiet."

Enguer wanted to slap the back of the rogue's head, if he could have found it, but he restrained the urge and waited more than a little impatiently for Reskalin to tell him what he had heard.

Seconds turned into a minute and then a little longer before Reskalin finally spoke again. "There are orks somewhere down that tunnel chanting. At first, I thought it was the hum of a subterranean river like the fast-moving sewage canals under Arre, but then the pitch changed. I almost missed it."

Enguer's heart sank to his stomach. They were so close to escaping this awful place. Yet he knew that humming meant a religious ceremony that would involve shamans, which suggested the possibility of discovering the information they originally came in here for in the first place and that meant they were not quite done here.

"I need to check it out," Enguer said it almost apologetically.

To his credit, Reskalin did not sound discouraged in his reply. How could he? He could have simply ignored the humming and told him about it later. Or never. "I know."

Resuming their previous caution, Enguer entered the dark tunnel, nearly devoid of any light, keeping one hand on the damp wall and his ears acutely attuned to the subtle sounds of Reskalin moving a pace or two ahead. To his surprise, it was several minutes before, he too, detected the faint humming that drifted over the stale air. If nothing else, Reskalin had the ears of a cat. The vaguely musical sound was still far away, but it seemed to be drawing nearer at a very deliberate pace.

Reskalin stopped and grabbed Enguer's cloak pulling him closer. "There must be several of them and this passage is too narrow not to stumble right over us. If we can t avoid them, run as fast as you can out of here and I will delay them long enough for us to escape."

Enguer was astounded at the ridiculous plan. "What do you mean delay? If they can't see us, we can both run."

"Just do as I say," Reskalin sounded heated and speaking fast. "If their shaman are like our priests they may have a higher sense that could detect our presence. I can put a dagger into the lead that will cause confusion and drop caltrops behind me if they pursue. By the time they recover we will be under your Soony again where they will be blind to our escape."

"Sunna," Enguer corrected him.

"What?"

"Her name is Sunna."

"Whatever."

Reskalin released his cloak and crept around the next curve in the passage. Still more concerned than agitated, Enguer followed close behind. They walked on, more slowly than before keeping close to the wall, all the while the humming, which had become distinguishable as a steady chant, was getting closer. Any expectation that the passage might suddenly widen or a side corridor might suddenly appear where they could hide when they passed was quickly becoming improbable in the time that remained and Enguer prepared himself for flight. He hoped Reskalin knew what he was doing. If the rogue miscalculated and found himself battling it out with the shamans Enguer resolved not to abandon him in this stinking hell. They would die together if one must die – a tragic tale of a heroic last stand that would never be sung. Sunna be praised.

The passage bent in a wide downward spiral and straightened out again for a few strides before it curved around to the right. The flickering light of advancing torches shown from around that bend and the chanting was loud. In seconds the procession of shamans would be in full view. They had run out of time.

"Door."

Enguer could hardly believe his eyes. Indeed, there was a door, two paces away, tucked into the uneven rock wall so shadowed that he had initially missed it. Immediately they made a dash for it. In the back of his mind Enguer realized that if it was locked, they would be literally face-to-face with whatever was coming around the corner with no way to avoid confrontation. Reskalin was at the door. Enguer could see the shimmering change of his cloak from the rock to the wood planks. There was a low creak of rusted hinges and Reskalin was through with Enguer right on his heels.

Inside, Reskalin slowly closed the door minimizing the noise from the hinges. Once shut, Enguer found a gap between the door and the frame and looked through just as the first of the orks rounded the bend. Walking three abreast, it was clear that their hunch had been right; they were indeed shamans. Slowly they passed by the door, not one paying a bit of attention to it and still more came, at least two dozen of them by his estimation. They wore long brown robes edged with rabbit fur, adorned their arms with gold and silver bracelets, their claw-like fingers with rings, hung bands of bone necklaces around their necks and pierced the center of their pig-like snouts with bone or bauble. Each of them carried either a torch or a blue-glowing light-globe that hovered a hand above their palm and they chanted in time with their steps. Under better circumstances the low intonation might have been soothing, reverent, perhaps a bit hypnotic. All Enguer felt was fear that they might be discovered.

A loud snort from behind shattered the still silence in the room sending a bolt of cold lightning up Enguer's spine. He spun to confront whatever was there and found himself facing the still form of an ork shaman in yellow robes slumbering over a pile of scrolls on his desk with quill still held upright in one hand. A single light-globe glowing dull blue lay trapped underneath the edge of the ork's loose sleeves bunched up around his folded arms forming a make-shift pillow to lay his head upon. All around the dim room shelves were packed with volumes of scrolls and a few tomes in a chaos of disorganization as if they were thrown there in a feeble attempt to keep them from falling on the ground. If not for the shock of the ork's presence, the scene might have been humorous. Less humorous was the fact that he had paid no attention to the room where they found refuge in his panic to get out of the passage. What if the ork had not been sleeping?

Enguer stepped back to the door and observed the end of the shamans procession passing by. The last of their number, an elder ork carrying a staff capped with a human skull with red rubies sparkling from the eye-sockets stopped dead in his tracks and turned his black-eyed gaze square on the door. For an eternal moment of rising terror, Enguer was sure the elder was staring straight at him. Somehow, he recovered enough to step away just in time to avoid the door slamming into his face. With a loud bang the door impacted the wall where the blurry form of Reskalin stood seconds before The elder shaman's arm stretched forward holding it firmly in place.

With a start, the sleeping ork nearly jumped from his stool in fright before rushing around his desk to kneel groveling before the elder. Harsh words followed that appeared to physically force the frightened ork to bow lower and lower before the elder cracked him on the top of the head with his staff for final emphasis. Sent nearly prostrate by the blow, the ork sniveled and whined pathetically while the elder surveyed the mess of the room. His gaze passed over Enguer without a flicker of interest and continued around the room before settling on a spot near a bookshelf. Following his gaze, Enguer caught the faint blur of the edge of Reskalin's cloak where the pattern of the rock wall changed to the more complex patterns of the bookcase filled with scrolls.

Don't move, Reskalin. Not a hair. Even the slightest sway would cause the pattern to shift abnormally and give him away. The waiting was interminable, more so he thought for his friend. Enguer gripped his dagger. He wouldn't wait for the shaman to realize the oddity. The elder might suspect already. Enguer slipped the dagger silently from the oiled sheath at his belt. He visualized the long blade plunging through the old shaman's neck below his voice box severing the spinal cord in a fierce strike that would kill instantly. Silently. He took a step . . .

A barking call came from down the hall. Enguer froze. The elder looked back and returned the call, spat a few parting words at the ork on the ground and slammed the door shut. For a few long seconds no one moved and then apparently satisfied the elder wouldn't return, the ork stood grumbling, brushed the dust and dirt off his robes and shuffled his way back to his desk.

He never made it.

Dark crimson stained the ork's robes where daggers held in olive-skinned hands slid from between the creature's ribs and retracted to disappear behind him. Mouth open wide extended to its fullest found no air to utter a cry, it stumbled forward, face stricken with terror and fell to its knees, one arm grasping the top of the desk for hopeless support. The ork collapsed after a moment, quivering briefly until it was left with no more life to give.

"Reskalin, watch the passage, I need to look through these scrolls." Enguer stepped over the dead ork and began rummaging through the dozens of scrolls on the desk. They were all written in a block-like scrawl of unfamiliar script. Some bore crudely drawn images and symbols that held no meaning beyond the comprehension of an ork and perhaps only the shamans themselves. Still, Enguer thought they might have some value in the hands of more worldly scholars in Arre who might have a better chance to translate their meaning. He packed as many as he could stuff into the small bag strapped across his back, less than half the total, and joined Reskalin by the door. His hood was down again, revealing a troubled expression on his face.

Enguer removed his ring. "What's wrong?"

"Did you know orks could read and write?"

"No," Enguer shook his head nonchalantly, "but why should that surprise you after everything we have seen here?"

Reskalin's furled eyebrows did not relax by even a little. "I know priests in Arre that can store power with words on scrolls such as those. Dangerous power."

"They appeared to be letters and simple drawings. I took as many as I could fit in my pack for Borath to take a look at. He might know someone that can decipher their meaning." Enguer felt something like a stone under his boot and shifted his foot to take a look. There, a red ruby flashed in the spare light. "What's this?"

He picked it up and held it in the blue glow of the light-globe hovering over the desk. "One of the eyes from the elder's staff."

Reskalin eyeballed the gem then swiftly strode over to the ork and motioned for Enguer to help him. "Let's move this fella behind the desk. That shaman may soon realize his ruby is missing and come looking for it."

Enguer agreed. It wouldn't be a stretch for the elder to realize it probably fell out when he struck the ork on the head. The gem was bigger than his thumb and of significant value. He had a hunch the elder would rip the enclave apart looking for it, especially if the staff served as a status symbol or part of an important ritual.

Together they shoved the ork behind the desk and mopped up any traces of blood with cloth ripped from the shaman's yellow robes. Whoever found him would immediately guess that he was murdered and hidden away, there was nothing they could do about that, but Enguer hoped they would be long gone before that happened. Even if they suspected their own, the place could turn into a roiling mountain of activity that would make it difficult for them to escape despite their advantages of stealth and concealment.

"Want to take a quick look at where the shamans came from?" Reskalin was looking through the crack in the door as he put his hood back in place obscuring his image.

"Why bother at this point?" Enguer was surprised at the rogue's sudden interest in exploring the cave further. "We should leave with what we have. Once that dead ork is found we might be stuck here until things die down from the commotion it will cause."

"It is still hours until sunset and most of them are likely asleep. Just a little further, I promise, and then we will head straight out."

Enguer wished he could see Reskalin's face. His tone was almost . . . enthusiastic, maybe a little excited. "Alright then. Let's be quick about it."

"Don't forget your ring."

Blushing slightly, Enguer set the ring on his finger imagining himself strolling boldly down the corridor thinking he was invisible. It was a momentary slip of his focus that sent a red flag up in his mind regarding Reskalin's motivation for pressing on. Something wasn't quite right.

The passage from where the shamans trudged snaked further into the lightless, silent depths. At one point it seemed to spiral downward and then straighten into a long corridor with smoothed walls. Enguer's hand slid across the surface, over ridges and depressions that might have formed carved images or symbols. He reached out with the other to grab at Reskalin in the darkness and snagged the back of his cloak.

Reskalin stopped, the soft shifting of fabric indicating that he turned to speak in a bare whisper "What is it?"

"The walls," Enguer didn't need to say more. He new the rogue would understand that there was something unusual about them.

A long moment passed and then Reskalin, sounding curiously anxious, pulled him closer, his breath sweet with the scent of berries they had found in the forest the day before, "Bring out your light-globe and shield it so only a bare cone of illumination comes forth."

Enguer smiled in the darkness. He had done this many times in The Wilds to avoid detection when a bit of light was needed. Removing the pack from his back, he quietly dug through the pile of parchment until his hand found the padded pocket that held the light-globe and a folded leather pouch. He retrieved them both and placed the orb inside the thick pouch sewn neatly to its size and held it close to his body.

"Spark," Enguer uttered the command and tapped the light-globe. Instantly, dim illumination shown through a narrow hole in the pouch about the size of a small coin. Light spilled oddly from the edges of the hole with it pressed against his invisible leather cuirass appearing as a miniature solar eclipse floating in mid-air. It was enough illumination for him to notice Reskalin had removed his hood and stood staring in awe at the strange illusion.

Swiftly, Enguer moved the globe to press the light against his opposing hand and raised his arms above his head. Slowly, he edged his hand around the light-globe far enough to allow a small sliver of the light to escape against the wall. What he saw caused him to rapidly draw his breath in a simultaneous reflection of the gasp he heard from Reskalin standing inches away.

Everywhere the light touched thick veins of red gold shimmered as if alive, forming outlines of vile creatures that stretched from floor to ceiling, across the floor and over the stone above their heads. Some appeared to be demons with eyes represented by blood-red rubies, ambers and garnets bringing attention to massive heads emphasized by horns and rows of sharp teeth or mandibles, grotesque bodies misshapen and distorted yet powerfully built with bulging, exaggerated muscles and long claw-like appendages that often numbered as many as a dozen. Other creatures appeared to be distorted versions of animals Enguer knew except that they were put together like dreadful puzzles out of order – the head of a growling lion on the body of a goat with feathered wings and chicken feet, an eagle with a unicorn horn, leather wings and the tail of a serpent, or a wolf with an ork's head and barbed tail of a scorpion were among the most vivid.

Enguer's eyes took it all in, following the figures down the passage as far as he could see until he brought the light down to the floor where more frightful images, smooth from decades of wear, still clearly represented their disquieting intent. Human skeletons, dwarf skeletons, elven skeletons, reptilian skeletons and even Atlantean skeletons were all represented in a neat row across the floor, identifiable by the caricature outline of their heads with haunting holes bored into the stone where their eyes should have been. And oddly, outlines of fish of various size scattered randomly among them that gave the impression the skeletons were under water.

"There is something unusual about these figures."

Enguer couldn't believe his ears. "Yes, everything about them is unusual."

Reskalin's eyebrows furrowed in an agitated line across his forehead. "What I mean is they are all facing one direction, back toward the way we came, as if they were leaving. And the skeletons," he gestured to the images on the floor, "have are all facing the way we are going."

Enguer recognized the pattern. Reskalin was right. "Maybe it is symbolic of whatever this is all supposed to represent."

"The end of days."

"Are you guessing?" Enguer knew of no legends or mythology that described anything like this.

Reskalin stood staring at the images as if transfixed, his disembodied head floating above his cloak struggling to camouflage against the complex patterns all around them. "There was a man that came to Arre with the manner and robes of a prophet a few months ago. He claimed to be from a village far to the east. A village he called Nukhu perched on the edge of a vast sea beyond the Thraix tribes." He turned troubled eyes on Enguer, a hazy gaze that saw more in the past than the present. "The man preached that the end of days was nigh and that when it arrived all manner of evil would be released upon the earth by a god in judgement of man. He described everything you see here and more. Much more." Reskalin reached out and slowly traced over the red gold outline of a demon on the wall with one slender finger. "He said it would begin with a scourge of demons and their fiendish minions spreading across the land like a dark storm cloud and end with fire from the heavens and a great flood that would lay low every city of man." Reskalin nodded toward the ceiling and Enguer followed with the sliver of light from the light-globe. Jagged lines of the red gold veins fashioned what appeared to be a giant ball of fire streaking across the ceiling almost directly above them in the direction they followed.

Reskalin hoarse whisper cut through the darkness, "He said his god had chosen him and his seed to spread the word to all parts so that everyone would be warned of his god's retribution and the reasons why."

"What reasons did he give?"

"That all the cities of man would soon be as defiled and corrupt as Ys and that mankind had forgotten the gift of life and free will so generously bestowed upon them, turning away from the One True God to serve and indulge themselves."

"One True God? I have never heard of such a thing. Was this man deprived of his senses?"

The rogue's head bobbed as if he had shrugged, "Perhaps maybe. Who knows? What matters is that many people believed him. Many left their homes and tradecraft to follow him although he never asked them to do so. He said his children's children would one day build great ships to carry those worthy through the deluge so that mankind could one day start anew. The Zilach grew so concerned with the rhetoric and the growing size of the movement that he forced the prophet and his followers to leave Arre. They fled into the Plains of Tarre and have not been heard from sense."

"No word of them in Provigi or Anzi?"

"None. Where ever they went, it wasn't Tarre. From the looks of this place they may have ended up here. But why the orks would allow them to create this . . . chamber . . . is beyond me." Reskalin looked back up at the images on the wall. "The strangest thing was how believable the prophet was. He had a charisma with the people that was mystifying. Hundreds were swayed to his side." Reskalin pulled his hood up. "We'll go to the end of this passage and if there is nothing of interest when we get there, we'll turn around and go home. I have had my fill of this place."

Enguer was fine with that. He was looking forward to seeing the sky again. And this passage with its strange tale of demons, floods and fire from the heavens did nothing to encourage him to stay a minute longer than he had to.

Chapter 22

Something Unexpected

"What a strange door to find so far under the mountain." Reskalin passed his hands lightly over the intricate relief that was etched in gold on the surface of the stout portal like a spider crawling over the delicate threads of a web.

The rogue had his hood down and cloak tied back over his shoulders allowing Enguer to watch with fascination the intimate movements of Reskalin's careful inspection in the shadowy illumination of the light-globe he held aloft. Whatever the symbols meant, they fit together to form the larger likeness of a clawed hand, open with palm facing out as if a warning to go no further. The image nearly filled the entire doorway and in the midpoint of the palm at the same height as the handle, five red-glowing gems were arranged in the shape of a pentagon with a sixth gem exactly at its center. These Reskalin never touched.

"Are you looking for an opening mechanism?" Enguer didn't understand why Reskalin was studying the door so closely. "The handle is right there."

"Traps," Reskalin whispered distractedly. "That symbol with the gems is exactly what the priest described so we must be careful."

This was new information and Enguer had the distinct impression it had been unwittingly revealed. Something was amiss. "Priest? What priest."

"What?" Reskalin glanced over, a blush touching his cheeks in the dim light.

"You mentioned a priest?" Enguer removed his ring causing his physical form to immediately become visible. If they were going to have a conversation, he wanted to look his companion in the eyes.

Reskalin sighed and brought his hands away from the door, "I'm sorry Enguer. I should have told you before. There was a larger reason that the Fat Man insisted that I come with you to find the orks."

"I'm listening."

Stepping closer, the rogue's slender eyebrows curved over brown eyes filled with trepidation. "A priest in service to Laran, our god of war, came from Lindium in the Spine of Cel to see the Zilach of Arre. It was about the same time as the prophet from Nukhu although I do not suppose there was any significance in the timing."

A head shorter than Enguer, Reskalin looked up at him in a way that made the little man look small and vulnerable. An image flashed through his head of a similar pose he often seen between his parents just before they kissed. Enguer shivered in spite of himself.

Reskalin placed a hand lightly on his shoulder. "Are you ok?"

Enguer shrugged it off. "Yes, of course. I am fine."

Peering at him sharply with those dark eyes, the rogue continued, "Anyway, the priest told the Zilach that he had a vision. He described that symbol on the door and a crystal disk rimmed in gold that would be found behind it."

Enguer was intrigued, "What does it mean?"

"We don't know." Reskalin's short brown locks fell over his eyes a little when he shook his head. "Only that it is the root of evil in this place and the reason for the orks recent aggression."

"So, you were sent to retrieve it."

"Yes. And I had nearly given it up thinking that it was a foolish tale told by an overzealous priest."

"Wait a minute," Enguer wasn't quite sure Reskalin's tale was any more believable. "You were ready to go back to Arre without ever having entered the enclave. It was only by my insistence that we are here in the first place. How do you square that?"

Reskalin looked away. "It is true. I would have left if you were willing and then in a few days I would have disappeared in the night and returned on my own." He looked back at Enguer, eyes intense. "I have grown to think of you as a friend and I didn't want you to put your life in jeopardy over something you knew nothing about."

Enguer smiled down at the rogue. It was good to have a true friend for the first time in his life. "That should have been my choice to make. Yet here we are anyway. Shall we go in?"

"Wait, there is one other thing," Reskalin's voice was laced with a hint of fear. "The priest said the disk is guarded by something powerful and evil, but he couldn't say what. We will have to proceed with care."

Enguer nodded and returned his ring to its place on his finger while Reskalin readjusted his cloak to cover his entirety. Then the rogue firmly took hold of the handle and slowly pressed down on it. The door did not creak with the first sliver of yellow light that spilled from the opening so he dared to push it a little further until it was wide enough for both of them to slip through one at a time.

And they stopped dead in their tracks.

The door opened into a large hazy chamber illuminated by a combination of faintly glowing light-globes floating randomly about and an oil lamp hanging from a hook on one wall. Through the clouds of vapor Enguer could see a large table in the center of the room cluttered with smoking vials partially filled with colorful liquids, interconnecting glass tubes on metal towers and various ceramic containers scattered about. It smelled acrid and harsh similar to a blacksmith's forge on a hot summer day with no breeze for ventilation. The back wall was lined with tomes and scrolls neatly arranged behind a desk piled with more of the same. Across from the desk blazed a hearth recessed into the wall. The heat it added to the humid warmth of the bubbling liquids was almost smothering in the caustic air. Between the door where they stood and the table with glass implements the space was empty except for a number of hides that covered the floor. Some of the animals he recognized, but to his consternation, many he did not.

"No one is here," Enguer whispered and took another step forward. He was relieved not to be staring at an army of orks wondering why the door had opened on its own.

Reskalin shot out a hand grabbing at his arm, "Wait . . ."

"I know you are there," a raspy, garish voice spoke from behind books piled high on the desk, "and I know why you have come."

Enguer froze. He felt Reskalin tense. Whoever it was, they might be assuming someone was there because the door opened.

"You are much better than I anticipated, most would have never made it this far," the voice cackled, "but I should have anticipated they would send someone that knew what they were doing."

A figure stood from behind the desk. He was an elderly ork, hunched and wrinkled with long stringy white hair that flowed down the front of his layered black robes and over a thick ribbon of gold that held a medallion adorned with red glowing gems set in a pentagon pattern matching the one on the door. His eyes, black as obsidian, stared unblinking in their direction glittering in the light from the hearth.

"Ah, there are two of you," the ork smiled showing a jagged row of broken and missing teeth stained with rot. "What wonder the magic must be that hides you. But not from the Eye. You have been marked."

Enguer didn't want to believe the ork really knew they were there but it was becoming increasingly clear that he must and he hoped Reskalin had a plan to deal with him. And whatever this business was with being marked by an 'Eye' he didn't like the sound of it. Not one bit. This ork was a shaman, of that he was sure, and that meant magic. Dark magic that could be used against them in ways he could only begin to imagine.

"What are your names, thieves?"

Unable to see Reskalin, Enguer sensed that he had moved away and a little forward. He did the same in the opposite direction. If they were separated it would be difficult for the ork to strike out at them both at the same time.

"Come now, I may be an ork but can't we be civil? Ah well, I don't need to know your names. You are humans, aren't you? Yes, you must be. The Enlightened Ones could easily destroy us all and take what they wanted and the dwarfs and elves would hardly trouble themselves over your race." The old ork was calm and appeared unconcerned with their intrusion. His arms hung at his sides with one hand on the desk to steady his sway and his eyes darted left and right marking their location.

"Do you know what you are here to find humans? It's closer than you might imagine! Right there in that small chest." The shaman motioned weakly to a small iron-bound box on the table adjacent to the smoking-bubbling glass vials.

"Go ahead, take it," he cackled. "I won't stop you."

Enguer silently removed the bow from over his shoulders. Something told him that the situation was about to come to a head and he was resolved to plug the arrogant ork with at least one arrow before he died.

"You can take it," the shaman voice changed – slowed, thickened –

and his black eyes rolled back into his head, "but you will never leave this room alive."

The door they had come through slammed shut. On the table next to the small chest, several glass vials shuddered and boiling violently, pouring forth a noxious green gas that slowly filled the room. Enguer took a deep breath of rancid air before the gas came near, he would have only a few minutes to get the box and get out before his lungs forced him to breathe again. He tried to sprint and found himself moving in slow motion as if through water. Two daggers buzzed by his head at high speed striking the ancient ork in the center of his chest.

And bounced away harmlessly.

The shaman stood straight and rigid, no longer hunched over. His face and exposed arms took on the look of stone rather than flesh and he moved stiffly like one might imagine from a statue. He held aloft one clenched fist and released a clump of shiny dust into the air while at the same time blowing it toward them through gray puckered lips with the force of a strong wind.

The dust filled the air with sparks and where it touched skin it burned for an intense second worse than a hornet's sting. Enguer did his best to avoid them in his slowed capacity, but many struck forcing a painful yelp that was echoed by Reskalin a few paces to his left.

Slowly, painstakingly, Enguer drew his bow. It was like a mad dream with everything moving around him at a normal pace while he desperately slugged through a quagmire of molasses. When the arrow was finally in place, Enguer aimed for one of the cracks that ran like a fissure through the orks stone skin with no way of knowing whether the missile would fly true through a chink in the stone armor or drop like a speared sparrow when it struck.

The shaman's hands crackled with electricity and he sent a web of lightning sparking and hissing across the floor to where Reskalin must have been. From the corner of his eye, Enguer saw the table where the chest sat abruptly shake with a strong tremor sending glass vials shattering on the floor and scrolls skittering in every direction. A blur of movement told him the nimble rogue had jumped on the table to avoid the lightning. The shaman realized it as well and sent another tangle of electricity in a higher arc.

Enguer released his arrow.

The table shook with another tremor. The lightning spidered over the spot where the small chest had been – now gone. There was a sharp cry and Enguer felt his freedom of movement return with a rush that caused him to fall prone. His lungs were burning. The green gas was expanding and thinning. He would need air soon.

Back on his feet, Enguer spied the shaman through the green haze bent forward, chanting arcane words, with the fletching of an arrow protruding from his left breast, nary an inch shy of his heart. Enguer notched another arrow. This one would go through the orks neck.

And then something heavy crashed into him from the side.

Instinctively, Enguer lashed out with his bow impacting the heavy body hard and sending it tumbling off to the side. Dropping his bow, Enguer pulled his short sword and long dagger in time to strike with a back-handed slash followed by the downward thrust of his dagger that cut deep into the next furry body. A quick glance told him the quivering remains of the giant rat would not be a threat again, but two more were quickly closing in on his scent unaffected by the green gas that hovered above the knee.

Enguer sped toward the rats. His lungs were on the verge of exploding and he couldn't get to the fresher air near the floor until they were dead. Noses fiercely twitching, they sensed his fast approach, but not quick enough to avoid the blade of his sword down the throat of one and a sharp rib-crushing kick to the side of the other. Enguer spun as a third came out of nowhere and planted its teeth in the leather of his boot, piercing deep enough to cut into flesh and muscle. He screamed at the pain and struck down with his blade separating the head of the little beast from its body. The motion sent him tumbling to the floor where his lungs finally gave out and he sucked in the putrid air for good or ill. He removed the ring and twisted to look at the injury to his leg.

"Enguer! Get off the floor!" The sound of Reskalin's high-pitched shriek was comforting and terrifying at the same time. He cast around quickly for more rats, none were near, but what he saw was far worse.

The shaman knelt on the ground where his desk once stood, the last of it melting into the sea of magma that was expanding out from the ork's blazing fists shoved deep into molten stone. It spread quickly around the perimeter of the room, the heat from it intensifying, unbearable, burning and destroying everything it touched. A rat screamed it's last when it was caught up in the fast-moving magma. Reskalin skipped scarcely a step ahead of it, his cloak trailing behind him in a bizarre display of shifting concealment. Enguer stood in the center of the room with only seconds before the entire floor was liquid death.

Everything in the room was burning, flames licking up the sides of blazing bookshelves slowly sinking, hides combusted along the edges stinking, the air turned black and the floor glowed red. Just like the gems. Enguer realized then that the pattern of the magma closing in on him was in the shape of a pentagon and almost laughed at the absurdity. He would be dead soon, killed by an ork that could control the properties of stone and obliterate every trace of his existence. What a story it would have been.

Only a few feet remained. Reskalin moved one way then another, eyes everywhere in a desperate bid to find a way out. There was no way out. The last piece of furniture in the room, the table that had held the glass vials and small chest, was sinking into the floor. It would be gone and then they would be gone. And there was nothing Enguer could do to save him.

From somewhere in the haze, the shaman laughed. The cackling-coughing laughter filled the flaming chamber with his triumphant glee echoing mercilessly. Continuously. It filled Enguer with rage. If he could find his bow, he would choke the laughter out of that freak of nature with a knot of arrows. His bow was already a pile of ashes. Less than ashes.

"Enguer," the calm voice beside him took all his rage away. It was Reskalin, somehow different, somehow the same. They would die together. He could see on his friend's face that he had accepted it as well.

"I'm sorry Reskalin. I wish . . ."

Reskalin put one slender finger over Enguer's lips. "I need to tell you something. Maybe something you should have known. I don't want you to die without knowing."

Enguer's anxiety rose. What did it matter now? It was so hot; the magma was only a few feet away and he couldn't breathe. He struggled to focus on what Reskalin was saying. Was he screaming? Enguer didn't understand. Where was Reskalin's cloak? Why would he leave it on the ground like that? Soo hot. Sweat stung his eyes. Why was Reskalin shaking him? He didn't understand. The fumes, the gas, the black dust that swirled around them – maybe the air was cleaner near the floor. Enguer fell to his knees and found himself facing . . . breasts. A woman's bare breasts.

Everything stopped. Enguer slowly looked up, over the leather cuirass on the ground, across the length of torn buttons and fabric and along the slender olive-toned neck to the face he knew so well. Reskalin.

She cupped his face in her gentle hands and leaned close. He could feel her breath on his skin, she was so close when she spoke, he could hear her clearly as if they were alone in a quiet wilderness glen, "Now you know the truth." And kissed his lips.

Enguer didn't know what to say. He wanted to say something. There were so many feelings going through him at the same time that he couldn't sort them out. And then she was slowly pulling away, releasing him.

Everything came back in a rush. The unbearable heat, the choking smoke and gas, the pain in his leg, the table just inches away from being consumed forever, the sadistic laughter and molten rock creeping ever closer. Reskalin drew two short daggers from a hidden sheath in the small of her back and slowly turned to face the vague shape of the laughing shaman over a dozen strides across a lake of magma. Enguer watched through eyes glazing, consciousness fading. He thought she would throw the daggers in one last act of defiance, but she ran. Enguer sank to the floor. She ran to the edge of what remained of the stone floor and jumped, landed on the sinking table, ran three strides across it and jumped again.

Enguer never saw where she landed.

~~~

Myrllin fell. Plummeting toward the earth with only seconds to live.

From far above, a rage-filled roar saturated with shock and pain reached Myrllin's ears. The wind caught the edges of his robes forcing his body to flip over roughly to face the sky. The reverse caused his long dark hair to streak along the sides of his face dancing in the air above him playfully framing his view of the heavens. Myrllin still had the sense of falling, but the stars didn't seem to diminish at all. And then there was something else. Fire. Hundreds of jets of fire streaking across the sky like a shower of meteorites with a winged reptilian creature prancing among them. No, that wasn't right. Not prancing. Avoiding. Evading. The fog over Myrllin's mind lifted. The creature was a dragon. A red dragon with smoldering scales and smoking holes burned through its leathery wings. Dergo.

Myrllin closed his eyes and spoke the charms. His fall slowed, then halted altogether and he willed his body to stand upright levitating barely a hundred spans over the rocky earth. Above him

Dergo plummeted from the sky trailed by a plume of smoke. All Myrllin could do was watch helplessly as he no longer bore the strength to save his loyal friend.

Where was Wodanaz?

Myrllin momentarily focused on the image of his brother and found his eyes drawn toward a deep cleft in the mountain range nearly a quarter of a league away. There was a flash of bright light from above compelling him to snap his gaze back toward the sky. The fiery plumage spun off by the Phoenix had not abated. Hundreds of blazing feathers darted out in a spherical wave that exploding against rocks, trees and the ocean indiscriminately while others flew wildly a league over the horizon or winked out against the night-time vista of stars. The Phoenix was spinning faster again, pulsating brighter and brighter with hot white light.

Something told Myrllin he had to find his brother. With what little strength that remained, he propelled himself toward the fissure where he would find Wodanaz. It didn't take long. From a distance Myrllin could see his burly form capped by a head of long blonde hair clinging to the edge of the narrow chasm. Sleipnir was nowhere in sight. Myrllin redoubled his speed avoiding the bursts of flaming feathers falling all around.

"Take cover with me!" Wodanaz shouted above the explosions.

Myrllin landed on the narrow ledge next to his brother, pressed his face against the icy rockface and released the levitation spell. He was exhausted. If they ever finished chasing down demons, he would need to sleep a thousand years to recover. Wodanaz looked like he had been through hell as well. His face and arms were blistered and burned, his clothing was scorched badly and his usually well-kept golden hair was nearly black from soil and ash.

"You're not so pretty anymore," Myrllin's throat felt dry and cracked and his voice sounded haggard to his own ears.

A white-hot feather flew over their heads and down into the rift bursting not far from where they hugged the rock. Both of them jumped at the concussion and Myrllin's feet nearly slipped off the ledge before a ripple of heat and blasted shards of stone cascaded over their stiff frames. Wodanaz grabbed him with one arm by the back of his robes to keep him steady. It reminded Myrllin that their protective bubbles were no longer in place and there was nothing he could do about it.

"Speak for yourself!" Wodanaz shot back. "We're both going to be a couple of roasted chickens if that thing doesn't run out of feathers soon."

Wodanaz, the taller of the two by more than a head, peeked over the edge of the rift and ducked back down quickly. Then he pulled the end of a rope out from a small pouch on his hip and wrapped it around Myrllin's waist tying a snug knot.

"What are you doing?" Myrllin protested.

"Our friend up there is descending," Wodanaz kept pulling rope out of the pouch that was clearly far too small to hold so much of it. "If it hits the ground it'll shake the whole mountain. Do you have enough energy to put a shield above our heads?"

"Maybe," Myrllin doubted that it would hold for long even if he did.

Wodanaz tied the rope around his own waist and pounded iron pitons into the hard rock with his war hammer. He pulled on them, then fed the ends of the rope through the round eye loops before knotting them together securely. Even before he was done, the ground above them and the ledge where they stood had already begun to shake.

Myrllin held on tightly to the rope where it was attached to the piton in case the shaking got worse. In the sky above, the fiery feathers tapered off to be replaced by crushed rock pelting down over them like rain. Seconds later, the shaking intensified to the level of an earthquake punctuated by waves of fire that roared over their heads with such heat that Myrllin's sweat dried almost instantaneously. He threw up the shield. It was sufficient to protect them from the worst of the high temperature and falling debris, but too small to surround them entirely.

It would have to be enough.

The dark night sky flashed with a blinding radiance of lightning and fire. Thunderous booms, the sharp crack of splitting rock and the rumble of compressed earth was deafening. Boulders the size of carriages bombarded their shield and bounced away like children's toys into the dark crevice under feet frantic to preserve their fragile footing even as Myrllin fought a desperate battle to keep the shield up and hold onto the rope.

"Put everything you have into the shield!" Wodanaz thrust his arm around Myrllin and grabbed the piton to hold them both flat against the rockface. "I've got you!"

It was a small relief that Wodanaz took over the physical struggle keeping them on the ledge. What little energy Myrllin had left could go into the shield, but he knew it couldn't go on much longer. When the shield failed, they would be crushed and roasted. Every second counted for a chance that they might be saved or whatever was happening to the Phoenix would end.verEvery . . . second . . .

A massive explosion rocked the world around them, too much for even the mighty strength of Wodanaz to oppose, sending the two flying wide over the gaping maw of the fissure. Their brief flight was abruptly stopped short by the length of the ropes and they plummeted screaming into the darkness. Myrllin lost concentration on the shield and it evaporated into ethereal mists. Fortunately, the fall was short, arrested once again by the length of the rope, but it was a harsh cessation that snapped his head back and momentarily interrupted circulation to his brain. In those seconds, Myrllin wasn't sure if he lost consciousness or the fissure had caved in on them.

~~~

Myrllin floated in a shallow arc like the pendulum of time or the slow roll of a ship over a cosmic ocean. Or was he flying? Free of the encumbrance of gravity, a cool wind playing through his weightless tresses with and invitation to soar effortless among the stars.

Pain flooded through his extremities ending the perfect dream and his eyes fluttered open. Hazy daylight shown swaying through a narrow crack of earth above him. No, it was he who swayed. His back was arched over the binding of rope from which he was suspended and his arms were splayed out to either side. Once in a while he would bump against something else swinging slowly next to him.

He reached forward to grasp the taut rope and pull himself upright. Pain exploded from his lower back and he screamed in agony letting go of the rope and falling back to his previous position. He tried to control his rapid breathing and relax. Sweat poured out of him despite the frigid cold while he hung motionless until the pain subsided to a bearable level. Then slowly he reached for the rope again and gently eased himself up. The pain was still excruciating, if not debilitating and he spent another long moment panting against the stretched rope.

A heavy groan from behind ended Myrllin's respite. He gingerly spun himself around to find Wodanaz hanging upside down with a similarly tied rope around his waist. Had it not been for his brother's wide hips, he might have slipped the crude harness and tumbled to the bottom of the deep ravine they dangled over precariously

Myrllin reached deep. He had to find the strength to get them free.

Chapter 23

Escape

"Wake up, Enguer," Reskalin's throaty voice cut through the darkness to the place where he waited. "For the love of Tivr, please wake up!"

The world shook all around him, light filtered through from a great distance as he struggled to obey the command and make his way back to the surface. It took some time and no little encouragement from Reskalin before he broke through the thin veil of darkness to rejoin the place where . . . he felt pain.

Pain!

Enguer groaned. His lungs raw and burning, his leg ached like it was impaled on a stake and his head throbbed setting his teeth on edge. He wanted to go back to that quite place where he was before. There was no pain there. No worries. No thought.

It was too far away.

Enguer reluctantly opened his eyes to find a pair of dark brown orbs staring back at him. "Reskalin," he wanted to say more but his throat was so dry.

The eyes smiled back at him. "Drink this and rest a moment until you are able to speak."

A cool trickle of water broke like a dam over his scorched throat. He coughed and sputtered a bit finding it hard to swallow, nonetheless the more he drank the easier it became and soon he was drinking freely once more. It was miraculous. Not only did his throat recover, so did his breathing become easier and the pain in his head and leg subsided to a mere annoyance and then no pain at all. In fact, by the time he had drank the contents of the waterskin, he felt restored and whole, invigorated with energy as if his injuries had never occurred at all.

He sat up on his own and faced Reskalin kneeling in front of him. The rogue's eyes were searching his own as if waiting for something inevitable, undeniable, to follow. Enguer looked past Reskalin. The room still carried a haze, mostly evacuated by cooler air circulating from the doorway now held open by a short wooden shaft jammed under the door. It was clear enough to see the devastation around them. He and Reskalin sat in a circle of smoothed stone that extended less than a span in every direction. There was a button on the floor. From where it came, he had no idea. Beyond that, the room was covered by the strange flowing patterns formed by igneous rock. It was cool and dry, no longer the red-hot glowing mass of liquid hell-fire that should have been his fate. What had happened? He shifted his gaze to the remnant of a wooden table frozen in the act of sinking into the now solid rock. It was the table Reskalin had jumped upon and then jumped again to . . . the shaman. There he knelt crouching forward with his arms sunk to his elbows in the rock. Blood pooled around them from wounds in his neck in a parody of the lava that once surrounded them. The shaman was dead. Killed in such a sudden manner that he never had the chance to move and would forever leave a part of himself entombed in the swirling flows of the stone floor. It would be one hell of a shock to the orks that eventually found him here.

Enguer looked back to Reskalin. "You saved us."

The rogue lifted a single eyebrow. He wore an intense expression tinged with anxiety. "Do you not remember?"

"Bits and pieces. I must have sucked in more of that green gas than I realized." Enguer carefully stood, his legs felt solid and strong. "What was in that waterskin? I feel almost completely recovered."

Reskalin stood with him. "A powder that mixes with water. It has magical powers of restoration and healing. I get them from a priestess of Leinth, our goddess of death if you would believe it. She owes me favors."

"The goddess or the priestess?"

Reskalin smiled slyly, "That's my secret." He bent to pick up his shimmering cloak and a small chest laying at his feet. "Let's see what we nearly died for."

Enguer walked with him to where the remains of the table stood, all four legs sunk into the stone floor. It was a little less than waist high and sat at a slight angle, but it was level enough to sit the chest without worry of it sliding off the side.

"Stand away," Reskalin warned. Approaching the chest from the back, he took a needle-pointed dirk from his belt and carefully popped the ornamental lock off the front. Before it hit the table a jet of flame shot out from the front where the lock had been with such intense heat that it scorched the surface of the tabletop.

Enguer jumped back a step and heat of his own making rose to his hairline. "Is there no end to the ways we can die in this chamber?"

Ignoring him, the rogue was intent on lifting the lid of the chest with the tip of his blade. A finger width at first and then a little more. A blue glow emitted from within. Half open, Reskalin flipped it the rest of the way and stepped back. Nothing. A crystal disk the size of a human hand radiating a soft blue luminosity and rimmed in gold lay within.

Enguer studied it from a distance. "What is it?"

"I have no idea." Reskalin flipped the lid shut and scooped the chest into his travel pack. "We better leave before those other shamans come back. I don't think we can hide what happened here."

Quickly, Reskalin strode back to the shaman, removed his bejeweled necklace and shoved it in with the chest. He shrugged at Enguer and then donned his camouflaging cloak.

Enguer smiled and said nothing. Reskalin was a rogue after all and the wealth purchased with that bauble wouldn't do the shaman any good anymore. He placed the ring on his finger and followed the blurred form of the rogue out of the hellish chamber and quietly shut the door.

They backtracked down the long corridor with the sinister outlines and scurried up the long sloping spiral and through the twisting turns of the dark halls until they found their way back to the main passageway that led out toward the cavern entrance. Nothing had changed. The corridors were still with few sounds reverberating from chambers far away.

"It must be only a couple of hours until sunset," Reskalin stopped to whisper. "Once we are clear of the cave, run for the forest as fast as you can even if there are a few orks lingering about. No matter if we make noise, they still won't be able to see us well."

"What if there are shamans outside?"

There was a long pause from Reskalin before he replied, "In that case we will make a new plan."

"I'm ready when you are."

The cavern exit was not far and they encountered only one ork along the way. He appeared drunk, stumbling from one side of the passage to the other nearly bumping into them. The sound of the bawdy song he loudly sang carried no tune whatsoever and echoed harshly from the darkness long after he passed. No long after, the temperature cooled and there was a hint of natural light from around a bend that signaled their deliverance from the long 'night'. Enguer's heart leaped at the sight and he reflexively quickened his pace, nearly running over Reskalin.

"Be still," Reskalin hissed urgently. "I can hear the chanting of the shamans ahead."

Enguer's heart sank into his stomach. The main passage was wide enough for them to pass, but far too narrow if any of them could sense their presence. And with so many of them he doubted a favorable outcome if such a meeting were to take place.

"Ok, be quick," Reskalin pulled down his hood and rushed forward along the wall.

Enguer trailed him close. They rounded a corner and then another. By the time the cavern opened into the blinding bright light of day, he could hear the chanting as well. It was coming from outside and not too far away.

"They are just outside." Two disembodied hands appeared and rubbed the eyes of a disembodied head. Enguer wondered if he would ever get used to the strange cloak Reskalin wore. "I can't see them yet, but they aren't moving. I would guess they are waiting to greet the night with some sort of ceremony. Let's wait a moment for our eyes to adjust."

Minutes passed by while they waited for their eyes to correct after so long in darkness. Fortunately, the sun was far past its zenith and the light was slowly fading. Enguer expected to see clearly soon, having gone through this exercise many times in the past, but it didn't stop him from anxiously counting the seconds.

"I can see well enough now. You?"

Enguer could see the camp immediately beyond the cave entrance and expected the need to squint when they exited. It was good enough for him. Every minute waiting in the cave just seemed like a nightmare waiting to happen. "I'm ready."

Reskalin donned his hood and crept along the far wall to the caverns edge. Enguer stayed close. The feel of the cool breeze on his face and fresh air in his lungs felt marvelous. Outside, the sky was overcast and a strong biting wind surged through the valley from the west bringing a light icy rain that chilled to the bone. He welcomed it.

Standing on a ledge overlooking the vale on the opposite side of the cavern's wide entrance stood the ork shamans lined up in five lines forming the shape of a pentagon. Between them, a light-globe affixed to a tall pole shone bright red marking the corners around a matching one at the center. The shamans chanted high and low at the direction of an ork that roamed the space inside the formation. He held aloft a scepter crowned by a skull displaying a single red eye that flashed in the failing light. Enguer fingered the skull's matching eye in his pocket. They had seen this ork once before.

"Follow," Reskalin was scarcely audible above the wind that was causing havoc with his shifting cloak revealing the occasional flash of his leather breeches and olive-toned hands.

Slowly, they slunk down the rocky slope toward the vacant encampment below. With the sun approaching the horizon, they had to hurry. Soon the orks would stir from their enclave and pour from the cavern to resume their daily tasks. In their haste, Reskalin stepped on a cluster of loose rock sending them clattering loudly down the incline. He dropped flat into a depression in the stone doing his best to keep his petulant cloak tight about him. Enguer simply halted in mid-step and turned his gaze back toward the orks.

The chanting continued unabated, but the ork with the scepter had noticed the disturbance and peered keenly in their direction. At fifty paces, Enguer hoped the shaman's senses were not so well attuned. Still, he calculated their chances of crossing the valley and into the safety of the forest on the other side if the shaman was so curious to investigate further. The ork's dogged stared lasted for long uncomfortable minutes before he finally returned to conducting his churlish chorus. Reskalin rose cautiously and continued down the slope.

Once they reached the bottom, Enguer tracked Reskalin through the cover of make-shift tents and wooden shacks that were scattered across the vale. Muddy puddles and overturned stands of leather over-tunics suggested that the worst of the storm had come through earlier in the day. Observing the racks of weapons and long panoply of leather armor once again, it occurred to Enguer that the number of orks they had surveilled inside the cavern and outside the day before did not nearly match. The only conclusion he could reach was a dark one - either there were hundreds of orks they had not seen or hundreds more expected to arrive.

When they reached the opposite slope, Enguer looked back toward the yawning maw of the cavern. Several clusters of orks waited inside, their faces painted against the darkness in the final few minutes before sunset while the shamans voices resonated across the valley rising in an irregular crescendo that slowly paced with the setting sun. It appeared to be a solemn and unholy occasion that Enguer had not witnessed the night before. What was different about tonight? He didn't have long to ponder as Reskalin's hisses reminded him that they needed to get into the forest and far away before the orks found their dead shaman with knife wounds in his neck and arms submerged in solid rock.

At first sparse of tree and dense with scrub, the forest gradually thickened the deeper they ventured into the wilderness. Out of sight of the valley they paused and Enguer put his magic ring away. Finally, his anxiety was melting away in the familiar surroundings of The Wilds.

"The sparks that damn shaman threw at us burned holes all over my cloak." Reskalin held the fabric at arm's length trying to asses the damage in the dark. "I hope it can be mended. This thing cost me a hoard of treasure and a few favors yet to be fully paid."

Enguer pulled out his light-globe and shined a thin spotlight of illumination over the cloak. Dozens of small holes peppered the shimmering fabric prompting a long groan from his friend. He moved the light lower, illuminating the front of Reskalin's leather cuirass where it met his waist. The white fabric of his under-tunic stuck out at an odd angle rather than tucked into his leather breeches as he typically wore it. One shiny button flashed in the light drawing his attention. It matched the one he had seen on the floor in the chamber with the magma. He hadn't thought to question it then, but now it struck him as odd.

"Reskalin, what happened to your buttons?"

The rogue went still as his entire body appeared to tense up. Slowly his head rose from examining his cloak to meet Enguer's eyes. Fear and uncertainty reflected from those brown orbs and his slim eyebrows flinched nervously. It was an odd reaction to have over the subject of a button, Enguer thought.

"What about buttons?" Reskalin spoke in a low whisper although there was hardly a need for it.

Enguer had the impression that his friend was on the verge of violence and he couldn't understand why. He pointed to the button on Reskalin's under-tunic sticking out from under his Cuirass. "A button matching that one was on the floor in the room where the shaman turned the floor to molten rock."

Looking down at the button, Reskalin visibly relaxed. "I must have lost it in the struggle with the rats. They were tearing at me from every direction." He flashed a cunning smile, "I guess I'm lucky all they got was a button."

Enguer supposed that made sense. Although something nagged at the back of his mind like an absent memory or faded dream that he couldn't quite grasp. Whatever it was, it couldn't be worth the aggravation and he let it drop. "If we hurry, we can get to the flats by morning and rest until nightfall to avoid a reunion with the wyvern."

Reskalin nodded and tucked his shimmering cloak into his travel pack for safekeeping. "If we go at a steady pace, I'm sure we can make it."

A horn sounded from the direction of the orks enclave three times in rapid succession.

Reskalin looked over at Enguer in alarm. "They found the shaman. If they come for us, we have only about an hour head start."

"I doubt they can track us, but they might not need to. Where else would we go but back toward the pass?" Enguer quickly strapped on his pack. "And they run far faster than we can. We'll be lucky to make it to morning before they catch up."

"What do you suggest?"

Enguer nervously tapped the hilt of the dagger at his side. "We hike into the mountains and circumvent the flats. If they go as far as crossing, they may find our mounts, but that is less of a price to pay then our lives."

Reskalin sighed deeply, "I hope that shaman's necklace I picked is worth a tidy sum, cause this journey is costing me a fortune!"

~~~

Three days of treacherous travel over steep ridgelines and narrow ledges just below the snowline, an unfortunate encounter with a massive cave bear that nearly ran them off a sheer cliff and constant worry over the orks left Enguer shivering and exhausted at the edge of an outcropping overlooking a shallow river about a league west of where they had left their horses days before. Reskalin looked in no better shape, maybe a lot worse, considering he had spent so little time in the wilderness and lacked the years of conditioning Enguer benefitted from. He was resilient, Enguer had to give him that. Pushing day and night without complaint in subfreezing conditions they were not prepared for. And despite all that, they had no idea if they were ahead of the orks, behind them or if they were still pursued at all.

"It's getting dark, we need shelter, warmth and fresh food," Enguer's voice sounded to himself like a croaking frog and he couldn't remember if this was the first time he had spoken all day.

"I can build a fire, but we must be careful not to attract attention." Reskalin's voice had lost its husky timbre, becoming soft and weak. It worried Enguer and he reconsidered how durable in this environment the little man really was. Perhaps more fearless than robust, he thought. Many courageous men and women had perished under far less harsh conditions.

"I saw a small opening in the rock a little way up. Too small for a bear," Enguer smiled, but he didn't think Reskalin noticed. "You stay here and keep watch. I'll clear it out and come back before dark."

Reskalin nodded without saying anything or turning his gaze from the sparkling river below. An army of orks could parade along its banks without the rogue noticing a ripple in the water. Enguer was saddened to see the state his friend was in. He had reached his limit, gave everything he could give and more, now his body and mind was slowly shutting down. If left on his own, Reskalin would sit there and die in a day or two.

Enguer had been in that place a time or two in his life and he thanked Sunna he had the strength of his father to get him through. He had grown stronger because of it and now he had to be there for Reskalin. If the rogue survived, he would be stronger for it too.

Trudging back across the stone shelf, Enguer followed the ridgeline to where he had seen the dark spot he recognized as an opening in the rock. He approached it cautiously, not knowing what, if anything, called this small den home. Near the entrance he sniffed the air. No strong feral smell – that was a good sign. Next came the most dangerous part. Crawling inside.

Removing the light globe from his pack, Enguer used the leather pouch to focus the light directionally into the cave opening. From what he could see, a narrow cavern opened up inside with a high ceiling and there was no fecal matter on the floor. He crawled through the fissure almost too tight for him to fit and stood erect on the other side. From all appearances, nothing had ever lived here. The elevated, jagged entry was likely too difficult to navigate even for small creatures, but it would serve his purposes perfectly.

He pushed back through the entry and made his way back to Reskalin. When he arrived, he found his friend in the exact position he had left him. Enguer didn't bother to ask if anything had passed, he wouldn't have noticed anyway. He just gathered Reskalin up and led him back to the cavern on the other side of the slope.

Over the next hour, Enguer gathered fallen branches to make a fire and set traps with ice-berry root in the scrub. Sunna must have been watching over him as he had a fat rabbit on a spit in short order, its plentiful fat dripping into the flames emitting a mouth-watering aroma in the air. With considerable prompting, Reskalin took a few strips of the hot meat and absently consumed them. The food would bring energy to his body and the fire would bring warmth, but he needed rest to restore him to his senses. When they were done with the rabbit, Enguer tried to help Reskalin remove his leather cuirass and feel the heat on his skin more acutely. The little man would have none of it and Enguer gave up rather than fight with him. He put his own leather chest piece aside and lay down on the other side of the fire. It didn't take long for the small cavern to warm up, yet Reskalin still shivered violently where he sat. Enguer expected this might happen. The frigid cold had lowered Reskalin's core temperature to a dangerous point that a campfire alone would never restore.

Enguer strode around the fire and gently lay Reskalin's head on the soft leather of his travel pack. The rogue instinctively curled into the fetal position and continued to shiver uncontrollably. As his father had done for him, Enguer lay next to his friend and pulled him close to share his body heat. It would have worked better without the leather cuirass, but it would have to do. Through most of the night Enguer lay awake keeping the fire going and his friend warm and it wasn't until the shivering finally subsided did he finally drift off to sleep.

Strange dreams were visited upon his disquieted slumber in the early hour before dawn. Images, stricken by fire and green haze danced over his subconscious mind in a whirling cacophony of strange voices screaming in terror. Or was it rage? Both perhaps and worse yet, one of them might have been his own. Through the chaos and confusion of one dreadful portrait of horror after another, Reskalin's calm visage appeared composed and determined at the center of the madness. He was there and then gone. One moment shaking Enguer desperately and another looking into his eyes telling him something important. Then his mind took an abhorrent departure from the pandemonium to reveal the overwhelming vulgar display of his friend Reskalin ripping open his tunic to lay bare female anatomy. Even his dreams could not absorb the shock to his psyche nor the discourteous method by which it chose to crack the cocoon of deception where he had carefully secreted away those confusing affections. Enguer jolted awake, unsure of what he had just witnessed. His eyes focused on the flickering shadows that played overhead and he listened to the whistling of the wind outside the cave that rose and fell in haunting relief. It reminded him a quieting hum like the peaceful lullabies his mother would sing to put him to sleep at night and it brought Enguer serenity again as he drifted off to a fitful repose.

The next morning Enguer, laden with cold sweat, was awakened by Reskalin roughly pushing him off.

"What are you doing?" the Rogue nearly shouted scooting to the other side of the waning fire.

"Saving your life," Enguer pushed the vile images from his dreams away determined not to be consumed by their meaning.

Reskalin had an incredulous look on his face. "By groping at me all night?"

"By sharing the heat from our bodies so you wouldn't freeze to death."

The little man's gaze dropped to the floor and his cheeks flushed red, "Oh. Thanks, I guess."

Enguer yawned and stretched his arms wide. "How are you feeling?"

"Tired, cold, hungry. Alive."

"Well, at least there has been some improvement!" Enguer stood-up unamused.

Reskalin gazed around the small cavern as if seeing it for the first time. "Where are we?"

"A small cave above the ledge overlooking the river. It was a fortunate find." Enguer didn't want to say how fortunate. Had he not found it he would likely be digging Reskalin's grave that morning.

"How did we get here?"

"We walked."

"I don't remember much from the last day or so."

Enguer pat him on the shoulder on his way toward the cavern exit. "Stay warm while I check the traps. Hopefully Sunna has granted us another meal."

Either Sunna really was looking out for them or there were a lot of fat rabbits in the area, for he returned with two of them and an arm full of dry branches for the fire. Enguer consumed most of one rabbit, which Reskalin happily finished along with his own. Where the little man put it, he had no idea, but he was glad the rogue had found his appetite.

"When you are strong enough, we will go find out if we still have horses."

"Where are the orks?"

Enguer tossed a branch on the fire. "No idea. They may not have gone as far as crossing the flatlands in their pursuit. And I doubt they would have followed us into the mountains even if they were capable of tracking our path."

Reskalin looked at him with about as much spirit as a withering flower. "If we are safe here, I could use one more day of rest. If not, then we must go."

"We are safe," Enguer assured him. "Another day or a week the orks will never find us here. You tend to yourself here while I scavenge for roots and rabbits and keep an eye on the river. If the orks pass that way, I will know."

It rained most of the morning, mixed with a few ice crystals that never took hold and the wind died down to a subtle breeze. Enguer set his traps with more ice-berry roots dug up from beneath heavy brush and searched the river banks for tracks. He located the faded traces of ork prints heading south along the riverbank and the hoofprints of their own horses from the first time they passed this way but nothing more recent. If they were lucky, the orks wouldn't come this far.

When the rain subsided in the afternoon, Enguer settled on the ledge overlooking the river and unstrapped his travel pack. Inside, he found the crystal disk that Reskalin had given him for safe-keeping in the off chance he fell on their journey over the mountains. Enguer thought to get a better look at it in the daylight hours and removed it from the protective wrapping of cloth and leather. In the hazy illumination of the sun, the gold trim around the disk shined brightly and sparkling specks of reflected light drifted slowly within the foggy crystal as if floating in water. Looking closer, Enguer could see strange symbols carved into the narrow gold edge that reminded him of the arcane script he had seen engraved on the stone walls of the tower in Courth where the Enlightened Ones resided. Could this be an artifact of their making? How would an ork shaman come into possession of such an thing? Too many questions for his liking. Carefully he wrapped the disk and stowed it back into his pack.

A flash of movement caught his eye down by the river's edge. A young buck stealing a drink of water. If only Enguer had his bow, they would have enough meat to carry them through the rest of their journey back to Arre. Assuming their horses lived. Otherwise, it would be a long walk. Icy drops pinched his ears from moisture-laden storm clouds moving off the mountains. Enguer hoped up. He barely had time to check his traps and return to the cave before it started coming down in droves.

"Only one rabbit for tonight," Enguer squeezed through the narrow opening to find Reskalin sitting next to the fire mending his shimmering cloak.

The rogue looked up, his eyes brighter and more alive than when Enguer left that morning. He must have slept some. "We still have moldy cheese and salted pork," Reskalin flashed him a brief smile.

"How is that working out?"

"All I can do is sew the holes together. It won't look pretty but I think it will work well enough." He tied the last stitch and folded the cloak up before setting it aside. "I'll be ready to leave in the morning."

"Good, we can head out at first light if . . ." Enguer's last words caught in his throat as the echo of a war horn sounded faintly in the distance.

Chapter 24

Rabbits

"We have to leave," Enguer rushed over to the narrow cave entrance to hear better.

Without a word, Reskalin hurriedly gathered his things and stamped out the fire. Then he joined Enguer outside the cave. "Where are they?"

A deep howl rose high in pitch, followed by a chorus of at least a dozen more and another long blast from the horn. Enguer couldn't believe his ears. "They are across the valley," he pointed up toward a dip in the fading outline of the mountain range. "We never would have heard them if not for the wind in our favor."

"How soon will they be here?"

"By morning."

"So soon? Didn't you say they couldn't follow us through the mountains? Or wouldn't?"

Enguer shook his head. "I was wrong. That trinket we stole must be very valuable to them."

"Why do you say that?"

"Those howls are not your typical mountain wolves; they are something worse – Dire Wolves. I can tell by the deep timbre. And the bad news is they are excellent trackers."

Reskalin hoisted his pack over his shoulder, "Let's get moving then."

"One second," Enguer wedged himself back through the cave opening and returned with the dead rabbit. "We will need a distraction. Go down to the river, be careful not to leave too many tracks and follow it south. Make sure you walk in the shallows so not to leave a scent. I'll catch up shortly.

Reskalin's eyes narrowed sharply, "What are you going to do?"

"Dire wolves can't resist a fat rabbit," he smiled. "I'm going to create a distraction. We will need the extra time."

Appearing uncertain at first, Reskalin finally muttered "Be careful," and faded into the darkness.

Enguer took the rabbit and dragged it along the ground sprinkling a few drops of its blood intermittently down the hill and across the river. There was a rise atop a sheer cliff that over looked a natural bowl thick with trees that he remembered. It was beautiful to behold in the daytime. When he reached the rise, he threw the rabbit as far as he could manage. It would take the Dire Wolves at least half a day to get to the bottom and back up again. He chuckled quietly as he imagined the look on the orks faces when they found out their pets had been following the scent of a dead rabbit.

Taking a circuitous route back to the river that he hoped would lead the orks further into the dense forest, Enguer ran south through the frigid water with the expectation that he would catch-up to Reskalin at the ork camp where they left their horses. He prayed to Sunna that the horses were still there. If they were dead or stolen it was doubtful he and Reskalin would ever make it back to Arre. Once the Dire Wolves picked up their scent, they would be hunted down relentlessly. Dire Wolves were fast, faster than horses, with strong constitutions that allowed them to keep going for long periods of time. Enguer was sure that if it wasn't for the orks travelling only by night, the Dire Wolves would have already had them holed up and trapped in the tiny cave he had thought so safe. It would have become their tomb.

An hour later, Enguer jogged into the ork camp. He could smell the stink of decay long before he could make out the dark shapes of the abandoned camp. He came to a stop and crouched, listening for any sound above the sound of his own breathing. Something rustled ahead of him on the right and out of the darkness strode Reskalin with his black mare and Enguer's Lambei in tow. He stood up, his breath exploding from his lungs in a sigh of relief as he walked forward and took the reins of his horse from his friend.

"They are in remarkable condition for being left out here alone for so long." Reskalin stroked his mare affectionately over the curve of its long neck.

"I'm glad for it," Enguer tried to sound upbeat, "the next several days will be hard on them if we are to stay ahead of the Dire Wolves."

Enguer retrieved their saddles from a nearby copse of thorn brush where they were concealed and in short order the horses were ready to leave the stinking camp. Enguer calculated the time it would take the Dire Wolves to cross the mountain valley and locate the cave where he and Reskalin had taken shelter the night before. They were going to have to pass by that place on their way back north if they kept to the river. The river was their best bet for hiding their scent.

"Six hours," he muttered under his breath.

"Six hours for what?" Reskalin trotted next to him.

"The Dire Wolves are at best six hours distance from our cave and we must be well past it if the rabbit trick is going to work."

"And at worst?"

Enguer sighed, "Four hours."

"We had better hurry, then." Reskalin kicked his mare into a quick cantor that was normally reserved for churning up long distances on roads or flat grasslands.

Under normal circumstances Enguer would advise caution when riding at night in the shallows of a fast-moving river with slippery stones and hidden hollows. A lame horse would get them nowhere fast. Not today. In fact, he pushed harder. These were anything but normal circumstances and their lives were hanging in the balance left to chance and fortune. Enguer thought to ask Reskalin if the Rasna people had a god for that, they probably did, but it hardly mattered to him. He would trust his fate to the benevolence of Sunna and hold her blameless no matter the outcome.

Less than an hour elapsed before they passed under the outcropping not far from their cave. No Dire Wolves. Not yet. The only sound was the clip-clop of their horses' hooves splashing through the shallow water. Two more hours passed, turning into four. Then they heard it. The blaring horn and rabid howls repeating over and over.

"Sounds like the Dire Wolves found the scent trail of the rabbit. The orks will probably be forced to follow the blood trail I left." Enguer shouted over his shoulder.

"You think they have them on leashes like dogs?"

Enguer snorted, "I can't imagine the wolves would tolerate that. I have no idea how they keep them from running off on their own. Those things are the size of my Lambei!"

From the corner of his eye he thought he saw Reskalin shudder.

Four more hours passed before the first signs of dawn lit the horizon and more than three since they had heard anything from their pursuers. Enguer knew they had to stop and let the horses rest, at least for a few hours, or they would become exhausted. They were still a day or more away from the Travini Pass and another two days to Arre. More than double that if they lost a horse. In the space of the next hour there was enough light filtering through the thick forest branches for Enguer to spy a small glen with long green grass only a few strides from the river. He was reluctant to leave the river where for the last several hours they had left no scent trail, but the horses needed the rest and the nourishment that would give them the energy to slog on.

"We will rest here a bit," Enguer removed the saddle from his Lambei and began to rub him down with a brush from his saddlebag.

"Do you think they have gained on us?" Reskalin was rubbing down his mare with short, gentle strokes that struck Enguer as exhaustive.

"What? Maybe. I don't know," Enguer heard his voice come out unsteady. By Sunna, he must be exhausted. A little sleep would do him good. "They are at least a day behind us if the rabbit did its job."

"I suppose we will find out," Reskalin yawned. "I am going to try and get a little sleep."

Enguer nodded. "I will keep the watch until you wake up."

He lay there in the cool embrace of the long grass with his head upon his travel bag. His eyes felt heavy and his mind wandered to distant places and times decades behind him. He was in a comfortable doze on the brink of sleep. Enguer was not worried, any threat nearby would be sensed by the horses and their snorts and pounding hooves would awaken him immediately. He allowed his mind to drift and then dream. Images from his past flitted across his subconscious; his mother, his father, Suri, Commander Duraunt. They laughed and smiled, fought wild beasts, drank and sang. None of this had ever happened. The dreams were strange interpretations of how he wished it could have been. And then Reskalin appeared. He was strangest of all, somehow seductive and threatening at the same time. He drew close and pressed against Enguer expectantly. Something about that felt different, inviting. Reskalin's face was close to his own. Too close. Yet, his slender eyebrows atop intense brown eyes framed by long lashes, and full lips over a smooth hairless chin made his heart quicken and blood turn hot. He was beautiful. Reskalin leaned in and flashed the smile Enguer secretly longed to see.

And then the rogue kissed him.

Enguer awoke with a start.

It was sometime past noon. Reskalin was not in the glen, yet his horse was still there. Enguer exhaled a deep breath stepped in relief. It was just a stupid dream. But where was Reskalin?

Enguer stood up and looked around. The rogues travel bag was there along with the shimmering cloak he had folded up for a pillow. He walked the perimeter and discovered fresh folds in the grass that indicated Reskalin had gone down to the river. Enguer thought that was a good idea. He needed a good wash to reinvigorate his spirit, clean off the dirt and grime of the last several days and give him a fresh start to a new day.

Enguer started toward the river. It was only a few paces through a light sprinkling of trees and leafy undergrowth. He could hear the rush of water and the light splash of a body moving within it. At the edge of the forest where it met the sandy incline of the riverbank, Enguer stopped. He did not know why, but what he saw next he would never forget.

Reskalin was swimming from the center of the river where the water reached his neck toward the shallows in the direction of where his clothing lay folded on the bank. Enguer raised his hand to wave and toss out some silly witticism about bathing. But he froze, his feet stuck firmly in the earth as if they had grown there and the words caught in his throat.

Smooth olive-toned skin glistening with thick droplets of water falling from every surface broke the plane of water and air like a dream moving in slow motion. Reskalin's short cropped dark hair dangled over sharp refined features that imitated the face in his dreams. But it wasn't enough to distract from the long neck and lean muscular shoulders that followed and less so the narrow torso and fine lines accentuating round full breasts dripping droplets from their cold-inspired rigid tips. Enguer's eyes traced a line down Reskalin's firm abdomen to curvy hips and well-developed thighs that captured between them the perfect absence of the fairer sex. Something inside him stirred raw, carnal desire . . . and joy. He allowed his gaze to linger in those forbidden places for a while and then back to the face and eyes familiar to him. Eyes staring back at him in shock and anger.

Enguer turned and fled back to the grassy glen, but there was nowhere to go. He begged Sunna to wake him if it where another dream. Or keep him in it forever to live with his desires. What was he to do? What was he to say? He ran his fingers through his hair gripping tightly at its roots and found himself pacing in circles like a madman.

"Enguer," the voice came to him soft and feminine. He snapped his head up and there he was. There she was. Bare to the world.

Enguer wanted to pull his eyes away. He wanted to run into The Wilds and deny everything he was seeing. How could he? Did he really want to?

"Enguer," she called again. "You know the truth now."

He spun around to face her, collapsing to his knees. "Why didn't you tell me? I have felt so much doubt and confusion since we met. I don't know if I can overcome that!"

She was suddenly next to him, her arms pressing his face against her smooth abdomen. "What about me Enguer? Do you think I wanted this? Do you think I ever wanted to be a woman? I cursed my sex from the day I understood the difference between a man and a woman!" She squeezed his head tight and sank to her knees, her forehead touching his, breathing each other's air. "You made me want to be a woman again, Enguer. I can't explain why."

Enguer lifted his gaze back to her face and found her steady brown eyes staring back at him. Those dangerous orbs were beautiful as always, although he never would have admitted it to himself before. Behind that fierce gaze he sensed the same fear and uncertainty that must have been reflected in his own. And then he knew. Enguer kissed her. And for the next little while he and Reskalin explored the depths of their newfound intimate friendship in ways neither of them would have ever expected.

~~~

"Wodanaz," Myrllin called, his voice echoed weakly off the sheer walls. "Wodanaz!"

He was answered by a series of startled snorts before his head popped up, long blond locks matted with drool stuck to his face, and his steely blue eyes locked on to Myrllin's. "We're alive. Huh. Thought we were dead for sure that time," his voice sounded cracked and arid. "How long have we been hanging here?"

"Hours at the least," Myrllin shrugged, sharp pains travelling across his shoulders. "Maybe days for all I know. It's cold again."

Grimacing in pain, Wodanaz bent forward and pulled himself upright using the rope tied around his hips. Myrllin guessed his brother must be in no better shape than he considering how rarely he had ever witnessed his brother react to pain. Wodanaz was right that they were lucky to be alive. Somehow the pitons had stayed intact during the earthquake and the ropes held firm, otherwise the frozen fissure would have been their grave.

"You think the bird is gone?" Wodanaz was staring up at the edge of the rift.

"We're about to find out. I think I have the strength to lift us out of here. Hold on tight to your rope in case I falter."

Myrllin spoke a charm and spread his arms to the side and slowly lifted his hands upward. Suddenly, the burden of his weight disappeared and he rose toward the surface with Wodanaz. He stopped them at the ledge where they had been standing before they were thrown off and stepped over to it. There, they untied themselves and Wodanaz returned the rope to the impossibly small pouch looped on his belt.

Carefully, Myrllin peered over the rim of the rift. The landscape was scorched black for as far as he could see and the heavy smell of burned Sulphur hung in the air. Nothing moved. The entire area was devoid of life in any form, except for the two of them. There could be no more desolate a place on the earth.

"It made a hell of a mess up here," Wodanaz took a sip from his waterskin and passed it to Myrllin.

"What the blazes is this?" Myrllin coughed and sputtered after taking a mouthful of the liquid.

Wodanaz laughed. "It's called 'ql grannligr'. Something like ale, but far stronger. The Vikja brew it to drink on long voyages on the sea. Keeps the hunger away."

"I'll never understand what you find so interesting about these people. Help me out of here."

Wodanaz grunted in reply, climbed out of the fissure and reached back down. Myrllin took his brother's outstretched hand and was easily lifted up beside him. He looked around at the devastation. *Where was Dergo?*

Myrllin closed his eyes and opened his mind to the world around him. He felt the dragon's presence nearby. He was alive, if barely and unconscious.

"Dergo is this way," Myrllin motioned to a hill covered in ash a few strides away. There was no hint of the green grass that previously grew unhindered up its slopes.

Leading the way, Myrllin trekked to the top of the hill and stopped. The bleak scenery remained unchanged to the limits of his eyesight. A black, trackless land that concealed a million deaths. Whether it be bird or toad or fox or wolf, nothing was left to mourn. Not even the trees. *Was this the kind of world the Phoenix wanted to lord over?* The only variation in the landscape were the countless hills.

One of them was Dergo and Myrllin thought he knew which one it was.

Slowly Myrllin descended, careful not to slip on the ash, while Wodanaz stayed behind to keep watch. He passed one mound and then another until he came to the mound he wanted. It seemed smaller than it should for what it held blanketed by the fine powder like a black shroud. Almost imperceptibly, there was a low rise and fall near the center and the occasional wisp of grey dust stirred up where two large holes expelled a shallow draft of air.

Myrllin gently touched the surface. Through the grit of ash he could feel the hard shell of scales and when he brushed a bit away the thick ruddy plates were undeniable. He had found his dragon. Myrllin summoned the wind and blew it from his lungs across the still form of the beast driving the ash away. Clearly visible, Myrllin realized why the huge dragon had appeared so small – much of its body lay inside a natural depression. It was probably what had saved Dergo from being consumed by the Phoenix's explosion of unnatural fire when it fell to the earth.

The great dragon lay on its side. There were terrible rents torn through scales down to cauterized flesh along the length of its body, rips and tears radiated from jagged holes in its leathery wings and the white of bone protruded out from one leg. Myrllin gasped. He and Dergo had endured more than a few scrapes in their adventures together, but never anything like this. He steeled himself and tenderly lay his hands on the dragon's horned head. It was worse on the inside. The long fall had taken its toll. A score of bones needed mending and all of the organs were severely damaged. Left as he was, the dragon would not have long to live.

Myrllin was no healer. He regretted never making the time to learn the craft from the druids. There never seemed to be enough time. But Wodanaz had.

"I need your help, brother," Myrllin spoke through the bond they shared and showed Wodanaz the extent of the dragon's injuries.

Moments later, Wodanaz put a hand on Myrllin's shoulder. "I will do what I can. Sleipnir has already been summoned."

This was no small sacrifice. He had seen his brother use healing magic before. Each time Wodanaz emerged exhausted, whether or not his life-saving efforts had succeeded, forcing him into a deep sleep that lasted a month and a day from which he could not be awakened. Fortunately, they were not far from Hy Brasil and Sleipnir could have them back at their cliff-side home in just a few days.

Wodanaz removed his shirt exposing a strange glass-like oval stone with a hole in the center where looped a leather thong that hung from his neck. Then he retrieved a small tub of pigment from another tiny pouch on his belt and with thick fingers, applied the blue color to his face and chest tracing mysterious symbols even Myrllin did not recognize. All the while, he chanted an ancient song in the language known only to the druids.

"Hore me, I me agus ag me,
Ansin atta bi beo.
I uile do fuissim, cloch agus duille,
Ansin atta bi beo.
Ag dobhar, gaeth agus teine,
Ansin atta bi beo.
Me atta tall freamh, Me atta tall mug ag domun.
Inso atta me tabhair, inso atta me tabhair,
Co uib con icc mair."

The verses repeated over and over until Wodanaz was finished painting and the symbols crackled with magic energy. So too did the glass-like stone glow bright with anticipation and it was this he took in his left hand while he knelt to place the other on the red dragon. The body of the great beast shuddered at his touch and a deep groan escaped its massive chest. Brilliant healing light radiating soothing warmth enveloped every hideous wound. Myrllin could feel it from several paces away and it made him want to sleep. The dragon calmed and appeared to agree – its breathing came slow and rhythmic, the shuddering subsided and groan trailed away.

Minutes passed, then an hour and two more. Myrllin waited patiently once again wrapped in a protective bubble to ward off the cold. He was dozing on the edge of sleep when Sleipnir stomped sharply rousing him from his comfortable respite. Night had fallen and the previously intense light embracing the dragon had dimmed considerably. Myrllin watched as it disappeared completely leaving unbroken scales and perfectly mended wings as if nothing had ever caused them to appear otherwise. Wodanaz stumbled backward and sat heavily on the ash-covered ground. He sagged as much as sat, holding his head in his hands, sweat glistening on his skin in the chilly air.

"He lives."

Myrllin could feel the strength of the dragon's beating heart, the pulsing of liquid fire through its veins and conscious awareness returning. It was a great relief. Dergo had resided in Hy Brasil for many centuries with he and his brother and although mostly reluctant to join Myrllin on his wild undertakings, the cantankerous dragon had proved to be a loyal friend and ally.

"Are you cold?"

Wodanaz's weary breath formed clouds of steam in the frosty air, "Not yet."

As did the dragons. Dergo opened his large golden eyes and lifted his head weakly out of the black dust to survey his surroundings. He gingerly stretched his wings and stood on wobbly legs testing his strength and balance. Myrllin waited patiently. Both Dergo and his brother needed a few moments to recover from the ordeal they had shared over the past several hours. Twice in the past, Wodanaz had brought Myrllin back from the brink of death and he knew well the trials of traveling that dark road of mortality.

The red dragon shifted his weighty bulk, lowered his massive head to gaze eyelevel at Myrllin and spoke in a deep rumbling baritone, "It seems I am in debt to your brother."

"I doubt he would see it that way." Myrllin reached out and lay his hand over the dragon's ridged brow, probing with his magic. Wodanaz had done his job well. With a few weeks of rest, he was confident that Dergo would recover fully.

"This exploit of yours has cost more than we bargained," Dergo's eyes narrowed shrewdly. "Your debt to *me* will be higher than we agreed."

One dark eyebrow shot high on Myrllin's forehead. "What shall it be then? More rabbits to fill your interminable appetite? You know how long it takes to grow giant fat rabbits suitable for a creature your size?"

The dragon snorted forcefully at the flippant reply, his hot breath blowing Myrllin's raven-black hair back from his bearded face. "I tire of your rabbits! The island is crawling with them. Grow a cow or a pig once in a while so I don't have to fly so far for a decent meal."

"Is that what this is about? You don't like rabbits anymore?" Myrllin pulled a silk cloth from a pocket in his robes and casually wiped the moisture off his face. "Shall I hire livestock farmers to feed, water, herd, groom and weigh your cows and pigs? Why stop there? Let's add a few horses and a brood of hens . . ."

"Will you two shut up?" Wodanaz growled. "My head hurts. And by the way, Dergo is right. There are too damn many rabbits on the island. It would take a dozen more dragons just to keep up with their breeding."

"I take it you are ready to go home now?" Myrllin smiled expectantly.

"Yes."

"Wait," Dergo stretched his neck to look high over the hill toward the south. "There is something you should see before we leave."

"What is it?" Myrllin had a feeling this had nothing to do with rabbits.

"When the Phoenix shattered, it left something behind," the grave tone in the dragon's voice sounded ominous. "I glimpsed it on my way down. If it's still there. We go south."

Wodanaz stood up with a groan. "We had better take a look. This might not be over yet."

Myrllin looked up at Dergo. "Are you strong enough to fly?"

"Yes," the red dragon crouched low on the ground. "Get on."

Flying low over the scorched earth, Dergo led the way south with Wodanaz riding Sleipnir close behind. Even in the dark, Myrllin could tell by the blast pattern seared into the landscape that they were nearing the epicenter and within minutes they passed over the lip of a deep crater no less than a hundred spans from one side to the other. Dergo banked right and then left settling into a wide counter-clockwise orbit above the lightless pit.

"Do you see it?" Dergo called back over his shoulder. "It is there in the center nearly buried."

Myrllin couldn't see a thing. It was too dark at the base of the hollow and he didn't possess the dark-vision the dragon enjoyed. There was something else he could do. He pulled a small pebble from a pouch beneath his robes and tapped it gently with the tip of his index finger. It glowed slightly at his touch drawing a chuckle from the red dragon eyeballing his endeavor. Myrllin ignored the slight and nonchalantly rolled the pebble out of his palm into the black void. Seconds later, an explosion of light illuminated the crater from end to end as if it were daylight. The reluctantly approving grunt he overheard from the throat of the dragon was more than a little satisfying.

"Yes, I see it now," Myrllin acknowledged.

It was a black thing smooth and shiny with only a small portion of it exposed and the rest hidden mysteriously under dirt and ash. Myrllin didn't know what to make of it. Although his instincts guessed that it wasn't meant to be found.

I'm going down to get a better look. Myrllin sent the message to his brother through their bond.

Right behind you. Came the wholly expected reply.

Heeding a mental prompt, Dergo angled steeply toward the base of the blackened bowl and landed firmly, his sail-like wings casting clouds of ash into the air a dozen strides away from the strange object. Myrllin waited for the ash to settle before he slid down the dragon's scales and joined Wodanaz who was already kneeling next to it with a perplexed look on his face.

"We can dig it out," Wodanaz had his hands in the dirt probing around the edges of the object. "It's round, I think. And very warm to touch."

"I'll help you," Myrllin sank to his knees on the opposite side of the dark sphere and scooped away the dry and dusty soil.

Excavating the thing took less time than Myrllin would have imagined. When they had cleared away much of the dirt, he stood out of the way to let Wodanaz lift it upright out of its hole and onto flat ground. There it lay, balancing on its bloated waist, knee high and an arm's length wide and thicker on one end than the other. It was blacker than night fragmented by jagged crimson veins that pulsed with a soft red glow from within as if it held something alive.

"I can't believe it," was all that Myrllin could think to say.

Chapter 25

New Beginnings

Enguer stared up at the clear blue afternoon sky. The clouds had cleared away allowing a hint of Sunna's warmth to stave off the cold mountain breeze just enough to create a cozy shelter within the forest glen. There was warmth from the body that lay nestled in his arms as well. It was new and inviting and . . . confusing. Reskalin. Enguer felt a strange attraction from the start, he had to acknowledge the truth of that, but having few friends in his life he thought that maybe that was it. But it wasn't. It was something else entirely and he lay unsure how to come to terms with the new-found identity of his friend.

Reskalin stirred at his side, "How much time do we have?" Even her voice was different now. No longer husky and deliberate, it sounded softer, smooth, natural. Like a woman's.

"Not long. The horses should be rested by now and we need to take advantage of the daylight hours to widen our lead."

"I'm in love with you, you know."

Enguer might as well have been struck by a bolt of lightning. Never in his wildest imaginings did he expect to hear that from him . . . her. He lay quiet for a long moment until he felt Reskalin slowly tensing up next to him. He had to say something.

"I want to say the same, Reskalin. But in a way, you are a stranger that I have just met and I need to get to know you again to be sure." Enguer certainly desired her. He had proved that over and over in the last hours, but love? He had never experienced love outside his family and this felt different.

To his relief, Reskalin relaxed and propped her head up on one arm. "Then we will speak no more of it until we are safely back in

Arre." She kissed him on the cheek and stood to walk back down to the river where she had left her clothes earlier.

Enguer watched her bare, lithe form walk into the forest. Hot desire surged within him and he nearly called out for her to come back. It was his first time with a woman in that way and he wanted to do it again, but there was no more time for that. They had to get moving as soon as possible. With no small reluctance, he suppressed his hungry cravings and cast around for his clothes.

By the time Reskalin returned, Enguer was dressed and fastening the last straps of the saddle on his Lambei. He helped Reskalin with her saddle and soon they were trotting up the river at a faster speed than the dark hours in hopes of covering at least eight or ten leagues before night fell. More often than he wanted to, Enguer glanced over at Reskalin. She looked so obviously like a woman, even with the short hair, that he wondered how he could have missed it. Apparently, everyone in Arre had. Once in a while he tried to think of her as he had before – the obstinate rogue, his travel companion, his friend – but no matter how he tried, he couldn't see Reskalin in the same way as he did before. A man.

They spoke little that afternoon which suited Enguer just fine. He wasn't sure what he would have said anyway. Yet he found pleasure in that she road closer to him than before, close enough that he could have reached out and touched her if he wanted and many times he almost did. It was the conflict inside that stopped him and although he had no doubt about his physical longing for her, he needed to be sure about the rest. That was his mother's doing. He didn't understand at the time, but she warned him not to play with a girl's heart, no matter how badly other parts of him wanted to be with her. It had always seemed so silly until now. He had almost forgotten it.

When the light finally dwindled to patches of illumination filtering through the trees, Enguer called for them to stop and allow the horses to rest a bit and drink water. Over the course of the afternoon, he kept an eye out for certain landmarks he had memorized when they passed this way the first time and he did a few quick mental calculations.

"If we keep to our current pace, we should enter the Travini Pass by tomorrow afternoon or early evening." He offered a piece of salted pork from his pouch to Reskalin.

She rolled her eyes at him, but took it all the same. "I hope you can track us down something better to eat on the other side. Other than a rabbit," she smiled sweetly at him.

It was the same rare smile that he had seen on Reskalin a few times before, but this time it was different. He liked her smile. "I'm sure we can find something that will please you."

The way they spoke to each other sounded different now as well; less guarded, familiar, a little intimate. It was nothing like before. He supposed that's the way it was going to be from here on out and he was not sure whether he liked that or not. It would take some getting used to at the very least.

The familiar blare of the ork's horn called out from the south. It sounded closer than Enguer would have expected and just as the night before the cry of the Dire Wolves answered its call. Both the mare and the Lambei stomped their hooves nervously. The orks couldn't be more than a few hours behind them, far short of the day and a half he anticipated.

Enguer mounted his Lambei and waited on Reskalin to mount hers, "We must go faster tonight and rest less in the day tomorrow, otherwise they will be upon us before we can escape the Travini Pass."

"They have gained so much ground?" alarm sounded in her voice.

Enguer nodded. "Either they are stretching the night into the late dawn to travel further or they are running faster than I have given them credit for. Maybe both."

Enguer kicked his Lambei forward through the shallow currents of the river and reconsidered the merits of staying in it. Either the Dire Wolves could somehow still track them by scent, or they just figured their prey wouldn't be heading anywhere but the pass. He decided to stick with the river for the time being and hold out hope the orks would become frustrated and call off their pursuit.

Throughout the night they fled, the horses pulling more than needing to be pushed as if they too understood the urgency. Just once, early in the evening, did they hear the howls of their pursuers again and Enguer speculated that the orks had come across their camp in the glen. After that there were no more horns or howls to tell them how close the orks might be, just the splash of their own passage in the quiet darkness. Enguer stopped their progress only when necessary to allow the horses to drink and rest a little bit. The night was long and he found himself muttering prayers for Sunna to bring the dawn the longer it went.

When Sunna at last brought forth her blessed rays to carry light and warmth to the cold dark earth below, Enguer began to watch for a suitable place to rest their exhausted horses. They would need a half a day to recover after the aggressive gait they kept all night with another night ahead that promised more of the same. He finally brought them to a halt at a rocky embankment between the forest and the river with enough grass and soft plants to satisfy the horses.

After brushing down the horses, Enguer built a small fire and pulled off his boots and leather cuirass to dry out the leather. So far, the clear weather had held and there was nothing but white puffy clouds in the sky. Rain would help cover their scent, a down-pour even better, but he doubted it mattered any more.

"You're not worried that the fire will give us away to the orks?" Reskalin removed her armor and leather breeches and sat next to him wearing only her under tunic. She looked as exhausted as he felt and as much as he wanted to do other things, they needed every minute of the few hours of rest they were going to get before mounting up again.

"They already know we are ahead of them." Enguer pulled a small net out of his pack and fastened it to the double pronged stick he had cut off a tree. "With all that howling last night they must have found where we camped yesterday."

She lay her head on his shoulder and quietly watched him fiddle with the net. "What are you going to do with that?"

Tying the last stitch, he held it up. "Catch a fish if I can."

Together they walked over to the bank of the river. Enguer had seen a few fish in the deeper parts that morning and with a little luck might manage to catch one or two. He stripped off his clothes, fully aware and a little embarrassed that Reskalin was watching him closely, and stepped into the frigid water. He swam to the center of the river and tried to keep still holding the net above his head ready to strike. A small splash drew his attention to the bank where he saw Reskalin entering the water to bathe. The sun reflected off droplets on her olive-toned skin unblemished and perfect in the bright light. Damn he wanted her. She paused when she discovered him staring and smiled. Feeling embarrassed, Enguer wanted to look away, but he couldn't. She was beautiful and she said she loved him. How lucky could he be that . . .

Something tugged at the net he was holding. Startled, Enguer realized he had unconsciously lowered his arm into the water and to his utter disbelief a fish had inadvertently swum into it! He pulled the net out of the water to reveal a plump yellow perch flopping inside.

"Breakfast!" he shouted triumphantly.

The fish was enough to temporarily satisfy their hunger while a brief explosion of activity afterward assuaged their craving leaving the two lovers spent and quickly asleep in each other's arms. Enguer had not planned it that way, it just happened and he wasn't about to make it stop. Every moment they spent together he was finding it easier to be with her and harder to remember how it was before. He had heard of people falling in love, the famous poet and lyricist Vyvyan wrote extensively about it, but reading and hearing of something was far different than going through it one's self. Maybe this was the falling part.

The sun was high over head when Enguer led the horses away from the embankment toward the river. He could have slept the rest of the day next to Reskalin if it were possible. But it wasn't. The Dire Wolves would be on their tails again in just a few hours.

"No need to ride in the river," Enguer mounted his horse and studied the way ahead. "We'll make better time following the tree-line."

Reskalin rode up beside him almost chirping with enthusiasm. "By this time tomorrow we'll be on the Plains of Tarre and only two days from home."

In his mind the thought formed, 'or dead'. He kept that to himself. Not that he was worried about scaring Reskalin, he doubted anything scared Reskalin, it was just too gloomy and she was too happy. Why ruin it by saying something stupid?

They trotted north through the wilds always keeping the river in sight. It would lead them straight into the Travini Pass where its waters gurgled up from under a mountain of rock. Enguer didn't bother trying to cover their track, there was no point to it anymore, and where they could safely push the horses into a fast cantor, they did. Time and distance were all that mattered. The chase would be on again when darkness fell and the stakes for not coming out on top would be their lives.

Clouds rolled in off the mountains again that afternoon bringing a driving rain that forced them to take cover and shelter under the heavy forest canopy. Even so, they were drenched and cold to the bone when it finally let up enough to continue. And no sooner had they stepped beyond the tree-line, horns and howls pierced the quiet pall of the sodden forest interrupting the persistent hum of the steady drizzle that had become something of a soothing backdrop.

Enguer was startled. There were still hours before nightfall. The orks should not be stirring so soon. "The heavy overcast must be enough that the orks eyes are not hindered by what remains of the day."

"They sound much closer than before." Reskalin's eyes were wide and fierce, but her voice was steady. She was ready to fight.

Enguer prayed it would not come to that. It would be their last battle if it did. Yet his hope was fading, somehow the orks had managed to gain ground on them during the night. They were so close that he was sure their camps that morning couldn't have been more than a league or two apart!

He looked into her eyes and knew he had to tell Reskalin the truth. She would need to prepare herself for the inevitable just as he would and he took a measure of comfort knowing that they would go down fighting savagely. Together. "They are only three or four hours behind us." He watched her closely, assessing her reaction. If anything, her expression turned harder, colder. She understood exactly what he was saying.

"Then we ride until our horses fall dead under us and face these monsters back to back." Shorter by more than a head, she reached up and grabbed the back of his neck and pulled his lips to hers kissing him fiercely.

There couldn't have been a more perfect moment in his life. Forehead to forehead and out of breath with the light rain trailing down their faces, Enguer locked his steady gaze with hers. There was no uncertainty left, no doubt, he knew. "Reskalin, I . . ."

She kissed him hard again, interrupting his words and bit his bottom lip at the end of it drawing a small trickle of blood. "I know. You will tell me the words when we are safe again."

There was nothing left to say. Everything that could be said was there in her beautiful eyes. They didn't need hope, luck, or even the gods. They needed each other. He was convinced that if they were going to somehow survive, it would be through their strength together and it energized him with optimism that it just might be possible.

Fast through the scattering of trees they galloped, recklessly vaulting over thorn bushes and dodging the remains of tumbled timber, heedless of the dangers that could cause their mounts to stumble or fall. Their horses reflected their urgency, never faltering, never failing. They ran for leagues in the haze of the darkening sky until night fell and they were forced to slow. The rain finally ceased by the time they came upon the end of the river and the beginning of Travini Pass, but the wind had picked up significantly. Enguer stopped them at the banks of the small lake that formed where the river drained from under the mountain and allowed their horses to drink and rest. It would have been a perfect spot to camp under different circumstances.

"The trail through the pass will make our travel easier, but it will benefit our pursuers as well and they see better than we do in the dark," Enguer looked back down the river. The lake that fed it was at a higher elevation and had it not been nighttime he could have easily seen a league or more in the distance. "Our only chance is to make it through the pass and into the open plain by sunrise before they catch up. If they haven't caught sight of us, they will have to make camp until nightfall and we can gain a few more hours."

"We will make it," she sounded confident. Enguer wanted to believe her. Desperately.

The trail that wound through the dark pass was soon straddled by a sheer rock face on both sides leaving a sliver of sky filled with stars as their only illumination. Reluctantly, they slowed their pace to a fast trot. The horses were already tired from the hard ride that afternoon and required a short rest every few hours to keep from succumbing to exhaustion. A strong wind pushed at their backs as it whistled through the gorge giving the illusion that they were moving faster than they really were. It was a frigidly cold gust, but Enguer was just grateful it was not in their faces carrying their scent back to motivate the Dire Wolves that he knew were close behind.

Not halfway through the pass, the ominous echo of horns resounded off the surrounding cliffs followed by a frenzy of howls inspiring tired horses to step quicker of their own accord. Enguer looked at Reskalin, meeting her intense gaze. Both knew what it meant; the orks had reached the pass.

The next few hours passed in silence. Enguer focused his attention on guiding his Lambei through a series of escalating movements from trot to cantor to full gallop and then back down again to balance speed with endurance. Still, after all afternoon and most of the night, the horses were tipping on the edge of exhaustion, Reskalin's mare more than his own. Her long next was hanging low and her breathing heavy. Enguer had little confidence she would last the night. If any of them did. They pressed on, racing to escape the pass and searching the sky for traces of dawn.

Sometime later they crested a hill and paused to rest their horses. A thrill went through Enguer as he looked into the distance. No more than a league ahead of them the high cliffs eroded into the open expanse of the Plains of Tarre. He only knew it by the frame of the clear sky dense with stars all the way to the horizon.

"We are nearly there," Reskalin whispered to her flagging mare as she stroked her neck. "Not far to go now."

Enguer looked east over the Asinippi Mountains behind them. He thought he could detect the faintest hint of the stars fading with the coming of dawn. It was nearly time for Sunna to awaken, but would she break the shadow of the mountain in time to save them? The wind was still strong from the east and he met its icy caress across his face and ears stoically as his watery eyes searched the sky. There was something else in the air that caught his attention. Unsure at first, he wet his lips and concentrated on the taste and smell of it. The gusty ebb and flow of the air current brought the smell again, stronger this time. It was feral and untamed that mingled with a familiar stench . . .

"They are here," Enguer rushed to his horse and mounted quickly. "Stay near me, if your mare stumbles, push her close and I will pull you to me."

Reskalin jumped into her saddle like a nimble acrobat, "How far?" She pulled around her travel bag and began searching through it.

"Half a league or less." Enguer was anxious to get moving. They had precious little time. "What are you doing?"

She pulled a pouch out and emptied its contents on the ground behind her. "Giving us a little extra time."

Enguer could see several small pods bounce briefly in the dirt. "What is that?"

"You'll see," she smiled slightly. "Now let's go!"

They charged down the hill toward the freedom of the plains as fast as their horses would carry them. Enguer knew this would be the final length of the race and even if they made it out of the pass it was no certainty that the Dire Wolves would not follow. Especially if they were sighted. Unlike the orks, Dire Wolves were not hypersensitive to sunlight and could see as well as they. Maybe better. He guessed the orks had somehow trained them to return to their masters, perhaps attuned to the particular pitch of their horns. It seemed impossible. No one had ever trained a wolf as far as he knew, let alone a Dire Wolf the size of a horse.

Halfway to the outlet of the pass, horns rang triumphantly from the hill followed by a frenzy of rabid howls. They had been spotted. Enguer looked over his shoulder and could clearly see dark silhouettes moving back and forth on the hill against a sky scarcely less dark with fewer stars than before. There were orks on the hill with the Dire Wolves. How could that be possible? Orks could run fast, but certainly not fast enough to keep up with a Dire Wolf over a long period of time. There must be shamans with them.

Suddenly, a score of flashes and bangs flickered on the hill amid a chaos of startled yelps and gruff shouts. Reskalin's rich laugh rose over the clamor of their hooves and trailed behind them into the darkness. Enguer was unsure what had happened.

"Flash-pops!" she called out gleefully. "It will take a while for their eyes to adjust to the darkness again!"

Enguer pumped his fist in the air, "You've saved us!"

They raced on. Their horses were heaving and puffing on the edge of collapse when they finally bolted over the last few strides of hard rock and dirt and onto the soft earth sprouting with tall green grass. The Plains of Tarre. The sun was rising, there was no doubt about that, as soft reds and oranges illuminated the western sky behind the dark outline of the Asinippi, but as overjoyed as Enguer might have been, they were still deep in the shadows of the mountain range.

"No, no, no!" Reskalin cried abruptly.

Enguer looked over to see her mare slick with sweat and struggling to keep up, her eyes rolled wildly and pink froth flaked from the corners of her mouth. Easing up a bit on his Lambei, he pulled up next to the mare and held out his hand to Reskalin.

"Grab my arm and jump!" he shouted.

Reskalin hesitated, shaking her head as if in denial about what was happening. The mare stumbled then, falling further behind and Enguer eased up a little more. It wouldn't be long; she would have to jump now. He thrust out his arm again and this time she took it and a second later pulled herself in firmly behind him. The mare kept pace for a few more strides before her front legs collapsed in the grass sending her end over end. Enguer felt Reskalin bury her head in his back and tighten her grip around his torso.

The Lambei sped on. As powerful as his massive horse was, it would be struggling soon with the weight of two riders. Enguer looked back over his shoulder and watched in dismay at the dark shapes slowly gained on them. At one point he could hear an eruption of barking and growling and the shouted commands of angry orks. They found the mare. Enguer looked up at the sky. Some of the reds were showing a hint of blue far behind them. Dawn would come to the plains too late for them. The orks wouldn't stop now. He was sure of it. With the Dire Wolves slowly gaining on them, his Lambei would either give out like the mare or the Dire Wolves would catch up and drag them down.

"Put on your cloak," Enguer called back to Reskalin. "When they get close, we will jump off and hide in the grass. Hopefully they will follow the Lambei for as far as it goes."

Reskalin wrapped her legs around him tightly to free up her arms and he felt the movement of her removing the cloak from her travel pack. After a few clumsy attempts she managed to get it over her and then folded her arms tightly around his torso once again. Jumping off the Lambei would be a foolish gamble. Even if they managed to land without breaking any of their limbs, it would take Sunna's luck for the Dire Wolves to pass them by. The cloak and his ring would offer visual concealment, but how long would it take for the beasts to sniff them out? Their only chance lay with the closest Dire Wolves ignoring their scents to continue the chase. And there was a chance that without their weight the Lambei might have enough left in him to outdistance these monsters and get away. He could hope.

"Enguer!" Reskalin shouted, drawing his attention behind them.

Two Dire Wolves, the swiftest of their pack no doubt, were advancing on them rapidly. Dim illumination was beginning to bring light to the plains giving Enguer clear sight of their outline if not their detail. There was something strange about them. He knew the shape of a wolf well and he knew that Dire Wolves were built much the same, still, there was a dark bulk over the center of its mass as if it were carrying something on its back.

It gained another stride and a long appendage extended from the mass holding what appeared to be a sword high and ready. Enguer couldn't believe his eyes. The orks were riding the Dire Wolves! He felt one of Reskalin's arms release him and a sharp movement followed. The Dire Wolf on their right yelped loudly and tumbled across the green prairie tossing its rider into the air.

"Good shot!" Enguer shouted. He hoped she had a lot more daggers on her.

The Dire Wolf-riding-ork on his left had also seen what happened and moved ahead of them to avoid any flying projectiles. Enguer drew his sword, and deflected a strike from the orks blade when it swiftly veered in and then away again. Something flashed off metal in the distance. The ork swerved back in for a second swing and Enguer swatted the blade away a second time. On its next approach, Reskalin bent low behind him and the Dire Wolf yelped in pain. The ork pulled away again and Enguer could see a bloody wound on the wolf's hind just above the long bushy tail.

The ork growled at him spitting words Enguer couldn't understand and urged the wolf further ahead. Again, there was a flash in the distance followed by another that demanded Enguer's attention. He didn't have the time. On the next approach, the eager ork tried to swerve in further forward. Enguer understood his intent right away. The ork raised his sword to bring it down on the Lambei's thick neck, but Enguer pulled sharply to his right and the forceful swing met only air and nearly unseated him from the Dire Wolf's back. Stumbling with the ork's weight off balance, Enguer was free to bolt past him unhindered. Reskalin was ready and after another sudden movement from behind Enguer glanced back to see a second Dire Wolf and rider tumbling through the grass.

"Enguer," Reskalin called to him.

Enguer twisted in his saddle to follow her gaze. The Lambei was still moving fast working wholly on adrenalin, but what he saw bearing down on them in the first dim light of the early morning sunrise crushed every ounce of hope in his body. The dark outlines of at least forty Dire Wolves, each with their own rider, would be on them in minutes.

Chapter 26

The Hill

Enguer now knew how he was going to die.

Only a few times in his life did he have passing thoughts about his end and mostly he fancied himself old and infirm at the end of a legendary life awaiting a final embrace in the light of Sunna. Never in his wildest dreams did he imagine his body torn to pieces by ork-driven Dire Wolves in some distant grassland far from home.

Home.

He didn't know where his home was anymore. Courth had been his home, people knew him there, he could have been a farmer or a ranger in service to King Francik. It could have been a good life. He could have raised a family. Yet he had rejected all that to die in the grass. Unremarkable. Forgotten. And despite everything that could have been, he wouldn't have it any other way if that meant his life didn't include Reskalin. The clutch of slender arms wrapped tightly around his torso and the press of her head on his back made Enguer smile. He was grateful to find love before he died. No matter how strange he may have come by it or how briefly he would enjoy the pleasure of it. It was a miracle he could have only guessed at before Reskalin and if it had to end, Enguer was glad it would end with her.

Sweat lathered the neck and flanks of the powerful Lambei, his breathing fast and deep, long league-churning strides cut massive clods of earth and grass in the wake of his passing. If there were a more impressive breed in any land, Enguer had surely not come across one. No wonder the Enlightened One's valued them so highly. Any other horse would have faltered by now, exhausted, drained of every last ounce of fortitude like Reskalin's poor mare. Even saddled with two riders, the Lambei had not slowed. The strength of its heart, lungs and haunches were all that remained between life and death for all of them. Still, it would not be enough. The Dire Wolves would not be out run and it wouldn't be long before even the mighty Lambei finally faltered.

Another glint of light flashed from atop a high green hill a quarter league or so to the southwest. Enguer turned the Lambei toward it to get a better look. It appeared to be a man in metal armor crouching or sitting on a rock. Most likely a scout sent from either Povigi or Arre to keep watch on the pass and forewarn of another ork raiding party. Enguer doubted that t man could see their approach since they, and the Dire Wolves, were still shrouded in the shadow of the mountain. It was an odd spectacle watching the line of light slowly advance toward him knowing that the sun was at his back. It lit up the entire hill where the lone man sat and the long stretch of grassland in front of him. Enguer thought that he would very much prefer to die in the light of Sunna rather than the gloom of shadows and fervently hoped his Lambei was up to the task of getting them there.

For a moment, Enguer thought to alter his course away from the lone figure on the hill. Why should he bring death upon the poor soul? *It must be too late,* he thought. If he could see the man the orks could as well and Enguer doubted they would allow him to escape their bloodlust. Maybe they could all make a stand together; a ranger, a rogue and an unsuspecting armor-clad scout selling their lives steeply against two score Dire Wolves and their ork masters. He kept his course true and unwavering, bringing death as certain as those that followed.

There was a brief stir of movement and then Reskalin spoke quietly into his ear, "They are less than twenty strides."

Her voice was calm and steady. She was ready to face her last moments just as he was. It was a great relief. His father told him once that a person's true nature came out when faced with imminent death. Often, they begged, less often they were defiant and sometimes, just sometimes, they faced whatever came with the calm clarity of acceptance that freed their minds from fear and inaction. Those were the survivors.

Reskalin was a survivor.

Still a few dozen strides from the boundary between light and dark, and with the wind in his face, Enguer thought they might be close enough for the scout to hear if he shouted.

"Make ready!" he yelled.

Nothing.

Reskalin shifted and rested her chin on his shoulder, her warm breath against his cheek. "I see him. Try again!"

Enguer filled his lungs and shouted again at the top of his lungs, "Make Ready!"

The Scout slowly stood. He had heard or at least thought he had heard something.

Enguer repeated his cry and was rewarded by the scout's startled reaction. The man must be sure now. He paced the top of the hill frantically searching the darkness, disadvantaged by the sunlight in his face. At least he was warned and would not be completely surprised by what was coming.

"Ten strides now," Reskalin warned.

Just a little further. Enguer wanted to dig in his heels to encourage the Lambei to even greater speed, but he knew it had nothing left to give. He would not panic. The light was within reach if they remained calm. Crossing its threshold was the last victory he was determined to take, even if it was a small one.

Enguer sensed the touch of warmth on his skin before the Lambei stepped out of the shroud of darkness and into the bright radiance of Sunna. It was hardly less cold, but the intensity of the light and the small heat brought with it was like a blanket wrapped around his soul filling him with rapturous exhilaration that could have been nothing short of a divine gift bestowed by his goddess. Enguer never felt more humbled and grateful for anything in his life.

A cry of alarm brought Enguer's attention back to the hill in time to see the scout disappearing over the other side. *He's running*, Enguer lamented. The man probably still couldn't see the orks and thought he was about to be attacked by a man charging out of the darkness on a massive Lambei. Enguer hoped the scout had a good horse. He might stand a chance of getting away if he did. Even Dire Wolves couldn't run forever.

Still at least two-hundred strides from the base of the hill, Enguer calculated that was where their flight would end unless his

Lambei failed them sooner. Only two-hundred strides. It seemed so far, yet they would be there in seconds and it would be done.

"Get ready," he called to Reskalin. "When we make the base of the hill, we'll both jump. Try to get to the other side and hide while I hold them off!"

Enguer knew it was a stupid thing to say as soon as he said it. This was Reskalin he was talking to. She was as likely to run off and hide as his Lambei was to sprout wings and fly.

Reskalin's sharp teeth nicked his jawline causing him to flinch. "I'm telling you for the last time, I go where you go." She pressed her lips hard on his face and kissed the same spot. "Five paces."

The irony of her reply was not lost on him. He might have found a subtle humor in it had he the time to think on it, but his attention was back on the hill where there were suddenly two men on the hill in metal armor. *Why have they not fled?* The Dire Wolves with their dreadful passengers had to be clearly visible to them in the sunlight. Either they were heroically suicidal or . . .

More figures crested the top of the hill. Many more. They formed a double row of mounted cavalry to the left and the right of the two men standing in the center. Like the scout, they all wore bronze cuirasses accentuated by red capes that billowed around them in the shifting breeze and carried long iron-tipped spears adorned with a pair of red streamers. They looked stunning.

A thrill went through him. There had to be more than a hundred!

"A patrol from Arre!" Reskalin exclaimed excitedly. She was right, they looked just like the cavalry Enguer had seen the night the orks attacked the city.

Enguer watched the two soldiers still on foot mount horses brought up the hill by what appeared to be a young boy. His Lambei was only fifty strides from the hill with the Dire Wolves nipping at their heels. The beasts were so close that Enguer could clearly hear the ragged breathing and low growls brought on by the snap of their rider's whips. Unless the cavalry from Arre did something soon, Enguer feared that they would be overrun by the orks in sight of their salvation.

A horn blared from up the hill that resonated across the plain brisk and clear in the cold air. In response the mounted soldiers moved forward together in perfect formation at a regular trot. Slowly at first, they flowed down the hill building speed as they went until they reached the bottom. Only ten strides away they bore down at full gallop with their long spears level and thirsty for blood. For a few panicked seconds Enguer thought they might run them through as quick as the orks. He closed his eyes in anticipation of the impact, but in the last second the cavalry narrowly split their ranks and thundered past.

As a boy Enguer had heard stories about cavalry charges. The Kingdom of Courth was widely known and feared for their mounted shock troops used in battle throughout their history. He surely never expected to face one. Yet, the terror of nearly colliding with the cavalry suddenly paled in comparison to the brutal crash of heavy bodies and cries of man and beast that echoed across the tranquil Plains of Tarre behind them.

Enguer brought his heaving Lambei to a halt a few strides up the hill and quickly dismounted with sword and dagger in hand. He was followed by Reskalin a second later bristling with blades that appeared to float in the air against her shimmering cloak. Barely had their feet touched the ground before they were flinging themselves away from snapping jaws and the downward thrust of battle axes. A pair of the Dire Wolves and their riders had managed to follow them through the charging lines of the cavalry and halfway up the slope of the hill.

Enguer rolled back down the incline completely out of control. When he finally came to a stop, he had to jump away again to avoid the flailing limbs of the orks and their Dire Wolves that came tumbling after. He picked himself off the ground a second time, quickly regained his balance and prepared to face the orks and Dire Wolves that landed twenty paces further down the hill. One of the Dire Wolves lay unmoving, a dagger planted in the side of its skull, but the other one, as well as the two orks, were still very much alive and moving with renewed haste in his direction. Reskalin was nowhere in sight.

Beyond the approaching danger, Enguer was vaguely aware of the pitched battle that raged back and forth a short distance away. The noise was deafening, a cacophony of unidentifiable screams of man or beast and metal crashing against metal combined with the disorienting blur of movement by a mix of bodies no longer separated by distinct lines. Enguer's mind gave it only a second of thought, his attention was engaged on the rush of violence that would be on him in moments. He gripped his blades tighter and resolved to greet them with fury contained over the leagues of their long pursuit, a final meeting that now held an ounce of hope if he could survive.

Five paces ahead of the orks, the Dire Wolf was nearly on him when it was abruptly thrust into the air from an unseen force that propelled it from the ground. Astonished, Enguer watched it topple back down the hill, the fur of its underbelly a shimmering mass that shifted unnaturally as it rolled with the beast.

Reskalin.

The joy Enguer felt was short-lived as the lead ork thrust awkwardly uphill with his heavy battle axe and sank its broad blade deep into the soft soil between Enguer's feet. The miscalculation cost the ork its left eye and its life. Enguer danced around the stinking brute, pulled his blade free of its skull and slid to the side over the slick grass to avoid a passing swing from the second ork. When they faced each other again, it was from only five strides, both standing precariously on the side of the steep hill. This time, the powerful ork advanced slowly, clearly taking measure of his opponent. Enguer did the same and determined rather quickly that this was not a creature he should trade blows with toe-to-toe. He would have to outmaneuver the ork to gain advantage and that would be no easy task from where he stood. Enguer decided to even the odds.

Turning, he swiftly ran down the slope toward even ground. Just as he hoped, the ork took his departure as flight and chased after him howling with glee. At the bottom of the hill Enguer turned to face the oncoming charge. At first, the look on the ork's face was triumphant, he held his battle axe high in anticipation of a mighty death blow that would cleave Enguer in two, until he tried to slow his descent. He couldn't. The ork's long strides became uncontrolled, his face contorted in panic and he threw his arms wide for balance losing his grip on the great battle axe which fell flat in the grass left behind. Momentum took over his heavy bulk. He was going too fast for his legs to keep up. The ork stumbled and recovered, stumbled again and fell. He fell headlong into the soft earth and plunged downhill end over end.

To where Enguer was waiting.

The ork came to a stop face-up at Enguer's feet. Enguer almost felt sorry for the creature. Almost. And then his blade pinned the ork to the grass through the soft cartilage of its throat and he watched the evil light fade from its shallow orbs forever. He felt no remorse.

"Enguer!" A muffled voiced called from nearby.

Enguer looked around, but saw no one.

"Enguer!" The voice called again.

It came from somewhere near the carcass of a Dire Wolf not far away. Enguer felt fear rise within him. If it were Reskalin, maybe she was injured and needed his help. He ran toward the dead wolf, desperately searching the grass around it for the tell-tale sign of Reskalin's shimmering cloak. Nothing. The call came again. This time it sounded as if it came from the Dire Wolf itself.

Or beneath it!

Enguer knelt down next to the wolf and searched the ground around it. He found a boot, attached to a slender leg that disappeared under a mass of fur. He tried to pull her out, but it was no use. She was stuck underneath the bulk of the wolf that was easily the size and weight of a warhorse. Urgently, he began to dig and stopped when he realized that it would take too long. She was suffocating under all that heaviness and he was running out of options. He sat down with his back against the wolf's chest and took hold of its front legs. He didn't need to move the whole body, just the front where Reskalin was buried. Then he pulled his legs up close and dug his heels into the soil and pushed. It took everything he had to move the bulky creature, even if only to slide it a few feet on the grass, but it was enough.

There was a gasp of air from beneath him and then arms struggling to pull free and there she was, sitting beside him, sucking in the sweet air . . . and smiling. She was saved. They were saved.

Enguer sat with his back against the soft fur of the Dire Wolf holding Reskalin tightly in his arms. No longer under threat, Reskalin reversed her cloak to display its mundane thread. Exhausted, the pair watched as the orks broke under the assault of the soldiers and ran back toward the Travini Pass leaving a scene blood and horror in their wake. The cavalry had done its job well. If at a terrible cost.

The trauma of the initial charge was evidenced by a forest of spears rising from the once lush green grass stained crimson between muddy pools of blood and bile where mangled bodies with contorted limbs, broken necks and crushed skulls revealed the savagery of the brief meeting between man and beast. The residual from the melee that followed was just as terrible with limbs separated from their hosts by the vicious curved blades of battle axes and flesh sliced to the white of bone from sharp-edged swords.

Cries from the injured and dying rent the air expressing their anguish to the gods, their loved ones and anyone that might relieve their suffering. In this the orks were no different than the humans. Only the animals suffered in relative silence, their occasional bleats and yelps the most sincere, calling for no one, accepting their fate with quiet dignity.

The cavalry did not pursue the orks. They would have been ill prepared to do so. They returned to tend to their wounded, put down injured horses and press their spears through the hearts of any ork or Dire Wolf unlucky enough to have survived with wounds too injurious for escape. Enguer and Reskalin watched the bloody work, sitting side by side, both in shock at what they witnessed and continued to witness.

"I have seen many terrible things in Arre over the years. No few of them as a result of my word or deed." Her small hand crawled into his. "The underworld is a very dangerous place where trust is a fairy tale and survival hinges on the shifting winds of power. But I have never been a spectator to war. Is this what Rasna, Tarre and all the Western Kingdoms can expect in the coming years?"

Enguer had never seen war either. He read about it. Heard stories about it. And always it was portrayed as an inspirational tale of righteous duty in service to Sunna carried out with honor and virtue. Never did it look like this. Reskalin's stark words filled him with fear. "Courth is a peaceful kingdom. We have not been to war in many years. I know little of war." He squeezed her hand for reassurance. "But isn't war common in Rasna? The rumors . . ."

"Not in Arre," she was quick to respond. "Clevi and Scratu, cities in the south that border the lands of the Enchele tribes, they know more of war. Maybe a few of the coastal cities like Funa and Tarca, especially Cara, they see raiders from the sea every season. But not Arre."

An impressive-looking soldier separated from a cluster of cavalrymen standing at the edge of the bloody meadow and rode toward them. He wore an open-faced helm with a high red plume of feathers sprouting arrogantly from the top, a bronze cuirass intricately worked with silver that matched his greaves and vambraces and a long red cape that snapped from side to side like an angry snake. Two more soldiers, typical in appearance, trailed close behind.

"I know that man," Reskalin hissed in Enguer's ear and jerked her hand away. "His name is Commander Artis and this must be his Cavalry Unit. He is arrogant and corrupt. Just follow my lead and don't forget he thinks I am a man!"

Reskalin stood at the commander's approach and Enguer pulled himself up beside her. He didn't know what to expect from this man, but he knew enough that a corrupt soldier with a little authority could be a volatile thing. Especially so when far from those that controlled *him*.

"Bring them to me," the commander ordered his men when he arrived at the base of the hill.

"No need, Commander," Reskalin spoke in the husky voice Enguer recognized from the time before he knew the truth about him . . . her. It sounded strange and unnatural to his ears.

A moment later they were met at the bottom of the hill by the two soldiers who grabbed them roughly by the arms as soon as they were within reach and pushed them to stand in front of the commander sitting astride his warhorse. Under any other circumstance Enguer would never have allowed anyone to handle him that way, but Reskalin had asked him to follow her lead and he had to trust that she knew what she was doing.

"You fools have cost me the lives of several of my men today," the commander spoke unnecessarily loud and his nostrils flared under furrowed eyebrows. "By Laran, you had better have a good reason for being in this place!"

Enguer wondered at the show. There was no heat in his cheeks or genuine anger in his voice. What could be the purpose?

"We are here at the bequest of . . ." her words were cut short by the commander's horsewhip across her face.

Blinded by rage, Enguer pulled his blades and burst into a fluid motion that would have killed the guard next to him and the commander in the space of a few short seconds had it not been for Reskalin's outstretched arm taking hold of his sword arm.

"Your man is fast," the commander hissed dangerously. "One of your assassins I presume?" He spoke low so that no one outside their small group could hear, "Yes, yes. I know you Reskalin. A creature of the Fat Man and a thorn in my side more often than I care."

"The Fat Man will be grateful for our safe return," Reskalin spat blood from her cut lip onto the ground. "No doubt he will reward you handsomely."

Commander Artis laughed and slapped the horsewhip on his thigh, "Surely he would, I do not disagree. But I wonder if his appreciation for your return would equal the losses I have suffered over the years because of his . . . and your, meddling in my modest enterprise?" He tapped the horsewhip lightly against his cheek in mock calculation before his eyes widened as if receiving an epiphany from the gods. "And what about the profits from my future ventures? Can the Fat Man afford a reward equal to the wealth of a Zilach?"

The two soldiers laughed as if on que. They had obviously seen their commander's show a few times before and were clearly employed in his 'modest enterprise'. Enguer seethed with barely controlled fury at their predicament and more so at what had happened to Reskalin. If he hit her again, Sunna herself could not stop him from killing the arrogant bastard.

"I'm sure we can come to an arrangement," Reskalin offered. "A partnership in one of our concerns that would make you a very rich man."

"An arrangement you say?" the commander was tapping his cheek again, this time in what appeared to be sincere thought. "An arrangement maybe. I will think more on it." He smiled again. *A practiced smile with no true joy that couldn't fool a half-blind old lady on a dark night.* Enguer couldn't remember exactly where he had heard that expression, but it applied fully here.

Reskalin nodded in acquiescence, "We will make camp next to yours and await your decision."

The commander rolled his eyes, "Take them to my tent and make sure that they stay there until I return."

The brutish soldiers eagerly complied, grabbing each of them by the arm and pushing them up the hill. Enguer glanced back to see the commander trotting back to his officers. The fool thought he had won two victories that day – a decisive battle against Dire Wolf-riding orks and, probably more important to him, a decisive card to play against an old adversary back home. None of that mattered to Enguer except where Reskalin was concerned and in that contest, he would bet on her.

The soldiers camp was well organized and ordered to maximize space and efficiency similar to those Enguer had seen from time to time outside the city of Courth. It was surrounded by a deep pit that the soldiers must have only recently begun to fill with sharpened spikes since so many of the rows appeared incomplete. These soldiers were planning on being here for a while. Perhaps months.

And it was far from empty despite the majority of soldiers still out in the field. Dozens of men and women in the same style of clothing he had seen in Arre went about their business with little concern for the newcomers escorted under armed guard through their midst. Enguer paid them just as much attention. His mind was busy memorizing the layout of the camp. On the north side, white fabric tents stretched in eight rows of ten with space in between to hang a pot over a small cooking fire. Each one appeared large enough to comfortably accommodate two soldiers. To the south, there were a dozen wagons dispersed among several large tents with their flaps tied open revealing temporary workshops. The smith's and their apprentices were busy mending boots and armor, sharpening blades on stone wheels and crafting a variety of mundane implements to make life in camp as near to normal as possible leagues away from the nearest city. From a fabric shelter stretch between four wagons on the west side a mild breeze brought the scents of spices and cooking. And in the center a cluster of high-peaked interconnected tents rose above all the others. That appeared to be their destination.

At the entrance to one of the large tents, the burly soldiers spun the two of them around and removed their weapons before shoving them inside. To Enguer's surprise, the tent was stocked with a number of fine furs and blankets and a small table holding a pitcher with several cups, a loaf of bread and a brick of cheese. Enguer's stomach growled audibly at the sight of it.

Ignoring the food for the moment, Enguer listened at the entrance of the tent. One of the soldiers was speaking to someone outside, "Go over the hill and retrieve their horse. You can't miss it, it's the big one."

"Yes sir!" a young boy chirped, followed by running feet.

"You think the Commander will keep that one or sell it?" One soldier asked the other.

"I wish he would give it to me!" The second soldier laughed. "But he'll probably keep that one."

"Come eat," Reskalin threw a piece at bread at him from across the room. Her tone had not changed from the husky quality she had adopted for her male persona.

Enguer quickly strode over and leaned close so only she could hear, "How can you be so calm? They're talking about stealing my horse."

Reskalin pat his cheek and smiled sweetly, "They are also planning to murder us and drag our bodies a league into the grasslands for the vultures to feast upon."

"So, what are we going to do?"

Reskalin shrugged, "When the boy brings your Lambei we are going to leave."

Chapter 27

On the run again

A trickle of blood slowly trailed down Reskalin's chin from the injury she had received from Commander Artis a short while earlier. Enguer pulled a linen from his cuff and pressed it against her lip which she summarily slapped away.

"What is wrong with you?" she whispered.

This was not like her.

She gripped the hair on the back of his neck and pulled his face close, "They are watching us. I am a man."

Enguer understood then. Her whole life Reskalin had chosen to identify as a man for her own protection and security. Because of him she had courageously stepped out of that familiar skin to bare her true feelings. She had admitted as much just a few days earlier! She never wanted to be a woman, never wanted to meet a man like him and fall in love. Enguer bore as much of the responsibility as she did, perhaps more, and who was *he* to fail *her*? Reskalin knew what she was doing. This was her element as much as The Wilds was his. How could he question her judgment? He had to follow her lead.

The familiar clip-clop of hooves roused his attention. The steps were heavier than usual, dragging from fatigue, but still a welcome sound to his ears. It was his nameless Lambei, brought from the other side of the hill. Less than an hour had passed since their desperate flight ended and Enguer wondered how much his father's mount had truly recovered it case he was forced to call upon its service again soon.

"Wait here and be ready," Reskalin strode to the partially open flap of the tent, poked her head out and spoke quietly to one of the guards.

The tent flap opened wider and the guard strode in, annoyance written all over his face, "So where is it?"

"Behind that," Reskalin pointed to large chest stuffed with folded blankets. "Be careful, an injured animal can react violently and you know how sensitive the commander is about his favorite pet."

The guard visibly paled, then gathered the courage to take a few hesitant steps closer to the chest. "C'mere little fella, your daddy's gonna miss . . . "

Reskalin planted a knife in the base of his skull and cradled his fall gently to the ground to avoid an excess of noise. Enguer never saw where the knife came from, but he was glad she had it and resolved to learn how to hide blades on one's person if they ever made it out of there. Then he watched as Reskalin positioned the body which, to his surprise, hardly bled from the fatal wound she had inflicted before she walked again to the tent flap.

"Your friend has fallen and knocked himself out," He heard her say.

The guard responded with a curse and stomped inside the tent, "Porteus, you idiot. Can't you catch a damn cat without stumbling over your own two feet?"

The man knelt down beside his friend and a second later fell unconscious on top of him after receiving a blow to the head from the pommel of Reskalin's dagger.

"Why didn't you just kill him like the other one?" Enguer was a little taken aback by his own cruel words.

"He was a cruel man that did bad things to young girls," Reskalin dragged the two guards to lay side by side. "I have something special planned for this one. Help me bind them."

"Both of them?"

Reskalin was hurriedly ripping long strips from the blankets to bind the two men. "I am leaving a message for Commander Artis. From this day forward he will fear for his life whenever he dares enter the city limits of Arre."

Enguer quickly helped tie the hands and feet of the two men, the living one was just beginning to stir when they finished and

Reskalin shoved a cut of the blanket in his mouth. After a moment his eyes fluttered open, they were filled with fear and pleading as he tried desperately to speak. Reskalin was clearly in no mood to listen.

When she spoke to him, it was in her natural voice, clear and feminine, not the husky male tone she took so often, "When you torture those girls, why do you always demand that they smile?"

The guard's eyes widened, tears slowly slid down the side of his face and his mouth moved wildly around the gag in an effort to respond. Reskalin just stared into his eyes like she was expecting to see something new and after a time she brought out her dagger and showed it to him.

"I will give you the smile you have always demanded of the girls you abused. Perhaps it will serve you well when you meet Leinth?" Reskalin held the struggling soldier's head between her knees and with slow care drew her blade across his neck from one ear to the other in the shape of a red crescent.

Enguer watched in stunned silence.

When the man went still, she repeated the act on his dead friend.

"Let's go," She said quietly when it was done and casually walked out of the tent.

Enguer followed without glancing back. He didn't want to remember what had just happened or why. It would be hard enough to reconcile that it was his Reskalin that had done it. It was a cruel way to die, even if the man deserved it.

To his surprise and pleasure, Enguer found his Lambei tied to a post next to the tent unattended. It stomped the ground when he emerged from the tent greeting him with excitement like it always did. He was about to climb on when Reskalin called him over.

"Your weapons are in the barrel," she was retrieving her own blades and placing them in sheaths around her body.

Enguer found his sword and dagger, he was glad to have them back again, and returned to his horse. "We better get out of here before the commander returns."

Reskalin jumped up behind him and pressed her chin against the top of his shoulder. "Follow the path of the sun west so we are seen to be riding toward Provigi. Don't rush. Once we are out of sight, we can turn south toward Arre unseen, although I doubt that we will be followed."

Enguer nodded, gently taped his heels against the flanks of his Lambei and rode from the camp as if nothing in all the world was amiss.

They travelled non-stop at a steady trot for several hours, following the glowing orb of Sunna across the sky until it began to fall toward the horizon. Reskalin slept at his back, her slow rhythmic breathing comforting over the leagues. It was long past the time they should have turned south and Enguer thought maybe that was just fine. He turned his tired Lambei then, knowing that there would be no rest until the next morning. Reskalin said Commander Artis would not follow, but he wasn't so sure. The man was arrogant and full of self-grandiose, especially after the defeat of the orks and their vicious Dire Wolves. If anything, he would probably feel emboldened like some fabled hero of Rasna and no doubt expected accolades when he returned to Arre in triumph no matter how hollow the victory. Hollow, yes. The orks numbered in the hundreds, maybe thousands. A few dozen of their number slain or routed would make little difference to them. Still, no one in Arre knew the truth and who might they believe? A victorious commander native to the city or a foreigner and a known figure from the underworld with a reputation for violence? He loved Reskalin for who she was but her industry held little credibility.

Reskalin stirred as if summoned by her name in his head, but she did not awaken. He was getting used to having her so close and it bothered him more than a little how things would change when they returned to Arre. Would she assume her previous role as a man? Did she have a choice? How would they fit into each other's life then? Enguer did not relish the idea of spending what remained of his days in a secret relationship with a woman pretending to be a man and roaming the streets of Arre waiting for the brief moments when they could safely be together. Something was bound to break. He was sure of it. He didn't want to think about it.

Sunna retired to her daily slumber inviting her sister to take over the nightly vigil. Luna did so happily, reigning supreme in the night sky until the first rays of Sunna once again brightened the morning sky. No signs of pursuit. It still felt something like when the orks came after them except that the feeling was less eminent, less assured of the expected outcome. They would only find safety once they made it back to Arre and the protections of the Fat Man. Enguer wondered if he and Reskalin would truly be safe even then.

"We must stop for a while," Enguer brought his Lambei to a halt and dismounted in the shadow of a high hill that would shield them from the view of anyone approaching from the north.

Reskalin hoped off the back and stretched her arms into the air. "I feel like I could sleep for days."

"I as well," Enguer pulled off the saddle and began to brush down the weary horse. "Will you bring some dry branches from that thicket of Yellowbur? Maybe you remember how to make a campfire?"

She gave him a level look, 'Of course I remember. When have you had to show me anything more than once?"

Enguer could think of a few things, but he decided it was probably better not to bring them up. He didn't know much about women, but he remembered how irritated Mrs. Eibhlin would get when her husband reminded her of something she should have known. And the last thing he needed was an irate Reskalin on his hands.

A little while later, Enguer was setting rabbit traps around other nearby thickets when he noticed the scent of smoke in the air. He returned to the camp to discover Reskalin triumphantly tending a small campfire. She smiled broadly when he arrived and waved a smoldering stick in the air like a magic wand. "You see? I have made the fire. Now you must produce the rabbits!"

Enguer burst out laughing. He couldn't help it. Never would he have expected the scene before him. And she had no idea.

"What's the matter?" Her slender eyebrows furrowed in quick anger and the tone of her voice shifted dangerously higher. "Do you think you could have made a better fire? Is mine not *good enough*?" She began to kick at the sticks to put it out.

"No, no! It's not the fire!" Enguer shouted to stop her from ruining a perfectly good camp fire.

Reskalin's face was red with fury, "Then what is it?"

Enguer looked at the ground, desperately trying to control his laughter. "You're covered in burs!"

It was true. Small burs clung to her cloak, her hair, her eyebrows, even her leather cuirass. She looked at him with confusion painted over her face. She clearly had no idea what he was talking about.

"Look at your cloak."

Reskalin looked herself over and then quickly removed her cloak, "What are these things?" She shook the fabric violently, but the burs remained intact.

"They are from the Yellowbur bushes where you got the branches for the fire," he couldn't force the smile from his face. "There are a bunch in your hair, but don't touch . . ."

She lay her hand on her head and yelped. "How did I get these on me?" She nearly shrieked. "Get them off! Get them off!"

All humor drained from his body as Enguer realized Reskalin was on the verge of fury. He rushed over to calm her down. "Sit down and relax, I will take them out of your hair. They are just a nuisance."

Reskalin calmed, but not by much and sat down with in a huff. "Are they poisonous? Will they ruin my cloak?"

"They will not harm you more than a little irritation from their tiny little spines. We just have to pick each one of them off carefully." Enguer gently began to remove the burs from her hair. "Pull them off your cloak. You will see."

Reskalin grabbed the cloak laying on the ground next to her and snatched off a little bur. She was still highly irritated. "Why didn't you tell me about them? I might have been able to avoid them had I known.'

Enguer was focused on the burs in her hair and didn't think much about his response, "I did say it was a Yellowbur thicket."

351

"Why would you assume I know anything about a Yellowbur thicket or any other kind of thicket?" Her icy response gave him pause to consider his next words carefully. He had, in fact, pointed out the yellowbur a few days earlier and mentioned how they stuck to anything they touched. Enguer decided that was probably not the best way to go with Reskalin teetering on the edge of violence.

He chose a different tactic. "I'm sorry. I should have warned you. I will be more careful in the future."

That seemed to do the trick. The tension faded and they spent the next hour removing burs from her hair and clothes. When they were done, Reskalin stood wearing nothing but her long tunic. It was the closest thing to a dress he had ever seen her wear and he thought she looked very pretty. Under the circumstances, he kept that to himself. The rest of her clothing and dismantled leather armor were scattered all over the ground, bur free.

The remainder of the morning they cuddled together next to the fire and slept. They both desperately needed the rest and the moderate weather combined with a blanket made it impossible to resist. Before he drifted off, Enguer kissed the top of Reskalin's head snuggled against his chest and wondered how fleeting days like this would soon become.

Enguer awoke an hour before sunset and left Reskalin undisturbed to check his rabbit traps. Sunna smiled on him again with the gift of two rabbits captured by his snares. When he returned to camp, Reskalin had already dressed and prepared their pack for travel. Together they cleaned and prepared their meal before saddling the Lambei for another long ride. Enguer intended to go all night and all the next day before they stopped to camp again and from the looks of his rested horse, he thought it would be up to the task.

Sometime during the night, when Luna was still a few hours shy of the horizon, Reskalin propped her chin on his shoulder with her cheek next to his ear. It felt nice to have her smooth skin next to his and her arms tightly around his torso, sharing each other's warmth in the cold air as they crossed the leagues of grassland astride the sturdy gait of the powerful Lambei. It couldn't have been more perfect.

"We haven't talked about what we're going to do when we get back to Arre," She whispered in his ear.

Enguer's heart sank. They had two more days before they arrived back at the city. Why did she have to bring it up now? "I don't know what to say about that." He really didn't. How could he decide what he was going to do until she told him what she planned? He supposed he was about to find out.

"I've decided to be myself again."

Enguer wasn't sure what that meant. "Does that mean you will be the Reskalin I first met or the Reskalin I know now?"

"It means I am going to be a woman." She nipped his earlobe with her teeth causing him to jump and then sucked on it to make it all better. Enguer was strangely aroused.

"Won't that cause a problem between you and the Fat Man?"

She kissed him on the cheek. "I will be tested, yes, even with the protection of the Fat Man. But there will be no problem with the Fat Man himself or anyone loyal to him."

That surprised Enguer. "He will not be upset when he finds out who you really are?"

Reskalin laughed and hugged him tightly. "Enguer, you are so naïve. The Fat Man has known my whole life. In fact, he wanted me to come out years ago and it is I who resisted. Until I met you, I had no desire to be a woman. I had no desire for . . . love," her words trailed off into a whisper.

"What about your father? Is he still alive?" Enguer felt her body tense up against his briefly and he regretted asking the question.

After a while Reskalin relaxed again and she spoke in a neutral tone with a hint of sadness, "I never took the opportunity to get to know him. Now he has passed and I will never get the chance."

"I'm sorry, Reskalin. I hope he was a good man and that he cared for you."

"He was and he did. You would know."

"You think maybe I have heard of him?" Enguer doubted it. He hardly knew of anyone outside of Courth.

Her voice lowered to a quiet pitch again, "Yes, you have heard of him."

"What was his name?"

Reskalin hesitated and what she said next shocked him to his core, "My father was the Arch Priest Tanais."

Enguer almost fell off his horse. The Arch Priest had referred to Reskalin as his *brother*. She was his daughter! No wonder he was tortured over the relationship with Reskalin. What could he possibly have to say about that?

"What made you pose as a man from the start?" Enguer thought that would be a safer line of discussion than the sensitive topic of her father.

She lay her head on his back and spoke over the steady clopping of the Lambei's hooves in the soft grass, "My father and the Fat Man agreed that it would be safer for me. At least in the beginning. They also decided to keep my identity a secret for the same reason. After a time, I realized how different a man's world was compared to a woman's. Other men, powerful men, respected and feared me. They would never cow to a woman the way they did to a man, even though both sexes are considered equal under the law in Rasna. I saw no future as a woman, no advantage or gain, so I resolved never to become one." Reskalin shoved a fist into his ribs. "Until you came to Arre. I knew my whole life was about to change the first time I lay eyes on you."

"What about those powerful men now? Won't they turn on you simply because you are a woman?" Enguer feared what that would mean to her life. To their life together. Would they be dodging daggers for the rest of their lives? Eventually one would find its mark no matter how careful they were.

Reskalin's voice took on a cold tone matching the wind in his face, "As I said, some will try and test me. They will find the old Reskalin inhabits this new skin. Many will die. There may even be a guild war because of it."

Her words sent chills up his spine. This could be worse than he imagined. Far worse. "Surely the Fat Man would not welcome a guild war. My father told me once that the masters of the underworld loathed attention and often went out of their way to avoid it because it was bad for their business."

"Your father was a wise man," Reskalin sighed, "and everything he said was true. However, the Fat Man likes to shake things up every few years, purge the industry of bad apples, find out where loyalties truly lay. I can't explain how, but I would not be surprised if he *expected* this when we returned."

Enguer didn't like this plan one bit. He was not a man of the city, nor did he want to be. His life was in The Wilds or at least not far from it. He would likely get himself killed in a guild war. Probably doing something stupid in an urban environment he did not understand. His ignorance might even cause Reskalin her life and that he could not live with. "Why do we have to return to Arre? There is the whole world for us to explore without the fear of guild wars and cavalry commanders and knives around every corner. We could be free to do anything we wanted. Build a life together. A family . . ." What was he saying? He felt Reskalin's body tense up against his back again and he knew he went too far.

"Shut up," she hissed. "You speak the words of a coward and I know you are far from it! I know you, Enguer Rand, and I see a man with the soul of a warrior. My warrior. If your Sunna demands your death then she will get the bargain of two. We are bound as one and where we go, we go together as one!"

It was strange, the reaction evoked by her final declaration. Enguer was at once thrilled at the prospect of Reskalin by his side no matter what they faced and alternately distressed like a trapped mongoose. It was better not to speak more on the matter until he worked out what he was feeling.

"I am just saying we should consider our options, that's all." That was not nearly all, but it would be all for now.

"You are worried about me. I get that." She hugged him tighter than before and nuzzled her face into his back. "Do not forget who I am in Arre. They call me the shadow of death, the bringer of darkness and the stealer of light. It is all true. All of it." She giggled a little as if even she knew how absurd it sounded. "In Arre, no soul can sleep with confidence if I am set against them and not once have I failed to produce the desired results." Reskalin trailed her untrimmed nails through the locks of his fine dark hair, pulling his head back a little to expose his neck. She kissed the sensitive spot above his collarbone before releasing her grip. "My retribution on our enemies will be swift and certain," she ran her tongue along the line of his neck, "just like the Fat Man taught me."

Suddenly she was gone. Enguer pulled his Lambei to a stop and turned fearing she had fallen off somehow. He couldn't have been more wrong. She stood in the grass a half-dozen paces behind, peeling off her leather armor, her breeches, her tunic and stood naked in the moonlight. Enguer, already aroused by her touch, slowly slid off his Lambei and started for her, desire hot in his veins, craving the feel of her skin hot against his own.

Luna kept watch over them in the hours that followed, blushing with approval to her sister Sunna who would bring the light of dawn. But for some it would never be enough. For some, it was only the night that mattered.

~~~

"An egg?" Wodanaz scratched at his short blonde beard.

"An egg." Myrllin confirmed.

To see it sitting there manifested in its physical form was unsettling. It was an image from a fragment of a dream, or vision, that came to him with other random meaningless snippets when he rested in extended hibernation. The last long sleep, from which he had awakened only recently, had lasted three hundred years and given him vivid premonitions of the future. These he had already served prophetic warning to those in the need to know. But always there were other images, arbitrary images with no hint of meaning, that flitted through his restless mind that functioned as unconscious triggers to something vastly important yet underrated. The tragic love affair between Drystan and Eselt had been one that nearly toppled two kingdoms. The egg that sat before him now was another.

Images crowded Myrllin's mind. Fire, the Phoenix, a demon and death. Each one spoke volumes. Each one told a story that ended with an egg. What happened next was up to him.

"We must destroy it," Myrllin grabbed hold of his brother's arm for emphasis. "Summon your hammers."

Wodanaz hesitated. "Why should we destroy it? Such a beautiful thing it is. We must take it with us to Hy Brasil and discover what it contains."

"Brother," Myrllin shook his head sadly. "This is the Phoenix. It destroyed itself to destroy us knowing that it would rise again reborn. But we survived and now we must break the egg and capture the demon so that we may cast it into the Ourea as we have done with the others."

"Ah, too bad then." Wodanaz snapped his fingers and a colossal short-handled war hammer appeared in each of his hands. "I am ready."

Myrllin wove his hands through the air in quick patterns leaving glowing trails in the air that lingered to form a radiant sphere. "Now."

A crackle of electricity ran through the war hammers when Wodanaz flexed his muscular arms to lift them high over his head. Their glow did not diminish in the least upon their brief pause, rather, they illumed all the brighter and when they struck, it was like the thunder of a world cracking in two, the egg sundered and a great force of howling air burst through.

"Back away!" Wodanaz leapt backward, his arms thrown wide sending Myrllin tumbling over the ashes.

Deaf from the concussion and disoriented from the sudden violence, Myrllin crawled to his knees and peered through the dust. The broken egg spilled a yolk of magma over the ground hissing and popping angrily at its demise. In stark contrast to its bright fury, a dark orb arose so black that it seemed to suck in all the light around it. Gloomy tendrils reached out from its center seeking something unseen and finding no living thing to perverse whipped around frantically. Myrllin had seen this all before and through some unforeseen miracle he still held his conjured sphere intact.

He lifted the golden orb high and spoke words the void, the black hole, the demon could not deny, *"Niis pambt."*

A shrill shriek ruptured the still air for leagues in every direction. It was a cry of rage and despondence, a lament of futility with aroused fury, a plea for pity with no redemption. But no matter the emotion it howled over the ether; the void moved inexorably into the golden sphere that quietly compelled its custody.

"It is finished," Myrllin breathed with relief. The demon was firmly trapped withing the magical sphere.

"You will take it straight away to the Ourea, then?" Weary concern painted Wodanaz features darkened by the ash.

Myrllin glanced over at the sagging dragon and back to his brother, "If you will allow Sleipnir to take me, then yes. You and Dergo can go back to Hy Brasil and rest before the two of you keel over right here like frightened goats."

Wodanaz crossed the space between them and wrapped Myrllin in a great bear hug. "It will be as you say, brother. Let it be done."

Chapter 28

Homecoming

"I see it, there is the Bodin River ahead!" Reskalin pounded happily on Enguer's back.

Enguer was glad to see it as well. "The ferry must be on the opposite side. Will they return tonight?"

"No, we will have to wait until dawn."

As was his usual routine, Enguer removed the saddle from the Lambei and brushed him down while Reskalin went for dry wood to burn. Later, he would set rabbit snares and they would sit by the fire until they fell asleep in each other's arms. Tonight would be a little different however, in that there was a river nearby that offered the opportunity for a bath. A frigid bath to be sure, but enough to get clean after weeks of travel. To his delight, Reskalin joined him in the cold water lending a bit of warmth against his skin. The resulting commotion left them heated and exhausted and more than ready for the evening slumber. The rabbits, if any, would have to wait.

"What do you think it's for?" Reskalin was snuggled up against his body with her head on his chest. She held the disk they had recovered from the orc shaman in her hand, the fire light reflecting off the gold rim encircling the thin crystal radiating a soft blue luminosity in the moon light.

"It must be some sort of magical device," Enguer yawned. "Do you intend to give it to the Fat Man?"

"That *is* the main reason he sent me with you. He will know those who can best puzzle it out." She held the disk higher, turning it this way and that, the glow from the crystal intensifying briefly when positioned parallel to the moon. "How strange . . ."

Enguer could barely keep his eyes open. He was under warm blankets on a bed of soft grass with her silky skin touching his and soft hair gently brushing over his chest and chin. Comfortable and relaxed, he was on the verge of slipping into a blissful slumber. If she would only stop talking . . .

Reskalin abruptly shifted against him. It was enough to shake him from his peaceful descent and when he opened his eyes he was surprised, not unhappily, to see her bare torso suspended above him. Enguer's gaze followed Reskalin's delightful curves, to her pretty face looking up toward the crystal disk she held with both hands high above her head. There his gaze stopped. It was curious to view the moonlight that passed through it amplified like a spotlight forming a luminous blue circle of light on the ground a few strides away.

Enguer sat up next to Reskalin still on her knees. They were both completely naked and the night was cold, but the chill barely touched his skin he was so intrigued by what he saw. Something moved within the blue circle of light, blurred images going back and forth like people walking in front of a dirty window at night. And there were sounds, distant and distorted, that reminded him of the cacophony of background noise present in any city. Reskalin shifted the crystal disk and the blue circle lifted off the ground to stand impossibly on its edge at least twice the height of a man and equally wide. The image within shifted and sharpened until it was clear enough to notice what appeared to be a large camp with numerous fires burning. Enguer thought he could smell the smoke and discern dark figures walking leisurely here and there. The camp was a distant background and the details were shadowed in the firelight, but the figures looked like men, large men and a few with long hair that might have been women.

There was a startled grunt and a body suddenly walked into the forefront of the image. It was an ork warrior wearing hide and leather armor with a fur cape draped over one shoulder and a great axe gripped loosely in one clawed hand that hung casually by his side. Enguer could smell him as if he were standing only paces away. The expression on the creature's face was that of confusion and uncertainty and Enguer wondered if the ork could see them as clearly as they could see it. He was about to tell Reskalin to put the disk away when the ork turned its head and spoke coarse words to someone nearby that they could not see. There was a distorted reply and a second ork appeared a little further behind the first. This one was dressed differently. He wore a hooded robe with a thick silver chain weighted by a heavy medallion on the end of it, a wide leather belt that cinched his clothing at the waist and a walking staff capped by a huge red jewel that glittered when he moved. Enguer knew he had to be a shaman and far from uncertain, he had a look of rage on his face. He lifted his arm, pointed toward them and spoke something to the other ork as he strode forward. The ork snorted forcefully and turned back toward them, a toothy smile between protruding incisors on his pig-like face. He too, strode forward.

And stepped through the blue-tinted image.

Reskalin yelped and jumped up, dropping the crystal disk on ground. Immediately, the blue circle disappeared, but the ork was still standing there only a few paces away. All three stared at each other stunned and undecided. Enguer uncertain if what they were seeing was real. The ork glanced back to where he had come from and then turned back to them again, fear and rage contorting his ugly features. Enguer's hand found his sword lying next to him under the blankets and slowly stood up. He was surprised to note that Reskalin already had a sword in one hand and a dagger in the other.

With the tension rising, Enguer hoped the ork would run away. It must have known it was alone and far from home. Unless it could work out how to use the disk. The ork looked down at the crystal at Reskalin's feet and then back at them and Enguer realized that two naked humans, even holding swords, could not have appeared very intimidating to the massive creature and they were the only thing standing between him and the crystal that might be his ticket back home.

The ork rushed forward, great axe thrusting ahead and down in a deadly arc that Enguer just barely avoided. Reskalin jumped away too, receiving a back-handed blow on her hip from the ork's fist that sent her spinning. He was far faster than either one of them had anticipated. The ork pivoted on the balls of his left foot and reversed his swing at Reskalin. Still a little off balance, she threw herself backwards and caught the leading edge of the great axe that drew a line of blood across her left thigh. The ork plowed on and had it been just the two of them, Reskalin might have met her end right then. Enguer saw it differently and before the ork could take another step he stretched as far as he could reach and chopped down on the back of the creature's booted heel with his blade.

The ork roared in pain, twisting to face Enguer laying prone on the grass desperately trying to get to his knees. It took a step forward on its injured foot and instantly stumbled to the ground, his forward momentum sending him crashing onto the grass where Enguer had just vacated, the axe cutting into dark soil inches from Enguer's leg. On the offensive, Enguer and Reskalin both started toward the ork. As quick as they were, the ork was quicker, throwing himself into a roll that ended with him upright and half-supported on one knee with the severed achilleas. Four paces away, Enguer could have killed him easily if he only had his bow. As it stood, they would have to do it the hard way and soon, judging by the blood flowing from Reskalin's leg.

"Back off and put pressure on that cut," Enguer shouted to her. "I will finish this."

Reskalin laughed, "The hell you will."

Enguer shook his head. She was so stubborn. "Fine, let's flank him Just watch that axe!"

The ork lifted his great axe above his head and spun it in a continuous circle that would be a dangerous obstacle with its long reach. Enguer considered waiting until the ork tired itself out if obstinate lover wouldn't bleed to death first. Which he was sure she would if just to spite him and prove she was strong enough to stay in the fight. And then suddenly Enguer was diving to the ground for his life, the spinning axe flying less than a hand over his head creating a whirlwind that ruffled his hair. When he looked up, the ork was swaying on its knees with the hilt of one of Reskalin's throwing daggers protruding from the side of its neck.

"Sorry about that."

Enguer hoped she was talking to him. He got to his feet in time to watch Reskalin limp over to the ork and shove her sword through its chest. When she pulled it out black blood dripped from the blade and pooled under the twitching corpse ruining the grass underneath. She retrieved her dagger and wiped both blades on the ork's furry cape before she limped back toward the camp. Enguer was quickly by her side.

"That will need stitches," he pulled a small kit from his pack that held several metal needles and a coil of fiber.

"You've done this before?" Reskalin sounded a little unsettled.

Reskalin smiled reassuringly, "Many times. Didn't you notice all the scars I have?"

"I wasn't paying attention to your scars earlier," the wicked smile on her face brought a rush of heat to his cheeks which he hoped she didn't notice in the firelight.

He quickly stitched up the wound on her leg and tied it off before wrapping it tight with a clean linen bandage. "The good news is that the cut was not as deep as I expected. The bad news is you stink like an ork."

"More you than me!" Reskalin poked him in the ribs. "Why don't we drag than thing off a way and then go jump in the river?"

"I'll have to change your bandage again if you get it wet."

She leaned over to kiss his neck and whispered in his ear, "I look forward to it."

~~~

The clang of a distant bell startled Enguer awake. The sun was up, less than an hour past dawn and Reskalin lay close up against him with her head on his shoulder. He started to rise, but she gently pressed him back down.

"It won't be here for an hour yet," she breathed in his ear. "We have a little while longer."

Enguer was happy about that. The last time he was on the ferry he spent half the journey with his head over the rail. It was a good thing his father raised him as a ranger instead of a sailor. That wouldn't have worked out very well for him.

"Will we go straight to see the Fat Man?"

Reskalin put her arm across his chest and one leg over his waist hugging him tight. "Yes. And I've decided one other thing."

"What is that?"

"I will return to Arre as a woman. From this moment forward this is who I am. Let the chips fall as they may."

Enguer stared up at the glow of the clouds touched by the morning sun. They had already talked about this and there was no point in discussing it any further. She warned him about what to expect and he was committed to sticking with her no matter what happened. Still, he held out silent hope that he could eventually convince her to leave Arre. If not forever, at least for a time.

A little while later Enguer was up strapping the saddle on his Lambei while Reskalin cleared the camp and packed up their travel bag. In the distance, farmers and tradesmen were lingering next to the small dock with their carts and wagons full of goods to take to market. The ferry was pulling up empty of passengers with room to spare for all of them. It reminded Enguer of the village and settlements a league north that the orks had burned to the ground a few weeks before. So many innocent lives lost for no purpose. He wanted to believe that he and Reskalin had brought them some small measure of retribution with what they had accomplished. It didn't feel like enough, but it was a start.

The journey across the Bodin River was far calmer than the last, to Enguer's eternal relief and he managed not to get sick in the three quarters of an hour it took to get to the other side. He watched as the elevated city of Arre came into view, as busy as he remembered, with crowds of people flowing through the northern gate headed for the markets.

"It is likely that we have been noticed already," Reskalin leaned close to him. "Be wary."

Enguer scanned the dock ahead with the masses of people passing over it. No one seemed to pay them any special attention and there were a number of guards in flowing red capes scattered in knots here and there keeping an eye on everyone coming and going.

"Let's go to the western gate," Reskalin suggested when they disembarked. "It will be less crowded and take less time to get to where we are going."

"Will I be blindfolded this time?" he snickered.

She shot him an unamused look, "This is how it works; if I can't trust you with my life then you will be blindfolded. If I can then you won't. You see, even my life would be worth nothing to the guild if you were to betray what you knew and saw. This is no small matter."

"I didn't mean to suggest it was," Enguer replied. He didn't even try to hide his embarrassment. "I just don't know how things work now that we are . . . What are we?"

"You are my lover," she smacked the back of his head from behind him on the Lambei. "We will see what else you become if you live long enough."

At least there was a hint of humor in that last part, if a little too much truth. "Then I choose no blindfold. Our live are already each other's, this will make no difference to me."

"Be careful Enguer. You have no idea what this world is you so glibly accept. It can be your worst nightmare, fraught with invisible dangers where your life and the lives of everyone you care about can hang on one misplaced word."

"It is your world, Reskalin. If I am going to be with you, then I must accept your world and try as best I can to understand it. Otherwise, I am nothing more than a liability. Neither of us would survive long like that. I will embrace your world in the same way you embraced mine when we first went into The Wilds. Look how much you have learned and how much we have changed since that day we rode from Arre." Enguer didn't realize until he said it that he had settled on his choice. Perhaps he made the choice the day he found out who she really was. Maybe even earlier. He tried to tell himself he needed to work it out, think further on it, but who was he fooling? He chose Reskalin and everything that came with her.

She responded with a tight hug and they rode on against the throngs of people in silence until they came to the western gate. Reskalin was right, the crowds were less by half. There was, however, one other noticeable difference – the guards on the walls, towers and on the ground were easily double what they had been before they left Arre. One guard in particular, an officer standing not far away on the other side of gate, Enguer recognized.

Once through, Enguer steered his Lambei over to the officer and waved his hand in greeting, "Captain Tineus! How are you?"

The captain looked up squinting in the morning sun and moved to stand in the shadow of the riders to see more clearly. A smile crept over his weathered face in recognition, "Enguer Rand, the ranger from Courth. It's good to see you again. What have you been up to?"

"Chasing down orks on the other side of the Travini Pass," Enguer smiled wearily, "we found their lair and got away by the skin on our teeth."

"I heard something about the Zilach sending out a foreign ranger to track those beasts. I had hoped it might be you." His gaze settled on Reskalin, "Who might this be?"

"I am Reskalin," she responded simply.

The captain's gaze lingered and his smile faded a little, "Have we met? Your name seems familiar to me."

Reskalin flashed a smile that accentuated her feminine features. Enguer couldn't put his finger on it, but aside from the husky voice, something else had changed about Reskalin's appearance that made her look definitively female, whereas before Enguer would never have doubted that she was a man.

"We have not, captain. I am pleased to meet you now."

"I as well." The captain appeared uncertain, but his smile returned when he addressed Enguer, "No doubt you are in a hurry to report your finds to the Zilach. I hope we can meet up again soon for an ale or two and you can tell me all about your adventure!"

"I look forward to that. See you soon." Enguer waved and prompted his Lambei to move forward.

After a few steps, Reskalin spoke into his ear, "Captain Tineus is a good soldier. I believe he was one of Borath's men. He has also been a bit of an obstacle with regard to certain business ventures. Despite that, the Fat Man respects the captain and even more so Borath and has forbidden any harm to come to either of them."

Enguer had not considered the possibility that men like Captain Tineus might be vulnerable to the ire of the underworld. Strange that the Fat Man would be concerned for their welfare given the business he was in. Maybe thieves and assassins had some bit of honor after all. A code or some such that they followed. It was a hard concept to accept if it were true. It could have been the defining reason that his father allowed himself to be associated with the Fat Man, if that too, were true.

"Turn here," Reskalin instructed.

Enguer turned the Lambei into a narrow alley that zig-zagged left and right on a constant sharp incline. It felt like a passage constructed to deliberately disorient and confuse, which was likely the point. When Reskalin called a halt, Enguer was not at all sure how high they had climbed nor even the direction they faced.

A boy stepped from the shadows and held out his hand.

"He will see to your horse," Reskalin gestured to the boy. "Don't worry, he is one of the finest horse handlers in the city. You Lambei is in good hands."

A child? Enguer hesitantly handed the reigns to the boy and was shocked to realize that he wasn't a boy at all. Rather, he was a small person with the body of a child and the face of an aged man. Enguer had never seen anything like it. *Was it a dwarf?*

"He's called a midget," Reskalin laughed. "There are many in Arre. Have you never seen one?"

"Never," Enguer. "How did this happen?"

Reskalin shrugged, "They are born this way. There is no reason. Some wealthy men and kings employ them as fools to entertain their guests. We give them jobs that earn a proper living. It is amazing what they hear and what they see. So many people are blind to their presence." She gestured toward a nondescript door, "Now, come this way."

Inside, the corridor was dark and twisting with no source of light to guide the way. Reskalin took his hand in hers and confidently led him forward through the maze. Minutes later they stopped and Enguer heard her rap on something solid. A door opened inward shedding a sliver of light from behind a thick tapestry beyond that caused Enguer to squint. Reskalin pushed it aside and pulled him into a dimly lit room with a long table filled with delicacies and one occupant seated half-hazard in a large plush chair.

The Fat Man.

"Hello my dear!" He thrust his pudgy arms into the air. "May I say 'My dear'"? It seems you have had a change of heart regarding your choice of gender. Do I have this young man to thank for that?"

Reskalin hurried over to plant a kiss on the Fat Man's cheek. The joy that came over his face was almost comical verging on ridiculous. "Your father would have been so pleased to see you this way."

"You are my father in every way short of the first act," Reskalin stroked his bald pate and kissed him on the forehead. "And yes, I have taken Enguer as my lover."

The Fat Man's gaze fell upon him, intense green eyes noting every detail, judging every blink and twitch. His life weighed in the balance in those few seconds. Or so it seemed to Enguer.

"As I expected," the Fat Man cackled. "The son of Gaurin and the daughter of Tanais, a worthy match don't you think?"

"What trouble should we expect?" Reskalin.

The Fat Man's wide grin stretched across his face. "The ripples of your return have spread through the city and some bear the news of your metamorphosis." His smile never wavered; he might as well have been describing the previous night's theatrical performance. "Ten men are already dead because of it, fifty more will join them by nightfall and the morning will see at least a hundred more."

Reskalin appeared crestfallen, kneeling next to his chair like a child, "I'm so sorry. You do not deserve this."

The Fat Man laughed and placed a heavy hand on her slender shoulder. "We knew this day would come. At least I prayed for it more often than you know! And it is long past time for a modest purge of the rats that have been working against me for far too long."

"What would you have us do?"

"Sit, eat, let the wheels of progress do as they must!" He gestured to the abundance of food arrayed on the table. "I have been preparing for this day for many years and I was glad when you returned to Arre that it had finally come!"

Reskalin flashed Enguer a sly smile. She had been right about being noticed before they ever stepped off the ferry. Why should he doubt her?

"Should we cower in the dark like frightened children, or will you let us join the battle against the opposition? You know better than anyone that I can take care of myself."

"This is not your fight, Reskalin." The Fat Man took a long draught of wine that was quickly refilled by a boy bolting out from behind a tapestry. "You have been my charge. My responsibility. And it is my weakness they seek to exploit. They have been planning a long time, this I know! You coming out as a woman, in the position as my second, emboldens them to risk everything to bet that even my most loyal 'Big Brothers' would turn against me. To some extent it is true and by now the disloyal ones are dead. It is unfortunate."

Enguer recalled Reskalin telling him that the 'Big Brothers' were like captains over the guild's various business activities. Reskalin was a 'Big Brother'. What would she be called now, he silently mused, a 'Big Sister'?

"What about the Zilach and the city guard?" Reskalin continued. "Will they stand by and allow us to kill each other in the streets? Won't they see it as destabilizing?"

"No. Borath has given me his assurance that the Zilach will not react as long as the common folk are not harmed." The Fat Man picked up a bright red apple and bit into it. "They understand that this is an internal affair with the guild."

"So, again I say, what part shall we play?"

The Fat Man leaned back and studied the apple in his hand. "You will play no part. Instead, you will go to Ys and learn what you can about the strange behavior of Princess Ahes. It seems that she has been stirring up a bit of trouble in the kingdom."

Reskalin had an incredulous look on her face that shifted into the red coloring of anger. "You want to send me away *now,* while you fight a battle that I created? I will *not* go to Ys! My place is here by your side, defending the guild!"

The Fat Man laughed, the long robes he wore over a partially unbuttoned scarlet tunic quaked with mirth, "This is *precisely* the right time for you to be away from here. Your very presence inflames the passions of those we have deceived for so long. They will not be pacified so easily." He raised his cup high in the air and let the silky red liquid slowly fall onto the stone floor. "In the beginning, blood will spill like wine in the streets. It will be a reckoning like none have seen before in Arre and long overdue. When it is done, a new order will emerge. Under my direction of course and that will be the time for you to safely return."

"Will that be the end of it?" Enguer cut in. "Or will Reskalin be hounded by assassins in the shadows for the rest of her life?"

"We are all on a tight-rope balancing precariously between life and death!" The FatMan shouted gleefully. "That is the nature of our business!" He shook his empty cup in the air and a servant boy dutifully rushed from behind a tapestry with a pitcher to refill it.

Enguer couldn't believe how glibly the Fat Man spoke of life and death. "Are you insane? You're ordering the deaths of hundreds and hardly give a care for the life of a woman whom you speak of as your daughter?""

"Enguer, you don't understand . . ." Reskalin started to say.

Wine sloshed on the floor from the nervous hands of the boy pouring the wine and he moaned audibly when a bit of the red liquid spilled on the Fat Man's tunic.

"Steady child," The Fat Man spoke soothingly and winked at his distraught servant. "Leave the pitcher and find a towel. It's not your fault."

The boy started to run out of the room, remembered he still had the pitcher and ran back to place it on the table. The Fat Man smiled the whole time until the servant was out of the room. Then his smile disappeared and he put the weight of his gaze squarely on Enguer.

"Do you know who you are defending?" The FatMan leaned forward in his chair agitation plain upon his face. "Murderers, rapists, assassins and child-killers! That is the evil populate that I must purge from time to time. They do not respect the rules or covet the balance of power that I alone have jealously protected for decades! As for Reskalin, I am sending her to Ys for her protection. And yours! In case you haven't noticed, she is more than capable of taking care of herself. I made damn sure of that!" He leaned back in his chair, calm again, in control. "If for that you name me insane then I gladly accept the title of 'Mad Man'. Your father understood."

Enguer felt as though he had just been slapped across the face. "My father? What does he have to do with any of this?"

The Fat Man glanced over at Reskalin, "You have not told him?"

"There was never a good time," her tentative reply sounded less than convincing.

"What haven't I been told about my father?" Enguer demanded.

"Apparently everything," the reply was honest without a hint of cynicism or malice. Enguer could see the sincerity reflected in the Fat Man's dark orbs. The respect. And sadness.

Enguer rubbed his weary eyes. "I am tired of all the secrets, the lies. From the moment I was compelled to come here by those two idiots in Courth nothing has been what it seemed. Now I learn that there are secrets involving my father that are sure to leave me shocked and surprised." He lifted his hands in the air in mock plea. "Where does it end?"

"There is no end until we die," the Fat Man chuckled. "There is only survival."

"So, tell me about my father," Enguer sighed.

"No," the Fat Man shook his head. "The telling deserves a better setting. When you are alone and relaxed with Reskalin, she will tell you everything. For now, I need to know every detail about your recent journey." He cast his gaze upon Reskalin. "Did you recover the artifact?"

"We did," Reskalin pulled the crystal disk with the gold rim from their travel pack and handed it over. "You're not going to believe what the orks were planning to use it for."

Chapter 29

Fufluns

Reskalin spent the better part of two hours detailing their journey to the orks enclave and back. Enguer added particulars when prompted, but of course, Reskalin did most of the talking, leaving out nothing except for their intimate moments together. Enguer was glad of that considering the Fat Man was the closest thing she had to a father and he might not have appreciated such specifics.

"Apparently the disk has the power to bring battle-ready forces streaming through a circle of light projected by the moon through the crystal," Reskalin was explaining.

The Fat Man turned the crystal disk over and over in his stout hands. "Where do they come from?"

"Who knows?" Reskalin shrugged. "Wherever there are orks. Let's just hope they don't have any more of those devices."

"Hmmm," the Fat Man's attention was fully on the disk so much so that he appeared to be barely listening. "Yes, let's hope."

Reskalin watched the Fat Man for a long time before she spoke again, "It is getting late and we are tired. Why don't we pick this up tomorrow?"

"Good night to you both." The Fat Man muttered, never looking up, his gaze intent on the crystal and his own private thoughts.

Reskalin stood from the table and lead Enguer out of the room. He expected her to take him to the room he had been given the last time he met the Fat Man, instead, they entered a large chamber well-appointed with a plush bed, a tall standing mirror, several comfortable chairs, a writing desk and multiple tapestries hanging from the stone walls for aesthetic insulation. There was a fireplace on the far wall and three small light-globes hovering around the room, but not a single window that he could see.

"Is this your room?" Enguer recognized the subtle feminine touches here and there that he would have otherwise missed if he never learned the truth about his companion.

Reskalin ran her fingers up his neck and through the dark locks on the back of his head. "*Our* room," she grinned.

"So," Enguer sat in one of the plush chairs next to the bed. "I am comfortable and I am relaxed. Tell me what you know about my father."

The heat from the fireplace beat waves across his face, warm and inviting. Enguer was tired and he wanted to sleep, but his curiosity would never allow it with the answers to his father's past so close at hand. Reskalin regarded him from near the door with a sympathetic look on her face. She removed her boots, her cloak and everything in between before she straddled him on the chair where he patiently waited. Her raw scent was intoxicating and the kisses she landed along the length of his face and neck promised something more if he would but wish it.

With every fiber of will he possessed, Enguer gently shifted her body to lay comfortably within his cradling arms. "Please Reskalin, tell me now."

She snuggled her cold nose into the creases of his neck and extended a leg and an arm across his body. Enguer realized that for a woman like Reskalin, this was the ultimate expression of trust and vulnerability. She placed her life in his hands, body and soul, so that he would know she spoke the truth.

"When I was very young, my father brought me to Arre and introduced me to a man I had never met," Reskalin's quiet whisper tickled the hairs at the nape of his neck. "He was the fattest man I had ever seen and with the few words I was able to speak at the time, I called him Fat Man. It was an innocent truth with no insult intended. I remember the pure laugh of joy that escaped his lips and he decreed that from then on that would be his name." Reskalin stroked the growth of Enguer's beard left unshaven since the time they left Arre. "That is my earliest memory."

Agile fingers made the buttons on his tunic undone and loosened the straps that held his leather armor in place. Moments later,

Enguer enjoyed freedom from material encumbrance with the only barrier remaining between them the heat from their skin. Reskalin felt soft and inviting, her every touch intoxicating to his senses.

"After a while, Tanais, whom you now know as my father, left Arre in the company of the Fat Man and I was sent to the home of an old woman to look after me while they were away." Reskalin's fingers traced smoothly over his nearly hairless chest. "She was a cruel mistress that beat me if I neglected my chores and fed me barely enough to keep me alive. She had two sons, both a few years older, that she allowed to have their way with me, even encouraged it. I was only seven and I blamed my father for the abuse. That was the time that I learned what it was to hate." A small tear ran down her cheek that she quickly batted away with her hand before barking an unexpected laugh. "A year later, Tanais and the Fat Man returned to find a scrawny little girl in thread-bare rags that could hardly be called a dress with a head shaved to deter lice and a dirty face. Their reaction was swift and violent. The old lady begged for mercy. She begged for her life. I watched them beat her then drag her naked into the street. When they hung the woman from a post, I silently observed her struggle, staring into bulging eyes that pleaded for release, watched as she desperately struggled for air. And I felt not the least bit of compassion."

Enguer eyed Reskalin as she spoke. He had not expected this. A pang of sadness and guilt formed in his chest. Guilt for never having given a thought to Reskalin's past even though she had made no secret of her bitterness toward Tanais and sadness to know that it was much worse than he could have ever guessed. He had grown up sheltered and loved and despite the loss of his mother when he was so young at least he had known her. His troubles were trivial next to Reskalin's and he felt ashamed for it.

"They cut the old lady down before she died and nailed her to a wooden frame erected in the market place. No one intervened, not even the city guard. My father tried to tell me he was sorry. He told me how much he loved me. I didn't want to hear any of it. I hated him as much as the old woman and I ran away."

Enguer gently scratched the back of Reskalin's head to sooth her and squeezed her tight in the crook of his arm. "Why did Tanais choose the old lad as your guardian in the first place?"

"He met a priest of Fufluns that recommended her," Reskalin released an acerbic chuckle. "Fufluns is our god devoted to the welfare of the people. Not all people apparently."

"Your father could not have known how cruel your caretaker would turn out to be," Enguer spoke softly. "Why did you blame him?"

Reskalin's body tensed. "Tell that to the little girl left with strangers, frightened, abused and abandoned," her voice rose with anger.

"I'm sorry," Enguer relented quickly. "I cannot begin to imagine what you suffered. Where did you go when you ran away?"

Slowly, Reskalin relaxed and she pressed her face closer against his chest. "I went to the market place and sat in front of the old woman. For three days I taunted her while she suffered. She demanded water and I poured it in the dust in front of her. I told her that her sons were sold into slavery and that everything she owned had been burned in the street. I promised to cut up her body and feed it to the dogs when she died. The first two days she shouted curses at me and I cursed her back. Then on the third day she wept and pleaded and begged for forgiveness. I cut her throat and watched her bleed out. That's when I learned what it was to feel the raw satisfaction of revenge."

Enguer listened in stunned silence. This woman, this rogue, this lover of his had profound scars that might never be healed. *How could they?* Yet, he knew how deeply she must have suppressed those memories to behave normally in society. Well, not completely normal. She had been a thief and a murderer for most of her life. She was still. And somehow, he loved her.

"The Fat Man found me sitting in a pool of the woman's blood," Reskalin chuckled again. "What a sight I must have been! Sitting in blood at the feet of a dead woman right there in the middle of the largest market in Arre! To this day I remember the exact spot where it happened."

"Why did no one offer comfort or take you away from that place?"

Reskalin grunted. "No one would dare. They were all afraid. I found out later that the Fat Man was nearby the entire time. Watching over me."

"What about your father?" Enguer almost dreaded asking. "Was he there too?"

"Hardly," Reskalin scoffed. "He was holed up in a temple somewhere praying to Sunna for forgiveness. Or so I heard."

Enguer held Reskalin quietly for a while and watched the flames flickering in the hearth with Reskalin draped over his body like a comfortable blanket. She was still and quiet, her breathing rhythmic, restful. Enguer's eyes closed and he dozed.

"I met your father for the first time a week later."

Reskalin's words brought him immediately awake.

"He came with Borath Mecrulican and an elf. I was so excited. I had never seen an elf before and this one was kind and funny. I remember his smile, he smiled a lot, and showed me magic tricks. He even let me touch his ears," Reskalin giggled. "His name was ArteliThalozin and everywhere he went in Arre people would stop and stare."

"My father told me stories about an elf he once called a friend when I was little," Enguer recollected. "I wonder if this elf is the same."

"He was the only elf I ever saw in Arre and your father definitely knew him well," Reskalin nodded against his chest. "They all seemed to know each other very well. They laughed and joked a lot, told stories and teased each other. It made me angry to see my father so happy with them. I couldn't understand what they saw in such a hateful man."

"Did he talk to you?"

Reskalin sighed. "Constantly. He begged for my forgiveness and wept when he spoke about what had happened to me. Sometimes he would bring up my mother and tell me how proud she would have been of me. That only made me angrier and I refused to speak to him."

So proud, thought Enguer. So proud and strong, even back then.

"Your father and the others were there for only a few days when a strange man came one night wearing long robes and carrying a staff that he didn't seem to need to help him walk. He had long dark hair and black eyes that glowed from within like a cat and a deep voice that rumbled like distant thunder. There was something about him that projected strength and power unlike anyone else I had ever seen. My father and the others treated him with respect and listened very closely when he spoke. I remember they called him Myrllin. He was gone by the time I woke up the next morning. I never saw him again after that. Maybe it was the wild imagination of a little girl, but my memory of him is more vivid than that of all the others for reasons I can't explain."

Enguer was intrigued by the strange visitor and the relationship he had with his father and the other men. "Did you ever find out why he was there?"

"Only later, but it should have been obvious to me at the time." Reskalin reached over the thickly padded arm of the chair, brought forth a blanket and pulled it over them. It had grown chilly. The fire in the hearth was beginning to smolder and neither of them wanted to get up and add more wood. "A few days after this 'Myrllin' came to visit, my father told me that they would be leaving for a while. I was terrified and begged the Fat Man not to leave me with strangers again. The sympathy and understanding in his eyes was unforgettable and somehow I knew he was a kindred spirit. Maybe he went through something similar in his childhood or maybe he just had great instincts, I suspect a lot of both from what I know today, but he showed me compassion when I needed it the most. The very next day I was brought to a large room where a dozen men and women were assembled around a table. My father was there, along with Borath, the elf and your father sitting shoulder to shoulder with the Fat Man facing several people I did not know. The Fat Man introduced me as his nephew and that I was to be taught how to read, use numbers, become an expert with weapons and learn how to ride a horse. It surprised me to be announced as a boy, but I was smart enough to keep my mouth shut and ask questions later. The Fat Man said the people at the table would be my tutors and he made it very clear I should be treated with respect and that they would be responsible for my safety."

"Did you feel safe?"

"I was a box of nerves at first, but I trusted the Fat Man," Reskalin yawned. "My father left with the others the next day. He promised to take me to Courth when they returned and settle in a house near the river. But that was not to be. It was several years before I saw any of their faces again and by then I was an older, tougher, confident and fiercely independent young man. And I had embraced the ways of the underworld."

Enguer felt a mix of pride and sadness for his lover. She had gone through hell, transformed herself into another person and come out stronger in the end, except for one thing. "What of your father?"

"He begged and begged for me to go with him to Courth," her languid tone turned sorrowful. "Of course, I refused and he finally went without me. He sent me letters nearly every week until the day he died. I regret that I could never let go of the anger I felt for him before it was too late."

"Life has not been easy for you, Reskalin. I am sorry for that."

"Life has made me what I am, what you are, what we all are," she laughed quietly. "And I have spun this long sad tale about my life without telling you much about your father."

"Do you know something more?" Enguer was eager to know.

"A little," Reskalin plucked absently at the few hairs sprouting on his chest. "Your father, my father, the Fat Man, Borath Mecrulican and the elf, ArteliThalozin, were all members of the Order of the FIVE. That's how they knew each other. You've heard of the FIVE, haven't you?"

"Only from the tales by Boeger Penhallow." Reskalin might as well have dropped a rock on his head. *His father was in the Order of the FIVE?* "How could my father have been a member of a group that existed generations ago? And why would he have never spoken of it to me if it were true?"

"The Fat Man explained to me that the members change every few years and that they are a highly secretive organization," Reskalin's gloomy bearing lifted and she sounded more like her old self again. "No one knows who the current members are and only a few are aware of the retired ones like our fathers, the FatMan and Borath. I'm not sure about the elf. I've heard they live hundreds of years!"

"As amazing as it sounds, what you are telling me is just another part of my father's life I knew nothing about." Enguer doubted he would ever know who his father truly was. It seemed to change with every person he met that knew him.

"Enough of our sad lives for one evening," Reskalin slid out of the chair and walked slowly toward the bed trailing nothing but the blanket on the ground behind her. "Put another log on the fire and come remind me again the pleasures of being a woman."

Enguer didn't have to be told twice.

~~~

Early the next morning, Enguer was awakened by a rhythmic thumping on his chest. "Wake up, dear one."

He opened his eyes to see Reskalin hovering over him. "The Fat Man wishes to see us."

How long had he slept? A few hours maybe? And now he was being summoned to the place where the Fat Man sat on his opulent chair like a king on a throne?

"What time of day is it?"

"A little after noon," Reskalin replied. "We must go quickly, otherwise we will miss the meeting."

Enguer squinted in the sudden brightness brought on by the light-globes, "What meeting?"

Reskalin laughed and kicked him playfully in the side. "Get up and you will find out!"

Enguer washed his face in the basin of water that had appeared overnight on the table and dressed in a tunic that was a little more clean than the one he wore the previous day and followed Reskalin back to the chamber where they had spoken with the Fat Man the night before. Something was different this time. The room was bright with light and heavy with the fragrance of exotic foods. Moreover, the Fat Man was dressed in fine silks and rare furs like a nobleman with means. It was an odd contrast to the casual nature in the room the night before. Enguer let it all pass and focused on the strange people that walked into the chamber from a door he had not noticed before.

Atlanteans.

"Welcome! Welcome, Rukmani of House Krsna! I am pleased that you were able to accept my invitation so quickly! Please sit, sit." The Fat Man grinned broadly like a cat that had managed to coax a bird from its cage.

Servants, dressed as formally as their master, practically sprinted to pull chairs for the two women and the man that seemed so strange and out of place. This was as close as Enguer had ever come to an Atlantean. Only a few strides across the room, their lean build, large almond-shaped eyes and blue-tinted skin distracted little from their most notable feature – an elongated skull impossible to hide under long dark hair. The one the Fat Man identified as Rukmani wore flowing green robes cinched by a belt at the waist that appeared to be made of pure white light and a heavy gold medallion that hung from a thick gold chain around her neck. Like most of her kind, she boasted of beautiful features reflecting a kind, but stern visage that might have been described as middle-aged in human terms. Behind her stood a woman dressed similarly in red robes and a man in green. Both appeared younger than Rukmani and equally as beautiful and intimidating. Enguer had heard that the colors and medallions held meanings of significance, rank or position, but he couldn't recall the details.

Rukmani met the Fat Man's gaze and for the briefest second Enguer thought the heavy man's eyes flickered with doubt. Whatever he was up to, Enguer had the impression that the Fat Man was uneasy about this meeting. That worried Enguer a little. A man like that could be dangerous if he didn't feel like he was in control. It was hardly different from the same look he had seen in the eyes of a cornered bear a time or two before.

"Thank you for your invitation," the Atlantean smiled coolly. "I trust that you have good news for me?"

No one made an attempt to sit down, leaving the servants awkwardly holding the backs of the chairs. The Fat Man quickly made a shooing motion and they disappeared behind the tapestries. It would all have been comical if the room were not so heavy with tension.

The Fat Man laughed nervously when the servants were gone, "Yes, of course!" He beckoned to Reskalin. "But first I would like you to meet Reskalin Alois, my Second."

Rukmani nodded to Reskalin in greeting, "Alois? Are you related to the former Arch Priest of Courth?"

"I was," Reskalin nodded in return.

"My sympathies," the Atlantean's expression softened considerably, "I met him once some time ago. He was a hero with a fine reputation."

"Thank you," Reskalin's reply sounded sincere if a little bitter.

Rukmani half-turned and motioned toward the two that came with her. "This is my son Sochu and my daughter Charumati."

Reskalin exchanged smiles and nods. "Did you come all the way from the Emerald Isle?"

The laugh that escaped Rukmani's lips sounded soulful and pure, similar to the way Enguer thought of a bird chirping happily on a warm spring day. "For a very long time, my family's home has been the Sindhu city of Dvaraka. My husband and I have been honored by the Emperor to serve as Consul and Keeper of the Source in the Great Vimana.

Reskalin bowed fully to the elder Atlantean, "You have come so far. I welcome you to our humble home."

Enguer was astounded by the Atlantean's words. In the Western Kingdoms, the places Rukmani so casually named were thought of as nothing more than myth and legend. He was also taken aback by Reskalin's suddenly submissive attitude. He was not sure which surprised him more.

"And, ah," The Fat Man gestured for Enguer to approach. "This is Reskalin's partner, Enguer Rand. Son of Gaurin Rand."

"Gaurin Rand. Another fallen hero," Rukmani's dark almond-shaped eyes seemed to bore through him. "and now the blood of two legends has united."

"*Noasmi gohed . . .*" Eyes wide and visibly shaken, Charumati spoke the strange words in a soft voice that defied her sharp, urgent tone.

Rukmani's hand shot up commanding silence from her daughter before she abruptly turned back to the Fat Man, "We must go. Do you have the disk?"

The Fat Man hesitated for the span of a breath, agitation clearly edged around his dark orbs, and then he double-clapped his hands together sharply. A well-dressed man hastily appeared from behind one of the hanging tapestries against the wall and strode forward carrying a silver tray with a purple fabric pouch on top. He stopped in front of the Fat Man and presented the tray.

"Here it is," his smile could not have been more contrived. "I assume you have brought what *you* promised?"

Her hand still poised in the air, Rukmani barely crooked her long slender index finger prompting Sochu to step forward and wave his arms in short circular motions parallel to the floor. At first, Enguer thought the Atlantean might be starting a fire as swirling tendrils rose from the carpet to form a thick column of smoke a little over knee-high that rotated in time with his hands. But then the short column began to glow with white light, growing brighter and gyrating faster and faster until it was far too intense to look at. Suddenly it was gone and the room seemed to grow dark with the absence of the brilliant illumination. In its place sat a bulbous ceramic jar, as blue as the ocean, its shiny glazed surface reflecting the glow from the light-globes that bobbed near the ceiling.

Sochu's right hand burst into flame and Enguer felt as much as saw Reskalin take a half-step backward. He could feel the heat on his face from across the room and marveled that the Atlantean could endure the scalding fire. Seemingly unconcerned, Sochu placed his burning hand over the lead seal that secured the lid to the jar causing the metal to liquify and run down the sides of the vessel in short rivulets. Seconds later the flame was gone and Sochu stood holding the lid of the jar in his unmarred hand. The glint of gold shined from the open container. Gold coins. There had to be hundreds of them.

"As we agreed," Rukmani stretched out her hand and the purple pouch gently lifted off the silver tray and floated over to her.

Enguer, still amazed at the jar full of gold, thought his eyes would leap from their sockets. He had seen magic tricks in the market, witnessed its use in battle and read stories about powerful wizards when he was a boy, but this was different. These Atlanteans used it effortlessly. Almost as if magic was as much a part of them as their arms and legs. Maybe it was, for all he knew.

Chapter 30

The Enlightened Ones

"If you need any help working out how to use that thing, Reskalin and Enguer might lend some advice," the Fat Man offered. His eyes kept shifting back to the jar filled with gold.

"Oh?" Rukmani pulled the crystal disk from the pouch. "How would the two of you know anything about operating this artifact?" Her stern gaze veered from the disk to settle uncomfortably over he and Reskalin.

"Luck, I suppose," Enguer shrugged. Then he and Reskalin told her about that night on the Plains of Tarre when they were nearly killed by the ork that stepped through the circle of moonlight magnified by the disk.

"I suppose you do have luck," the Atlantean echoed. "Both kinds."

"Do you know what the orks were planning to do with it?" Reskalin shifted to lean back against the edge of the table.

"They planned to move armies through it," Rukmani's tone was dispassionate, like she might have ordered tea, but the look in her eyes was dead serious. "The last attack on Arre was nothing more than probing your defenses to gauge how quickly your soldiers would react and how they would respond. With this thing," she held up the disk allowing the light to cast prismatic rainbows on the walls, "they could put an army outside your gates without a hint of warning. Your city would fall. Your people would be slaughtered."

Silence hung in the air for a long moment.

"Can they make another one?" Reskalin whispered. Her eyes were round with fear. She and Enguer knew well how dangerous and cruel the orks could be.

The sides of Rukmani's lips turned up in a slight smile, "They didn't make this one child and there are no others like it. It was a relic created by the Tuatha De to use in the civil war they called 'The Breaking' centuries ago. How the orks came to have it is anyone's guess."

"Will the world be safe from the disk now that it is in your hands?" The words sounded accusatory when they came out of his mouth. Enguer didn't mean them to be. Reskalin poked him in the back and even the Fat Man ripped his gaze from the gold coins to lift an eyebrow in his direction.

"That is a very wise question," Rukmani tilted her head back without taking her gaze from Enguer. "A good sign, wouldn't you say, Charumati?"

Her daughter responded with the briefest of nods and she too stared across the room at Enguer.

Rukmani raised up the disk again. "A relic with this kind of power is safe in no one's hands. Not even ours." With swift motion she sent the disk crashing onto an open patch stone floor not covered by carpet or fur. There was a sound like glass breaking, but higher pitched and far louder than it should have been. The crystal shattered hurling a thousand shards into the air, but before a single piece could fly far away, they erupted in a shower of sparking of light, disappearing into oblivion. Everyone, except for the Atlanteans, jumped back and shielded their eyes.

"That's why we destroy them," Rukmani finished in a calm, smooth voice.

A torrent of laughter erupted from the Fat Man that had him nearly double over. ,I . . . I could have saved you the trouble!"

"You would have never been able to destroy it," Rukmani's slight smile appeared again. "Even if you could I would have had to see to it myself to be sure. Besides, I would never have wanted to miss the looks of shock and disbelief all over your faces."

"Yes!" The Fat Man laughed all the more. "Quite right! Quite right, indeed!"

Humor, the Atlanteans had a shred of humor under their austere exterior. This was as much of a surprise to Enguer as what Rukmani had just done with the disk. And apparently the Fat Man, who Reskalin had been warned was a notorious prankster, also appreciated the irony of the situation as much as anyone. Except Reskalin.

"Why did you destroy it?" She shouted with rage. "We travelled to hell and back, nearly costing our lives, for that thing! We could have used it to destroy the orks for good!"

Rukmani's calm gaze settled on Reskalin, the smile disappeared, but it was not replaced by anger. "And then what, child? Who keeps the disk in their possession? The Zilach of Arre, the Lauchme of Rasna or someone else? Do you trust that your own rulers would not use it against the Enchele tribes or the Tarre?"

"The Tarre are our friends," Reskalin shot back.

"Today perhaps," Rukmani's eyes narrowed. "What about the next ruler that controlled the disk? Or the next?"

Reskalin shrank back against Enguer, confusion and uncertainty plain in her voice, "They would use it only to protect our people."

Rukmani's smile was back if a little sad. "Sometimes rulers believe they must conquer others to protect their people. No one can say the lengths powerful people might go to gain more power, nor how they might justify it."

Enguer recognized the truth in the Atlantean's words and he knew that Reskalin understood abuse of power as well as anyone. Men like Commander Artis, among a host of others, had been a constant force pushing against her and the illicit enterprises she operated under the Fat Man's umbrella. It was a power struggle every day from within and without. A game of survival and control. A contest of wills that Reskalin practiced with skillful domination. And after everything they had been through together, Enguer wouldn't hesitate an instant to bet on her every time.

Reskalin held her silence.

Rukmani turned back to the Fat Man. "We must go now. The assets of your organization have proven worthy and for that, you have my gratitude. Perhaps we will meet again one day." She shifted the scrutiny of her oval orbs again to Enguer and Reskalin. "You have talented young people in your service who are wise and curious. Beware that they may eclipse even your power and prestige one day."

"I should be so lucky," The Fat Man laughed nervously. "I welcome your employ and the opportunity to earn your gratitude and trust." The bow he performed was remarkably elegant and well executed for a man of his bulk.

Rukmani nodded, the translucent blue rings on the ends of her long braids chiming musically with the sudden movement of her elongated head. She flowed from the chamber followed closely by Charumati and Sochu leaving behind a strange absence of personality that Enguer had only experienced in the wake of King Francik . . . or the Arch-Priest Tanais.

"If she were anyone else, I would consider her an arrogant fool," the Fat Man mused after the Atlanteans had taken their leave. "But I am not so sure Atlanteans have arrogance within them. I like that woman. I think history will remember her well."

Enguer was struck by the Fat Man's pensive thoughts. He had always come across as impulsive and artless whenever they met previously. It gave him the idea that maybe that's what the Fat Man wanted everyone to think. There were animals in The Wilds that did the same thing by feigning injury or vulnerability, drawing in a predator confident of an easy kill. Then they would strike taking the predator-turned-prey completely by surprise. Enguer was learning quickly that nothing was ever as it seemed in the dark bowels of the underworld.

"The Zilach will be pleased that you have saved his city from invasion," Reskalin's words sounded more like a question than an observation.

She took a seat at the table and filled her plate with heaps of heavily sauced meats and vegetables that Enguer did not recognize. He sat down next to her and took in the varied aromas. It all smelled delicious and he wasted no time filling his own plate.

"Hmph," the Fat Man coughed a sarcastic laugh and returned to the comfort of his chair. No sooner had he sat down than a servant was filling his cup with burgundy liquid. "The Zilach is a fool that will try and take credit for the whole thing once I tell him about it. Of course, no one will believe him. Your rats will spread the truth well in advance of any announcement. As usual, he will be left wondering why he has little credibility in the eyes of the council and scurry back to my teat for protection."

"Spread the truth?" Reskalin chuckled between bites, "I'm not sure we have ever done that before."

"First time for everything," the Fat Man raised his glass in the air, "and the last order you will give the Sewer Rats."

Out of the corner of his eye Enguer saw Reskalin freeze in place and suddenly the tension in the room was shooting through the roof again. It was amazing how quickly her mood could change and more so how it affected everyone around her. Enguer had no idea what to expect next, but he was sure to stay out of it. This felt more like the makings of a family squabble that he wanted nothing to do with.

"Am I being relieved as your second?" She stared straight ahead. Her response was calm if frosty.

"For a time, my dear," the Fat Man replied cheerfully. "You are going to Ys, remember? Do not underestimate how important this task that I ask of you."

Reskalin snapped her head to the side, daggers of anger in her eyes. "Are you *asking*? Do I truly have a choice in the matter?"

The Fat Man met her dangerous gaze with cool confidence. "You know you have a choice in the matter. You also know that the underworld in Arre is about to explode in violence, but we have discussed that already." He flippantly nodded toward Enguer. "Besides, you have an obligation to this one. We promised to teach him the ways of the city when you returned."

Reskalin, visibly deflated, strode angrily from the room.

Enguer told himself it had nothing to do with her 'obligation' to him. At least he hoped it didn't. The guild war, or civil war, or whatever it was should have been enough reason to want an escape from the place. If only temporary.

Enguer glanced over at the Fat Man. They were alone in the room sitting at the massive table heaped with food enough to feed at least a hundred. The Fat Man returned his gaze and grinned broadly. Seconds passed in awkward silence. The Fat Man took a sip from his cup and continued with the grinning.

"So how do I get out of this place?" Enguer couldn't take it anymore. "I need to see a friend."

The Fat Man's laughter echoed eerily through the chamber.

~~~

"Good afternoon, young Ranger. I am pleased to see that you return from your adventures alive and well."

Borath sat in the same garden where they had met previously. The sky was overcast with the promise of rain later that night and it was cooler, otherwise nothing had changed. The elder man's welcoming smile stood out in sharp contrast to the one bordering on crazy he had so recently departed.

"Truly, I am glad to be back," Enguer was happy to report.

"So, tell me all about it. I'm sure it is a telling worth a bard's song!" Borath laughed heartily.

Enguer sat on the bench opposite the elder and lay out all the details of the harrowing journey to the Orks Enclave and back skipping only the part about Reskalin and their relationship. And because he now knew about Borath and the Order of the FIVE, he included the meeting with the Atlanteans and the final disposition of the disk. Borath listened quietly without interrupting, nodding his head from time to time until Enguer was done.

"It seems the Fat Man gave the Zilach a full accounting for once," the elder folded his arms and sat back expectantly.

"You knew everything already?" For a moment confusion reigned in Enguer's mind before the truth dawn on him. "Of course, you knew. And you wanted to be sure the stories matched up." Heat flushed his cheeks. He didn't like being taken for a fool. "You know, the Fat Man considers the Zilach a fool," he spat angrily.

Borath's eyes lit up with amusement. "He *is* a fool, but a clever fool and he knows it. That's why he keeps men like me on his council to advise and guide him."

"Why didn't you just tell me from the start? It wouldn't have changed anything that I told you."

The elder spread his hands apart and shrugged. "Because the Fat Man and I needed to be sure we could trust you."

"What?" Enguer was growing more agitated by the second. "What does this have to do with the Fat Man?"

Borath ran his hand through his thinning grey hair and sighed. "Do you recall the last time we met? You asked me to get a message to a man named Reskalin. He found you, yes? And you and he went to track down the orks."

"What are you getting at?"

"When you returned to Arre a woman was on the back of your horse wearing Reskalin's armor and Reskalin's clothing." Borath's eyes drilled into him accusingly. "We both know who that was and what that means."

"What that means?" Enguer repeated, somewhat confused.

"That she is in love with you and you her," Borath shook his head incredulously. "What other reason could there be for her to reveal herself? The Fat Man expected it to happen eventually, but none of us expected it would be the son of Gaurin Rand to do it. Yet, here you are. And by now the news has reached every dark corner in Arre. There will be many that believe her to be a chink in the Fat Man's armor that could bring him down. Maybe they are right."

"The Fat Man told us as much," Enguer dug the back of his heel into the ground creating a small divot. "We are leaving for Ys in the morning."

"Good," Borath's smile was back. "You should know that Reskalin means the world to him and if anything should happen to her because of you . . ."

"I know," Enguer interrupted.

"I'm sure you do," the elder pat him on the knee and stood up, the joints in his knees cracking from the effort.

"Oh," Enguer dug into his pouch and produced the magical ring the elder had lent him. "I have brought you back the ring as promised."

Borath squinted at the ring in the failing light and waved his hand at it. "Keep the ring. I am long past the days it will do me any good. Better that a young explorer such as yourself put it to the use it deserves."

Stunned, Enguer didn't know what to say. He managed a meager, "Thank you," before the elder turned to slowly shuffle from the garden and down a corridor newly lit with torches.

Enguer sat for a long time watching the shadows grow taller in the fading light of the garden. He thought about the Fat Man, Borath and the Order of the FIVE. One controlled the underworld and the other held influence over the Zilach. There was no question the two collaborated. Probably had done so for years. There was a guild war coming and those with the courage to line up against the Fat Man had no idea the power they were up against. What Enguer didn't know until that day was there were two men who ruled Arre and neither of them was the Zilach.

~~~

A cold wind whipped around the conjured bubble that protected Myrllin from the elements. The great ebony stallion he sat astride needed no such protection being that it was a conjured thing itself. High over the Atlas Mountains Sleipnir's eight powerful legs slowly churned through the air, hovering in place, while Myrllin stared into the golden orb where a dark swirling shadow, blacker than the blackest hole in the cosmos, roiled with rage at its confinement. Myrllin could almost feel the hatred it displaced . . . and the desperation. He knew that it knew its life in this world was nearly at an end.

"How did you manage to become so powerful?" Myrllin tapped on the orb.

Myrllin was genuinely perplexed by the question. This was a simple Chaos Demon they had captured, not one of the greater Named Demon's that he had expected. In the few years since the demons had been released from the prison of the Pithos that once held them, they had somehow evolved, grown stronger, developed in complex way that he would have never thought possible. And it frightened him terribly.

There were still more of the Chaos Demons out there somewhere and more of the Named one's as well. Too many for he and Wodanaz to find and destroy on their own. It would take the determined efforts of all mankind, the dwarfs, the elves, the Atlanteans and others to put an end to their evil purpose. Whatever that was, Myrllin was still unsure. Perhaps to rule over the kingdoms of the world, dominate the races, covet their magic or just sew chaos. From what he had experienced already, their motivations were wildly varied.

"What about you?" He asked the shadow inside the orb. "Was it your desire to burn the world to cinders?"

The trapped demon no longer had the faculties to speak vocally, but Myrllin knew that it understood what he said. It understood all too well.

"It's almost time to return to the Infernal Planes and become a slave again to jealous masters that I'm sure hold no resentment for your centuries of squandered freedom in this world."

Myrllin felt a new wave of hatred from the orb in response to his sarcasm. It was far more raw emotion than he had experienced from the other Chaos Demons he had confined and it caused him a moment of pause to consider how much longer he would be able to capture them in this fashion. He and Wodanaz would have to puzzle out an alternative when he returned to Hy Brasil.

Myrllin cast his gaze down at the smoking ten-league wide maw of the massive volcano the Atlanteans called the Ourea. Few knew that below the sea of glowing magma that it occasionally belched to the surface was a one-way portal into the Infernal Planes. The Atlantean wizards discovered it a century or so before and to this day no one could explain its existence. All that mattered to Myrllin was that the portal allowed him to send the demons back to their own world rather than trapping them for eternity in their own as his father had done more than a millennium ago.

He hefted the golden orb in his hand and stared one last time into its dark depths. It was time. He would have liked to study one of the demons one day but they were too dangerous to keep around even trapped in a prison. The folly of the Pithos had proven that beyond a doubt.

"Tell your master to expect more of you soon."

Myrllin did not wait for the demon's expression of rage. He dropped his arm to his side and let the orb roll across his palm to fall free and disappear into the Ourea's hot flames of purgatory.

~~~

"I have something for you," Reskalin pointed to a table where a blanket concealed a bulky item beneath it.

Enguer strode over and slowly pulled off the cover to reveal a long bow made from a timber he did not recognize constructed by a hand that must have been a master in its class. He picked up the bow and ran his fingers over the perfect curves of the upper limb and down the taunt string to the grip that felt like it was made for his hand. It was the most finely crafted bow he had ever held in his hands.

He looked over to find Reskalin grinning like a milk-maid with a new pail. "Where did you get this?"

"The elf I told you about," Reskalin eased up beside him and kissed him on the cheek. "He gave it to the Fat Man as a gift a long time ago and well, you know, bows are not his thing so, he thought you might like it instead."

"It's extraordinary, thank you." Enguer put down the bow and started toward the door. "I should thank the Fat Man as well. Will he be in the dining room?"

Reskalin rushed over, took his hand and led him back into the room. "The Fat Man has gone already. We will not see him again until we return from Ys."

"Ah, I see." Enguer wasn't really disappointed. Spending time with the Fat Man was always a strange experience.

"How was Borath?"

Enguer froze. *How could she know where he had gone?* He shook his head in surrender. This was Arre, of course she knew. "He was happy that we returned alive and that we are together."

Reskalin emancipated one of her rare, full-throated laughs. Enguer was so surprised by her reaction that he nearly dropped the bow. "What is so amusing?"

"Borath Mecrulican approved of you, did he?" Her laughter barely let up enough to speak, "That man has been after me to change into a dress and find a proper man since the first day I bled."

Trying hard not to allow his mind to linger on her shameless reference, Enguer was curious how she knew the elder so well. "Is he around so often?"

"Every week for as long as I can remember!" Reskalin laughter faded to nostalgic reflection, "The two of them, always scheming and planning together. Giggling like little girls with a candy. Steering the fate of Arre to the benefit of its people!" She barked a sarcastic laugh. "And lining their pockets thick with gold in the process."

Enguer just shook his head. He supposed it made sense considering the long history the two men shared together. Reskalin's comments also served to confirm his thoughts earlier in the garden. Enguer marveled at the layers upon layers of politics and intrigue in Arre. *Was it the same in every city?* He wondered to himself. *Even in Courth?*

Enguer walked over to the hearth and stacked enough wood to keep it burning through the night. "We leave for Ys in the morning?"

Reskalin had already striped off her clothes and crawled under layers of colorful blankets. "If you ever come to bed," she spoke in the husky voice she had used when she was masquerading as a man and giggled.

"That is hardly the honey that will draw the bee," he grinned and slid under the covers next to her.

She snuggled up close and rest her head on his shoulder. "We can travel the passes that cut through the Spine of Cel and then follow the coast down to Funa where we can catch a ship west. Don't worry, there is a tea we will buy that will calm your belly. I know how much you love travelling over the water."

Enguer let out a long sigh and stared up at the shadows dancing across the ceiling. "So much has changed since the day I left my home, Reskalin. I have changed. From chasing Demon Beasts and watching friends die to them, to stabbing a dying woman through the heart in a village I don't even know the name of. When I came here and found you, I thought it would be different. All I had to do was tell you the sad news about Tanais and I could get on with becoming an explorer, a wayward adventurer, living without a care. But soon enough I am killing orks and corrupt soldiers, cavorting with thieves and murderers, even falling in love with one." He absently stroked her dark, silky-smooth hair that had finally grown down to her shoulders. "The innocence in me has gone forever replaced with the certainty of uncertainty and the fear that despite my best intentions there has come into me the manifestation of a monster just as real as the Lukánthropos. A beast cruel and unmerciful, capable of unspeakable acts of violence and death to rival any rumor or legend that has been spoken in the haze of taverns or smoke of a campfire. The beast is real Reskalin. It is real and it is present. No matter the convictions of friend and ally it is a realization that I must live with. For it is the beast, the beast that craves the life of others, revels in their demise and feeds upon their souls. The beast is I, or what I have become and for it I shall suffer for all eternity to be known as Enguer Rand, the true Beast of Courth."

Reskalin punched him sharply in the ribs with her fist. "We are all monsters inside, Enguer, to some extent or another." She lifted her head to whisper playfully in his ear, "Now why don't you roll over and show me this beast you spoke of."

Enguer laughed. Reskalin had a way of making him feel silly when he took himself too seriously. Someone once told him that the best matches were people who balanced each other. His parents were like that, so were Mr. and Mrs. Eibhlin. Enguer and Reskalin would balance each other as well. There was another jab under the blankets, this time a little lower and Enguer quickly rolled over.

<u>Glossary and Cast</u>

Arid Fellowship - A professional guild of assassins based in Eriu.

ArteliThalozin – Elf from Avalon and former member of the FIVE.

Atiod-bherto - Cult of Druids defeated in the one-hundred-year Oak Wars by the combined forces of the Druids of Sunna and Eriu and the allied cities in both Eriu and Lyonesse. The Atiod were infamous for ritual sacrifice of animals and humans on stone altars and wickerwork structures. Their stone circles are identified by the center recumbent stone and flankers used for astronomy, ritual, and sacrifice. Now outlawed by the Western kingdoms, they continue to practice their dark arts in seclusion. The Atiod are chiefly located in the extreme north and south of Eriu.

Boeger Penhallow – Famous author of myths and fairy tales.

Borath Mecrulican – Former Commanding General of military forces in Arre and later an elder and advisor to the Zilach and his council

Buadhach – Eriu Druid.

Captain Tineus – Commander of the west gate guard in Arre.

Commander Duraunt – Commander of the First Expeditionary Force.

Dhroghan – Legendary hero of the Tuatha Dé (deceased) and founding member of the original FIVE.

Dyzig and Gigot – Masters of the Thieves Guild in Courth.

Enlightened Ones – The formal name applied to the Atlanteans by the people of the Western kingdoms.

Filberzh the Risen - The Arch-Druid of Sunna.

Gaurin Rand – Legendary Ranger, member of the FIVE and Enguer Rand's father.

Hydruntin Ass - An ass common throughout the Western Kingdoms, Hella, and the Capsians.

King Sarou Francik IV – Ruler of the Kingdom of Courth. He reins from the capital city of the same name.

Kiltullagh – Ancient city where, according to legends, the Sphere of Elements is hidden.

Lauchme – Elected King of the confederation of city-states in Rasna.

Liafal Stone – The magically imbued stone in Teamhrach where all the High-Kings of Eriu are coronated.

Myrllin - The Mad Bard, the Prophet, the Sage, the Steward of Hy Brasil. He has the ability to foresee the future with varying degrees of clarity. He is a powerful wizard with an obscure past. Myrllin lives in a castle on the mystical island of Hy Brasil, which is not always visible. When he is not needed, he has the ability to hibernate without aging for hundreds of years at a time. Son of the legendary Tuatha Dé hero Dhroghan and a Nymph, and a twin brother, Wodanaz, whom he is older than by one minute.

Nightstalker – a massive predator similar in form to a black panther with a much larger head, double rows of dagger-like teeth and two long protruding horns on its head.

Ourea – Massive active volcano that rises from the Atlas Mountains on the Emerald Isle. It is purported to serve as a one-way portal into the Infernal Planes that the demons call their home.

Pithos - A traditional vessel for transporting wine, olive oil and other liquids in Hellas

Purple Porphyry – An extremely expensive purple marble from TaShemau that appears 'dusted with the stars.

Ql grannligr – 'Slender ale'. A strong ale brewed by the Vikja for long sea voyages. Replaces the need for much food.

Reskalin Alois – Talented rogue and Second to the FatMan in Arre.

Suri Privou – Experienced Ranger of Courth.

The Eibhlins – Farm family with land adjacent to Enguer Rand's home. Mrs. Eibhlin looked after Enguer for a time after his father died.

The FatMan – Former member of the FIVE, well connected GuildMaster in Arre.

Tanais Alois– Arch Priest of Sunna in the Kingdom of Courth, godfather to Enguer Rand, older brother of Reskalin and a member of the FIVE.

Tuatha Dé - A mysterious, magical race of people who reside in a kingdom of four cities far to the north.

Tuatha Dé Blood - The pure race of Tuatha Dé that comprises the leadership, scholars, and wizard class of their people.

Valiant Keep – The massive fortified manor-house at the heart of Tintagel where the Duke and Duchess reside.

Vyvyan – Famous poet and lyricist.

Wodanaz – The Wanderer, Famed Poet and Minstrel, Seeker of Wisdom, Chronicler of the Fourth Age, Son of legendary Tuatha Dé, Dhroghan and a Nymph, and brother of Myrllin.

Zilach – Governor of a city in Rasna.

Enochian Translations

"Dooaip oiad iadpil bvfd idoigo aqlo mahorela tia butmon de zonrensg cnoqod hoath." – In the name of god, he that lives forever, in the glory of him that sitteth on the holy throne in thy dark heavens.

"Oi amma de homtoh vorsg malpirgi sa teloch sa oln tia levithmong gmilcalzo ioiad!" – He hath opened his mouth to deliver unto his servant, the true worshipper, this curse to triumph over life and death and made unto us beasts in power and presence forever.

"Noasmi gohed." – Let them become one.

"Micma nanaeel! Solpeth bien ialpor a ivonpovnph. Toatar a ciaofi! Ol iolcam croodzi. Zirenaiad. Zorge sa noas hoath. Q adoian teloch aaf ialpvrg!" – Behold my power! Hearken unto my voice burning with wrath and anger. Listen with terror! I bring forth the second beginning of all things. I am the lord your god. Be friendly unto me and become the true worshipper. Or face death among the burning flames!

"Kures gi biab." – Here you are

"Zir Kures," – I am here.

"Niis pambt." – Come unto me.

Celtic Translations

"Hore me, I me agus ag me,
Through me, in me and of me,

Ansin atta bi beo.
There is life.

I uile do fuissim, cloch agus duille,
In all creatures, stone and leaf,

Ansin atta bi beo.
There is life.

Ag dobhar, gaeth agus teine,
From water, air and fire,

Ansin atta bi beo.
There is life.

Me atta tall freamh, Me atta tall mug ag domun.
I am the vessel; I am the servant of nature.

Inso atta me tabhair, inso atta me tabhair,
This is my gift, this is my offer,

Co uib con icc mair."
So that you may live.

About the Author

Born in Homestead, Florida, Ravek Hunter grew up in the United States and Belgium. He earned a bachelor's degree in marketing from Florida International University and went on to become a sporting goods executive. He currently serves as a consultant in the same industry and occasionally assists his wife of fifteen years at her floral design company. The proud father of two boys, Ravek counts reading, exercising, and family travel among his leisure hobbies.

Over the past thirty-five years, Ravek's passion has been researching ancient civilizations with a focus on the origin stories behind their mythology. His writing style attempts to immerse the reader into the story by bringing to life historically accurate and rich details of the culture and time period that frame the narrative.

Inspired by classic fantasy authors like Robert Jordan, Terry Goodkind, and R. A. Salvatore, Ravek writes to entertain and provoke his readers, who, he hopes, share his fondness for mythology.

<u>Connect with Ravek Hunter</u>

Thank you for choosing this work of blood, sweat and tears by *Ravek Hunter*! If you enjoyed reading this novel, please consider posting a review, telling me what you think on one of the social media platforms listed below or reach out via my direct email:

Friend me on Facebook:

https://www.facebook.com/Ravek-Hunter-Literary-LLC-238417183579740/

Follow me on Twitter:

https://twitter.com/RavekHunter

Subscribe to my blog:

https://www.goodreads.com/author/show/17885196.Ravek_Hunter

Visit my website:

https://www.WorldsofAtlantis.com

Email: Ravekhunter@gmail.com